HARD RAIN

Also by Samantha Jayne Allen

Pay Dirt Road

HARD RAIN

Samantha Jayne Allen

MINOTAUR BOOKS
NEW YORK

This is a work of fiction. All of the characters, organizations,
and events portrayed in this novel are either products of
the author's imagination or are used fictitiously.

First published in the United States by Minotaur Books,
an imprint of St. Martin's Publishing Group

HARD RAIN. Copyright © 2023 by Samantha Jayne Allen. All rights reserved.
Printed in the United States of America. For information, address
St. Martin's Publishing Group, 120 Broadway, New York, NY 10271.

www.minotaurbooks.com

Library of Congress Cataloging-in-Publication Data

Names: Allen, Samantha Jayne, author.
Title: Hard rain / Samantha Jayne Allen.
Description: First edition. | New York : Minotaur Books, 2023.
Identifiers: LCCN 2022052808 | ISBN 9781250863812 (hardcover) |
    ISBN 9781250863829 (ebook)
Subjects: LCGFT: Detective and mystery fiction. | Novels.
Classification: LCC PS3601.L4355 H37 2023 | DDC 813/.6—dc23/
    eng/20221104
LC record available at https://lccn.loc.gov/2022052808

Our books may be purchased in bulk for promotional, educational,
or business use. Please contact your local bookseller or the
Macmillan Corporate and Premium Sales Department at 1-800-221-7945,
extension 5442, or by email at
MacmillanSpecialMarkets@macmillan.com.

First Edition: 2023

10 9 8 7 6 5 4 3 2 1

For my mother

Shrill, the sound cut through the steady drum of rain on tin. One of those Amber Alerts, Bethany thought, yanked out of deep sleep. She picked up her phone to silence it and saw a flash flood warning from the National Weather Service. It was four in the morning, and despite being on the charger, the phone's battery was at 2 percent. She reached for the bedside lamp and clicked it twice before realizing the power was out.

Rain lashed sideways against the window and she sat up straighter. There was a *whoosh*, a humming noise in the air, as if the wind outside were frothing the water into something more solid. She pulled her husband's old college sweatshirt on over her tank top and pajama shorts and walked out into the hallway. Lightning lit the A-frame in flashes. Water rushed in through the seams in the back door. She froze, not quite believing what she'd seen. Jesus, the cabin was up on pilings twenty feet high— how, even? Legs shaking, she stumbled to the bedroom for the big hunting flashlight John David had thrown in the bag and stumbled back out again. It was hard to tell, but Bethany figured the water on the first floor was three to four inches deep, as little waves lapped the bottom rung of the dining room chairs. Without the air conditioner or fans, the humidity had crept up. Condensation fogged the windows, and already, the smell was strong—like wet soil, mildew. Her bare feet felt sticky against the hardwood as she descended the slatted stairs. She stopped two steps up from the first floor and leaned over the rail to bang on the door to the other couple's room.

"Y'all awake? Michael? Kendall?"

She looked down at the rising water, mesmerized, halfway wondering if this was a bad dream. Oh, God, they would hate her for this! It had been Bethany's idea to rent a cabin by the river Friday and Saturday for the four of them not even an hour's drive away. Just something different, fun—that is, if John David had actually been able to step away from church duties for once. The cabins on the Geronimo River were tiny, old and bare-bones, maintained by the state park. The green linoleum counters and seventies-style paisley curtains were exactly the same as they had been when she'd stayed here as a kid, some of the few times she remembered her mother and stepfather ever laughing together. She'd felt buoyed this afternoon, stupid now. Had known the river was too high for swimming, had seen it might come a storm, but had simply wanted to be here this weekend, somewhere that felt—what, nostalgic? It was clear to Bethany from the moment the others stepped foot inside the cabin that they were disappointed, only going along because that Sunday was her birthday. It was even more awkward without John David here. God, she could've killed him just then for leaving, but mostly she wished he were here to handle this mess. John David always knew what to do.

Thunder boomed and ricocheted off the windowpanes.

Bethany ran back upstairs, slid into her sandals, and walked out onto the small balcony off her bedroom. Rain hit her face so hard it stung, and the beam of the flashlight made the rain look white like ice pellets. Brown river water rushed between the trees and swept over the hood of the truck in the driveway. Maybe she should call 911. But, nearly dropping the phone— her hands were so wet and shaking so bad—she saw it had died. None of them had had much reception anyway and there was no landline. The river sounded like a freight train. She waved the flashlight in front of her, flicking it off and on, then yelled out into the darkness, a pitiful cry for help that died in her throat. And quieter, she tried to shush the dread in her heart, that voice telling her they were certainly fucked, but she'd heard it now and she couldn't not hear it. She wiped her eyes and smoothed her hair back. They still had the kayaks. Could they paddle out? Should they try and climb the roof?

It sounded like a bullwhip hit the house. Then, splintering.

The rest happened so quickly. All Bethany remembers is being lifted off her feet and the wind knocked out of her. She spun, muddy water filling her mouth and nose. No way to tell which way was up or down. She briefly surfaced—not because she swam up, more that she happened to land that way—coughed and struggled to fill her lungs with air. The river roared in her ears and rain kept coming down hard, blinding her. She kicked and pumped her limbs, but was pulled under again.

Lungs searing, heartbeat slowing, she stopped struggling.

But the river spat her out. Slammed her hard on her back. She wasn't moving anymore, and her head was above water. She'd hit some kind of barrier. With a surge of adrenaline and one handhold on the side of what she thought was a big rock, she spun and reached behind her. It was a slab of broken concrete, part of a road or bridge maybe, and a bent piece of rebar jutted out above her head. She grabbed the rebar and pulled herself up so only her legs were submerged, and then shimmied up so she could perch on top of the concrete, waves beating just below her feet. Coughing, gasping, she vomited up what seemed like a gallon of floodwater followed by the taste of blood in her mouth—her lip was split, her face cut and throbbing. Her sandals were knocked off, cell phone gone, Michael and Kendall God knows where, but all she could think about was the flashlight. Damn it, she'd lost John David's expensive flashlight. Her mind churned with static while her eyes scanned the pitch dark for a light.

The rain stopped, and eventually, the rising sun pinkened the cloud-dense sky.

Bethany felt calmer now—numb, maybe—and her teeth had finally stopped chattering. Yet, she noticed her perch had begun to shift. The pale brown water, though slowed, was steadily rising. She remembered once being a very small child, her mother distracted at bath time, leaving Bethany alone with the tap running. Not knowing she could turn the knob herself, she had sat scared and frozen while bathwater seeped over the sides. Now she shivered and sucked in her breath. Gripped the rebar and raised herself up again. She had no idea how far downriver she'd traveled, no idea where the Geronimo ended and land began. Water went as far as her eyes could see, only interrupted by the tops of a few trees and a tin roof up a hill in the distance.

She swallowed hard, a sinking feeling in her stomach, when she thought she heard a man's voice.

Was that Michael? No.

Was she hallucinating?

No—someone called to her, she was certain. She carefully

4

turned herself around and saw a man on a tree branch hanging over the swirling water. She stared open-mouthed—had he been there in the dark this whole time? He was maybe twenty feet away, asking her to swim to him.

"The tree! Get to the tree," he called. "Lady, you'll be swept off if you don't!"

They stared at each other for a moment. He wore jeans and a red T-shirt, sopping wet and stuck to a thin body corded with muscle. He had a narrow face, strong brow, shoulder-length honey-blond hair, and a short beard. The biggest, roundest blue eyes she'd ever seen. He looked to Bethany in that moment like Jesus.

"You have to swim! Launch yourself off it! Swim to me and I'll catch you," he called.

"I can't," she screamed, but as she did, most of the concrete submerged.

Cold water drew up to her neck. The current pulsed against her, grit and debris stung the cuts on her skin, but she was able to position her feet against the concrete. She took a deep breath and let go, her fingers curled and sore from gripping the rebar so hard for so long, propelling herself off the concrete with her legs. She stroked her arms as hard as she could, so close to the man that he leaned out of the tree and reached for her. Focused on only his outstretched arm, ignoring her fear and the rough sweep of unknown objects against her bare legs.

A whirlpool formed around her, pulling her below the surface.

He was in the water. He flung her backward by the sleeve of her sweatshirt and she was out of the whirlpool, surfacing, reaching for the branch overhead. She hoisted herself up and hooked her legs around the jagged bark of the tree and inched forward, hugging the branch, summoning what felt like the last of her strength to turn upright.

He wasn't there.

She yelled out for the man, but only the rushing of the water called back. Scanning the horizon, she briefly spotted the top of his head bobbing downriver, swiftly out of reach. He was gone, gone—the current carried him until he was gone from her sight—and she sobbed, knowing it should've been her out on the river dead drowned.

Part I

ANNIE, TWO WEEKS LATER

Chapter 1

The flood drowned our pastures, battered and broke our houses, left the roads out damaged and all the low parts slick with mud. The water even rose over the graveyard. Headstones knocked loose floated into people's yards. Caskets, like our secrets, unearthed, reinterred. Now every time it rains, I think about the surface of the river and the alternate universe below it—the living and the dead, all things obscured yet still a part of ours. How that spring the water stole from us and rearranged what we knew of as home. Map the land after a storm like that: Garnett County, split by the fault line and riddled with rivers. My family's place out in the country, away from all the lights. The old library building and the live oak behind the football field where I used to sit and eat my lunch and dream my dreams. Home back then was also the shitty third-floor unit I kept imagining someone had died in, the place where I'd been holed up until Bethany Keller called and asked me to meet her at the office downtown.

Outside, the world had a violent shine to it. Overgrown grasses electric shades of new green, puddles streaked with silver.

The edges of the old downtown street were mostly dry, but if you looked closely at the side of the courthouse you caught the ghost of a waterline, a fine coating of silt. Opposite the square was a century-old redbrick building, and on the second story, our office: McIntyre Investigations, founded by my grandfather Leroy and his former partner in the sheriff's office, Mary-Pat Zimmerman. Leroy had retired, so I was the McIntyre on the door—I always puffed up a bit at that, though Mary-Pat was still my boss.

I walked up the narrow staircase. Opened the pebbled glass door and startled to see Bethany inside and already seated, tapping her finger on the edge of my desk. Her nails looked bitten down, and her face—"Oh, Annie," she said, turning to look up at me. "I look worse than I feel. It's all right. I'm all right, now."

"No, it's not all right," I said, instinctively touching my own cheek. "I'm so sorry." Despite her skillful makeup, I could see Bethany had a nasty shiner. Four black sutures over her eyebrow. Most of her exposed skin had scratches, and on her forearm was a yellow-green bruise the size of an apple. She wore a gauzy pink blouse over a high-necked camisole, white jeans with purposefully frayed hems, and matching heels, giving her the appearance of a beaten-down Barbie.

"Door was open," she said, shifting in her seat. I nodded and took the chair across from her. I was still working on this tendency I'd developed since being hired: no matter how big or small my clients' losses were, it was difficult to meet their eyes at first. To allow myself to feel what they were feeling. Growing up, I used to wish for danger and intrigue to greet me, foolish wishes conjured from endless, sleepy nights in this small town. Six months into my work as an apprentice investigator, I knew enough about loss—real loss—to be afraid of it, and yet, there was some part of me that kept tempting darkness. That wanted to look at the monster under the bed. Maybe I was a voyeur—why else be drawn to this line of work? Or maybe, I hoped, there was another, better version of me, braver than I felt most days, who would come to life if I dared peer back.

Bethany wouldn't let me look away. She moved her face up and down until our eyes locked. "Annie, I—I feel like I'm sleepwalking. Like, how can this be real life?"

The tragedy had made national news. In our county and to the northwest, upriver, thirteen inches of rain had fallen in a matter of hours. The Geronimo crested at a record forty feet. A wall of water had knocked out an entire concrete overpass, killing three stranded motorists. It lifted an entire house clear off its foundation. The house—a vacation rental adjacent to the state park—had floated only a short distance before hitting a stand of cypress at the riverbank and splitting in two. The couple who'd been staying on the first floor had been trapped inside, but Bethany had been shot off a balcony and into the raging river. County search and rescue had spotted her from a helicopter clinging to a tree branch. Kendall and Michael Davis's bodies had been recovered several days later.

I heard Mary-Pat coming before I saw her. She had long legs and a distinctive gait, a way of dragging her boots when she walked, and she ambled around the corner holding a Styrofoam to-go box from the café. Her ice blue eyes widened. "Bethany Richter, I'll be damned. I'm awful sorry for your losses."

I had to remind myself Bethany Keller was Bethany Richter now that she'd married John David. Bethany was one of my cousin Nikki's closest friends, and before she became a full-time preacher's wife, had also been an aesthetician at the salon my aunt owned in town. We'd known each other since elementary school, but my most vivid memories of her were at sixteen, seventeen—she and my cousin had been cheerleaders who'd gotten themselves kicked off varsity on several occasions, mostly for back talk and drinking, and Bethany notably one final time for getting caught fooling around behind the buses with the away team's quarterback.

People change, I've been told.

"Annie, Ms. Zimmerman," Bethany said, pausing until Mary-Pat was seated at her big desk in the opposite corner of the room. "I want to hire you. I—"

"Yeah, Nikki already told me that," I said. And there was my instinctual tic, reminding her that I was best friends with Nikki, too. Growing up, it had never been the three of us. Nikki and I had a sisterlike dynamic, close enough in age to be equals. She and Bethany were only a grade above me, but together acted like I was a baby, teasing me mercilessly, or worse, excluding me altogether. Add to that I was not a cheerleader—in title or in spirit. It was silly, I knew, but I had to remind myself to not be so defensive now. "She didn't tell me the details, though. I'm sorry, Bethany."

Mary-Pat unwrapped her cheeseburger and shot me a look. "Tell us why you'd like our help. And don't mind me—got to eat and run, but Annie'll take notes."

Heat crept up my neck as I fished in the desk drawer for a steno pad and pen. "Yes, go on."

Bethany nodded. "Well, it's about this man I met out on the river that night. I don't know who he is, or if he's even still alive. He probably isn't. He got pulled away by the current and I lost sight of him," she said, exhaling like she'd been holding her breath. Her brown eyes watered and she dabbed them with the ruffled sleeve of her blouse. "He saved my life. I want you to help me find him, or at least figure out who he was. If I can't thank him 'cause he's gone, I need to speak to his family. I need to tell them how sorry I am."

"Oh," I said, surprised. Nikki really hadn't told me the details and I'd assumed it was related to Michael and Kendall's estate and the church, which would have been a bit less daunting. Before the flood, Mary-Pat sent me to Houston to track down a distant relative needed to probate a client's will, and I'd finished the job alone. I'd had an inverse trajectory with this line of work: solved a homicide then shot back to square one. Had no right to expect otherwise. No law enforcement experience, no special training, I'd been swept up—my role in the investigation equal parts circumstance and sheer will—though part of me had been longing for credit, for recognition of what I'd done. In the months since the homicide case closed, everything had slowed down. Before the Houston assignment, Mary-Pat only tossed me the occasional missing-pet case, my big win locating an ill-tempered spaniel that kept getting out. The last half a year was spent taking notes, taking lunch orders, taking calls Mary-Pat would rather ignore. When I'd told her that Bethany would be coming by, that Nikki had referred her to us, she hinted that even if it was technically under her license, she might let me take lead. A straight-A student at heart, I liked the feeling of being teed up for a promotion. But this—this was not what I had in mind. This was bigger. An actual missing person case. And maybe, a chance to really prove myself.

"Have you talked to the law already?" I asked Bethany.

"When they were looking for those drivers from the bridge and for Michael and Kendall, they did aerial searches and went down the river by boat, but they didn't report any other victims. I told the fire chief about the guy, to keep looking, but they stopped. The sheriff's department says I don't have enough information to file any kind of report, but I figure someone must be missing this man. Someone must miss him," she said.

"Well." Mary-Pat put down her burger and wiped her mouth with a napkin. "We don't want to get your hopes up."

Bethany inched toward the edge of her seat. "But you find personal records and stuff like that, right? Couldn't you figure out who he is, and even if he's dead, like, locate his next of kin?"

"You don't have a name or much for us to go on," I said. "What else do you know about this guy?"

"He was white, had long, straight, parted-in-the-middle honey-brown hair. A short beard, round blue eyes. Honestly, he looked just like the paintings you see of Jesus. Like, kind of sad and long in the face, heavy brow, but attractive. Probably late twenties, early thirties."

"Huh," Mary-Pat said just as her phone started buzzing in the belt clip she wore. "Hold on, girls," she said, and answered the call with more of a grunt than a hello. I assumed it was not a new client.

"Aw, little Annie." Bethany pointed at the wall. "That's such a sweet picture."

It was a photograph of me sandwiched between Mary-Pat and Leroy on the day he bought the office space. Twelve years old and head turned sideways, I stared wide-eyed up at my grandfather. That summer Leroy and Mary-Pat had solved a cold case that was extensively covered by the media, bringing them notoriety across Texas and allowing them to open the firm. The case had now grown distant in most people's memory, but Mary-Pat and Leroy had maintained a reputation and got a lot of business through word of mouth, the basic website I'd helped them make, and reruns of an episode of *Dateline*. I looked back at myself in the picture and winced. All knobby knees and braces. Being around Bethany, even now, added to this feeling of adolescent unease bubbling up in me.

"You were always the smart one out of the three of us, Annie," she said and looked back at me. "If anyone can help me, it's you. You've always been a nice girl, a good friend to me."

"I'll try," I said, blushing a little though I knew better than to be flattered. We were friendly, but I wouldn't go so far as to say friends. The last time we'd spent significant time together was when I'd been forced to tag along with them at cheer camp in fifth grade. If I had to guess, the truth was closer to Nikki having already told her I'd be able to find the man, and she now worried at the uncertainty inherent to such a case.

"I've always trusted you," she said, looking like she might tear up again. "I posted the whole story right after I got out of the hospital. Did you see?"

I had, actually. That was how I'd known she was the woman referenced on the news. And after I read it, I couldn't stop thinking about it. A wall of water, the river roaring in her ears, plunged into total darkness—my palms had started sweating, scrolling the hundred or so comments attached that were all some variation of condolences. Adding my own felt like a drop in the bucket, but I'd typed something out anyway.

"It got shared a bunch of times, so I know people around here have seen it. Still, no one's stepped forward with any information about the guy. Everyone thinks I'm making it up," she said.

"Who said that?"

"Oh, you can just tell—'bless your poor heart,' they'll say, or 'have you tried talking to someone?' They all think I've lost my mind."

"I'm sure that's not the case," I said, biting my tongue. Describing him as looking like Jesus come to save her didn't help. "So, can you remember anything else more specific about the man you didn't already share? What was he wearing?"

"He had on a red T-shirt that said 'PAWS Garnett fundraiser 5K.' Like from the animal shelter, I guess? He also had a tattoo on his right forearm," she said, and reached out her own arm, tracing it with her finger. "A single stemmed blue rose.

Right here, pretty big. No other tattoos and no piercings, that I could see anyway."

I nodded, writing it down. The shirt made me think he was probably local. A rose tattoo wasn't that unique, but a blue rose, and one that large, might be memorable.

Mary-Pat came back into the room and sat heavily in her swivel chair. "How's John David holding up? What does he think about all this?" Mary-Pat lived near John David's parents, the Reverend John Richter and his wife, Colleen, in a small unincorporated area north of town settled by German immigrants at the end of the nineteenth century. Rhineland was now nothing more than an antiques store and a handful of farms, and for the most part had remained in the hands of those same founding families. Hillview Christian was the evangelical church out that way, set far back off a county road, but from what I'd heard, it had doubled its size in recent years. John David was an executive pastor under his father. The friend who'd died, Michael, had been the church's youth pastor. Mary-Pat shook her head. "I can't imagine how everyone must be feeling."

Bethany looked down at her hands in her lap. "John David's not really processing all that's happened. He's like on autopilot. I mean, we all are. Trying to get through one day at a time."

"Where was he that night?" I asked. "It was just you, Pastor Michael, and his wife, Kendall, at the vacation rental that night, correct?"

"Yeah. A lady from our church, Mrs. Parsons, was dying," she said, looking between me and Mary-Pat. "John David took the call and went to the county hospital to be with her. By the time he could come back, the roads were already flooded. He's so wise, John David, he has such a strong faith. But even he is just like, how on earth could this have happened? *God, why them? Why me?* I keep thinking. When I told John David about the man and wanting to find him, he seemed kind of upset. Still, I think he gets why I need to do this."

Mary-Pat narrowed her eyes. "The two of you are in agreement, though? He knows we'll require a payment here soon?" Mary-Pat would be the first person to say it was old-fashioned to ask that her husband was on the same page, but she'd also been stuck chasing down a contested bill too many times to not ask. That and she wasn't much for emotional speeches.

"Yes. And he doesn't care about the money," Bethany said, a little irritated-sounding. "Not like it'll make what happened to Kendall and Michael hurt any less. But I need to do this so I can sleep at night."

Mary-Pat nodded. "I understand. We'll find out what we can and will be following up with you throughout the course of the investigation."

"Good, that's good," Bethany said, loosening her vise grip on the arm of her chair. "Thank you."

"It's traumatic, all that's happened to you," I said carefully, trying my best to not sound like everyone else she'd shared her story with. I was pretty sure I believed her, but Nikki's warning when we'd talked on the phone echoed: Bethany nearly died out on that water. For two days after she was rescued, she didn't even speak. She'd said Bethany was on edge, but I could see now that was putting it lightly—it wasn't just the loss of her friends that had hollowed her out, given her the manic energy of someone trying to fix the unfixable. She'd lost the person she was before and there was no going back. "I'm not saying you were mistaken, Bethany, but Nikki said you were in shock when they found you and I wonder if—"

"She did, did she? Come on, Annie. You of all people should know she's the crazy one, not me," she said, letting out an exasperated sigh. She was right; Nikki could be erratic, wild—often the instigator when the pair ran around in high school, and now, set to be married to a man she'd only known six months. Bethany reached to pick her pink suede purse up off the floor, clutching it tightly under her arm. "If there's nothing else now, I'll get going. Speaking of Nikki, I need to call her. Heard the happy couple settled on a date."

"That's right," I said. "Should be a great party." I led her to the door, the big smile I'd plastered on my face making my jaw ache.

Why? We had been in a drought. The soil grew saturated too quickly, couldn't handle so much water after nothing for so long. Garnett's always been prone to flash floods because of the rivers, all the limestone hills and creeks up over the fault line, but never like this. A flood of this magnitude should statistically only occur once every five hundred years. *Why me?* Bethany had said. *Why anyone?* I wanted to say back. From the second-story window, I watched her exit the building and get into her car, a pearlescent white SUV with a fish sticker on the window and a yarn and Popsicle-stick lanyard hanging from the rearview. God's eyes, I remembered the lanyards being called. I'd made one once in vacation Bible school as a kid.

"What do you think, Annie? Should I let you take this one?"

I turned back from the window. Mary-Pat watched me intently, arms crossed over her chest. I trusted her. She wouldn't take on a case for the firm that she didn't think was solvable and she wouldn't let me go solo unless she thought I was ready. I knew, in my heart, I was ready.

Why, then, did I hesitate?

Bethany's honey-haired Jesus man—I couldn't picture him, couldn't wrap my head around him being alive at this point if he'd been swept downriver as she described. Then again, she

18

didn't necessarily need me to find him, she only needed to know who he was.

"Yes," I said. "I'll take it."

The truth was, I'd felt it coming. Like when you trip, that split second before you hit the ground, know you're going to fall, and know you can't stop it? For the past two weeks, ever since I'd heard what happened to Bethany, how she'd nearly drowned, her face—brown eyes wide with fear, that long, chestnut hair dripping muddy water, mouth rounded in a scream—it was all I could see when I closed my eyes. The case already chose me.

Chapter 2

"Wait a minute, darlin'," Leroy said as I pulled into a parking space at Walmart. I let Ray Price finish crooning before I cut the engine. Fine by me. There was an earnest, turned-out sound to the old songs and I loved the way the steel guitar sent a shiver down my spine. Or maybe I loved the music because it was loaded with associations. Moments like now, sitting here quietly with him. Leroy had his eyes closed and his Stetson pulled low over his brow.

"Feeling all right?" I asked.

"Fine. Only daydreaming," he said, but grimacing as he opened the passenger door. I drove a used Pontiac Grand Prix I called the silver bullet, both for its color and my superstitions. It had a lot of get-up-and-go, but got terrible gas mileage and rode too low to the ground. I came around to hand Leroy his cane and help him out of the seat.

I read somewhere that people who survive heart attacks often suffer from depression. I don't know if Leroy was depressed. He'd always been a melancholy person. He still acted himself, only more so—if he was down, he closed himself in his bedroom, drew the curtains, and listened to his records. If he was up, he called me and asked me to take him driving, wheedling me until we went across the river to see the ponies or to the VFW bar so he could have a cold beer in the company of the two-steppers and barflies. He seemed to me just tenderhearted lately, though I hadn't seen him since the flood. His house in town only took minor damage, but we hadn't been to see his land across the river, "the place," as my family called it. The creek would be running, the stone cistern full, and the mesquite would have leafed out, vibrant as the bluebonnets and Indian paintbrush dotting the hillside. I knew he ached to go. I also knew his leg wasn't strong enough to walk it yet.

"You got your list?" I asked. "Didn't the doctor say you should get some vitamins?"

He mumbled an affirmative and stretched his arms, looking up at the sky. The morning was bracingly clear—it amazed me how quickly things could change. How after all that destruction, it was possible for a day to be this beautiful. At the far end of the Walmart lot sat parked a jumble of RVs and campers, some with awnings and couples slumped underneath in camping chairs. Travelers and truckers frequently stayed overnight since it was right off the interstate, but I wondered if some were displaced by the flood. Transients were not uncommon, either—two men lay on the strip of grass between the parking lot and the entrance to the Greyhound station, duffel bags propped behind their heads as pillows and an old yellow dog curled at their feet.

Barely dodging the overenthusiastic door greeter, Leroy and I split up to get our respective groceries and met back in the produce section. Despite the list, he loaded up on canned Vienna sausages, or "veenies," as he called them, crackers, beer, a stereo that was on sale, circus peanuts, and chocolate-covered cherries.

"So much for your DASH diet," I said.

"Come on, Ears. I'm fine."

He'd lately taken to calling me Ears, which I rather disliked, but that didn't seem to matter to him. His first day back from the rehab facility following the car accident and heart attack that nearly killed him, he looked between Mary-Pat and me, said we were his eyes and ears now that he was resigned to using a cane, now that he had a pacemaker and two stints. He never explained why I was Ears and she was Eyes, though in a weird way I got it.

"Any thoughts on my case?" I said, tossing a bag of salad greens—one vegetable, at least—into the basket attached to his motorized scooter. *My case.* The words felt funny in my mouth. Mary-Pat hadn't stuck around the office much longer than Bethany had yesterday, leaving without giving me any to-do list. I spent the rest of the afternoon finishing up my usual clerical tasks, which had accumulated over the time I'd been stuck at home, then worked into the evening combing through records, but as Bethany had said, there wasn't anyone else reported missing during or right after the storm that hadn't been accounted for by the law, either in Garnett or the neighboring counties. I didn't quite know where to keep looking after nothing came up in the file search. I woke that morning so anxious I felt like I was vibrating.

Leroy stopped and looked up at me. "Be careful with it. Shoot, not saying you would, but take care to not cause more distress."

My palms around the buggy handle felt clammy. "You don't think I should take the case, then?"

"No, no. Didn't say that. Just be careful, sounds like this woman has been through a lot," he said. "Talk to the fire chief first. He leads all search and rescue."

"Right," I said, and wiped my hands on my jeans. "There's a

flood relief drive at the high school tomorrow. Think I'll have Mary-Pat introduce me to Chief Harkness then. I also heard the humane society will be there—Bethany described the guy as wearing one of their T-shirts. The shelter got destroyed and no one answered their phone line. But that shirt and a tattoo is about all I have to go on."

Leroy was quiet for a moment, after some contemplation adding a sack of oranges to his basket. At least he wouldn't get scurvy. "You ought to look for a person no one would miss, sounds like."

"I thought about driving over to interview residents from those complexes off River Road," I said, my voice rising, hinting it was more of a question than a statement. "There was so much destruction there, I wonder if it might've gone unnoticed that someone hadn't been accounted for since the flood."

"Do that and return to the scene when you can. It'll look different as the water's receded, but you never know what you might come across," he said, and I nodded, breathing a little easier with some sense of direction, some sense of his approval. Doing Leroy's job had seemed at times both natural and strange. I come from several generations of lawmen, and notably, one woman, my great-great-grandmother who'd been one of the first female sheriffs in Texas. But I'd never dreamed of being a cop. I'd dreamed of doing big things in an amorphous way that mostly translated to getting the hell out of Garnett. I'd come home from college expecting to leave soon after, but when I took Leroy up on his offer to work for the firm, desires coiled tight and hidden in my heart sprung free. I didn't know what I thought I knew— about him, this place, me. More than anything, I wanted to find the truth. And for a time, I thought I wanted to be him.

I motioned for Leroy to follow me toward the men's clothing section and he rolled alongside me in silence. Wandering the aisles—really, going to Walmart for anything other than a quick errand—reminded me of the hours and hours I spent here in high school. Wasn't much else open after 7 p.m. Me and Nikki, we'd go cruising around the parking lot, buy gum and sticky lip gloss, meet up with boys, do a lot of nothing, fall in and out of love in the span of a single night. Nearly everywhere in this town reminded me of me back then, and I was still deciding if that was a good or a bad thing. I stopped in front of a rack of sweatpants, handing a pair to Leroy. "Why don't you let me get you some of these?"

"No, thank you," he said, the buggy beeping as he put it in reverse.

"I don't get how you do physical therapy in Wranglers and a collared shirt. That can't be comfortable. At least get some slippers or tennis shoes," I said, and pointed at his stiff leather boots.

"I'm comfortable as I'll ever be."

I grabbed a T-shirt from the sale rack that said 24 HOURS IN A DAY, 24 BEERS IN A CASE . . . COINCIDENCE? and handed it to him. "Well, nothing else, this one suits you."

He laughed and put it back, nodding toward the registers. "Let's get on up there before I miss the early bird discount. You got work to do enough without dressing me. And don't worry yourself so much, Ears. I reckon you'll find him."

My face felt warm and I smiled. That was about as effusive as Leroy ever got. I followed behind him, scanning my buggy one last time for anything I might've forgotten.

"Whoa, whoa. Back it the hell up, lady," a man's voice boomed from the front entrance. "Get off of me!"

I looked down the long aisle and recognized one of the two men who'd been sleeping on the grass out in the parking lot. His camo pants sagged at the waist and knees and he'd donned a gray oversized hoodie stained with what looked like motor oil. With deeply tanned skin weathered from the sun, he looked older than he probably was, and his brown hair was bunched and matted into something resembling dreads. The door greeter's face flushed—she was starting to cry—and she pointed at his torso. "I saw you put it under your shirt!"

A small crowd formed around the two. A teenage girl aimed her phone at the door greeter to record. "Help!" the woman hollered and flapped her arms. "Thief!"

The manager hurried toward the pair, blue-and-yellow vest flapping open behind him. "What's going on, Rhonda?" Sweat darkened his polo shirt under the arms and around the collar. He huffed and pointed at the alleged shoplifter. "This'll be the last time, son."

"Aw, come on, man!"

"He done took a bag of chips," the woman said, lifting eyeglasses that hung from a beaded chain around her neck to her nose and frowning. "He's a thief."

"We got cameras," the manager said, his voice tired.

"You got cameras, then you should know I didn't take nothing," the man said, and unzipped his jacket. He shook it out and lifted his shirt to reveal a concave stomach and faded blue boxers. He spun around to show the others. "See?"

"Fine, go on then. Just get," the manager said as though he were shooing a stray dog. He waved away the onlookers and shrugged. "Nothing to see here, folks. Thank you for shopping."

Leroy laughed. "If the door lady would've paid attention, she'd have seen it."

"She needs to calm right down," I said, and rolled my eyes. "Seen what, that the chips were jammed down his pants?"

"No. Well, yes. But the two of 'em got a system. He got her riled up on purpose. While the door greeter was fussing over him, his partner walked out with a whole mess of things."

Sure enough, I looked through the door and saw not one, but

two men out in the wind. The pair untied the yellow dog from a post, stuffed their duffel bag with food, ditched the handbasket, then hopped the curb. Turned toward the station, and in an instant, were gone. "I didn't notice the second man, either," I said.

Leroy used his cane to stand, reaching into the buggy and placing his items on the conveyor belt. "Little darlin', you've always been a good listener. Don't forget to keep your eyes open."

Chapter 3

I dropped Leroy off, stopped home to put away my groceries, then drove to the bridge near the center of town and parked, setting off on foot to canvass the area. The Geronimo River was to the west—long, winding, rocky. In the center of the county near town it broke off to the Salt Fork River going northeast, and due east, where I now stood, it became the Angel River. Normally clear as glass, with a soft, cold current, the Angel was aptly named. But on that day the water was a milky brown. Mud-rich and chock-full of debris from the flood, even weeks later. The level had only receded under the bridge a few days ago.

I kicked a stone into the water. Though the Angel was spring-fed, what flowed down the Geronimo found its way here and intermingled. A body might easily pass underneath me, unseen in the murky depth. A corpse held fast in a tangle of upturned roots. I loved the river and felt somehow betrayed. I'd floated this river before I even knew how to swim, before I even had memories, and later, after I'd gone away to school, it was the steady pulse of its current I dreamed of, its forks and creeks branching from the center of town like a web of veins. I hadn't feared it like I did now. What if the water rose as violently again? Weather patterns were growing more extreme. I had read about this, had felt the words "climate change" hanging over our heads, but it wasn't a talking point anymore. There wasn't an "if" anymore.

Shivering despite the heat, I walked off the bridge and onto the city park path. A dozen people had reportedly drowned in the flood. Two were of course Michael and Kendall Davis, three had been motorists—another, a man who'd tried to aid one of the motorists—but the other six, including two children, had all been residents of two section eight apartment complexes in Garnett, River Oaks and Rancho Vista, which were located not far from the city park. I'd gone door-to-door in the closest neighborhood, a handful of mud-stained houses bunched together in the shade before the land opened up into cleared-out, empty fields, but no one had known of a still-missing man. I saved the apartment complexes for last. Knew I had to prepare myself. Past the railroad trellis I came around a bend to where the city park path became private, ending at a short picket fence with all but two or three of its boards cracked in half or gone altogether.

The units closest to the river were gutted. Nothing but red-brick shells and dark, gaping holes where windows and doors should have been, yellow caution tape strung across them. A bank of construction dumpsters sat overflowing with pink insulation, plaster, shards of glass, stained and sodden mattresses, and rolls of ripped-up carpet. I walked uphill toward the front of the first complex, mindful of the fact I'd left the bullet at the city park and would have to practically slide down the muddy embankment on my way back.

I stepped inside the empty unit closest to me. My shoes squished in the muck as though I were walking outside, not on an apartment floor. The once white walls were stained and coated brown, nothing left hanging, though there was a bright red *x* and a few numbers spray-painted on one. Scattered to the corners were odd bits: a toothbrush, plates, two broken chairs, a baby doll with the head bent at an odd angle. A deep blue feeling coursed through me, heavy and strange. I thought about what Leroy had said, thinking that looking for someone missing wasn't just keeping your eyes open—it was drawing shapes from the void. The air was so still in there. It felt wrong to linger, knowing this was someone's home. It wasn't safe, either; exposed wires jutted out from empty sockets and there might be dead animals and other hazardous waste deeper inside.

The sun shot straight into my eyes, disorienting me. The surrounding parking lot was not half full, and I walked until I spotted an elderly woman with a younger man, maybe her son, leaning against the hood of a dark green Corolla and waved them down. The man was in his late thirties or early forties, heavyset, and wearing a Spurs jersey. "Let me guess, you get locked out of the laundry room? We left some stuff in there, too," he said.

"Nope, don't live here. But I heard a lot of people from this complex got displaced last month. Was wondering if either of you had heard about anyone still missing? Someone never turn back up?"

The man looked me up and down for a moment, jingling his keys in his pants pockets. "You a reporter or something?"

"Private investigator," I said, squaring my shoulders. Technically unlicensed, but close enough.

His eyes got big. "For real?"

I nodded, used to this reaction. People expect a man in a trench coat. Dog the Bounty Hunter, maybe. One of my weaknesses as an investigator is also my strength: I'm unintimidating in appearance. I'm young, a woman, soft-spoken and on the small side, have long hair that I wear loose around my shoulders, and freckles. An open, sympathetic face that makes people, strangers even, want to tell me things. Not have a conversation necessarily, but get things off their chests. That is, if they notice me in the first place.

"Huh. That's cool."

The woman, much less impressed, pushed herself off the hood of the car and said in Spanish that she was hot and she was going inside to wait. The man argued with her a bit before she grabbed the keys from him and left. I cleared my throat to bring his focus back.

"Sorry, management is just now letting a select few people back into their apartments to get whatever's not ruined. Mom's real upset about the whole thing," he said, eyes trained on the woman's retreating figure. "But missing? No, can't think of anybody still missing. You heard about that family, though?"

A knot formed in my throat. Two children and their parents had been sleeping soundly when water cascaded into their home. The parents, like a lot of people, didn't have a landline installed, so they didn't get the reverse 911 call an hour earlier telling them to evacuate, and tired after working a double shift, they'd turned their cell phones off and didn't get the National Weather Service warning, either. By the time they were awake and had gathered the children, they were trapped. I hadn't let myself think about what I assumed would be the worst part: the knowing. Had they told the children what was coming when they realized it? Those last few minutes, water up to their necks—I inhaled slowly, trying to keep my nausea at bay. "I heard. I'm really sorry," I said, and squinted up at the nearest unit, the older woman staring out at us from the open, paneless window. "Y'all got evacuated in time?"

The man nodded and turned to look where I was, his face

scrunching up in the sunlight. "We happened to be at my uncle's place for the weekend. That's where we're living now. Thank God. Our neighbors were up on their roof for eight hours waiting for rescue. The other woman here who died, she was my mom's friend."

"God, I'm so sorry," I said.

"I have nightmares about it. The water came so fast, they said it burst through her front door."

"Shit. Those units down there?"

He shook his head and pointed a little farther up. "The surge came all the way up there. That one was Lucia's, the other, two down, is where those kids and their parents . . ." He paused and let out a wet cough, turning his face away.

The unit he pointed at was the one I'd walked into a few minutes earlier. My stomach lurched again. The numbers on the wall must have been for the bodies—I hadn't known. But hadn't I felt it?

"Anyway." He sniffed and looked up. "I better help Mom."

"Of course," I said, staring for a moment before I snapped out of it and handed him one of Leroy's old business cards with my name and cell number penciled on the back of it. "Thanks for talking. If you hear about anyone missing, either officially or through the grapevine, you can call or text."

He pocketed the card, then walked toward the hollowed-out building. His mother came to the window again. I looked to where she looked, through the trees and toward the swollen river. But water has no memory. Unlike the trampled brush and those left behind, the quickening current bore no witness to the dead.

Chapter 4

After leaving the apartment complexes, what was left of them, I texted my cousin. Heart heavy and tired, I needed a break, or at least to sit in the air-conditioning for a few. Mixer's was a dive on the east side of town that had dollar margaritas from two till five. Nikki carried one in each of her hands, licking her wrist where one sloshed over the lip of the cup. "I realized why everything looked wrong when I pulled up. Sign's gone from the parking lot," she said, motioning with her chin toward the dingy window outlined with colored string lights.

I turned and looked out at the live oak at the edge of the lot, at the blond wound on its trunk and the cracked lower limbs. "Heard a giant branch fell. Toppled the sign and landed across a row of cars. It's lucky no one was hurt," I said, then scooted out a chair for her with my foot.

"Well, cheers," she said, and tapped her cup to mine.

"To what?"

"To being lucky," she said, and drank, pushing aside her straw to get to the salt on the rim.

"Cheers," I said. Despite being frozen and throat-stingingly

full of well tequila, dollar margaritas went down pretty easy. I
shivered and blinked back a dull ache from the ice. "So, your
buddy Bethany—"

"I know, right? She and I hadn't been talking much since she
quit the salon, but God, when I heard what happened, it just
broke my heart for her. It's a miracle she's alive. What do you
think about this missing person she's talking about? Think you
can find him?"

"I'm going to try," I said, the whisper of hesitation I'd felt
in the office creeping back in as I met Nikki's gaze. Mary-Pat
liked to say don't shit where you eat when it comes to taking
work in a small town. There was room for me to be taken advantage of if Bethany saw this as a favor, not a job. But what
bothered me more, I realized, was that if for whatever reason I
wasn't successful, I couldn't bear to let Bethany—and by extension my cousin—down, that I'd be reminded of such a failure
for a long time. Plus, could Bethany handle a disappointment
in her current state?

"She needs help, Annie."

"I know," I said, sitting up straighter. "I just worry she's not
remembering it all correctly. Trauma does that, you know. She
said this mystery man looked like Jesus."

Nikki fooled with the platinum curl that had come loose
from her topknot before answering. "Yeah, like I told you, girl's
had it rough. Wouldn't be surprised if she had hallucinated him
or some shit. But, then again, I also know Bethany's not crazy."

Nikki was right, Bethany was not crazy. I bit back a laugh
remembering her comment in the office, that Nikki was the
crazy one, not her. Nikki's engagement ring, a white gold band
with a round center stone and a bunch of tiny ones circling it,
caught the light and shimmered. *Halo style,* she liked to say.
Calls me his angel. It had been a little over a month since her

boyfriend, Sonny, proposed, but it still felt surreal to me. Part of me expected them to call it off—in the six months they'd been dating they'd broken up twice—or at least postpone. Sonny had completed his military service, was set to start college in the fall at State, and they planned to marry in early August.

Just then, I caught a glimpse of Sonny walking across the parking lot. "Thought this was just the two of us catching up," I said, and nodded in his direction.

"Aw, shit. I'm sorry. Want me to tell him to leave?"

"Of course not," I said, and laughed. But I had to look away from her, feeling my face heat up. She hadn't meant anything by inviting him, but it stung—it had been weeks since we'd hung out, and didn't she miss me like I missed her? Didn't she have things she needed to tell me, too?

"Why don't you call the professor?" she asked, referring to my boyfriend, Wyatt, who was not a professor, but a graduate student and TA in the geography department at State. "It's been a minute since I've seen him."

"He's probably in class," I said. "It's fine."

She motioned to me pressing my hand below my collarbone. "You okay?"

"Yeah." I smiled and clasped my hands together, though I did feel as though something uncomfortable had lodged in my chest. That was one of the things I'd wanted to vent to her about: me and Wyatt. I didn't exactly know what to think; lately he and I had been going days without speaking. He really was busy with his coursework. But me? I felt like I was spinning in smaller and smaller circles, my restlessness harder and harder to explain, easier to not. It probably was this town I swore I'd never come back to that stirred up my anxiety. I needed to just talk to Wyatt, but I didn't want to raise the question—surely, part of my restlessness was also about him, the same boy I'd dated in high school. I didn't want to hurt him, and I didn't want to lose him. That and I'd always felt the need to keep parts of myself for me—a hand cupped over a tiny flame. Fire dies without air, I also knew. Still, I couldn't open up—to him or to anyone—not all the way.

Sonny sat down and presented us with a cardboard box full of nachos. Mixer's didn't serve food and didn't care if you brought stuff over from the Mexican place down the street. He leaned over to kiss Nikki. "Figured I'd better get y'all something to soak up the tequila."

The worst part about disapproving of Nikki's wedding was that I genuinely liked Sonny. He was kind and had a sense of humor. The nachos made me realize how hungry I was, a partial explanation for my mood. "Smart man." I sighed and reached into the box. "Thanks."

"No problem," he said, and motioned to the bartender for a beer. "What's Wyatt up to?"

"Oh, you know. Finals week."

"Annie's got a new case helping out that poor Bethany," Nikki said, and then covered her mouth with her hand. "I'm allowed to tell him that, right?"

"It's no secret," I said, glad to change the subject away from Wyatt. "Sonny, I'm looking for a man who disappeared on the night of the flood. You were with the volunteer fire department out in Parr City for a while, right?"

"Just for a few months before I left for basic, yeah."

"So how extensive is the county search effort during and after a natural disaster?"

"I don't know. In Parr City we hardly ever got called out. I remember we set a fire out in some guy's back pasture once just to practice," he said, and laughed a little. "Garnett has an actual fire department though, and in this case, they definitely had help from surrounding counties and the state. Heard they searched the river for days looking for that preacher and his wife. I do know that a lot of times people are never found."

"That's what I heard, too," I said. "Heard they were in pretty bad shape by the time they were located."

"The water, it—yeah—you know." Sonny winced. He looked up at the television mounted on the wall behind the bar. "Best not to picture it."

Nikki leaned her elbows on the table. "I hope that Bethany and John David can support each other through this and grow stronger after."

I took a slurp of margarita. "Has to be hard."

"They were already having problems," she loud-whispered.

I raised my eyebrows. "Like what?"

"She doesn't tell me half of what goes on these days. Think I gave her too much crap after she quit the salon to work at the church, so now she feels like she can't complain around me. But I think she's had a hard time adjusting to married life. She's so tightly wound around John David. You know they live at his parents' place? It's like a separate garage apartment, but still."

"Seems like they haven't been married that long to already have problems," I said, an unexpected hitch in my voice.

"I know. That won't be us, will it, babe?" Nikki said, and squeezed Sonny's bicep. He diverted his gaze from the baseball game and smiled, though I could tell he hadn't been listening.

I looked between my cousin and her fiancé. Nikki would be turning twenty-five in a few months. She was still a kid, wasn't she? Why the rush? Maybe I felt this way because I was only a year younger and nowhere near getting married. Maybe I felt this way because we were at a dive bar on a weekday afternoon, because I hated the pet name "babe," or because I was jealous, but instead of feeling happy for her I felt that inconsolable restlessness back again. Finishing my drink in one long pull, I went to the bar to close our tab, ready to get out of there.

At home, I saw the crickets were back. They'd come with the rain. Black little suckers that leapt behind the fridge when I swatted at them with my rolled-up junk mail. They were harmless but made me feel itchy, compelled me to constantly check food containers and shake out my shoes. One bounced against my leg when I dropped my car keys on the coffee table and lay on the couch, one my parents had given me after they finally bought a new one after thirty years. The apartment was as old as the couch and appropriately priced, but I hated its paper-thin walls, even more the smoke smell that lingered no matter how much I cleaned or left the windows open. I'd moved out of Nikki's house two months before, hadn't minded since Sonny was moving in. It was time I got a place of my own. Still, I felt as though I'd been banished here. Since the flood, I had, however, come to appreciate being on the third floor. My downstairs neighbors had to have their carpets replaced, while I'd only had to sit up here alone for three days, just me and the crickets, no power, no phone service, and no way of leaving until the water receded.

Feeling a headache, I slid off the couch, poured a tall glass of water, and surveyed the contents of my galley kitchen. When the power had gone out, everything in the fridge had spoiled. I'd had enough ramen and canned soup to last me a few days, but the loss of modern conveniences had stoked some primal fear in me. I'd felt like an ill-fated pioneer doomed to die of dysentery. And now, how was it that with all the groceries I'd bought that morning nothing seemed to fit together for a proper meal? I settled on a box of macaroni, turned the water on to boil, and relocated to the dining area a mere two feet away where I had another hand-me-down, a pine table and chairs still nice but for legs chewed up by my great aunt's poodle. I turned on my laptop, my fingers hovering over the keys until I decided to open Facebook.

There was an invitation to like someone's brother's screen-printing company turned clothing brand, tank tops and trucker caps emblazoned with sayings like MAMA NEEDS WINE or BUT FIRST, COFFEE—and more from another girl I'd gone to high school with who was deep into an MLM scheme peddling essential oils. I ignored the notifications and went back to my original mission of searching for any neighborhood groups with posts that weren't private. There were detailed chronicles of raccoon problems, but only a few posts related to the flood, mostly recommendations for drywall repairmen. There was, however, a post on the City Hall page with over three hundred comments, dated the night of the storm. People had been commenting in real time, asking where to go once they evacuated, worrying what to do about food, pets, important medications left behind. The admin replied over and over saying to not go back, just head to the high school gym, and that they would have food, water, and shelter for the night.

Nothing about a missing man.

I clicked over to the sheriff's department page. They typically posted alerts and advisories, things like that, and it occurred to me someone might've left a telling comment. The night of the flood the posts were accounts of being overwhelmed by high water rescues, and more people commenting in real time, wondering where the boats were, why no one had come to save them. The poster repeated the warning to motorists: *Turn around, don't drown!* People around here all know the saying, know that even six inches of moving water can float a car.

I knew—I just hadn't been thinking that night.

Several miles outside Garnett, you can spot the water tower on the horizon. There is a subtle incline as you cross the county line, and Leroy used to always pull this trick on me when I was a kid—he said he could make the water tower disappear. Knowing every small hill, he'd wave his hand at the exact right moment and instantly the tower would poke up on the horizon. Wave again, and *voilà!* the tower would fall off the edge of the earth. Wait a couple seconds and he'd bring it back with a flick of his wrist. I never learned the trick as well as him, but whenever I came into town from the east, I tried my hand.

The tower never appeared to me the night of the flood, but I had seen the mean cloud coming. Driving home from Houston and headed west into the setting sun, I'd seen it—blue-black, like a bruise thumbed on the sky. The cloud broke and a sheet of water fast-walked over the prairie as night fell. The deluge was so heavy I couldn't see two feet in front of the high beams, much less my beacon, the lighted tower, and I worried I'd missed the turnoff onto the back road that skirted town and led to my apartment. When I saw the road sign, I was nearly on it. I made a quick turn, picking up speed. Completely forgot about the creek that crossed under the road, normally bone dry. The bullet slowed and the engine made a low, whirring noise. Individual raindrops shone when lightning struck, tiny mirrors catching its quick flash. Black water over the road came steadily, like a cup overflowing under a faucet. I felt the wheels lift off the pavement. It happened so fast—I tapped the brakes, tried to see well enough to steer, but it was no use. The wheels needed to meet the road or I risked being swept into deeper water. I hit the gas and said a prayer. Charged up an incline and straight into a fencepost. The impact damaged the bullet, but I was unharmed and able to drive home not long before the county turned into one wide, impassable lake.

Wasn't until days later that it really hit me: I could have drowned. Could have met the same fate as the others who'd driven into water that night. I had faced the disorientation of near-death not long before, and the pain and guilt I felt—still feel—when I thought about last fall was immobilizing at times. "You don't owe anything for your life, Annie. Stop waiting for the other shoe to drop," my mother said when I confided my fears in her. But those were the thoughts that motivated me as an investigator: never taking life for granted and the constant wonder of what I could do to keep deserving it. And now the shoe really had dropped—the flood introduced a new level of chaos into all our lives. I think part of why I took Bethany's case was, on some level, wanting to rein in the chaos of the storm. This man with no name, this enigma, he had to be brought into the light.

I closed the laptop and stepped out onto my balcony to look at the moon rising. It was nearly dark, and the green-tinted lamps in the parking lot flickered on as my neighbor called her kids inside. *You were right,* I thought, remembering Nikki's toast. *We're lucky.*

Chapter 5

Much of the next day was spent finishing up paperwork for Mary-Pat, a due diligence case she'd taken on behalf of the HR department at a big company up in Austin. When it was three, I locked up our office and walked across the square. Piles of spilt-open sandbags leaked out onto the sidewalk, leaving thin trails of mud to dry in the late-afternoon sun, and I felt claustrophobic in the way 3 p.m. often made me feel, but worse. Even the building's shadows looked wrong—the live oak shading the square had been uprooted, and the sun beat down on my back as I headed into the café.

Soon the tables would fill with kids bored after school, flirting with each other and cutting up, but now the place was near empty except for lunch stragglers and the coffee klatch ladies. I scanned the narrow, high-ceilinged room for Mary-Pat, who'd wanted to grab a bite before the flood relief drive, at which point I'd be granted an interview with the fire chief. It was the café's owner, Marlene, who caught my eye first. Her smile sagged a bit, and it hit me how strange it felt to come out on the other side and continue on like normal. Marlene and I were friends, but not the type of friends where we would've checked in during the aftermath. My heart surged—I felt relieved knowing that the world was still spinning in a way I couldn't quite put into words.

"Hey girl," she said, and pulled me close, her hair-sprayed, teased-up curls scratching my cheek.

"Missed you," I said, and before I could blink them back, tears stung my eyes. It took me by surprise—I laughed and inhaled sharply at the same time, the sound pained, and Marlene squeezed me tighter.

"I've been worrying over you, too," she said, and let me go, let me look down and collect myself.

I cleared my throat and nodded toward the menu board. "See you've got Dr Pepper cake today."

Marlene made all the desserts from scratch, and her chocolate-and-soda concoction was an under-the-radar favorite. I'd waitressed here for about eight months. The café felt like home—and it was home, not just to me, but to everyone in Garnett. Open 24/7, even during the storm. When the building lost power, Marlene had made sandwiches till all the bread was gone and the fridge sat emptied, keeping the doors propped open all night, becoming a secondary way station for the first responders.

"Well, you better have you a slice. Your buddy's waving to you," Marlene said, and turned my shoulders. Mary-Pat sat alone in a booth by the window, looking at me in a way that might be classified as rude if you didn't know better. I knew better, but it didn't mean I wasn't unnerved by her icy stares. She was Leroy's best friend, had known me since I was born, but I'd always had the feeling she was holding back. Probably a detective thing, or maybe the result of growing up queer in an often-small-minded town like ours. It was also just her nature. She could be aloof, which was not the result of shyness, but almost the opposite: she didn't require an audience. I loved her and I loved that I didn't quite know her—that she couldn't be pinned down. If while growing up I'd ever had the notion to paint her as my cool, older aunt, she swiftly rejected it. Her role in my life was peripheral but constant, like a migratory bird that I might track across the sky, reliably gone and back again.

I slid into the booth across from her. "Thanks for setting this up."

"Wes Harkness is a busy man these days," she said, and opened the menu as if she hadn't memorized it over the decades she'd been eating here. "Might only have a few minutes with him before the event starts."

Our waitress approached the table, one thin, penciled-in eyebrow raised in greeting.

"Hey, Dot, how are you?" I asked. She hadn't liked me when I'd waited tables, and since I'd quit had doubled down on her disdain. Thought I was high on myself. Maybe I was—I'd been pretty glad to hang up the apron.

"Sick and tired of being sick and tired," Dot said, then scratched behind her ear with her pen. "What'll you have?"

"Just a grilled cheese. Thanks."

"I'll take a BLT and side salad—aw, no, make it fries," Mary-Pat said. "Go ahead and bring me the check for both."

"In that case, Dot, I'll get an iced tea and the special. The meatloaf and mashed potatoes and green beans," I said to her retreating figure, then nudged Mary-Pat's foot under the table and laughed. "Thanks, boss lady. I didn't know you were buying. Shoot, I'm ordering dessert."

Mary-Pat drew her foot back. We were not on the level of equals, sometimes to the point where I didn't feel I could joke around with her, though it rarely stopped me. This time, at least, she smiled. "Don't call me that. Speaking of which, now that you've got the training and the required six months under your belt to apply for your own license, I should go over some things," she said.

So, this was why she wanted to meet early. My palms started to sweat. If I got my own license, it would be official. Being a licensed PI meant I could do this job anywhere in the state. I looked up at the pressed-tin ceiling, the fan mounted in the corner slowly rotating. I'd often thought that working for the firm could be a stepping stone to something else, someplace else. Law school, maybe. Or maybe just a fresh start in the city after I had a chance to figure things out. Still, I hadn't envisioned the day when I'd have to make the choice. "Will I have to go out on my own?" I asked.

"Course not. But once you're licensed you can be an independent contractor like me and choose your own work. Mostly, though, we'll continue under the same model if you stay working for the firm. You, Leroy, and me share resources, and when one of us accepts a case we all do. We each take a share of the profits. Which I would strongly advise—as you've seen, there's not *that* much work to go around in a town this size—and he and I have the name and reputation that you don't. This way when you don't have anything coming in, you're still working. Eventually you'll make your own connections and bring *us* work. There's a new criminal defense attorney in Parr City. Might want to make inroads with them, for example."

My shoulders loosened. "Right. Makes sense," I said. "I can start networking."

Mary-Pat focused her pale blue eyes back on me. "You'll apply for your license here soon, then?"

"I think so—"

"You *think* so? Why've I been training you if you only think so?"

Dot wordlessly slid our plates onto the table. I had an odd, tight feeling in my chest. Like a balloon inflating so I could hardly breathe. During the homicide case last fall, when I started working for Mary-Pat and Leroy, I felt alive in a way I hadn't before. All my senses heightened; outlines sharpened and colors seemed deeper. I had a singular purpose: the truth. Yet after the killer was arrested, things didn't seem much clearer, only changed, and it was hard to come down from it. There was a constant buzzing under my skin. Even with the low-stakes work Mary-Pat tossed me I had this anxiety. It wasn't that I didn't want to be an investigator. It was that I wanted it badly. Badly enough that I was afraid of making a commitment to it, when honestly, I might fail. My plate was steaming hot and I stared at it for a moment. If I could solve this case, *my* case, I'd know I could keep going. Mary-Pat grumbled and took a bite of her sandwich, eyeing me.

"I'm going to apply, of course I will," I said. "I'll do it before the end of the month."

Garnett High was housed in a squat brick building the color of sand, two blocks off the courthouse square. I backed the bullet up to the side door of the gym and some boys from the football team, all of whom looked less than thrilled to be stuck here after school, unloaded the two cases of bottled water from my trunk that I'd brought to donate. Half the county was still on a boil notice after the flood had contaminated the groundwater supply.

Game day banners in purple and gold, with the ubiquitous popular girl handwriting that turned a single sentence into a page, and the smell of the gym—recirculated air, rubber mats,

Lysol—sent me right back. In a good way, mostly. Reminded me of basketball games, late-night trips to the café afterward, and Wyatt's arm slung over my shoulder. He'd played forward, and while he wasn't bad, he wasn't good. But he made it fun, an uninhibited enjoyment of the game that had made me relax around him. Even without our shared history, I thought, there was an ease with which we fit together. He'd come stand next to me at a party, or meet my eye across the bar when we were out, and we'd just start laughing, immediately knowing without saying what stupid shit had set the other off. Yet that ease sometimes went the other way—there was often an opaqueness between us. We didn't argue much, but we didn't always go deeper.

Stations had been set up around the court. One was the Kiwanis Club, loaning out dehumidifiers and giving away cleaning kits with gloves, mops, buckets, and mold spray, then the church groups with pantry staples and their literature tucked inside paper sacks. I looked around and didn't see Mary-Pat yet, who'd left right after me. The stage at the half-court line where the fire chief and the city council would speak and conduct the raffle was empty. I had someone else to talk to in the meantime, anyway. Near the entrance to the locker rooms was a row of kennel cages set up by PAWS Garnett, the animal shelter whose logo Bethany had seen on her rescuer's T-shirt. But there was no one manning the booth. A sign taped to the folding table read: STORM DAMAGE WAS TOO GREAT TO REOPEN PAWS. LOCAL SHELTERS ARE AT MAX CAPACITY. WE ARE WAIVING ALL ADOPTION FEES—THESE ANIMALS MUST BE HOMED!

Three pit bulls, a litter of black kittens, and one older tabby cat crouched in the corner, laminated cards taped on their cages. The kittens were all named after different sugary cereals: Lucky

Charm, Honey Smack, Cocoa Puff. The old cat was named Tater Tot—he had mottled, brownish-yellow fur, and a chubby body with stub legs, so the name fit. I'd thought about getting a pet when I moved out of Nikki's—she was allergic—but wasn't sure it would be a great idea given my unreliable schedule. Plus, how long would I stay in my apartment? In Garnett, long term? As I leaned over the table to see if there was a bag, phone, or some indicator a staff person would be back soon, Mary-Pat caught my elbow.

A tall, broad-shouldered man in suit and tie, maybe in his early sixties, stood at her side. She nudged his arm. "Wes, this is Annie McIntyre. Leroy's granddaughter."

"Nice to meet you," he said, and loosened his necktie. Wes Harkness had been Garnett's fire chief for over a decade. I remembered him visiting my elementary school for those terrifying assemblies in which a house fire was simulated and you were forced to find an escape route. He smiled at us warily. "Now, how can I help you ladies?"

"A client of mine says a man disappeared in the flood. She doesn't know his name or anything about him, but says there's no missing person report and that no one searched for him. She encountered him on the river that night. I'm wondering if that's true or not, about the lack of search for him—"

"Lack of search? This is the Richter woman?" Harkness grimaced and waved with his index finger at someone trying to get his attention.

"Yes, Bethany," I said. "I didn't mean to imply—"

"No, no, I understand. But, you see, we were running helicopters as soon as the sun came up. That's how we located Mrs. Richter. It's possible we missed someone else caught up in a different tree, but I don't think so. She's talked to me, her father-in-law approached me, too—was just talking to the Reverend actually, he's on the city council, you know," he said, and motioned toward the stage set up at the half-court line where the charity raffle would begin soon. "But I'll tell you what I told him. In that first intensive search where we found the other victims, we had boats, cadaver dogs running the banks, more helicopters. We don't have the resources to keep looking indefinitely."

"Must've been a living nightmare, what y'all saw," Mary-Pat said.

"In a single twenty-four-hour period, we had three hundred high water rescues. *Three hundred.* These guys were amazing—I mean, you know how hard that is? Floodwater running three, four miles per hour is about the same force against your body as F-5 tornado winds. Will knock you right over. I've never seen anything like it since that El Niño storm fifteen years ago, and that wasn't as bad as the flood. We got out those armored vehicles, basically tanks, and drove them through a few neighborhoods, getting folks off roofs, but mostly we were out by boat that night." He shook his head. "Longest night of my life."

The waterlogged El Niño year. Momma and I had evacuated in the middle of the night, barely making it out. I remembered it had been an unseasonably warm late October, the day before Halloween. Disasters often happened in the transitions—spring, fall—the air was hot and cold, too volatile. To hear the fire chief rank the two events coalesced the utter chaos of the past two weeks in my mind. What had happened this spring would be *the* flood, the one that when you said the word no one questioned which. "I'm sorry," I said. "Is it plausible you missed someone, though?"

"Well, of course. Children, for instance, have gone missing on the river and we've never found them. Smaller bodies, they," he said, and winced when both Mary-Pat and I did. "It happens, I mean to say. It's possible someone never was reported missing because no one's missed them yet. Or they never will. If there was a report from law enforcement, we'd reinstitute a search. Or hell, maybe he made it. You think about that?"

One of the high school volunteers breathed into a microphone and ear-screeching feedback echoed in the hollow rafters. The head of city council, the Reverend John Richter, walked onto the retractable stage and took it from him, attaching it to the stand himself. Bethany's father-in-law was a large man with a thick mane of white hair. He wore a deep purple dress shirt and starched, pleated khakis. His face was stern, his mouth set in a frown, but his lively eyes and relaxed shoulders gave him an air of confidence and authority rather than stiffness.

"Unless you have more questions, I better get up there," Harkness said.

"Thanks, Wes," Mary-Pat said, patting his back. "And thanks for being here."

"Yes, thank you," I called after him as he joined the city council onstage.

Harkness towered over the mic stand. Wagged a finger at the crowd, and forgetting the mic was on, hollered, "If you haven't purchased a raffle ticket yet, run over and see Miss Terri by the door!"

Looking around, I estimated there were about sixty people in attendance, a majority of whom were obligated to be there because they worked for the city or were manning a booth. But it was a bigger crowd than I'd expected. The drive was for funding to clean up the area, along with aid to families who'd lost their homes. It would be months before all the FEMA aid came through, and even then, it likely wouldn't be enough. "This is a season of loss for our town," Harkness said, his voice cracking.

"On a grand scale and on an individual scale. So many have lost so much . . ."

"You hear about his daughter?" Mary-Pat whispered to me.

"No—oh, God, is she okay?"

She leaned in close. "Overdosed last week in the school parking lot. EMT gave her Narcan, saved her life. Apparently, Wes and his wife, even her boyfriend, didn't know she was taking pills."

I looked down in disbelief. Ms. Harkness had been my algebra teacher. She was young, fresh out of school herself, and kids often saw her as a confidant, eating their lunch in her room, always picking her for games played during pep rallies. She had the same kindhearted yet intense energy as her dad, only about equations and getting kids to join Mathletes.

"It's important to remember those that helped. If I know anything, it's this: natural disasters bring out the best and the worst in humanity. When normal life gets interrupted, when fear sets in, you see people's true colors. Everyone, please give a hand to our first responders and to your Garnett fire and rescue," Harkness said. He looked at his boots and waited for the applause to die down before nodding toward Reverend Richter to take over.

The Reverend's stare was piercing. He sighed and the gym went silent but for the air conditioner's whine and the ragged, dead-tired sound of people's breathing in, breathing out, like we were one big wounded animal. He held the room in his outstretched palms. Spoke the names of the drowned, never breaking eye contact until his voice steadily commanded us to bow our heads, as he did, asking that the dead not be forgotten.

When the raffle ended—one of the names drawn was Mary-Pat's, to her horror—the crowd thinned. The Ford dealership had donated a service check and car wash to the raffle, Marlene a gift certificate, as had several other local businesses, including my aunt's salon, the Beauty Shoppe. The Reverend stepped down from the stage and approached Mary-Pat with her coupon for a half-price pedicure. Standing before us, I noticed how massive he was, both in his height and his girth. He took her hand in his, pulled her in for a hug, and she patted him on his wide back. "If there's anything you or Colleen need, you know I'm just a stone's throw away," she said.

"Bless you, neighbor."

The Reverend turned to me and I stuck my hand out. "Annie McIntyre, sir. My condolences. I'm a friend of Bethany's, and—"

"Yes, I know," he said. His tone was neutral, but his gaze somber, his mouth set in a tight line. "She's requested your, ah, services."

I nodded quickly. "We'll do our best to find the man."

"Of course, you will," he said. "Excuse me ladies, we have a meeting here shortly."

I looked at Mary-Pat as he retreated out the side door of the gym. "Just me or was he—"

"He's a little weird," she said. "For someone who makes his living getting up in front of hundreds of people every Sunday, he's always been standoffish. Maybe 'serious' is the word. Nothing personal."

"I wonder if he thinks it's a waste of money or something, especially after what the chief said. Bethany said everyone keeps acting like she made the guy up."

"Maybe," she said, and yawned. "Anyhow, think we're about done here. Been a long day."

"I'll catch up to you later," I said. "I've got one more person to talk to."

An older woman wearing tie-dye and her hair in braids had taken over the animal shelter booth, yelling at the high school boys to help her put the folding chairs away and stop horsing around. I tapped her on the shoulder and she faced me. Her shirt had the shelter logo, and her yoga pants underneath were matted with animal hair. "Hey there," she said. "Mind?"

"Not at all," I said, taking the pile of flattened cardboard crates she'd handed me. She pointed to a rolling cart behind me where I stacked them. "Do you have any volunteers or staff who're in their late twenties or early thirties, male, with light brown hair? Tattooed?"

"Hmm, no," she said, frowning. "All female staff for at least the last five years that I've been working here. We've had volunteers who were guys but they were older, retirees. Why?"

"I'm looking for someone who might've gone missing during the storm. He was last seen wearing a red 5K fundraiser T-shirt, from PAWS. Maybe you kept a list of last year's participants?" I said, and met her gaze.

She squinted so the wrinkles around her eyes deepened. "The 5K never happened. Only three people registered—myself, Wes Harkness, and my husband—and then that morning there were those dry, high winds. A fire out west of town near the route. We called it. Lord knows we could've used the donations, though."

"What happened to the T-shirts?" I asked, ferrying a box she'd filled with towels and cleaning supplies.

"I brought them to St. Thomas's to put in their holiday baskets. They hand out donated clothes and a few dry goods every year at their—human—shelter. We had about a hundred made. Don't know what I was thinking. There's probably a bunch still stuffed inside a closet," she said, stopping and turning toward a loud crash. One of the high school boys had fallen off the step-ladder he was using to take down the banners zip-tied to the side of the bleachers, and another boy stood beside him laughing. "God bless America," she muttered under her breath, and when I didn't immediately think of a follow-up, she set to the task of packing up the dry food.

"Thanks," I said, inching away. I had a lead. A small lead—I imagined the church didn't keep a record of who'd taken a basket, or even who stayed there one night, two, but it was better than nothing. Buoyed, I fast-walked toward the exit. "Hold up!" the woman from the kennel called to me just as I was rounding the corner of the bleachers. "My husband'll have a fit if I take anyone else back to our house."

All of the animals had been adopted except one.

The days were getting longer. Light through the trees was a warm-tinted silver. The rush I'd felt leaving the gym dissipated as I drove home past the wreckage on River Road, past two sets of front steps leading to nowhere, the accompanying houses diminished to rubble. "Tater Tot," I said to the mewling cat in a cardboard box on the floorboard. "A bit undignified, isn't it?

He hissed.

"I'll call you Tate, okay?"

He let out a low growl, which I took for resigned agreement, quieting as I drove. War zone images flashed past. Downed telephone wires. Chain-link fences bent back by the force of the water with kids' clothes caught in them. Tires stuck in trees. Ruined furniture and black garbage bags piled at every curb. Standing water in the fields, the river the color of coffee—after the aftermath, this purgatory stretched on. It felt like a long time of living in the meantime. And it would take even longer, I knew, before I understood the ambivalence about my life as it was right then. But for now, I'd settle for safety for me and for this stray. For sun slanting through the windshield, warming my face.

Chapter 6

I was right to think that St. Thomas's didn't keep records of who'd stayed in the six-bed shelter they kept in a small, old bungalow a few doors down from the church, much less taken a holiday basket. I had to knock several times before an elderly man with round glasses and a scowl came to reluctantly greet me and tell me as much. He also said that a lot of the folks who came to stay the night were not local, but passing through town. If Bethany's rescuer were transient, I thought, that might explain why no one had reported him missing. I hung around outside the old Catholic church, growing warm in the sun, but it was slow, not a food pantry day, and that tight feeling in my chest returned, that feeling like I'd struck out again. Then I noticed a sign taped over the door next to the pantry. THE INTERNET CAFÉ IS NOW CLOSED, it read.

Where else could you access a computer, if you didn't own one?

I walked the mud-slicked shoulder of the highway, cutting east down a tree-lined side street toward the public library. I remembered once when I was maybe twelve or thirteen, I'd spent most of a Saturday afternoon sitting on one of those hard, round footstools in front of the mystery shelf reading an Agatha Christie. At a table on the end of the aisle sat a homeless man. At one point, he fell asleep. The librarian, Mr. Brown, came to tap him on the shoulder and the man startled awake. Yelling, swinging his arms, he hit old Mr. Brown in the face. I stared unabashedly until he was subdued and asked to leave. When he got up, Mr. Brown and I made eye contact—I said something along the lines of that he had been scary—but instead of agreeing or saying something unkind, Mr. Brown said, "Hush, now. Libraries are for everyone."

Mr. Brown had since retired, but the Garnett Public Library had the same distinctive smell—like pencil shavings, paste, and general dampness—and much of the same dark oak furniture upholstered in a nubby, forest-green fabric that scratched your legs. I veered toward the new-release shelf but stopped midstride, reminding myself I was working, and went up to circulation instead. When she came out from the back room pushing a shelving cart, I saw that the new librarian was Heather Ellis, a young woman whose family was friends with mine. Her father was my mother's boss at First Bank of Garnett.

"Annie McIntyre!"

"Heather, hey, it's great to see you back in town," I said. "I didn't know."

"Yep, here I am." She gave a tired, rehearsed smile like she had told this story a lot recently. "I was living in Dallas, then my partner and I split up, and, well, I saw the position open up and it seemed like the perfect time to come home and help out at my parents' place. Back in my old room, even."

"That's good—good for us, anyway. I mean, the county is lucky to have you," I said, my cheeks tinting. I realized too late I couldn't quite tell if she'd been sarcastic. Heather had been a senior in high school when I was still in middle, but she'd been kind to me whenever we came over to her house for her family's annual Memorial Day cookout. She was someone I'd looked up to, had finished at the top of her class and gone away to college. I remembered the last time I'd seen her, at the cookout after her graduation. Giddy and distracted, she'd floated on a plane high above us. Later, I got it: that in-between time felt like a door had opened and all you had to do now was walk, careful not to look back. "If you're not too busy, mind if I ask you a few questions?" I asked. "Guess I should fill you in, too. I'm working for my grandfather's investigation firm now. Working on a missing person case."

"Oh, wow. I remember hearing something about that from my dad. Uh, sure," she said, and motioned to the cart full of worse-for-wear children's books. "Let me hand these off to the aide to shelve, then we can sit over there."

I sat at the table closest to the desk so she could see any patrons that needed help. To my right was the children's area, and on the left was the adult section and the computer center, like it always had been. But I also saw that one of the study rooms had been turned into a "career center," which was new. Heather returned, perching on the edge of her chair. She fidgeted and darted her eyes over my shoulder—I figured she probably either had had a lot of coffee or had a lot of work to do, but after the breakup disclosure I wondered how it all had been weighing on her. "Everything okay?" I asked.

"Yeah, just a long day. Long week. I'm sure you know it isn't always story time and recommending books," Heather said. "Honestly, they could have hired two of me and there would still be work to go around. There's a lot of need in our community for programming and outreach."

I nodded sympathetically, noting how she tended to grind her jaw when she wasn't speaking. She wore her thick brown hair in a flattering, layered bob, and glasses with trendy Lu-cite frames, but her conservative blouse and slacks in two drab shades of gray swallowed her tiny frame and made her look older than she was. A far cry from the girl I'd remembered. Back then, she'd had her hair dyed blue or purple, a nose ring, wore thrift-store clothes (ironically), and was the first vegan I'd ever met, all of this a study in contrasts—or protest, more likely—to her straitlaced, bank president dad's big barbeque parties. Though, she probably looked at me now and wondered why I still dressed like a teenager: T-shirt (dark, to offset spillage), jeans, the gold hoops I got for my sweet sixteen, and my white Chucks, which were mud-stained.

"You end up helping with things like emergency housing applications, job interviews, just navigating around people's is-sues, and it breaks your heart when something goes wrong," she added. "There's already a children's librarian here, and anyway, I always wanted to focus my outreach on adult education, digital literacy, career skills, things like that."

I pointed to the old study room. "You have a jobs program now?"

"I think it's working out pretty well so far," she said, her smile this time unforced. "Our programs have great attendance. That and the new community garden out back are my pet projects. But enough about me, you wanted help."

"Might be related to what you're talking about, actually." I stopped, hearing a loud noise like someone had dropped a stack of books. I turned to see an older man wearing a stained white undershirt and brown, too-loose cargo shorts standing with his backpack thrown onto the ground right behind me. He heaved into his chair with a massive sigh, winking at me as he did.

Heather chuckled and rolled her eyes. "Don't mind him. He's

here every day, makes it his special mission to drive me to distraction."

The man grinned. "Aw, c'mon."

I nodded over my shoulder before turning back to face Heather. "I'm trying to locate someone I think might be transient, and who would've been in Garnett about a month or so ago. Or more recently, someone displaced by the flood. A younger male, white, blond-brown shoulder-length hair, same color beard, blue eyes, narrow face. A large blue rose tattoo on his forearm. My client has described him as looking kind of like Jesus," I said, my voice trailing up into a question.

Heather's brow furrowed. "We do see a fair amount of people who are passing through who are houseless, or just newly arrived to town, maybe from the jail and need to apply for work, or just need to use the internet," she said, gritting her teeth at the sound of the man's chair screeching on the laminate again. "Sorry. Do you know his name?"

"No, I don't," I said. "Figured it'd be a long shot, but I thought he might've come through here. Or thought you might've noticed someone like that, maybe one of your regulars, who'd gone missing."

Heather bit her lower lip. "It's definitely possible, but sorry, I just can't place a person that looks like that. If I see someone matching that description, I'll call you," she said, and handed me her unlocked cell phone to punch my number in. There were a pair of older women now waiting at the desk, the aide nowhere in sight. "I've got to get back to work, but we should hang out sometime soon," she said, smoothing the wrinkles from her slacks as she stood.

"All right, thanks for your time, and yeah, I'd like that," I said, and handed back her phone. I walked toward glass-paneled doors smudged with fingerprints, bracing myself for the late-afternoon heat. The sun on pavement was blinding after the yellowy dimness of the library, and I quickly turned the corner of the building, about to trek back toward the street near the church where I'd left the bullet parked, when I nearly ran into the paunchy older man who'd been sitting behind me at the library.

"Whoa," he said, and puffed cigarette smoke into my face. "Where're you headed so fast? Thought you was looking for someone."

On closer inspection his shirt and cargo shorts looked like they hadn't been washed in some time, or maybe ever, and he had a strong body odor that cut through the smoke. His eyes were watery and red like he hadn't slept. I wasn't sure if he was homeless, though. He had a sandaled foot propped on the bumper of a burgundy Lincoln Town Car and fiddled with a set of keys in his other hand, his backpack resting on the hood. "That's right. How much did you hear?" I asked.

"Enough for me to think you were looking for Charlie," he said. "'Specially when you said the rose tattoo."

"Please, tell me more," I said. "Charlie—what's his last name?"

"Dunno. Seemed like the crunchy, off-the-grid type at first look. Come to think of it, he did look a bit Jesus-y with the beard and long hair. Come to find out he was released from prison. Been drifting. I'm surprised Heather didn't think to recall Charlie. Hung around here every day from opening until they kick you out at nine."

I caught sight of Heather through the window. She was smiling and helping a little girl count out change for a late fine. "When was this? What did he do all day?"

"Use the computer, stay out the weather. It's been a while,

but I remember him. Quiet, good-looking kid. Think he found something through that church group."

"Which church group?"

"There's this addiction recovery group, not anonymous, it's called something else. But anyway, they meet at that big church out to Rhineland. Last time I seen him he said they'd gotten him a job. Don't know doing what. Say, he's *missing* missing? Some folks like him are just missing—you know?"

I nodded, getting what he meant. People ran just to run, missing because they didn't want to be found. I knew better than to over-romanticize, but I wondered what it would be like to up and leave. Sometimes, I wished no one knew who I was. It was why I'd chosen to go out of state to a private college I was now majorly in debt for, even with scholarships. But even a thousand miles away I had still been me. Stealing looks over my shoulder, both out of fear and longing to go home, realizing that these new people had a sense of who I was, only they didn't feel a kinship when they detected an accent or clocked my one good outfit, worn over again. But that desire to walk through the door—to not spin around—returned when I was idling in the bullet, stuck waiting for a train to pass at the red-light rail crossing, or on clear days like today when the sky stretched wider than seemed possible. "Yes, this guy, I think he's *missing* missing," I said. "Last seen during the flood."

"Shoot," he said. "Wish I could help more."

"No, this has been really helpful." Of course, I couldn't be certain this was Bethany's man, but it felt good to have even a hint of a lead. What made my scalp tingle, though, was the mention of Bethany's church. "Can you think of anything else about this Charlie? Know if he had any family, or where he was from?"

"Like I said, he was quiet. We talked a few times since we had to take turns with the computer when it got busy, but nothing too personal. None of my never mind," he said, flicking ash onto the sidewalk, and averted his eyes. "Gonna head back in. Hot out."

"Okay, thanks," I said, and walked down the sidewalk toward the highway, the lowering sun hitting my face.

"Hey," the man called after me. "Charlie ain't in trouble, is he?"

"Quite the opposite." I spun around. "Might've been he saved a woman's life."

Chapter 7

I nearly forgot I'd promised to pick up Leroy's prescriptions. There was a pharmacy inside Walmart, but Leroy preferred the locally owned compounding pharmacy off Ranch Road 30, which closed at five, so I had to speed. Heading back from the pharmacy toward town, I called the Hillview Christian Church offices to see about the addiction recovery group meeting, but was sent to voicemail. If the man really was affiliated with Bethany's church, it might be the case that she'd encountered him before the night of the flood. Maybe his was a face she'd pulled from her memory while in shock. Then again, Hillview was huge, hundreds of members if not a thousand. I knew that if I called Bethany, though, I'd be forced to give her a status update, and I didn't want to do that until I knew for sure if this was a viable lead.

Leroy's house was on the west side of town, on a quiet street lined with other houses like his: low-slung and single-story, white limestone, with spindly live oaks and pecan trees shading small lots. He stood hunched over a walker at the top of the gravel driveway. The roof of the carport had fallen under the weight of a downed tree branch, crushing the top of his pale blue pickup. My dad had promised to come and fix the carport and get the truck towed, clean up the mess. That he hadn't yet didn't surprise me; he and Leroy weren't on the best terms and the truck was a touchy subject. Leroy hadn't driven it since the accident that nearly killed him.

"Ears, go on and get me a refreshment," Leroy called as soon as I stepped out of the bullet.

"Hello to you, too," I said, handing him the paper sack with his medication, and went up to the front porch where he kept a beer fridge. When I came back with a cold can of Budweiser, I noticed his ruddy face looked a little pale. "You all right?"

"Thank you kindly, darlin'. Might have to pop a nitro," he said, swallowing his beer.

"Let's get you inside," I said, figuring heart medicine and alcohol wasn't an ideal combination, but there was no point in going there. Thinking about the recovery meeting had stirred me up, I guess, and Leroy, I was certain, had never tried to stop drinking. Never apologized for being anything other than he was. For the most part, we all accepted it. Leroy was high functioning, of course. But if you looked closer, if you knew better, you could see that there had been losses—his post as sheriff, for one—losses that no feel-good fix could replace. My dad, on the other hand, didn't drink, didn't smoke, and barely drank caffeine, only allowing himself a Diet Dr Pepper once or twice a day. He and Leroy were opposites in every sense. Dad never wanted to work in law enforcement again and he didn't see the appeal of holding onto a hundred acres out across the river. Would sell if given the chance. Dad wasn't humorless, as Leroy often accused him of being, but he wasn't a romantic. They were of differing natures, but part of me believed Dad's habits had been formed specifically in resistance to Leroy's, especially when it came to drinking. "You sure you're okay?" I asked, noticing Leroy's hand shook. "What're you doing out here?"

"My constitutionals," he said, and stopped at the porch swing, shooing a mangy, one-eared cat to sit. "Down to the mailbox and back a few times. Need to build up strength in this goofy leg so I can go on back to work."

"Speaking of work, you were right about looking where others wouldn't," I said, sat next to him, and told him about the former library patron, Charlie.

Leroy nodded along, leaned back into the swing, and rested his free hand on his round belly. "And have you driven out to the area where the client was found and claimed to have seen this fellow?"

"No," I said. "Should I? Don't think the water's receded much. Plus, don't know exactly what I'd be looking for. I'd go around asking if anyone saw something, but it's pretty isolated out that way. It's the state park."

"The state park isn't that big. Lot of the land on that stretch of river is actually private property. Could have impeded the law's search. It's not a bad idea. Mostly I like to walk the place where an incident occurred. See if I feel any sort of way. Know what I mean?"

"Think so." Leroy was willing to let details swirl around in his head before worrying about piecing them together, trusting his intuition when it suited. I was like that, too, I supposed, but I'd always considered my tendency toward abstraction a lack—of seriousness, of drive—not a quality to be cultivated and honed. I liked his way of doing things. Listening to him talk made me question myself less. "Wish you could come with me," I added.

Leroy shrugged, took a long pull of his beer. "Talking about drifters and such got me to thinking about the time my cousin

Del and me hitchhiked all the way to Mexico. Dropped every-thing and left."

"I can't imagine doing something like that today."

"It wasn't a great idea then, either," he said. His laugh came slowly, rising from someplace deep in his chest. "We'd got-ten out of work on the road crew and needed to feel free of it. Sometimes I miss being completely free of things."

I nodded, imagining the sun on the horizon, wind through an open window coursing through my hair. I knew he also meant that he hated being unable to do what he wanted, unable to do what he needed to do. "Let's go in so I can see what all you have in the pantry," I said, worried that if I left then he wouldn't eat, just sit out on the porch all night drinking.

By the time I made us supper—I'd found canned salmon and saltine crackers so decided to fry croquettes like my mamaw used to—did the dishes, and drove back to my apartment, it was after nine.

A full moon hung in the sky so big it looked fake. Still, I liked to park under the lamppost, in the spot closest to my build-ing. My phone buzzed in my purse and I stopped to check it before pulling out my house keys. Nikki had tagged me on In-stagram—a shot taken my first weekend back home from college, the two of us posted up on some barstools wearing tight tops and boots, the warm neon making the ringlets she'd coaxed my bone-straight hair into shine. *Throwback Thursday! Lol Annie is that still a thing??* So, she had sensed my irritation at Mixer's—this was her way of testing the waters without confronting me. I liked it but didn't comment, which was my passive-aggressive way of keeping her guessing. Being her and Sonny's third wheel wasn't all that irritated me—it was the conversation we'd been fumbling toward, about her wedding. Probably why she'd been avoiding alone time with me. I also had a text from Wyatt that

I hadn't responded to. Hey was all it said. That kind of fishing made me more annoyed than if he'd texted nothing. Without overthinking it, I knew I wanted to see him—laugh and talk, that heady mix of relaxation and heightened awareness, anticipating his touch.

I heard a faint rustle behind me, but the contrast between the bright screen and the dim stairwell made it hard to focus at first. There was a man below me, midway down the stairs, looking up at me through the railing.

I nodded in his direction, but he didn't respond. Drunk or high, most likely. He had heavy-lidded eyes and brown hair knotted into a greasy bun. I was pretty sure he lived with a girlfriend directly below me, but that's all I knew. That and I often was woken up at four in the morning by the sound of their door slamming. Propping his boot on the opposite railing, he blocked the stairs, still eyeing me. I reached for my keys, but my shaky fingers slipped against them. I scrambled to the ground, all the blood rushing to my head when I bent over to retrieve them. He was at the top step now. I jammed the key into the lock, and when I was inside, I turned the dead bolt and watched him through the peephole. He staggered around the landing, stopping in front of my door. We stood eye to eye for a minute, maybe less, and though I knew he couldn't see me, my heart battered against my rib cage. I couldn't move until he left.

Mine was the kind of complex where folks come and go. There was a freedom in living here I'd never had before. I liked being accountable to no one. Yet ever since the flood, I wondered how long it would take for someone to know if I'd died. That night I'd woken at three to a disembodied voice yelling, "Evacuate now! Seek higher ground!" It was the police driving down the road, waves of water fanning out in their wake, loudspeakers affixed to the roof racks. But by the time I'd gotten my bearings and prepared to leave, the parking lot was under four feet of water.

"Tate?" I dropped my purse on the table, clicked my tongue, and called again. He'd been hiding from me since I'd brought him home, and sure enough, two yellow eyes flashed when I peeked under the couch. Fresh food in the bowl, baby-talking to him—none of it worked. I left him to his own devices, a little wounded.

Turning on the television for background noise, I put my feet up, then googled Hillview AA and Hillview NA. Nothing. Opened Facebook and searched again. This time, a result came up for an event, a meeting of a group called New Beginnings that billed itself as a drug and alcohol recovery group. The man from the library was right that it wasn't anonymous, and yet as written in the event's description, their philosophy was similar: they believed that addiction was a spiritual problem, and the program seemed to be based around milestones and account-ability. I scanned the list of attendees for "Charlie" or "Charles," but no dice. The event was from several months ago, but I was willing to bet they'd continued to meet weekly on Monday evenings.

The Facebook event had been created by the Hillview Church's main page. I clicked over and saw the church's last post was a photo album from the memorial for Michael and Kendall Davis, the couple who'd drowned. Some pictures were older; one was of the whole church leadership and their families, Bethany in-cluded, another of just the couple. Michael had been handsome in a nerdy way: reedy and tall, flannel shirt and hipster glasses, nice teeth. Kendall, his wife, was a fair-skinned blonde who at first glance looked kind of anemic compared to Bethany's curvy, dark-haired, red-lipstick-wearing good looks, but in the photo with just her and her husband you could see she was pretty, with big, blue-gray eyes and high cheekbones. There were hundreds of comments attached to the post. I tried to imagine how being at the memorial must have felt for Bethany. Maybe she felt pulled under by an invisible current, to someplace dark, muffled, in between the living and the dead. Maybe she felt such sweet relief to breathe, to simply be alive. 'Did she somehow—even there beside her husband and all the other people who loved her—feel utterly alone?

Tap, tap, tap—the tapping mingled with my dream sounds. I sat up, not remembering falling asleep, no idea when I'd turned the television and lamp off or closed the laptop. My phone said five past midnight. No new texts, no calls. My stomach felt hollow. The tapping started again. Goose bumps broke out over my arms. Something was hitting the sliding glass door on the balcony. Keeping the lights off so I could see out, I pulled aside one of the plastic blinds. Nothing. I chalked it up to the wind throwing grit from the parking lot and lay back down on the couch for a moment, too unsettled to sleep, too tired to move. Someone knocked on the door. My heart leapt into my throat as I stumbled toward the sound—

Wyatt leaned against the doorframe. "Hey, you."

I pulled him inside the dark apartment without a word. Not realizing before that moment how badly I wanted it to be him.

Lying awake in my bed, I studied Wyatt's profile. His straight nose and his long eyelashes, his fuller lower lip and round chin. He was someone so familiar to me and yet I always felt the need to pause, look again. He got up to get a glass of water and then I heard his sharp intake of breath, his knee knocking into the table.

"What the hell, is there a cat in here?"

"Yeah, that's Tate," I said, not getting up, afraid the poor thing would run back under the couch if I did. "He must like you. He's still warming up to me. Sorry I forgot to warn you."

"Scared the shit out of me. He's, uh, huge," he said, as he sat on the edge of the bed and sipped his water, not looking at me.

"Hey, did you throw something at my window?"

"You wouldn't answer my text," Wyatt said. He shrugged, then lay back. "It was just a pebble, wouldn't have hurt anything."

"I was working. Guess happy hour was pretty fun?" When he didn't answer, I nudged his arm. He was drifting off, way too tipsy to have driven over here I realized.

He put his hand on his forehead. "Shit, just remembering I totally embarrassed myself in front of the dean and his wife. She was at the table and I was looking for a seat, standing behind her, then a couple bumped into me and I spilled my drink right on her head. I'm pretty sure she was wearing a wig and I ruined it."

"Wait, I thought it was drinks after class like normal, not some sit-down dinner at a restaurant with your boss and plus ones and all that."

"Yeah, pretty much everyone was there at the dean's house. Nicer than I'd expected. Today was the last day of finals, kind of a formal wrap-up to the semester and to celebrate the graduates. They had catering, even busted out the expensive wine."

My face felt warm. "Why didn't you say so?" I hadn't talked to him all week, so I don't know what I was expecting. Still, it stung that he didn't invite me or at least let me know about an important dinner with all his colleagues and their significant others. "Right, guess I'm just your last call now," I said when he didn't answer. My voice sounded all weird and croaky—*don't you dare cry.*

He sat up and pulled his T-shirt over his head. "Do you want me to go home? You're the one who didn't text me back earlier."

"You texted me 'hey.' Not exactly an invite to dinner, which also would have been a thing to ask me more than twenty minutes in advance."

"So, you did see my text, you just ignored it," he said, crossing his arms. "And it's whatever, but also weird you didn't even tell me you'd gotten a pet? I don't know, Annie. You seem to want it both ways and that's not fair—"

"This is not all on me."

"I know." He looked at me for a moment, and I couldn't tell if his eyes were wide and glassy because he was tipsy or he was upset. Either way, my heart panged. He kept staring, like he could see right through me. It was dark, and the ambient light from the parking lot through the blinds striped him with bluish shadow. "Maybe there'd be less guessing between us if you moved in with me."

"What?" My throat felt dry and tight, and I reached for his water glass on the nightstand. Being caught off guard made me weirdly angry. But also, deep down, even if I didn't know what to say now, I felt relieved the question had been put out there. Whatever the answer, maybe it would be better than this in-between feeling. "You're drunk," I said.

"I'm serious," he said. "My lease is up soon. Why not?"

I had this out-of-nowhere, gut-level dread. And yet I wanted to be his, for him to be mine. Maybe he was right and I wanted it both ways. Or rather, that there could be more than one way. I was too tired or too immature to articulate that—or to question it—so I didn't say anything, only gave a dramatic shrug.

"Just think about it," he said. "Shit, I'd rather eat glass than live with Drew again."

I squeezed a pillow to my chest. "Wait, do you want to live with me or do you not want to live with your roommate?"

"Christ, Annie. You."

"Forgive me for wondering," I said, deflecting now. "You didn't even invite me tonight—"

"Come on, really? It was a boring dinner and you didn't miss anything. You can be so goddamned crazy."

"No, I'm not. And if I didn't think you'd get a DUI, I *would* tell you to go home," I said, and turned to face the wall. Squeezed my eyes shut until I felt him lie back down, until I heard his breathing slow. I wanted to sleep so deeply that when I woke up, I'd forget for a moment where I was. That delicious, half-conscious moment where I had no memory.

Chapter 8

The Geronimo was sometimes referred to as the poor man's river. Often dry, or low, its current was unpredictable. Not like the spring-fed Angel that drew the town's settlers, sustained farms and commerce. You could swim the river here or go tubing—people did—but it was wilder. Could be sunny out and come a flash flood, all because a hard rain fell thirty miles northwest. That morning the Geronimo was running fast and high, barely receded enough for me to park at the rental property where Bethany had stayed the night of the flood.

I cut the engine and reached for my thermos. Despite being the sober one, I'd overslept. Wyatt had made a pot of coffee and left me a note: *I know you require a written invitation, so how about dinner on Wednesday? I'm visiting my grandparents this weekend. Hoping this is enough advance notice for you.* Nothing else had been said about moving in, which made me both relieved and anxious. Maybe he was drunk and hadn't meant it, but either way we'd have to talk when he got home. I considered texting him yes to dinner and to drive safe—and probably would've if he'd just written "sorry"—but it was too much of a game now. Besides, I had work to do.

I put my phone in my pocket as I stepped out of the bullet. Figured if I walked in the direction that Bethany had traveled the river that night, I might come across a house or two and ask if they'd seen a man matching the description of her rescuer. His origin point couldn't be much farther away than the tree where Bethany had been located by helicopters. And, if by some miracle he'd survived being swept away, how far could he have traveled without seeking help? The sun shone, and from where I stood the surface of the river was a brittle silver, like crumpled aluminum foil. The air smelled like river water—brackish, slightly of fish guts—and it was already warm. Eerily quiet but for mourning doves cooing in the brush. The bridge that used to cross a half mile back was gone—the same concrete-columned bridge that had split in half and killed the motorists—and as a result, traffic had been diverted and I'd seen no cars. It had taken me over an hour to get out here. It occurred to me now the man might've been on or under that bridge before the surge. Maybe was fishing and had gotten stranded.

Closer, the water looked murkier, dirt brown. Recent, deep tracks were impressed in the mud from trucks and skid steers, the lot where the cabin had stood having been cleared of any big debris. Left standing upright were several wooden beams set in concrete. The pilings. Broken and blanched white like splintered bone, they were all that remained anchored to the foundation. Tucked under a rock a few feet away was a fragment of paisley-patterned curtain that pinched my heart for some reason. Michael's and Kendall's bodies had been found downriver, but Bethany was rescued less than a mile from here.

I walked back toward the road that hugged the river. It's true what they say about your body knowing something before your mind catches up—the hair standing up on the back of your neck, butterflies in your stomach. All this land had been underwater and the memory of it altered the air particles somehow. I sensed the water like a high tide. Incoming. That I ought to turn back. But this was what Leroy had meant by feeling the scene, wasn't it? He had wanted me to remember the weight of the task at hand. To not avert my gaze, though the memory of violence, so imprinted on this place, made my pulse thrum and my head feel light. Cypress trees with roots like an old man's knuckles lay on their sides, ripped from the soil. Smaller trees and shrubs looked stomped, and a tangle of debris and wild new growth blocked easy access to the river. What I could see of it was a wide brown ribbon, the surface unbroken but for branches carried fast by the current like half-hidden cottonmouths.

According to my phone I'd walked about three quarters of a mile, and though I had no way of knowing exactly the tree Bethany and the man had been stranded in, I could guess. There was a tall sycamore with long, overhanging branches up a short hill on the side of the road farthest from the river. I touched my hand to its rough trunk, trying to imagine only the highest canopy above water. This was a remote area and I was barely out of the state park, so I hadn't expected much, but the road led nowhere. As I was about to turn back and see if there was an alternate way across the river, I saw a patch of white caliche fanning out onto the asphalt—a driveway? I came around the bend and saw that the road dead-ended at a metal fence with a wide iron gate. Not one, but three bright orange PRIVATE PROPERTY, NO TRESSPASSING signs posted along the fence.

The signs didn't stop me, and neither did the gate, which had a chain but wasn't locked. The virtue of being young and female is that I appear unthreatening—which can be a bad thing, depending on the situation—but it's gotten me into places that another person wouldn't feel safe going into unannounced or unarmed. If someone caught me wandering up their driveway, they'd likely assume I was lost or needed help. Still, fear gnawed at me—*no, no, no* my legs seemed to say as they carried me up-hill. The whoosh of blood in my ears and the crunch of gravel under my boots seemed incredibly loud. When I reached the top of the hill, I made sure my hands were out of my pockets, and paused, listening for dogs, or worse, the cock of a rifle.

There was a barn-red, two-story wooden house shaded by a large pecan tree, and about twenty feet away, a detached ga-rage that looked like a miniature version of the house. Both had been nice at an earlier point, but the paint needed touching up and the grass in the yard was overgrown. The house was square, simple, but slightly off; the porch jutted out too far and the gap between it and the ground was too high, the metal roof an odd choice with all that overhang. They'd probably built it them-selves. No vehicles were parked in the driveway. I also noticed that the windows of the garage were covered with what looked like bedsheets, the floral pattern faded by the sun.

I knocked on the front door to the main house and walked backward down the porch steps. Didn't want to crowd them. I waited a few minutes, knocked louder, and called hello. Again, no answer, so I walked around the side of the porch. I couldn't see the river through the trees anymore, but could feel it puls-ing, muddy and menacing. The wall of the garage had a line of silt about five feet up. I walked downward toward the side of the garage where the door was, to knock, and if no answer, at least see if there was a car inside, and that's when I smelled it—rot. Worse than rot, something dead.

Oh, God, if this person lived alone . . .

I pulled my T-shirt up over my nose, pushed the door slightly, and it swung open. Using my phone's flashlight, I saw that the garage was empty except for a metal gun safe and a white, old, but well-maintained-looking Mercedes parked to one side. The car had a large sticker in the shape of a Christian fish on the windshield that jogged my memory. It was the logo, if you'd call it a logo, for Hillview Christian. The same one I'd seen on Bethany's car. Hillview was a big church, not a megachurch, but I could see it fitting the designation in several years—all that to say I wasn't surprised, but it felt uncanny to me in the way that when you first become aware of someplace or someone, the name will keep popping up everywhere you look. Nothing was amiss that I could tell—except, of course, the smell—and the sheets tacked over the windows were creepy, as was the emptiness. Where were the boxes and random crap that accumulates when you have this much space? I spun around, making up my mind to leave, feeling unproductive and a little nauseated.

Then, I nearly stepped on it. A dead raccoon. A big one, too. "Holy shit," I said aloud, laughing a little as my shoulders untensed. I walked out into the hot noon sun, checking my surroundings in case anyone had returned home. There was no fencing along the river, only more NO TRESPASSING signs tacked to the trees. I thought I might take a shortcut back along the river toward the road instead of going all the way around the house and down the winding driveway. The riverbank was nearly impenetrable, but a wide path mown in the grass was tamped down enough to make me think the owners might drive out this way themselves, or at least take ATVs down it.

A shadow fell on the grass, and I looked up in time to see a turkey vulture circling the brush. The bird cawed, and I looked closer through the trees, toward the water. My heart leapt into my throat—a tan-colored pickup truck was in the river, submerged up to the wheels, not far off the shore. The front bumper had slammed right into a makeshift dam of two fallen trees.

Before I could think better of it, I scrambled down the bank. Half stumbled, half swam out the ten feet or so the truck was from the shore. The water was cold, moving, but not so fast that I was in danger of being pulled under. I stopped and stood upright, and the water only came up to my waist. If a person had been inside, they'd have easily been able to get out. I took a deep breath, rested my hands on the tailgate, then slowly waded up to the window.

A bloated corpse sat strapped into the front seat.

BETHANY, TWO AND A HALF WEEKS EARLIER

"Knock-knock," Kendall said in a singsong voice from the open doorway to Bethany and John David's room. "It's only nine—you're not going to bed yet, are you? I made brownies!"

You would whip up a damn dessert, Bethany thought. "That's so sweet of you," she said, wiping her nose. She'd stopped crying, but knew her face must be red, her mascara runny. She hunched over—had already put on her pajamas and taken off her bra—and crossed her arms over her chest until she could cover up. She'd always felt weirdly exposed in front of church girlfriends, Kendall especially. Kendall, so thin, so delicate, she made a midriff and cutoff denim shorts look modest. Bethany grabbed John David's hoodie from the overnight bag and pulled it over her head, sensing Kendall's eyes scan her breasts and that stubborn roll over the elastic waistband of her shorts.

"It's your birthday and you can eat whatever you want. Those are the rules," Kendall said, her voice taking on a mock sternness. "Come on downstairs."

Bethany took a deep breath and walked toward the door. "I'm not that hungry, honestly. I'll stay up for a bit though, if you two want to watch a movie or—"

"Oh, honey! Are you crying?" Kendall stepped over the threshold and put her arms out. "What's the matter? Did you and John David have a fight?"

"Yes, but it's nothing. Me being silly. Selfish, really," Bethany said into Kendall's feather-soft hair. Kendall squeezed her harder when Bethany sniffed and the tears started fresh. It felt good to be hugged. Bethany could be so defensive—and why? Kendall was nothing if not sincere, and she always made an effort to include Bethany, even when Michael and John David carried on about some dumb thing that happened when they were all at Baylor, which was often. Kendall could sense when Bethany was edging on hurt by their inside jokes, would change the topic or at least explain the reference. Bethany wiped her eyes. "Thanks, Kendall. I just—I wanted him to stay."

"I know. But I guess that's kind of what we signed up for, hitching our wagons to these two," Kendall said, and motioned with her chin toward the landing. Michael was downstairs in the living room strumming on an acoustic guitar, singing to himself. Her face turned serious. "They're called to serve. It's bigger than you and me. And being understanding of that is part of how we serve our husbands. You know that."

Bethany stepped back, nodding. "Told you it was selfish."

Her new pink swimsuit poked out from the top of the overnight bag. She ought to try harder to relax around Kendall. To be her friend, trust that she wasn't judging her. Who else could she talk to about being the pastor's wife, this role she wasn't entirely sure she'd signed up for? Kendall had confided in her, after all. If there's one thing Bethany had learned working in a salon, it was that friendship between women was transactional. It wasn't enough to keep someone's secrets, you had to share yours. "I think the rain's stopped. Want to lay out on the deck with me tomorrow?"

"Oh!" Kendall grinned. "Sure!"

And as if on cue, rain started knuckling the tin roof. Bethany raked her fingers through her hair in frustration. "Well, jeez. Maybe not."

Kendall laughed and looked up at the ceiling. "Don't worry, hon. It'll clear up."

Bethany stayed downstairs a bit after Michael and Kendall had excused themselves. She could hear them giggling before the light under their bedroom door turned off. Annoyed and wide awake now, she scrolled through her phone. There had been no word yet from John David since he'd left. "She's dying," he'd said in the driveway before backing out, one arm out the open window of the SUV, gently squeezing her shoulder as if to say, *buck up.* Bethany was ashamed now that she had felt no pity for old Mrs. Parsons. Death's doorstep sounded scary as hell. She knew that in the end she should have no fear, for she had accepted Jesus in her heart and had been saved. Still, her stomach tightened.

She rolled off the couch to turn off the lamps and get a glass of water. Standing in the dim light of the kitchen, she remembered the last time she'd been here. Momma's laugh coming in bursts like she'd been holding it in—and she had, hadn't she? Her mom never laughed back then. She and Bethany's stepdad had only been married three years. They split not long after that vacation and Bethany never saw Doug again. She had thought—prayed— she'd never see his son, Eli, again either. Out the window, a pair of headlights bobbed down the dirt road, blurred by the rain. They were driving awfully fast—and who would be way out here, this time of night? The hair on her arms stood up. Then, she heard a crash followed by a scraping sound. Heavy footfall, she was sure. Someone was out there, and whoever it was had been able to see her this whole time, but she couldn't see them.

The crash came again, and before she could think better of it, Bethany grabbed the flashlight off the table and opened the sliding door onto the cracked concrete pad. She stood under the mold-spotted awning and held the flashlight out in front of her with both hands, as though it were a loaded gun.

She swept the flashlight to the left, right, and that's when she saw the trash can tipped on its side and a big ugly possum frozen in the beam of light. The poor thing blinked once and flattened itself like roadkill. John David told her once that possums have extreme anxiety. Playing dead's not a trick, he'd said, more like a panic attack, which rather endeared them to her. She had to laugh at herself—God, she could be such an idiot. A walk to clear her head would be nice, but the rain was coming in heavy sheets now. She hurried back inside, locked the doors, and with the flashlight still in her grip took the stairs up to her room. Lay down and said her prayers before drifting off to the rhythmic drumming of the rain.

Part II

ANNIE, TWO AND A HALF WEEKS LATER

Chapter 9

The morning after I'd found a bloated corpse inside a truck, it was Leroy's voice I heard replaying over and over in my mind. I kept thinking about this one Thanksgiving when I was fourteen or fifteen, and Dad, Leroy, and I had been drinking from Momma's fancy amber-colored glassware—they'd let me try the wine, but Dad doesn't drink so must've had water in his— playing dominoes, when I remember getting up to take the yams out of the oven. Yams topped with brown sugar and little marshmallows that had browned and pillowed over chopped pecans. I set the steaming dish on the counter, when Leroy out of nowhere said, "Dead people. They smell kind of sweet." Then he left, pacing the backyard alone until supper. I don't know if he was talking about his work as a lawman or he was remembering the war. Neither of us asked. Dad had turned up the radio and I followed suit, folding napkins as if it hadn't happened, letting the moment dissipate into the loud family banter.

But now, sitting in my aunt's kitchen the day after I'd seen my first dead body, the memory came rushing back—Leroy's face that day, and the sweet, wet earth smell of candied yams.

"Annie, hello?"

My plate was getting cold, the eggs and the bacon grease starting to congeal. I took a bite of a biscuit that caught in my throat. "Sorry," I said, washing it down with the last of my coffee, knowing I could not talk about what had happened yesterday without getting upset. Knowing that if I got upset, they'd only be scared. So, I forced a smile and tossed a balled-up napkin at Nikki. We were supposed to be going over preparations for her and Sonny's engagement party next weekend.

Nikki grinned. "You can't be trusted to do the decorations, no offense. Why don't you be in charge of picking up the booze."

"You'll also help out Aunt Jewel with the cleanup and setup. She said the other day you haven't been to see her in a while," Momma added. "Awful sweet of her to host. Then again, she's the only one who has that kind of room."

"She'll hold it over me till kingdom come if anyone spills on that ridiculous white carpet," my aunt Sherrilyn said.

"Booze and cleanup. Done," I said. "Any coffee left?"

Sherrilyn got down my grandmother's recipe box from the shelf and placed it at the center of the table. "A little. Put a new pot on while you're up. Jewel's making dessert. We'll do relish trays and sandwiches, Tina. You think deviled eggs?"

Momma nodded. "What about dips? Who doesn't love a good dip?"

I got up and kept my back to them, taking my time measuring the grounds and looking for the sugar.

I couldn't get her out of my head.

She was presumably female—there'd been a muddied pink blouse and long hair, but the body hadn't been otherwise recognizable, decomposition far along, skin puffy and discolored. Part of the truck's cab had been filled with water, but it looked

86

sparse, clean. A single gold cross had hung from the rearview mirror, glinting in the sun. The river water had come up to my waist and was cold, dark, but I didn't think about snakes or metal or debris. I'd simply pulled my phone from my pocket and called the police. It took a while for the EMTs and one of the sheriff's deputies to find me, I believe, but I'd lost all sense of time standing there in the river. I knew I could have waited on the shore for the law to arrive, but I couldn't leave her there unprotected. I had the sudden urge to cover her face when the men arrived.

I put the cream back in the refrigerator right as my phone buzzed with a text. Nikki picked it up off the kitchen table where I'd left it. "Old Mary-Pat says—wait, what the hell? Dead woman?"

"Shit." I put the mug down heavily so it spilled over the side and burned my hand. "Give me that," I said, reaching toward her with the other.

Momma looked up from the recipe box. "Dead—who died?"

I ignored her and opened the text.

Dead woman's name is Jacinda Moore. Think it's the same Moore as the local builders. Knew her husband way back. You were on their property. Will let you know what else I find.

The first thing I'd done yesterday after leaving the scene was call Mary-Pat, then Leroy. The two of them knew what I meant when I said I needed to know who she was. Finding the dead woman was simply being in the wrong—or right, depending on how you saw it—place at the wrong time, but because I'd been working, I needed to parse out my sense that Bethany's man and this woman were somehow related. It wasn't irrational to think so, but like everything with this case, there was a certain murkiness that made it hard to see, to know what I was even doing.

"Oh my God, Annie," Nikki said, and grabbed my arm. "Tell us what happened."

"I was out by the river yesterday and I saw a truck in the water. A woman trapped inside," I said, my voice cracking on the last syllable. "Dead, she was long dead. I— There was absolutely nothing I could do."

In an instant, Momma, Sherrilyn, and Nikki enveloped me. The mixture of their floral, familiar scents was comforting, but I felt like I couldn't breathe when they murmured *oh, honey,* in my ear, said *you did what you could,* and *rest her poor soul.* A fat tear blurred my vision. Jacinda. What I'd seen yesterday wasn't Jacinda anymore, her soul had long departed, but I felt a connection to her in death. An invisible rope rubbing rough against my wrist if I dared pull away from her. Nikki, Momma, Sherrilyn—they didn't understand.

I don't think I wanted them to. I needed to talk to someone who already did.

When I pulled up at Leroy's, Dad was standing in front of the collapsed carport, hands on his hips, while Leroy sat on the porch. They had their backs to each other, but I sensed a charge in the air between them, a push and pull. I came up beside Dad. He had taken a chainsaw out of the shed and laid it on the ground by his feet.

"What's the plan of attack?" I asked.

"Hooo boy," he said. His eyes were tired and sunken looking. "Well, I was fixing to cut the branch into smaller pieces, but I can't find the ladder, my back's killing me, and I can't deal with his riddles and his BS today. Trying his damndest to make it harder for me to help him."

I looked up at Leroy on the porch. He still had his back turned. "That doesn't sound like him at all."

"You already picked up his prescriptions? I was going to do that, honey. You're not responsible for his care," he said, touching my arm. "You okay? You look a little pale."

"It was no big deal, and yeah, I'm fine," I said. "Sorry about your back. I can help, or maybe I can ask Wyatt and Sonny to come over later this week to help you lift—"

"Naw, naw," he said, looking up at the clear blue sky. "I'll be okay." Dad had been a cop up until he was injured while on duty. It was a car accident, and the driver had been Leroy, still sheriff at the time. Leroy wasn't charged with anything, but it was insinuated that he'd been intoxicated. He subsequently took early retirement and opened the private investigation firm, while Dad took disability and had worked only odd jobs since, his back injury never quite healed. I was a baby at the time, so I knew no difference, but I'd picked up on the fact that the accident was a turning point in their relationship. There was resentment on my dad's part, and on Leroy's a refusal to change his ways. At least that's how I saw it. Though neither disclosed much to me, I knew it was more complicated than that, and there was a force—love, or at least loyalty—that kept them if not close, perpetually in the other's cold, outer orbits.

"Come on up, little darlin'! Have yourself a beverage," Leroy called from the porch swing without turning around. "And get me a freshie."

I looked back at Dad. "Sure you're okay?"

He nodded and waved his hand before walking back into the shed to dig around again for the ladder. My dad had never really

approved of me working for Leroy, was of the mind that I was
wasting my degree. He also seemed to think—though he didn't
say—that by doing so I'd chosen sides in the ongoing battle between him and Leroy. By virtue of silence, we skirted around it,
most times, and I wasn't about to change that. I walked up the
porch steps, sat next to Leroy, and lowered my voice. "Why'd
you make him so mad? He's trying to fix the place up."

"So he says."

"What ulterior motive do you think he possibly has?"

"Nosy. He's plain nosy. Aw, but what do I care." He took a
long pull from the fresh can. "It's not him I'm worried about."

"What're you worried about?"

"Might be I'm losing my mind."

"Well, I could've told you that," I said, and though he chuckled, I noticed his fists were clenched.

"Someone's been prowling around here."

I sat up straighter, scanning the porch for anything amiss.
"Did someone steal something? I heard there were a lot of
break-ins around here after the storm, while people were away."

"No, just a sense. Swore I heard someone," he said, and
took another sip of beer. His eyes were puffy and red-rimmed.
Knowing Leroy, he'd probably sat up half the night, keeping
watch. I walked to the opposite end of the porch and looked
over the fence. Sunlit puddles in the yard looked like the metallic streamers we used to put in fruit trees to scare the birds.
There was something menacing now, too, in the way the sun
hit the surface of the water. I sat back down, and Leroy studied
me for a moment. "This woman you found, have you seen her
again?"

"You know she was dead—"

"In your dreams. In your thoughts," he said.

"I can't stop picturing it." Tears welled up. This time, I let them fall. Leroy knew a thing about ghosts. And he knew a thing about me—if he and my dad were distant stars, Leroy was my sun. "Can't help but feel like I stumbled into something I didn't bargain for. Also, I— I don't know that this woman and my missing person are connected but, what if? Am I crazy?"

"You know how I feel about coincidences," he said, leaning forward.

"What, that you don't believe in them?"

"Wouldn't say that." He sighed and stretched his arms, but his eyes were more alert. "But I do believe they're usually not."

My phone vibrated in my bag. It was a local number so I answered, only somewhat surprised, then, to hear the sheriff's voice on the line.

Chapter 10

Sheriff Ray Garcia slid a grainy, resized photograph of a woman across the table toward me. Mid-to-late fifties, with a round and pleasant face, her brassy, reddish-blond hair was thick and came down past her shoulders—it was the long hair that I recognized, now, the rest, well, had been beyond comprehension.

"This is Jacinda Moore."

Garcia was both Leroy's successor and an old friend, also Mary-Pat's former boss. He knew me, so I felt relaxed though we were seated in metal folding chairs in a damp old storage closet, or what passed for an interrogation room in the Garnett County station. The walls were thin enough to hear the phones ringing, the static of someone's radio left on as they walked past the door. Garcia respected the work Mary-Pat and Leroy did, even asked for assistance at times, but his dark brown eyes were cold and hard now. His opinion of me was shakier—when I discovered Victoria's killer last fall, he'd acted like it was less a product of my investigative work, more situational, which was fair enough. He knew I'd been in over my head, had barely made it out alive.

That said, I always felt he'd been wrong to underestimate me.

He uncrossed his arms and laid his hands on the table. "Tell me, Annie, what were you doing out on her property?"

"I've been hired to find a man who disappeared on that stretch of the river the night of the flood. I came onto her property because I thought whoever lived there might be a person to question. Nearly didn't see the truck," I said, and shivered as though I were still standing out in the water.

"You're still working for Mary-Pat and your granddad then. How is he? I've been meaning to grab a beer with him."

"He's taking it easy, doing much better," I said. In truth, Leroy was waiting outside in the bullet, but at the last moment had refused to come inside. Pride, I figured. He didn't want Garcia to see him using the cane. "I told him what happened," I said.

"Seeing a dead body like that, it's hard to explain how it affects you . . ." Garcia trailed off before locking eyes with me. "I know you know that now."

I nodded, a lump forming in my throat. I drank from the Styrofoam cup of water he'd handed me, my fingernails digging into the sides.

"We believe the truck had been in the river since the flood. Jacinda hadn't used her cell phone or her credit cards since that day. The truck must've been held fast by all the debris at the narrowing of the river. I pray to God there aren't more discoveries once the levels recede, though I'm sure there will be," he said, and leaned forward. "Now, who's this person you're looking for?"

"I don't have many leads yet, unfortunately. He was a stranger to my client. She came to you first, I believe," I said, and recounted Bethany's story.

"She must've talked with one of my deputies. First time I'm hearing about any supposed missing man. I can see why they didn't file a report, though," he said, resting his hands behind his head like it was no big deal. But wasn't Jacinda Moore's truck being in the water this long proof that search and rescue could have missed Bethany's man the first time? Just as quickly, Garcia's face shifted back into that same hardness from earlier. "Anyway, I called you in because I needed to formally rule you out."

"Rule me out of what?"

"Involvement in Jacinda Moore's death," he said, pushing the photo closer.

Jacinda's eyes had been a soft shade of hazel. Warm and inviting, even flattened into a crappy computer printout. I felt like I might be sick. "Involvement? She was murdered?"

"She didn't drown, anyway. Took a bullet to the head. If I had to guess, gun's probably at the bottom of the river. That and the keys."

"Keys? How, then—"

"They weren't in the vehicle. Truck was in neutral." He cleared his throat and clicked his pen. "So then, night of the flood, where were you?"

My mouth opened and closed a few times before words came out. "Uh, driving home from Houston. Made it back to my apartment just in time."

He nodded, waiting for me to get uncomfortable with the silence. An interrogation technique I'd also learned from Leroy. Did he really think I had something to do with this woman's death? Sweat beaded on my forehead, and I wondered if I should shut my mouth. No—he was just doing his job, and besides, I had already made up my mind on the drive over here. I needed answers. By fate or sheer bad luck, I was in this now, too. I matched Garcia's stare for a moment, hoping *he* might divulge more than he intended. When he didn't, I bit first. "Do you have any ideas of who might've killed her?"

"No, not yet," he said, almost imperceptibly rolling his eyes. "And I don't want you to go around telling this to folks who aren't your grandfather and your—whatever Pat is to you, okay? I need to locate the woman's next of kin."

"What can I do?"

"I dunno, Nancy Drew." He smirked and shook his head. "Did you happen to see the car keys, a gun? Anything you can think of that looked out of place?"

"No. But I wasn't looking in that way," I said, hedging for a second before I spoke. "Maybe my missing person could be linked. He was last seen right near the truck."

"Who knows at this point? I'm going to call you to keep tabs. And if you remember anything, you have my cell now."

"Of course." I stood slowly, hoping we were done. Garcia nodded and I inched toward the door, eager to get out of the small, stale-aired space.

"Be careful, Annie. Whoever killed her did so in cold blood, pushing her truck into the water like that to cover it up," he said, his voice lowered. "Natural disasters, any kind of big disruption like this that has folks feeling desperate, it tends to bring out the worst in them. Our cases might not be connected, probably aren't, but all the same, keep an eye out."

Tall weeds sprouted through the cracks in the asphalt path that led to the family burial plot. We took our time getting down there. Leroy's leg was stiff from riding in the bullet, my mind preoccupied with all that Garcia had told me, and both of us were afraid of what we might find. Leroy had insisted we check, though. He'd heard tell the floodwaters had eroded the soil that homed the graves, disturbing what lay beneath. The area, a wedge of land between the rivers that ended in their confluence, had gone totally underwater. Aerial footage on the local news had shown what looked like one big lake, and even now, the ground was wet and spongy. In the low spot nearest the river were mud piles and lacerations in the grass where heavy equipment had been used to reinter a casket.

"Here." Leroy pointed west, into the late-afternoon sun. "Over yonder."

"I don't come to see her often enough," I said, squinting at the flat horizon. Mamaw was buried with the rest of her kin. My mother's people were here, too. When Nikki and I were kids, a visit to Aunt Jewel's often included a visit to the cemetery. She'd tell stories, then fuss when we inevitably got bored and chased each other between the headstones. I'd always gotten spooked coming out here. Thinking about death, the great equalizer. Realizing all of us are important and none of us matter. I wished I'd have paid attention when Jewel rattled off the names. Reliving the past has always been my family's preoccupation, memories our currency. Maybe I'd come along the next time she drove out, listen to her talk, help her replace the plastic flowers in their cracked, sun-faded vases.

"Looks to be dry," Leroy said. "Surely, he would've told us had there been damage, but I reckon you can't trust the little dummy. Bryant kid's the new groundskeeper. Heard when he saw a casket float by his place he waded out, tied a rope around it, and secured it to a tree. Course, when the water went down, he realized he'd suspended it in midair."

I nodded, knowing Leroy wanted to come out here, flood damage or not. He wouldn't say what I believed—what I hoped he secretly meant—which was that he missed my grandmother.

Next week would've been her birthday. At the base of the short hill, several of the simple white crosses were askew. "I just remembered that when I was first poking around Jacinda Moore's place, I noticed she had a Hillview Church sticker on her car."

"Richter's church," Leroy said, and scrunched up his face. "Don't care much for John Richter."

"Why not?"

"Shoot, this had to have been thirty years ago." He leaned heavily on his cane. "I was called out on a domestic and by the time I got to their house his wife had changed her tune. Didn't happen again. I didn't get a good feel from it, though. Guy was a smart-ass, didn't seem to take it serious that I was there. Been skeptical of him ever since. Though, seems like everyone else in this town has a high opinion of him."

"He and the city council were at the flood relief drive," I said, thinking now his reaction toward me might be because I was Leroy's granddaughter. Preacher or not, it was hard to imagine the old man hitting anyone. I thought back to a photo I'd found of him when combing the church's Facebook page. His white hair had once been red, his face chiseled and square. One of those cheesy, velvet background studio shots that had been retouched, he wore a polyester brown suit and had a thick mustache, but there was a forcefulness in the way he had leaned into the shot that made the picture unsettling, rather than the funny throwback it was intended to be. "He seemed a bit cold. Wary of me," I said.

"He's high on himself is all."

"Yeah, I can see that, too." I'd always thought that to be a big-time pastor—or politician, or CEO for that matter—you must be, on some level, full of it. How else could you stomach all the self-promotion, the constant awareness of how you were being perceived? Maybe the Reverend was not put off by my investigation, rather, he didn't see a need to give me the time of day.

We came to the end of the path. There was a small courtyard, and beyond it, the river running fast. A placard next to an old stone bench said the Geronimo was named for Saint Jerome. I'd also heard it was after the Apache leader, or maybe Geronimo Lopez, one of the original landowners back when Texas was still Mexico. This was the last stretch before the Geronimo split into the Angel and the Salt Fork. If you kept going southeast, and down this road, you'd hit the apartment complexes that got destroyed, and beyond them, town. Hook west and slightly north at the fork and you'd see the abandoned railroad crossing, then the highway, and across the river, our family's land. It all followed that long line of water. All connected.

I looked north and across. A cluster of newly constructed town homes, mercifully undamaged, had been painted a clean shade of white that was near blinding in the sun. Bright white offset by black window trim and front doors painted a retro-hued blue. I knew enough from watching *Fixer Upper* to think it was trendy.

"Heard they're going to be expensive," I said, and pointed toward the development. "I remember seeing a Moore Construction sign out front when I drove by a few weeks ago. Must be the same."

"It is. Jack Moore was Jacinda's husband," Leroy said. "I had some business with Jack back when people were stealing copper and timber from some of his work sites. Turned out it was an inside job; usually is. Don't reckon I ever met Jacinda."

"I'm going to learn more about her," I said, recognizing the odd resolve in my tone. Beyond simply being the one to find her, I think now I had assumed a certain responsibility for Jacinda. I'd never, ever stop seeing her—it wasn't like I'd done anything special to find her, I didn't deserve thanks, but maybe I was owed access to her life for how she had taken up residence in mine. "Bethany's guy was last seen in that tree right by where her truck was. What if he's not this hero—what if he's a killer?"

"I can see where your mind's going. But the connection—the place they were last seen—might only be because they're victims of the flood, so to speak," Leroy said, stopping at the row to his left. "That storm shook everything up, turned it upside down, swept it all right into the river."

"Yeah, I know." Mamaw's headstone was near flush with the ground, a pink granite marker that had a smear of dried mud across it that I bent to scrape off. Leroy had his matching headstone already made and nestled in the dirt beside hers. I shuddered, seeing his name, and grabbed a fistful of the tall weeds that had grown up between them. "You know, maybe it wasn't the wisest idea to put a cemetery by the river," I said.

"Water's never come up this high before," Leroy said, and coughed into his fist. He'd struggled with the walk, and I could tell by his tone he felt blue. I should've known better than to agree to take him here and to the sheriff's station, but he'd yearned to leave the house. Lately he reminded me of those zoo animals that get released and then perish because they don't know how to be wild anymore. He'd grow stronger, I was sure of it. And soon as the low water crossing was passable, I could take him out to the place across the river, the home of his heart. Until then, this would have to do.

"It feels like a betrayal, the flood. We all wished for rain for so long," I said.

"A hard rain after a drought—my uncles used to say it's like medicine after death."

He stopped and looked down, now standing over his own grave.

"Tell you what, little darlin'. Leave the stone, but don't put me in the ground here. Take my ashes out to the place. That's where I always wanted to be. Mix me up with a bit of our dirt, scatter the rest to the wind."

We were in a cemetery, after all, but I didn't want to talk about Leroy dying.

"I often wonder why I'm still here," he said.

"Maybe don't spend *all* your time wondering," I said, and nudged his arm. "Come on, Mr. Cheerful."

But hadn't I felt the same way, after all that happened last fall? I looked down at my right hand, as if the purple scar across my palm might open up and bleed. I couldn't let go of that fear I'd felt when I nearly died, and the scar was the reminder I kept clutched in my fist. Leroy, too, had come out the other side marked.

He shook his head, then turned to walk back to the bullet. I hurried after him, an urgency swelling in my chest. What else should I have told him? That I loved him, I realized later. "Hey," I said. "I need your help with this, okay? You can't go quitting on me now."

He stopped, turning back to face me. "You're right," he said. "One thing's for certain, it's that there's always work to be done."

Chapter 11

The shot was a toxic shade of red. Tasted like bubble gum mixed with grain alcohol. "What the hell is this?" I asked Nikki, chasing with a draft beer. "It's gross but I also kind of like it."

She shrugged. "I think it's Big Red and something else plus vodka. Asked him for something sweet. How're you feeling? Did you hear anything else?"

"Better now," I said, and closed my eyes for a second, glad for sepia-tinted shadows that might hide me, for the loosening in my limbs as the drink burned through. "But no, haven't heard much," I lied, remembering the sheriff asked me to not say anything about Jacinda's apparent homicide yet. Not like I hadn't taken Nikki into my confidence before—and hadn't I longed to reclaim that intimacy with her, my best friend? We had a lot of ground to cover—the case, Wyatt—but I was too on edge now, ready to lash out if she said the wrong thing. The sadness I'd felt when I discovered Jacinda, the fear—it was hardening, sharpening.

We were back at Mixer's. The tables were almost full and

cigarette smoke wafted inside from the rickety back deck. The band was usually the same tone-deaf State kids driven over from Colburn. Part of me wished we'd gone to the old VFW bar. They often had a country band. Honky-tonking, swept up in the candy-colored neon and the two-stepping, a place that felt to me out of space and time. It didn't really matter, though. Even if we didn't talk, it was nice to be out with my cousin, only us two—we'd done our makeup and gotten dressed at her house in boots and short black sundresses so we kind of matched.

"So scary," Nikki said, rubbing her arms.

"Yeah, it was. I needed this," I said, not meeting her eye. Only after I'd texted Nikki back did I realize seeing her would make me flustered, embarrassed—I felt no closer to finding Bethany's rescuer, and with the discovery of Jacinda, like I'd tugged on the wrong loose string, unraveling all sense of order. I'd gone home and closed my eyes after the cemetery, only to wake in a panic from the scene unfolding in my head: Bethany, water up to her neck as she gurgled out a scream, Jacinda floating facedown beside her. I did my best to shove the image to the back of my mind, and forced a smile in Nikki's direction. "Wonder who's playing tonight."

"They're called the Four Horsemen," she said. "Country covers."

"Grim," I said, looking toward the stage. Four young guys wearing all-black retro western wear started to play. The guitar player and the lead singer looked like brothers. Tall and skinny, Adam's apples bobbing up and down when they sang, their harmonies airtight. A haunted, old-timey sound. They weren't half bad, but no one was paying them any mind, and the noise of the crowd soon drowned them out.

"Let's have another of these," Nikki said, and pushed her

way to the bar without waiting for me. She'd also been acting kind of twitchy, I'd noticed. While she bought the next round, I staked out a table, noticing a guy on the opposite wall follow her with his eyes. When he caught me twisted around in my chair to stare at him, he nodded and smiled.

"See that guy with the dark hair and blue shirt," I said when Nikki came back, careful to not get caught again. He looked like someone. But so did everyone in this bar—I concluded that I did not know him, but that I'd likely known of him at some point. Early thirties, fairly good-looking, with a forgot-to-shave look that was definitely intentional. On either side of him were two other men of about the same age and level of attractiveness, and who were now watching me, too.

Nikki took her shot and handed me mine. "Yeah, I see him," she said, and flashed him a smile.

"Nik," I said, checking her left hand. She was wearing her engagement ring, though as we'd recently discovered, diamonds only deterred nice guys. A not-so-nice guy had been the reason for one of Nikki and Sonny's breakups. He had a girlfriend who caught wind first, proceeding to slash Nikki's tires and yell "whore" at her window—on a night Sonny was staying over—and then, after Sonny and Nikki broke up, the guy ghosted Nikki.

"Ladies." The bartender came over to our table with a tray of tequila shots. "From your admirers."

"Aw, Christ, Nik."

She rolled her eyes. "I'm going to take one. Come on, it's free."

I took the shot and sucked the lime. It irritated me that there was an expectation now to speak to them. Emboldened by the buzz that had gone straight to my head, I bit down on the pulp and moved it over my teeth so the rind covered them, turned toward the man and his buddies, smiled, and flipped them the bird. It felt good to be a little mean, but it wasn't really about those guys. I felt like there were tiny spikes under my skin, a pressure building in my chest the longer we sat here. Maybe I shouldn't have come out. The case, the way the brown river water lapped at the truck tires—I couldn't get it out of my mind.

Nikki laughed. "Girl, what's gotten into you!"

"Yeah, well, I think they thought that was flirting," I said as the men sauntered over.

The guy in the blue shirt sidled up to Nikki. His friend sat on the edge of the table beside me with his legs splayed open, then nudged my arm with his knee. "Hey pretty girl, what's good?"

"Hey yourself." I considered asking him to get his crotch out of my face, but instead I turned to Nikki on the other side of me. "Should we go get a beer at the bar?"

Nikki ignored me, and put her hand on the man's forearm, using her finger to trace a tattoo of a Gaelic cross inexplicably doused in flames. "This is new. When did you get this?" she asked, her voice teasing.

Then it hit me. She'd known the whole time they'd be here. The room seemed to tilt as I stood from my chair. "We just spent the morning planning her engagement party," I blurted out to the group. "So, excuse us. We need to consult again about her flowers."

At the chorus of the men's *oooohs,* I yanked Nikki with me toward the bathroom. My face felt tight and hot as we pushed through the crowd at the bar. For some reason, *I* felt bad—guilty, also embarrassed to be the killjoy—and it suddenly made sense to me why I'd always been monogamous as a goose when it came to boyfriends. I was nothing if not loyal.

No one was in the bathroom, so I latched the door. "Do you want to marry Sonny? If you don't, it's fine. I'll support you. Just be honest with me, Nik."

Maybe she also felt bad, or maybe it was the greenish fluorescent bulb over the sink, but Nikki looked like she might puke. "I love Sonny. I really do. But you know how it is, sometimes, right?"

"I'm not a cheater, no. And I'd burn Wyatt's house to the ground if he cheated on me," I said, my fists clenched at even the thought—of him wounding my pride in such a way, but more so the look on his face if he'd been hurt by me. I didn't think I could stand that.

"Oh, please, like you've never thought about it. You hardly bring him around anymore."

I paused for a minute, standing in front of the sink mirror. She wasn't wrong, but what was going on between me and Wyatt wasn't about wanting to be with someone else. "This isn't about me," I said, chin raised. "If you aren't worried about hurting Sonny, fine, that's your problem. Just don't make me your accomplice."

"He's cheated, too, remember?"

"Okay, so again, why are you marrying him?"

"Nothing's happened since we got engaged. We're serious this time," Nikki said, meeting my eyes in the mirror. "I wasn't going to actually *do* anything, but I'll block that guy's number if that makes you feel better."

"You made me look like an ass back there."

"I know. I'm sorry," Nikki said, slumping against the stall door. "Sometimes, I dunno, I like to see what's out there. I like to see that I've still got it."

Forgetting my makeup, I splashed my face with water and

stung my eyes. "It's one thing to go out and flirt a bit, another to meet up with the guy. Do I need to sober up and drive?"

"No—I mean, yeah, let's go, but no need to drive."

The moon was full, bright enough to see clearly the path toward the rodeo fairgrounds. We sipped our beers as we walked—we'd paid our tab and left out the back door, Nikki managing to sneak two open cans inside her purse without spilling—and were quiet. There was a ringing in my ears, the silence a muffled sound in itself.

The fairgrounds were empty now. It was a flat expanse of land off a dirt road a few blocks behind the high school. The bleachers and chutes looked flimsier without the livestock and the fans. The arena was still a mess from the flooding; deep puddles remained, and mud-caked panels that had local ads still pinned on them from last year's festivities were starting to disintegrate. Trash piled everywhere. The rodeo was a Garnett institution, and though I knew it would be back this summer, seeing the fairgrounds beat to hell by the flood gave me a blue feeling that was hard to fight. Nikki took my hand and pulled me to the right, off toward a large pavilion with open sides and a flat metal roof. A dance was held here every year after the rodeo, along with barbeques and bingo tournaments throughout the day.

"Here," she said, and hopped onto the concrete. She let go of my hand, then twirled while holding out the sides of her dress. "I decided this will be the reception venue!"

"Yeah?"

"It'll be hot as hell in August, but we can set up big fans in the corners to keep the air moving and the skeeters out."

She danced, her smile wide and guileless. Like earlier hadn't happened. I was annoyed, but really, I didn't want it to be another way. I wanted for Nikki the perfect, future selves we'd imagined, like in the dress-up games we'd played as girls. For fancy paper place cards, for creamy white cake and pink bouquets. I sat on the ground, leaned back on my elbows, and closed my eyes. Tried to call back that old feeling where make-believe was real as anything. "Well, what's your song going to be?"

"Is it too corny if I choose 'You're Still the One'?"

"Yes," I said, and took out my phone to play her some Shania when I heard a car engine that was too close to be road noise.

Nikki walked to the edge of the pavilion and peered around the metal beam, waving me over. Two dark-colored sedans were parked next to each other. They had their headlights on, so it was hard to tell the makes of the cars or the exact color, but we could see the profiles of two men standing in front of the lights. One wore a red ball cap. We crouched behind a picnic table so they couldn't see us, in case they turned around. The one in the ball cap handed the other a brown paper bag, the other man passed some cash. Looked to me like a drug deal. I first thought they were harmless teenage stoners—when I was in high school this was a popular place to skip and smoke weed after lunch—but even at a distance they looked bigger, more filled out than high school boys. I wished I could see better, and inched forward on my hands and knees. The wind lifted the man with the red ball cap's T-shirt, and I saw a handgun tucked into the waistband of his jeans.

Nikki's beer can tipped onto its side. "Shit."

I looked back at her and put my finger to my lips. Turned forward right as the men looked back in our direction—they still couldn't see us, but they'd definitely heard us. I realized then that I knew the man who'd handed over the cash. He'd been a year ahead of me in school, was both valedictorian and a football player. He'd also been captain of the soccer team, and had gone on to be a kicker for Texas Tech. Heavier now, his face looked puffy, and he kind of slumped his shoulders in a way I hadn't recognized. I didn't know if he'd moved back to Garnett or was only home visiting, but there was something efficient, mechanical about the way the two interacted, and I sensed he'd bought from the man in the red ball cap before. Nikki and I crouched even lower behind the bench and waited an agonizing minute or two before they each got into their cars and drove off.

"Did you see that was Tyler Thompson?"

Nikki audibly gasped. "One with the sweatpants? Damn, he looked terrible. I didn't even recognize him."

"I'm surprised, too." I dug my nails into my palms, and again, some misplaced shame made my face grow warm. I think I'd had a bit of a crush on Tyler in high school—a lot of girls had—and like the rest of this town, I'd been proud seeing him on TV that first fall after graduation.

"What do you think he was buying?" Nikki said.

"Could've been anything," I said. "But probably drugs, right?"

"Yeah. Think they'll come back?"

"Even if they did see us, why would they?" I said.

"Snitches get stitches," Nikki said.

"You think that was El Chapo selling to him?"

"Whatever, you should know better than me there's some shady shit going down in good ole Garnett these days."

She was right. Despite the gun, I hadn't been scared—I was drunk now, for one, and two, nothing could shock me after a dead body at the river—but I knew we should've been more careful. Tyler Thompson, damn. And who was the other man, and why was he armed? I shivered with a rush of adrenaline. "Let's get out of here."

Nikki was faster. She passed me, running full out into the flat field toward the road and the streetlights on Main. The pounding of my heart made me feel more alive than I had in a long time. The uncut grass, already damp with dew, whisked against my bare calves. Nikki's blond curls bounced on my horizon and I had an image of her as a little girl, us playing tag in the backyard, me pumping my legs hard as I could to try and catch her. If I ran hard enough, if I let the darkness and the wind blur my vision, maybe I could go back there again.

Chapter 12

Overdressed for church, of all places. I tugged on the stiff, navy-colored dress I wore, my toes pinched in sensible heels—an ensemble I usually reserved for funerals. On the rare occasion I'd attended Aunt Jewel's church, First Baptist, she said she'd tan my hide if I wore jeans. At Hillview, half the congregation wore them.

Hillview, aptly named for the rise the sanctuary sat on above the river and to the west of the fault line, used to be a Congregationalist church, but in the decades since John Richter took over, had broken off to become nondenominational and evangelical in their ministry. The church campus was surrounded by scrubby ranchland, and on one side of the property was a cleared-out and graded section of dirt with some heavy equipment parked on it, and a sign that read FUTURE HOME OF THE PARSONS MEMORIAL RECREATION CENTER. I wasn't surprised; the church claimed to have more than doubled its membership in recent years. Hillview now had multiple Sunday services, a newly built fellowship hall, church offices, and a freshly paved parking lot full of cars, all with that same fish sticker on the windshields.

I took a paper bulletin that was handed to me and moved up the receiving line. As I rounded the corner, I spotted the young pastor. He stood in the narthex, multicolor light from the stained-glass window bathing him in a soft orange glow. He greeted each person with either a firm handshake or an embrace, most by name. When it was my turn, John David took my hand in both of his, and despite myself, I blushed. His hair was longer than it had been in the pictures I'd seen, and he wore well-fitted khakis and a pale blue dress shirt rolled up over his forearms. No robe or stole. He was tall like his dad, but must've gotten his mother's eyes—dark and round and kind of bruised-looking—and an easy smile. "Welcome. We're always happy to have new folks joining us," he said.

"Actually, I'm a friend of your wife's—"

"Yeah? That's great. I'm glad she invited you," he said quickly, his eyes ever so slightly drifting to the line behind me. It was five till ten o'clock and the start of the service.

"I'm very sorry for your losses, Pastor," I said. "My name's Annie McIntyre. I'm a friend, but also the investigator she hired. I won't keep you now, though."

"Is that right?" His smile tightened a little. "Well, Annie, make yourself at home and take part in any part of the service you feel comfortable doing so. We'll be catching up with you after?"

"That'd be great, thanks," I said, turning toward the rows of wooden pews. Dark red carpet covered a center aisle, sloping down to a stage bordered by massive white floral arrangements, with cameras and speakers nestled in between.

On the wall behind the pulpit was a stained-glass window. Beams of morning light silhouetted a massive golden cross suspended from the rafters. A full band was warming up stage right, and combined with the buzzy, crackling energy of folks filing in, all big grins and bear hugs, I felt like I was waiting for a show at ACL rather than a church service. I considered looking for Bethany, but worried it might seem like I was ambushing her—I hadn't told her I was here yet—plus, it looked to be completely full up near the front. So, I ducked into the back row. Behind the pulpit sat the elder Reverend, clad in a heavy black robe and velvet stole. I knew from the church website that he had given the earlier service at eight that morning. I tried picturing a younger version of the man, his blue eyes narrowed and red-rimmed, his fist raised in midair. His face searched the back of the sanctuary, and though I was certain he hadn't recognized me—hadn't even seen me—I felt weirdly self-conscious, and I slumped lower in the pew.

A woman plopped down next to me, hitting me in the arm with her purse, then fanning herself with a collection plate envelope. "I always think since I'm going to the second service, I'll have all this time, but I'm still always late," she said, shrugging the purse off her shoulder onto the floor.

"Know what you mean," I said, and stood as John David walked down the aisle. "How long have you been coming here?"

"Oh, forever. I was raised in this church. Honestly, I only started coming back regularly after the younger one"—she nodded up at John David clipping a mic onto his shirt—"took over the later service. He just has a way. And change is really good." She bit her lip as though to stop herself from gushing even more.

John David greeted the full sanctuary, his voice booming through loudspeakers. He began with people added to the prayer list and other announcements, and when he was done, sighed heavily and patted the arm of his father, who'd come to stand by his side.

"Last night we received tragic news about one of our church family. We've learned that Jacinda Moore has been called up to heaven. I don't have more details other than what is in the news reports—as those of you who knew her are aware, she was preceded in death by her husband, Jack, and had no children—but she was found in the river. This flood has been a wrecking ball to this church and this town . . ."

"Called up to heaven" was an interesting way to say murdered. The story had broken overnight—I'd seen it on the local news site that morning, pictures of the beige truck strung with caution tape, along with that same picture Garcia had shown me of Jacinda and her long coppery hair. Jacinda must have been a longtime member, not an only-goes-at-Christmas-and-Easter type, for John David to have made an announcement. From where I sat, I detected a few muffled cries and some murmuring. Did my best to look around without gawking. It didn't seem to me that anyone in particular was overcome with emotion, but there were easily three hundred people there, so hard to say. What was clear to me was John David's seriousness. It wasn't a coldness or stuffiness, but the sympathy he conveyed now without a hint of sanctimoniousness. His deep and melodic voice, the perfectly timed pauses, his fluid and decisive movements across the stage.

As John David transitioned into a prayer, the woman beside me started rocking and nodding with her eyes closed. Without thinking, I inched away from her. It wasn't that I was uncomfortable. In fact, I think I wanted to be moved as she was. When the band played the first hymn, she and the others looked to be swaying in the same steady current. But I still didn't feel as swept up. I remembered how as a kid I'd felt churlish and mean when we went to church. Instead of paying attention, I usually spent the hour or so thinking up questions I knew the pastor had no answer to—how do you know that you're right and they're wrong were the gist of most—arguing with only myself and counting down the minutes until we got home and I could change out of my dress tights. It was exhausting. At one point during John David's sermon, the woman began to cry, and if anything, I was envious. Like watching a wave crest from the shore, I wondered how I might swim out and ride it.

The fellowship hall, I'd learned, was built by Jack and Jacinda Moore's construction firm. There was a glass case near the entrance that held framed photos of youth group mission trips, women's quilting projects, and a ten by twelve of Jack, Jacinda, and the Reverend Richter wearing hard hats and wielding shovels to break ground on the new building. I walked inside the open, airy space full of natural light from a wall of windows, and found a bunch of people milling around a long table topped with fancy-looking silver coffee and tea carafes, real glass cups and saucers, and a sheet cake precut into small, even squares.

"I'm totally shocked," a man's deep, radio-announcer voice said from behind me. "I hadn't heard from Jacinda, not since, gosh, probably March."

I turned to see that the voice came from the bandleader, a middle-aged man with a faux-hawk and a blazer over jeans who I'd heard referred to as Pastor Brad. I tapped his shoulder. "Hi, I'm Annie. Sorry to interrupt—it's just that I heard you talking about Jacinda Moore?" I balanced my piece of cake over the top of the coffee cup to shake his outstretched hand. As I did, the woman he was speaking to nodded politely and left to refill her coffee cup.

"Pastor Brad Little, pleasure to meet you," he said, gripping my hand a few moments longer than was necessary. "It's such a shame. Jacinda was a good woman. Always giving back. How did you know her?"

"I, um, found her body. In the river," I said, lowering my voice. "I didn't know her personally."

"No way," he said, his jaw hanging open. "That's awful."

"I suppose I wanted to know a bit more about who she was."

"Lord help us. She was one of a kind. See, Jacinda had a wicked sense of humor. Eccentric, sure, like a lot of smart people are. Could talk to anyone," he said, and laughed like he was remembering one such interlude. "I, for one, will miss her."

It sounded like he'd found a nice way of saying Jacinda was more than a little out there. I nodded encouragingly.

"She and Jack were always willing to lend a helping hand. And not just to folks in Garnett. Took a group down once a year to build houses and churches in Mexico. They were big into missionary work." He bit his lower lip and shook his head. "I just can't believe it. I guess we don't know His plan."

I was about to ask more, when I smelled a sweet, freesia-heavy perfume and felt a soft touch on my arm. It was Bethany. "Annie," she said, pulling me into an embrace. Her voice lowered as she said into my ear, "How is you-know-what going? You could have called, you know."

"I know, I just—" I spun back around, to tell Pastor Brad to hold up, but he had already walked off and was talking to a couple and their teenage boy. I looked over Bethany's shoulder and saw John David and his father holding court in the center of the room, a dozen or more people circling them and held in rapt attention. "I guess I wanted to hear the service. Is there someplace quiet the three of us could talk?"

Bethany led me into a large office lined with bookshelves. One shelf was full of baseball memorabilia and a wooden bat. John David had played ball at Baylor, I remembered. Another shelf was filled entirely with hardcover copies of his father's book, *Walking by Faith,* and the accompanying DVD set, which I'd gathered had been a fairly big hit in evangelical circles. On the wall was a framed diploma, a green-and-gold pennant, and an old-looking oil painting of the Last Supper. In the center of the room was a large wooden desk with two plush leather chairs in front of it. Bethany sat in one and offered me the other, and as she did, John David entered the room and closed the door behind him.

He looked between the two of us and sat behind his desk. "Anything to drink? Coffee, tea?"

"I'm fine," I said.

"Think I'll have a water," John David said, but didn't move to get up. He smiled at Bethany, the tiniest bit of tension in his brow.

Bethany stood and hurried over to a side table topped with a basket of snacks, a Keurig machine, and a mini fridge stocked with drinks. She pulled out a water bottle with the church's logo printed on the label, cracked the lid, and handed it to him. It took a measure of self-control for me to not ask if his legs were broke.

"Thanks, honey," John David said, then turned back to me. "So, Annie, have you found the guy?"

"I have a lead I'm checking into," I said, folding my hands in my lap.

"That's great," Bethany said. If her outfit—a blindingly pink Lilly Pulitzer dress that was tight on top but hit below her knee—made her look more conservative, when she opened her purse and pulled out a scented lip gloss, rolling it on her lips then wiping the edges with her thumb, it reminded me of the teenager I'd known. Something about the motion was familiar, or maybe it was the lack of self-consciousness when she'd made a kissy-face for a split second.

John David toyed with the edge of a picture frame that lay facedown on his desk. He turned it upright and I could see from the side that it was a shot of him with Michael and Kendall Davis. My stomach twisted, imagining them trapped inside the cabin with water rushing in. I remembered what Bethany had said about John David not quite processing it all yet. He smiled half-heartedly at me when he caught me staring and raised an eyebrow. "Big break in our case then?"

"Well, I'm still working on it," I said, not wanting them to lose confidence in me, but knowing better than to take any credit yet. "I wanted to tell you both that it was me that found Jacinda Moore. I found her body in the river when I was out, uh, canvassing I guess you'd say, around the site where Bethany was found the night of the flood."

"Oh my." Bethany shivered and sucked in her breath. "That must have been terrifying."

"It was really upsetting, if I'm being honest," I said, my throat tight, trying not to think about the thirty seconds between me reaching the truck's tailgate and coming up to the driver's side window, the moment death smacked me in the face. I still felt affronted—like when you hit your head on a cabinet and blame the cabinet, or how when you fall the ground seems to have risen up to greet you—because those thirty seconds were a beginning and an ending, and I'd never stop replaying them.

"I can't imagine," John David said. "I was so upset to hear she'd been killed. The news reports say it looks like a homicide?"

"Yes."

"Jacinda was—well, back when she was a member here—she was quite loved. This is shocking."

"Oh." I leaned forward in my chair. "She was no longer a member here?"

"Jacinda had come less frequently—understandably so—once her husband's diagnosis required her constant caretaking, but after he passed, she stayed away, even going so far as to officially leave all of her committees and small groups." John David sighed. "I regret not reaching out to her more while she was still alive."

"Must have been a little awkward given her work on the new rec center?"

"She wasn't part of that," John David said quickly.

"Oh, I suppose I assumed because of the construction firm—"

"Nope. Lost the bid. Came in way high. We got a much better offer elsewhere. It wasn't personal, but she took it personally. Understandably so, in retrospect," he said.

Bethany's heel tapped on the tile. She'd been unusually quiet, and it startled me when she cleared her throat. "But is that why you're here, Annie? Jacinda? It's terrible she's been killed, and terrible you found her, but I don't see what she has to do with our guy," she said.

"It doesn't, not necessarily." I paused, not quite sure what to say, surprised by her tone. "I was curious given her connection to the church. Mainly I'm here because I wanted to see if either of you could tell me more about the group New Beginnings?"

Bethany frowned and looked at John David. "That's the drug and alcohol recovery program, right, honey?"

"Yes," John David said. "They meet in the old fellowship hall Monday nights at seven. That's Brad's project. He's really passionate about leading people away from drugs and alcohol through Christ, and by all accounts the group really makes a difference in these people's lives. Some real success stories," he said. "Brad's a recovering alcoholic. He'd tell you that himself."

"Pastor Brad?" I asked. "Your musical leader?"

"Yeah, I saw you talking to him earlier," Bethany said.

"So, is there crossover between the recovery group and members of your congregation?" I asked.

"Occasionally, I'm sure. Brad, for one. But no, it's really a separate entity. We get some regular folks, along with a lot of folks only sent our way by recommendation of a parole officer. But what does New Beginnings have to do with your work for us?" John David looked at Bethany, and a flicker of recognition passed between them—they'd had this argument before. "Honey, are you sure this investigation, if you'd call it that, is really leading us anywhere? No offense, Annie."

Bethany's shoulders shot up to her ears and her eyes darted back and forth between us, landing on her husband. "Maybe you were right. I just feel like I'm losing my mind," she said, her lip quivering.

"Hey, come on," I said, and looked at Bethany. John David kept saying "us," I'd noticed—as far as I was concerned, she was my client, not him. "Bethany, I think the man who saved you might attend, or used to attend, New Beginnings. Does the name Charlie ring any bells?"

She and John David frowned and shook their heads.

"I've got my work cut out for me then. Like I said, it's a small lead, but it's what I've got. I'll keep after it." When they stayed frowning, I lied. "I've got an additional source I can't disclose quite yet. I'll let you know more soon."

Bethany let out a deep breath and reached across to squeeze my hand. "I knew you could do it, Annie. Thank you."

"Don't thank me yet," I said, standing, smoothing my dress out. "Just wondering, what's the story behind the decal on everyone's car?"

John David's eyebrows raised, and then I could see the lightbulb go off. "Oh, you mean the parking pass."

"Aren't they cute?" Bethany stood to walk me out. "When the new construction was going on, the parking lot being paved, we held Sunday services in the big conference center at State. The stickers let campus cops know not to ticket us."

"It became a thing, though—people kept 'em on, still like getting new ones. It's a way of spotting the like-minded out and about in this crazy world," John David said. He locked eyes with me and I felt a flush of heat on my neck. He opened his desk drawer and smiled. "Want one?"

Chapter 13

I propped my elbows on the counter and breathed in the café smell: a distinct mix of bacon grease, batter, and a musty, metallic tang emanating from the motor of the ancient drink cooler under the register. Earlier I'd been out to the railyard and the Greyhound station, hoping that I might ask some of the transients about having known a Charlie who'd passed through. I'd had no luck, and by the time I called it I was sweaty, mosquito-bitten, and starving. I'd also been distracted by thoughts of Jacinda.

I wasn't the only one.

Retired ranchers always staked out the café at dawn, stayed posted up here the entire morning talking weather and cattle with several pots of coffee between them, but today the conversation veered toward gossip. "Heard it was execution style," one of the old men seated at a table behind me loud-whispered. "Cartel style."

"Heard tell she had a lover," his companion said. "A lover she'd been seeing since before Jack took the cancer."

"Cops in here this morning were saying something about

her finances. So, I'm thinking she owed someone a buttload of cash," added Dot in a breathless heave. Ice cubes plopped into water glasses as she poured from her pitcher. "The few times she came in here she was real rude. Pushy. Not to dance on her grave, but I can see someone being pissed is all I'm saying."

I was glad my back was turned so they couldn't see me roll my eyes, though it occurred to me that they wanted an audience—me, specifically. They'd probably heard I was the one to find Jacinda Moore in the river. But I wasn't going to indulge them. In a town this size, most had already heard it all via the game of telephone, and this was the part where truths got twisted to satisfy the appetite for fresh details. There was something different in the pitch and fervor now, or lack of it, rather—an unsolved homicide on the heels of a deadly flood added a weariness to the chorus, a leadenness to the air.

"Here you go, hon," Marlene said, and placed a paper sack in front of me. "Three burgers, and a little something for Sheriff McIntyre, on me."

"Aw, you know he loves these," I said, spying a couple of fried pies wrapped in wax paper. "Thank you." As I pulled out my wallet, I heard the bell on the door and turned to see a small-framed woman rushing in from outside, making a beeline to the register.

"Heather, hey," I said, and waved to get her attention.

She turned, gripping the strap of her black leather purse so tightly her knuckles whitened. "Sorry, Annie, didn't see you there. I'm doing mock job interviews for high school seniors in half an hour and hurrying to eat beforehand," she said, smirking. "I need my strength."

"Well, I won't keep you," I said, motioning to the to-go bag. "But I was planning to come back and ask if you remember a patron, possibly homeless, named Charlie? Another man stopped me that day we talked, the one who sat behind us? He said he'd been eavesdropping and this Charlie guy fit the description we went over."

"Uh, no." She bit her lower lip and sat on the stool next to mine, picking up a menu. "Charlie doesn't ring a bell."

"This other guy said that Charlie was a regular for a few months."

"Big, older man with a backpack? He told you this?"

I nodded.

"He comes in a lot. Bless his heart, he means well, but, uh, has a few issues. I can tell you, though, that a lot of the transients who come and spend time in the library don't have a local address or ID and can't get cards, can't check out materials, and I never know their names. They come and go, so it's possible, but I can't recall specifically," she said, shrugging.

"Here you are," Marlene said, back with my card. "What'll you have, Heather?"

"Chicken fingers, please. I'll also get mine to-go," she said, handing her cash. "I don't need change."

So, she wasn't vegan anymore. I noticed then that she had bags under her eyes, her skin dry. "Things going okay at your folks'?"

"Well, my brother is fifteen and a little shit, and my parents can't keep up. What he gets away with blows my mind. They act like old people now—I guess they kind of are. And they go to bed at like nine," she said, laughing a little. "It's fine, but I've started looking into buying my own place in town."

"It's good you're there to help, sounds like."

Heather made eye contact, and her face softened. "Yeah. I keep telling people I came home to help out, but the truth is they're helping me. I was in a bad place and needed to regroup. I finally accepted that everyone needs help, even me. Everyone deserves a bit of saving grace—I really believe that."

"There's no shame in it," I said, though I knew I'd had a hard time accepting it myself. Sometimes I couldn't tell if my problem with coming back home after college was just that I worried what other people would think. That no one understood the pull of my family, or the land itself, so imprinted on me. That without them I would lose all equilibrium. "And the library?"

"Pretty great, actually. Feels more like home than home. All the time I spent there as a kid is the reason I became a librarian in the first place."

I smiled. "When you mentioned story time the other day it reminded me—there was this author that spoke a few times when I was little. Wrote kids' books about Texas history and came in costume? Like, hoop skirts and her hair all big—that part probably wasn't historically accurate."

"Rita Kerr! I still have my signed copy of *Texas Rose*," she said, laughing. "Or *The Ghost of Panna Maria*."

"That's right," I said, remembering how I'd been drawn to the tales of pride and courage, tradition and legend. Stories of frontier girls, set during the fight for independence from Mexico. Sanitized stories, of course, but even in my fuzzy recollection I now sensed the menace lurking just below the surface. War, epic storms, snakebites and disease: ours was always a history shaped by violence. I felt that way now, too—it was easier to see murder and disaster as aberrant, but I couldn't quite believe it anymore.

Marlene came through the swinging door to the kitchen with Heather's order. "Here you go!"

"Thanks, Marlene," Heather said, standing. "Nice seeing you, Annie."

"Wait," I said, touching her arm to slow her down. "You mind if I come by later to talk to your staff? Your patron, he seemed pretty sure about this Charlie fitting the description."

"Yeah, yeah, of course. Anytime." She checked her phone and raised her eyebrows. "Sorry, but I've really got to hurry."

"Right. No problem," I said, gathering my things to follow her out, then cut across the courthouse lawn to the office.

"I said no pickles." Mary-Pat sighed. "I always say no pickles."

"Sorry," I said, and bit into my cheeseburger, which I then realized was the one out of the three without pickles, but wouldn't say so now.

Mind reader that she was, she narrowed her eyes at me. "Yours, right?"

I took a big bite to stop from laughing. Wiping my hands with a napkin, I took out my notepad. In addition to me bringing them lunch, Mary-Pat had told me she wanted to offload one of her assignments onto me.

Leroy paced, clicking the mechanical pencil he kept in the pocket of his pearl-snap shirt. A police siren blipped outside and he looked toward the window of our office. "Heard anything else about the Moore case?"

"Only gossip," Mary-Pat said.

Leroy turned and caught the toe of his boot on my desk—his desk, but the one I'd been using—and stumbled. I was out of my seat to help him in an instant, but he gripped his cane and waved me off. This was the first time he'd been up the stairs to McIntyre Investigations since his heart attack, and watching him take the narrow, rickety stairs had nearly given me one. "Careful," I said.

Mary-Pat nodded in his direction as she peeled a pickle chip off her bun. "You all right?"

"Most certainly am," Leroy said. He sat behind the desk and fished in the drawer for a bottle of Wild Turkey to pour into his Coke. I'd left all of his things intact, only adding some pens and a phone charger to the clutter. "How're you feeling, Ears? I think the AA meeting tonight will be useful," he said, no hint of irony in his voice as he dribbled whiskey into the Styrofoam cup. "Nothing else you can cross this Charlie off your list."

"I hope not. I mean, flimsy as it is, the name Charlie is my only lead."

"Even if he's not Charlie, you're right there's a good chance he was a drifter. He had folks around, or a job to get back to, someone would've reported him missing by now," he said, pausing for a sip. He shivered and wiped his mouth with his sleeve. "Shoot, though, think about the Moore woman. No one missed her."

I nodded, remembering how everyone at Hillview had seemed uncomfortable at the mention of her name, their feeble words of regret for not keeping in touch. My heart hurt for her. But then again, it sounded like she'd alienated herself. Maybe her aloneness was by design. I wondered what would prove to be the case for Bethany's man. Charlie, or whoever he was. After seeing Heather, I felt uneasy putting much stock in the name. It nagged at me—either she or the man I'd spoken with outside the library was off the mark—and I couldn't help but feel there was something she wasn't telling me. She'd practically run from me when I brought it up a second time. "I'll go back to the library, also back to the shelter where the T-shirts were donated. Someone else might be working who remembers," I said. "What's the thing you wanted me to do today?"

"Yes, so while you're out, I need your help on a case for the insurance guys," Mary-Pat said. "An injury claim they think is fraudulent. I was tailing the guy for a bit, but had to cut out early to take a call for the prosecutor. Instead I'd like you to run surveillance on him. Name is Bud Nelson. Not just today, but for the week. Can you do that in addition to your casework?"

"Sure," I said, knowing that she wasn't really asking so much as she was telling me.

"Good." Mary-Pat crumpled her cheeseburger wrapper and tossed it toward the trash can by my chair, missing by a foot but not getting up to throw it away. "Now Annie, the main reason why we're meeting, and why me and your granddad are both here, is that we wanted to formally ask you to be a partner in the firm."

I'd bent to pick up the wrapper off the floor and stood too quickly. Felt the blood rush to my face, heard my pulse pounding in my ears. "Oh, um—"

"Well, say something," Mary-Pat said, eyebrows raised. Leroy smiled with what looked like genuine happiness, a smile I hadn't seen since before his heart attack.

"Sorry, I, um—thank you," I stammered. "I'm honored." *But I haven't even fulfilled the promise I'd made to myself,* I thought. Not only had I not solved my missing person case, I had barely made progress, so swept up I'd been in my discovery at the river—how could I sign up for this, too? What if I let them down? Plus, being a licensed investigator was not the same as being partner in this firm. Being partner meant staying in Garnett.

"Little darlin', you want to be a partner, don't you? Pat told me you were applying for a license."

"I am—I do," I said, breathing fast. The warm air combined with the smell of the full trash can twisted my stomach. "I'm surprised is all."

"You know, right, that even for us a case doesn't solve itself? It takes time and it isn't easy," Mary-Pat said.

My chest had that tight feeling again. "Okay, but—"

"You're feeling in over your head. I get it. But, Annie, we're all in over our heads. Every time we take a new case we have to start over," she said.

"Yeah, I know, it's just . . ." I trailed off, plucking my shirt for air. "I don't feel like I'm getting anywhere, period, and y'all have these high expectations of me."

Mary-Pat shrugged. "Either you're up for it or you're not."

"I'm up for it," I said, and went to open the window. "I just want to temper your expectations." The sky was hazy and hot-white, and somewhere, in some kind of multiverse if one existed, there was another version of me. Grinding away at grad school, most likely. Maybe in Austin, working at a downtown office, writing boring copy but making enough to rent a quirky bungalow, enough to buy new clothes and eat out at restaurants every night. Or maybe I was up and leaving this town without an agenda or a dime to my name, never looking back. A partner—there was a path in front of me now, real as any of those things. But it seemed to me dim, unlit. I didn't know how it ended. Yet in my head, but mostly in my heart, I knew I wanted to keep going down it.

"Don't know if 'expectations' is the right word," Leroy said. He stood and leaned on his cane, eyes meeting mine. "More like good faith."

Maybe he was right. Maybe the restless feeling, the shake in my hands, the tightness I'd been feeling would lift—I could breathe deeply, way down in my diaphragm, chest expanding, even my heart growing larger, stronger, if I could prove myself worthy now. If I could trust in myself, trust that what I was doing here really mattered.

Mary-Pat pulled a cardboard box from her desk drawer and handed it to me. "Here."

I opened the box and felt my face grow warm. "Thank you," I said, admiring the weight of the creamy white cardstock. My first ever business cards. I ran my thumb over the embossed, bloodred font: *Annie McIntyre. Private Investigator.*

"I'll do my best," I said, swallowing the lump in my throat. "I'll find this guy one way or another. Promise."

"The lonely, the lonesome, the gone. That's our lot," Leroy said. "That's who we try and see after. But you already knew that."

Chapter 14

It's different out in the country. You can't parallel park your car on the street out front and wait for someone, not without being seen. Bud Nelson lived off a gravel road that, luckily, was near a creek bordered by thick gama grass and a stand of trees. I parked off the main road a quarter of a mile back and approached on foot. Found a spot that was hidden from sight but with a clear view of the property. A beige, single-story ranch-style house, an overgrown yard, and a white Dodge truck with a busted fender in the driveway. Bud claimed to have injured his neck in a car accident and had hired a personal injury lawyer in hopes of a big payout. If he came out in the yard and, I don't know, did a cartwheel, I'd take a picture to send to the insurance company as proof of fraud.

I leaned against a live oak hung with wisps of Spanish moss and saw a water moccasin slide down a branch right in front of me and drop into the creek. The water was muddy, slow-moving, and stunk in the high heat. Beer cans and an old tire had collected in the piles of broken branches. I didn't see more snakes. Still, I moved away from the tree and pointed the lens of Mary-Pat's expensive camera toward Bud's house. It wasn't just the snakes and the fire ants making me jumpy—I didn't like this for other reasons.

It was hard to quantify pain, I thought.

My dad's back, for instance. He didn't complain outright too often, but sometimes it seemed to vibrate off him. Days like that, he reminded me of walking past one of those fenced-off transformer stations, emitting a low buzz. *I'm fine*, he'd lie, clicking his teeth together, his dark, live-wire eyes blinking fast. He knew, I knew, people judged you when you told them you were hurting. At least, that's how I'd interpreted his shame at taking disability, even though he rightly qualified. I would've been annoyed if Bud was gaming the system, I supposed, but I also wanted to give him the benefit of the doubt.

The afternoon fell away. I needed to go home, change, and feed the cat before the church meeting. I was eager to get back to my own case. Five o'clock sun slanted right across my eyes and Bud still hadn't so much as moved a curtain. Maybe he really was laid up. Maybe asleep or watching television. The insurance company had hired us for a week's worth of surveillance, though, so I'd have to come back later. It's what you signed up for, I reminded myself—the unglamorous, too. I stood and touched the business card I'd slipped into the back pocket of my jeans. It felt something like a promise.

The placard over the doorway read ENTER INTO HIS COURTS WITH PRAISE. And as I reached for the handle, I did feel something like elation. Bethany's man very well might be here, right on the other side of this door—I pushed through on an upswing, a quick flutter in my chest. From the foyer of the old fellowship hall, I caught the low rumble of voices and the legs on metal folding chairs being popped out, screeching on the linoleum tile.

"Welcome!" called Pastor Brad from a dimly lit room with no decoration except for a large wooden cross, a lectern, and a standing whiteboard with *New Beginnings* written in its center.

It appeared the new fellowship hall and sanctuary was quite the improvement. This room was square, windowless, and the yellow cinder block walls had the gunky look that comes from being repainted many times. The floor and the ceiling seemed to retract—white tiles were low above our heads, warped and streaked with brown from water leaks, and the faded green carpet frayed and curled up at the edges of the baseboards. Pastor Brad was seated at the front with a guitar in his lap, a Bible in his hand. He knitted his thick eyebrows together and squinted, recognizing me—if he was confused or surprised by my presence, he quickly recovered. "Make yourself at home. Annie, right? Grab a coffee, stay for the fellowship. We're just about to get started."

"Thanks," I said, faltering a bit. It hit me that Brad thought I was here because I had a problem—why wouldn't he? I suddenly felt like I was standing in front of a dressing room mirror at an awkward angle with bad lighting. Alcoholism was mapped onto my genes, and being here made me think I ought to feel worse about it than I did. I drank too much, knew that. I also knew I could stop. It was the out-of-control feeling I disliked—I remembered once when I was a little girl spending the night at Leroy's, my mamaw got me out of bed and put me in the truck still wearing my pajamas. Startled, I wanted to know why we had to go to the store even though it was after supper, already dark out. Why Leroy couldn't do without his beer for one night. Mamaw had looked at me in the rearview, her face serious. "He can't," she'd said. "He just can't."

The folding table along the back wall did not hold the catering-style carafes of the new fellowship hall, but a cheap old drip coffee maker with a plastic tub of Maxwell House, powdered creamer, and a loose stack of paper filters beside it. There were leftover slices of the sheet cake in a Tupperware beside the cups and napkins. The coffee tasted watery, but would do. I scanned the group of fifteen seated in a semi-circle, and didn't immediately see anyone matching the description of Bethany's rescuer. I made eye contact with one of the only two women there. She was in her early forties if I had to guess, still wearing her work uniform from the Texaco. She nodded toward me shyly when I took the seat next to hers.

Brad stood and it quieted. His hair was extra spiky today, and I noticed his habit of fiddling with his wedding ring as he paced the room. He gave off the energy of a spooked cat. "Today, y'all, I want to talk about anger. That itch, that heat under your skin! That bitterness that don't go away! Y'all know what I mean? I'm talking about *rage*," he said.

A man seated nearest Brad nodded, raising his hand and removing his Cowboys ball cap. He had the look of someone several years beyond their real age because they've lived hard; big and fit, but with deeply lined skin, sun-faded tattoos. "Rage and crank," he said, and stood, holding his ball cap over his stomach. "When I got geared up it was this pure rage come up in me and—" He paused again, taking a deep breath. "It was just unstoppable. This energy, this mean, jerky energy took over me. I don't know if I was already angry and that got me started getting high, or if getting high made me angry, but we had this old woman neighbor used to get on me about crap all the time. One day she wasn't home, so I kicked in her door and stole her TV. Didn't need it, didn't sell it. Just broke it. Then went back a second time to smash up the rest of her place. And that's just one thing—one thing I remember. Jesus, please forgive me for that rage. Every day I'm sober I plead His mercy."

The woman sitting next to him clapped, as did several others.

Brad had had his eyes closed, and he opened them slowly, staring wide-eyed around the room. "Brother, do I know what you mean. Whiskey drew out all the wrath in me. Made me fight and act without thinking." He pressed his palms together and pointed his fingers at us. "Now, friends, I ask that when you feel rage, remember that the Scripture asks us to pray. Psalm 4:4 says 'Tremble and do not sin, when you are on your beds, search your hearts and be silent.' Remember to wait and take a deep breath, friends. Whoever did you wrong or is after you, pray for them instead of retaliating, pray instead of reaching for that bottle!"

"I'm two years sober and I still get angry," said the woman sitting next to me, rising shakily from her chair among the chorus of amens. "But thing is, I get angry at me. Whenever I was using it was like everything I touched turned to water in my hands. Everything I loved slipped through my fingers like water. I can't get it back. I'm hurting real bad and it's like, life goes on. It's just awful."

"Linda, I pray for you every single day. We love you, Linda," Brad said, and the room was quiet but for Linda's shaky breaths. "You're allowed to pray for yourself, too. You'll be forgiven, sister."

She sniffed and wiped the stream of tears from her face with the sleeve of her polo shirt. Without thinking, I reached for her free hand. She looked down at me, completely unguarded and unbothered by this stranger touching her, and for a split second, I felt as free. I didn't want her to be alone, that was all. I let go, hot with embarrassment, and let the moment pass. She sat down and Brad started playing his guitar again. Hummed a few bars that seemed familiar, though I couldn't place them, before launching into a mix of song and spoken prayer. The rest of the group closed their eyes and nodded along. I kept mine open. Some stragglers had come in, and I studied each face, every tattoo, but no. Maybe it was a dead end. Maybe this Charlie never existed and now I'd come crashing into this vulnerable, softhearted space without giving anything of myself in return.

When the song and prayer ended and everyone was moving about for a break, I approached Pastor Brad.

"Thanks for letting me be here this evening. It was, uh, good," I said, reddening. "But I actually came here looking for some- one."

"Okay, Annie, okay," he said gently, and his face twisted into a half grin. Thought I was fibbing. In some ways, now, I think he was correct.

"Do you know a man in his late twenties or early thirties, white, who has dark blond, shoulder-length hair and a short beard? Blue eyes, kind of a thin build and narrow face? He may or may not go by Charlie," I said, and raising my voice, turned to the others who'd starting milling around Brad. "Anyone know a Charlie used to come here?"

An older man wearing thick coveralls came closer. "Sounds like that Kingman kid."

Brad sighed. "Shoot. That does sound a bit like Charlie King- man." He pulled out his phone and scrolled for a few moments before handing it to me. "This him?"

I'd have to show Bethany, but the picture was of Brad in front of Richie's BBQ with his arm around a man who looked, well, exactly as Bethany had described. Like a honey-haired young Jesus. On his forearm was a blue rose tattoo. I could've reached out and hugged Brad's neck.

"Okay if I send this to myself?" I asked, and when he nodded, texted myself the picture. "Charlie Kingman," I repeated, and handed back the phone, my heart now pounding. "I'm trying to locate him or his next of kin."

"He's probably dead or back in jail." The man in coveralls grunted, affronting me with his coffee breath. "Boy got himself a paycheck and fell right off the wagon. Wouldn't answer my calls or nothing. I tried."

Brad put his phone in his pocket and sighed again. "We all do our best to offer support, but everyone's on their own journey to accept Jesus as their savior. At the end of the day, everyone's got to face their own demons, painful as it may be." He looked back at me. "Charlie's a nice kid. We found him a construction job with—wait, you knew Jacinda, that's right."

I felt like someone poured ice water down my back. "Charlie knew Jacinda?"

Brad nodded. "She hired a lot of folks who needed second chances. Anyway, Jacinda gave Charlie a shot after I asked her to, but maybe a month later had to fire him. Relapsed, I gather. Shame. I haven't seen or heard from Charlie since he was let go. His phone goes straight to voicemail."

"Maybe he went up home," added the man in coveralls.

"Up home. Where is that?" I asked.

"Said he grew up in Idell." He harrumphed. "I'd a left, too. Say, what you need him for anyhow?"

"I'm a private investigator," I said, and took out my new cards, running my finger over the embossed lettering. "He's missing, so if either of you hear from him, call me."

I sat in the bullet a few moments before dialing Bethany. I needed her to confirm this was in fact the man who'd rescued her.

Windows down, it was still warm. Dark out now but for the parking lot lamps, and quiet but for the bullfrogs. I held the phone out in front of me, staring at Charlie's picture, my hand lightly trembling. Jacinda had fired him, and later, she'd been murdered. Shot and left hidden only several yards from where he'd been spotted by Bethany.

Dead or alive, it didn't look good for Charlie Kingman.

I fidgeted in my seat as Bethany's phone rang.

"Annie," she answered, her voice hoarse, almost a whisper.

"Hi, Bethany," I said, my own voice trailing up awkwardly as I heard her sniff—had she been crying? "If this is a bad time, I—"

She blew air into the phone like she was trying to stop herself from hyperventilating. "I feel like I'm having a heart attack, Annie. I know I'm not, but— Oh, God, please help me," she said, and sobbed, the rest inaudible.

Chapter 15

Bethany and her in-laws all lived on the same large property, which was about six miles down the farm-to-market road from the church. I had to pass it on the way to Mary-Pat's place, so knew the route. I turned off onto a smaller, unpaved road that cut up through the low hills and onto a wide plateau of farmland. An iron gate under an archway that said RICHTER marked the top of the long driveway. I hopped out, unlatched the gate, and sped down the gravel without closing it behind me. To the side of the main house was a flagstone path that led to a small, wood frame in-law suite with the porch light on. Small being relative—it was the size of a normal house, but dwarfed in comparison to the three-story, 1890s limestone farmhouse with a wraparound porch. Bethany's SUV was the only car parked in the driveway, and it was quiet, only the creak of cane-back rockers and wind chimes carrying on the breeze.

I knocked on Bethany's door and she flung it open. The porch light overhead cast a halo on her crown and drew moths around her. She wore gym shorts and a neon-pink sports bra under an old Garnett High Cheer shirt with the sleeves and the collar cut off. Her unwashed hair was pulled into a lumpy ponytail, and splotches of red blossomed on her chest. It was completely dark inside the house.

"Is he out there?" she said, her voice shaky.

I spun around. "Who?"

"I was too afraid to go out there, but I heard someone," she said, and fanned her face. "I turned the lights out in case they were watching me, got all dizzy with my heart racing, and then you called."

"I didn't see anyone when I pulled up, but I'll look. Just wait there," I said, feeling for my phone, and walked around the side of the house. I'm the kind of person who, when scared, or in a situation where others are scared, can detach from my feelings and move. A lot of people freeze like deer in the headlights. You don't really know which kind of person you are until the moment arises, unfortunately. I'd learned that the hard way. As I walked the wind blew at my back, making the hairs on my neck stand up. I heard a tinny screech and spun around. But it was only the chain of a tire swing suspended from the tree at the back of the yard, spinning in a strong gust. After I had walked every inch of the yard, checked the perimeter of her in-laws' house, too, and latched the gate, I came up the driveway toward Bethany's.

She stood on the front step with her arms crossed. "See anything?"

"No. And I remember the gate was latched when I came to the driveway."

"Oh, God, I really am losing my mind—"

"No need to panic," I said, hoping she wouldn't melt down again. "Earlier, you said 'he'? You asked if 'he' was out there."

She bit her lip. Nodded, letting out a long sigh. "You should just come in," she said, and opened the door wider.

"Where's John David?" I was reasonably sure no one was out there, but I turned the dead bolt behind me anyway.

"He and his parents are off at this big conference," she said, flipping the light switch. "I think I need a drink. You?"

"Sure," I said. The house had an airy, open floorplan, the downstairs one large, softly lit room. While Bethany found me a wineglass, I pulled up the picture I'd texted myself of Charlie Kingman. I debated whether or not to show her now, given the panic attack. Maybe she should call John David, see if he could come home early. Maybe I could come back in the morning. She sat cross-legged next to me on the leather couch—real leather that smelled like leather and was supple, not sticky and peeling like the one Nikki and I had shared—and smiled wearily. Heart beating hard, I watched as she filled our glasses, and tucked my phone under my thigh. "You were saying, Bethany? About a guy?"

She swirled the wine and smelled it, looking at me with one eyebrow raised. "So, I've been worrying that my stepbrother—ex-stepbrother—might be trying to contact me. He showed up at church maybe a month and a half ago out of nowhere. Leaning against a pillar in front of the sanctuary like it was no big deal. He was looking for me—why, I don't know, and I don't plan to find out. Probably money. I ignored him and kept walking. But I keep worrying it's only a matter of time before he comes back."

"You seemed pretty shaken up. Has he threatened you?"

"No, but, Eli's not a nice guy, Annie. Absolute trash. I don't need ghosts like that coming back into my life. Like, you remember how I came up, don't you?"

I nodded. Her mother had been abused by Bethany's stepfather, Doug, and for a time, Bethany had lived in foster care. Right when she left Doug and things started to stabilize, her mother had had a heart attack and died. Luckily, Bethany's grandmother stepped up and took her in, but her high school years had been wild and unsupervised. She'd barely graduated. I didn't remember ever meeting Bethany's stepbrother when we were kids, but based on what I knew of Doug, I could imagine his son might be rough around the edges. "If he's harassing you, we should call the police."

"No," she said firmly. "No, I don't want to blow this up. I don't even know that it was him out there just now. I just had him on my mind. Please, don't."

"But Bethany, you were having a panic attack at the thought—"

"No. It's not even that so much as—as I can't stop thinking about the flood," she said, her bloodshot eyes searching mine. "Why were you calling me, anyway? Did you find my man?"

I hesitated for a second, but this was also bigger than Bethany now. Searching for him had become my mission as much as it was a job done on her behalf. Charlie was my man, too. Now that I knew he was affiliated with Jacinda, I knew there wasn't time to wait. So, I unlocked my phone. Handed it to her with the picture zoomed in. She stared at the screen for a moment, the soft blue glow emphasizing the shiny tissue on her face where the stitches had recently come out. "That's him," she said. "That's totally him."

"His name is Charlie Kingman. He used to attend New Beginnings. Pastor Brad knew him."

"You're kidding. Really?"

"Yep. Here's the deal, though: I need you to not try and contact him yourself. Let me handle it. Let me find out if he's even alive," I said, and touched her arm. Her skin had broken out in goose bumps though it was quite warm inside.

"Honestly, I don't see how he could be," she said. Her hands started shaking, and no longer the sommelier, she polished off half of her wine in one gulp, setting it on a wooden coffee table crowded with hurricane glass votives and a basket of what looked to be decorative tumbleweeds. "Why can't I try, though? Maybe I could contact his family."

"That's what you're paying me for, right? He's an ex-con who may or may not be on drugs," I said, weighing what I would say next. "Mostly, I'm worried he might have had something to do with what happened to Jacinda Moore. Either way, he could be dangerous."

"Jacinda? Seriously?"

"I don't know, but it's possible. Turns out they knew each other."

"Holy crap." Bethany hugged her shoulders and rocked back and forth. "I still can't believe someone would do that to her. But God, she was such a— Wait," she said, sitting up straight. "This man saved my life, Annie. Why would he do that if he was some cold-blooded killer? That doesn't make sense."

"Maybe he felt guilty. I don't know. I only brought you in now because I needed you to confirm that was him before I went any further. There's so much I still need to figure out."

"It's funny." She looked down at her feet, her pink polished toes digging into the white rug. "I was dreaming about that night. Was drifting off on the couch when I heard the noise outside and, like, shot upright. I can't even relax when I'm asleep. It's the weirdest thing—you know when you've been at a water park or on a boat all afternoon and then that night you feel like you're still rocking? It's like that, every time I try to sleep."

"It hasn't been that long," I said, topping off her wineglass, then mine. There was a sweet smell I couldn't place—I looked over my shoulder toward the kitchen and saw an open carton of Blue Bell and a spoon next to it, a sticky puddle forming on the black granite countertop. The kitchen was messy, but overall the house was well-kept. White subway tile and open shelving, ship-lap accent walls in the living and dining area, brass hardware and vintage light fixtures, and a mostly neutral color scheme with pops of blue. Again, I was reminded of my *Fixer Upper* binge-watching. I grabbed a bohemian-printed throw blanket off a chair and offered it to Bethany. "I don't know how you're handling things as well as you are. Seems perfectly normal to feel disoriented. Plus, you're here all by yourself—"

"I think John David wants to get away from me," she said with a big huff of air, shrugging off the blanket. "I think he's mad at me or something."

Tears spilled down her cheeks. Not seeing any Kleenex, I got up and came back with a paper towel. "That can't be true," I said. "Also, you know, people handle grief differently."

She blew her nose and nodded. "John David and Michael were best friends. And Kendall, God, he loved her as much or more."

"Michael and Kendall didn't grow up in Garnett, did they?"

"No, Michael was John David's roommate at Baylor. John David introduced Michael to Kendall, who he knew from a camp they worked at, and the rest is history." She dabbed her eyes and cleared her throat. "Kendall was good friends with John David's ex, so I worried it would be weird between us, but she was always really sweet to me. When John David took the executive pastor role and they were looking for a youth pastor to replace him, he immediately thought of Michael."

"You must miss them, too."

"Just when the day feels normal, I mess up and think, 'Oh, I'll ask her about something at small group,' or 'I'll see Michael at the office,' and I collapse all over again. John David, though, it's like he has a switch he can flip on and off. Compartmental-ize, I guess? But I'm worried it's going to build and build and then he's going to have, like, a massive meltdown."

"You're probably right," I said. There was a grandfather clock—it must have been a family heirloom—hanging on the wall, its ticking both calming and maddening. "Hope I'm not out of line here, but Nikki shared with me y'all were fighting, even before the flood, and—"

"She shared with you? Talking shit, you mean," Bethany said, a laugh at the back of her throat. She gulped her wine and set the glass down hard enough I thought it might've cracked. "There's no fight with me and John David, not really. It's just, like, tense sometimes. I've always been an outsider with his family."

"If they're unkind to you because of your past, or whatever, that is probably the least Christian thing I can think of," I said, my face getting hot.

"No, no. They're really nice. Too nice. Which is worse, in a weird way. John David, like, intellectually understands not every family is like his, but he doesn't *get it* and I can't explain it to him. And who wouldn't simply smile and slip into this beautiful life," she said, waving her hand around. "A total crazy person. All I know is I've got a lot to pray over, and a lot to work on."

"It is a nice place," I said. There was a gallery wall behind the dining table with their framed wedding pictures, some an-tique mirrors, and a blown-up black-and-white photo of the old farmhouse. An Instagram-worthy letter board prop with Joshua 24:15, "But as for me, and my house, we will serve the Lord." Another, "The Richters" and their anniversary date.

Bethany smiled, and bit her lip. I had the impression that she was holding a thought in, and when she finally spoke her voice had leveled out. "Yeah, it is. When John David and I came back from our honeymoon his mom and sister had renovated the kitchen and decorated the whole house for us. They've been so kind. His dad's pretty stern, but underneath it he's a big softie. They really are lovely people."

"Yeah, but they're not perfect, either," I said, wondering if I should share what Leroy had told me about her father-in-law. "Bethany, I know it's probably not my place to say this, but it's not just the Richters, or Jesus, or even this Charlie Kingman who've saved you. You've also saved yourself, over and over. I've seen it myself."

"Oh, Annie," she said, and leaned over the cushion to hug me. "Thank you."

My face flushed from the wine and Bethany's embrace. She let her arms go limp and her chin rest on my shoulder. Maybe because I usually had my guard up—an image of her and my cousin as kids snickering behind my back flashed past—I felt suddenly uncomfortable with my own earnestness. I patted her on the back to let go, then set my wineglass on the table, meeting her gaze. "Earlier, Bethany, you were going to say something about Jacinda but stopped."

"Yeah, um." She looked down again, pausing. "Promise you won't tell anyone?"

"Of course."

She ran her finger along the rim of her wineglass and reached for the bottle. "I feel bad talking crap about a dead woman, but Jacinda could be such a bitch."

"Oh—"

"Texted me that she knew a secret I didn't want getting out. Power play, basically. I think she knew some dirt about my ex-stepbrother, and like, wanted to hold it over me."

"What about your stepbrother do you think she knew? And besides, how do you know that's what she meant?"

"I don't know. Guess I never will. Anyway, some of the

women in my small group, including Jacinda, saw Eli that day he was at church. I was shaken up and Jacinda noticed. Acted all weird around me ever since then." She locked eyes with me. "John David doesn't know about Eli, and doesn't need to. Okay? I'll tell him eventually, but with everything going on now it's just—"

"Got it," I said, aiming for as neutral a tone as possible. "Did any of the other women have problems with her? Or just you?"

"Jesus, Annie, I didn't hurt Jacinda. And no, I don't think so." Her face turned red again like she might cry. "Oh, God, I keep forgetting there's this luncheon with those same women tomorrow. These high school grads came home from a mission trip and are supposed to do a presentation for us. I'm hosting and I haven't even started planning. I've got so much to do before bed I can't even bring myself to start."

My eyes landed on the overflowing laundry basket by the stairs, dishes stacked around the sink, the dining table covered with books, papers, shopping bags, all the junk you don't want to throw away and yet don't know what to do with. "Anything I can do?"

She gave a helpless shrug of her shoulders. "Kendall was the original host. She used to coordinate the youth group trip down to Mexico."

"Oh, jeez—"

"Annie," Bethany said, reaching for my hand. "Can you take a break from work and come? Or I can pay you for the hour, count it toward my bill. Please? I promise it won't be weird. I won't try to convert you or anything. I'm nervous and I just need a friend there, you know?"

There was that word again, friend. It felt different now—less like she was deploying the term, more like she meant it. "Fine," I said. I felt for her, but it also occurred to me that the luncheon would be a good opportunity to interview people who knew Jacinda. "You know, I don't think you should assume these women will be so hard on you. You're obviously a bit preoccupied. They're all your friends, too, right?"

"I guess. They're all so frickin' *nice*. They tell me they love me, and I think they mean it," she said, her voice nearly a whisper. "But, Annie, they barely know me."

I left when she fell asleep in front of the TV. I tucked a blanket around her on the couch, then rinsed a few dishes, remembering what she'd said about the rocking feeling, her body understanding what her mind knew to be false—that she'd never left the river. Held fast, unable to quit reliving that night. She needed a sense of closure. She needed me to find Charlie. Even then, I knew, it would be hard to move forward. Six months on, I was still getting to know the new me, and that in-between feeling was a lot like treading water.

Again, I saw no one, and it was quiet but for the kind of night sounds you hear out in the country. The wind had kicked up. Branches clicked in the trees, and I stopped on the flagstone path to lift my hair off my neck and feel the cool air on my skin, knowing it wouldn't last long. The moon was mostly full, and the clouds drifting in and out made the sky an ambiguous swirl, like a cheap mood ring. I wasn't sure what to think yet. Leaning against the hood of my car, I took out my phone and dialed the sheriff.

Chapter 16

Mary-Pat ambled down the steps from our office onto the courthouse lawn. She looked up at the morning sky stippled with pink clouds and took a deep breath. "Nice day. Weather holds out I might go fishing. Then again, you want to go early, while it's still cool. Now would be the time. You like fishing?"

"Uh, sure," I said, stopping to readjust the printouts I'd made, which were falling out of their folder in my haste to catch up with her long gait. After I got back to my apartment last night, I'd tossed and turned, too wired to sleep more than a few hours. I'd gotten up to head to the office at four, to drive and clear my head, to start digging into Charlie Kingman's past. "He went to prison on a drug charge. Possession with intent to distribute meth," I said. The fact that he was a felon—a dealer—made him more dangerous in my mind. And when I'd read the word "methamphetamines," I thought *anger.* I thought of the man who'd stood up at New Beginnings, Cowboys cap clutched in his hands, telling of that mean, jerky energy that overtook him. What if Charlie had been high out of his mind—resentment combusting with the poison running through him, crackling like fire under his skin?

Mary-Pat faced me. "You said this arrest happened in Austin?"

"I'll get a request out for arrest records, but yes, the conviction was in Travis County," I said. "He did time in the prison out toward Parr City, so I imagine that's how he ended up in Garnett. At the very least, he's not the knight in shining armor I think Bethany wanted him to be."

"Most people aren't so simple. All right, look alive," she said, and nodded in the direction of Sheriff Garcia exiting the old stone courthouse and walking in our direction. The sun peeked over the greened-out copper roof, warming my shoulders, giving me a fresh surge of energy. I always thought of the courthouse as a place out of time. People like to say that nothing ever happens around here, that nothing ever changes, but it's not true. What they really meant was that it wasn't getting better. The changes that had come to Garnett were like erosion—of occupied houses, open businesses, maintained lawns—and the courthouse, the square, and the nice parts fanning out from it like an island losing land mass.

"Thanks for meeting so early," Garcia said, and tipped his cowboy hat. "I've got a guy out on long-term sick leave, Pat, and another hit retirement, so we're short on manpower. I'm fixing to offer you a contract, if you're for hire."

"That so?" Mary-Pat was hard to read, but at this point I knew her aloofness was in direct proportion to her eagerness. "I suppose we could talk," she said.

Garcia sat on a stone bench in front of the courthouse and motioned for us to join him. There wasn't enough room for all three of us, so I stood in front of the two of them and hugged the folder to my chest. Garcia took a sip of coffee from a thermos and looked at Mary-Pat. "We have a strong lead in the Moore case," he said. "That said, this Charlie Kingman Annie spoke to me about last night needs to be further investigated."

When we'd spoken on the phone after I left Bethany's, Garcia seemed surprised I'd gotten as far as I had, and it occurred to me again that people really thought Bethany was making her rescuer up. "I doubt you want to run another wide-scale search of the river, but with the water lower now, it stands to reason you might find him easier," I said as steadily as I could muster. "I really think you need to look in the river again."

Mary-Pat looked up at me, tapping her chin. "Just thinking. Why would this Charlie kill her now? He was fired several months ago, right? Why wait?"

"Maybe it was a crime of opportunity. Maybe he saw the river rising and knew it would flood. He realized he could cover his tracks easily," I said, heart beating faster. Again, that sense of chaos—what Chief Harkness had said about disaster bringing out the best and the worst in people echoed in my head.

"Right, right. And even if he's not involved, obviously you'd want to make sure that the man's body is recovered," Mary-Pat said, turning to Garcia. "Ray, what do you say? You gonna drag the river?"

"I'll talk to Harkness. Crew will be out first thing tomorrow," he said, his eyes darting between me and Mary-Pat. "So, what do you two say? Keep after Kingman and report back to me? Any legwork you do for my department, invoice it?"

Mary-Pat looked at me. "It's Annie's case. Annie, what do you say?"

I nodded, and she turned to Garcia and patted him on the

back. "We're happy to be of assistance. You're close to an arrest you said?"

"Not there yet." Garcia's eyes darkened. "Jacinda Moore was hard up for cash. Had a gambling debt. We're talking six figures. There was a big gun safe in her garage, turns out it was full of drug paraphernalia. We understand she'd started selling her late husband's prescription painkillers."

"Oh," I said, and shuddered, remembering that eerie, empty garage. I was genuinely surprised—I don't exactly know what secrets I thought Jacinda Moore might've kept, but a middle-aged church board member and owner of a successful business selling pills was not what I'd expected. Selling pills to fuel a gambling addiction, at that. "So, you think it was a drug deal gone bad?"

"Could be. We're looking at a man she was seen with in the parking lot of a casino in New Mexico the day before she died. Last place her credit card was used. In the security camera footage, it looks like they were arguing, then he grabs her hard and jerks her toward a vehicle. Problem is, the footage is grainy and the guy was wearing a ball cap and had his head down. It's our best lead, so I'm driving out today. Will see if anyone got a good look at him. Owing that much money made Jacinda Moore very unpopular in recent weeks. The list of potential suspects is longer than I'd like it to be."

When I'd spoken to Garcia earlier, I didn't tell him about Jacinda's supposed threat toward Bethany. I thought about saying something now, but again stopped—if I brought it up to Garcia, he'd most likely ask to question her, and then John David would find out. I could do a little digging on my own first, couldn't I? Bethany's face last night flashed through my mind—lip trembling, her eyes puffy and red, searching for reassurance in mine. Bethany had been through hell and I felt I owed her the respect, as my client and, I realized, as my friend.

"Jacinda was known for her big personality," Garcia said, fiddling with the lid of his thermos. "A real piece of work. Outspoken to the point of rudeness and a bit of an embellisher. She had alienated herself in recent months. In other words, we're hard up for people she might have confided in."

I bristled slightly at this description of Jacinda—she still felt mine in a way. A bond that made it both easier and harder to see clearly. Last night before I'd given up on sleep, I lay in bed and stared at my phone, scrolling through everything I could find on her social media accounts. She'd only had Facebook and LinkedIn. The LinkedIn hadn't been touched in some time. A lot of Facebook friends, but no one interacted with her frequent posts. Selfies in the car after leaving the salon, her coppery hair fried straight, or bullshit screeds about lack of work ethic and poor customer service, cancel culture, political correctness—I didn't agree with any of it, but there was something about the defiant tilt of her chin, the hard look in her eyes and sly smile on her lips, that made me look again. She was holding something back, I'd thought. What was really bothering her, perhaps. Charlie Kingman was listed as one of her friends, but when I clicked on his profile, it was empty. His only picture was of a dog with a blue bandana, and the only "like" was from Jacinda. They were both loners, it seemed. But if Charlie had turned into legend in absentia, I worried now that Jacinda was quickly becoming demonized.

"If Jacinda was selling and Charlie Kingman was a former dealer and a drug addict himself, doesn't it stand to reason that they might've been more involved than boss and disgruntled former employee?" I said.

"Could be," Garcia said, and turned to Mary-Pat. "That's why I need you to focus on finding him, if he's alive, that is."

"Annie's a few steps ahead of you." Mary-Pat nodded in my direction. "She's done some good work."

"Annie McIntyre." Garcia studied me. "How's your grand-father's place out across the river? He been out to see it? Heard it was a mess out west of town."

"We haven't been out yet with the low-water crossing, and of course, his leg is still healing up," I said, my face still warm over the rare compliment from Mary-Pat.

"The man has nine lives." He shook his head and laughed a little. "Good ole Leroy. Whenever we worked together and I had an idea, if it was any good, he used to grin at me, say, 'Ray, you say jump, I say how high.' Though in reality he rarely took cues from anyone. Good thing he was usually right. Anyhow. We'd better get on with it."

"We'll pass along your regards to Leroy," Mary-Pat said, an eyebrow raised.

Garcia turned back to me, wagging his index finger. "Remember, Nancy Drew, keep me posted and don't do anything illegal."

When he was out of earshot, I looked at Mary-Pat. "I really wish he didn't talk to me like I was seven years old."

She patted me on the back. "You know how it goes. Let him tell you a thing or two, nod and smile."

I rolled my eyes.

"Or don't," she said, checking her wristwatch. "Personally, I don't care if he likes me."

"Garcia likes you, though. Or respects you, anyway. He kept deferring to you, even after you said it was my case," I said.

"It's not the same thing, and no, he doesn't like me. But I'm used to people not liking me. I'm an old woman with a potbelly and an opinion. A lesbian, to boot. Half of his deputies used to call me a man-hater behind my back," she said, and the laugh building in her voice burned down to a sigh. "But honestly, Annie, other people's high estimation of me is none of my business."

"Sounds like a solid strategy," I said, tucking the papers under my arm so I could take my car keys out of my purse. I admired her stance, her integrity above all else, even if truthfully, I knew I couldn't not care what Garcia thought of me. That deep down, I wanted his approval. Hell, all their approval—Leroy's, Mary-Pat's, all the powers that be. I followed behind her as she walked toward her truck, knowing I'd better not screw this up. A line of cars, and what passed for morning traffic around here, rolled past us down Main Street, and I could see in the café window all the regulars lined up at the counter drinking coffee.

"The strategy is to focus on the work. Find Charlie Kingman, find out who killed Jacinda Moore. It's important work you're doing," Mary-Pat said, squinting at a sunbeam shot through the trees. She moved a loose strand of silver hair behind her ear and fanned her face. "Damn hot out already. So much for fishing. Be good now, Annie."

I nodded, watching her get into her truck and go, knowing that she was right. Likeable or not, people mattered. The truth mattered.

It all came back to the night of the flood. To the dark, deadly water. I still couldn't see the surface or how all these pieces fit together. I felt as though I were being pulled under by a fast-moving current, unable to fill my lungs with air. Charlie Kingman was a felon, a hero, a drifter, dead or alive I didn't know—and possibly a killer. Jacinda Moore was, at least on the outside, an upstanding

Christian woman. An upstanding Christian woman who gambled and sold pills and was murdered in cold blood. Bethany, or at least Hillview, somehow figured into the equation. I, too, had a part to play in all this, but I had no idea yet what it was.

Distracted, wishing I'd stopped by the café for a coffee to go, I nearly missed the bend in the road where I could park the bullet out of sight and walk toward Bud Nelson's house. I had time to kill before the church luncheon, so figured I better drive out to his place and clock a few hours for the insurance company before I got back to work on finding Charlie Kingman. The creek looked lower this morning after a full day of sun, but the shaded ground in my hiding place was soft and damp. I spotted a broken tree branch and pulled it toward me, but right when I was about to sit, it rolled down the slope toward the water and I landed hard on my ass. Fine, I'd stand. Bud's Dodge pickup with its own busted bumper was still parked in the driveway, and his faded blue curtains were closed.

I felt antsy planted here, waiting and watching. I shifted my weight from one foot to the other, taking a deep, slow breath. Maybe the quiet and the solitude would be revelatory. I'm too much of a worrier by nature to actually empty my mind, but I did like to let thoughts waltz around my head a bit without judgment. Wyatt liked to do that when he was working on his thesis, drive out to nowhere and stare up at the aimless clouds. And sometimes, he said, he just needed to be away. Alone. Maybe part of the problem between us was how alike we were in that regard. But he'd pushed through his solitary nature by asking me to live with him. Why couldn't I reciprocate? I gave up on my half-assed meditation and looked at my phone, thumb hovering over our text thread. Then, a new message popped up—but from Heather Ellis.

*Sorry I rushed off yesterday. Any luck with your search?
I asked my staff about a Charlie and no one seemed to
remember him* ☹

No problem. A lot has happened . . . I typed, and sent her the picture of Charlie Kingman. If you see this man, please let me or the police know.

Three dots appeared then disappeared a few times. Ok, she finally said. Will keep an eye out.

I heard a door slam and looked up from my phone.

Bud was out the front door, squinting into the midmorning sun. He was in his late sixties, bald, a big guy with a beer belly and ruddy face, wearing Wranglers, boots, and a short-sleeved button-down Hawaiian shirt in a mustardy shade of beige. He held his neck brace in his hand and turned his head with ease. I snapped a few pictures right before he unlocked his truck and squeezed himself into the driver's seat. Squatting behind the oak tree, I waited until he was at the end of the driveway so I could see which way he was turning. He made a left, gravel spitting as he peeled out, and I sprinted from the bushes. Luckily, the gravel road was long with no side streets to turn onto until you reached the highway intersection toward town. Panting, I got in the bullet and sped until I caught sight of the truck.

Wherever he was going—I hoped somewhere public—I wanted to see if he put on a show with the neck brace. He turned onto the highway, camping out in the left lane while a guy in a truck passed him on the right, giving him the finger out the window. I wanted to speed around him myself; he drove excruciatingly slowly, weaving, and didn't use his signal. Begging to be rear-ended. He turned into the parking lot of Bluebonnet Drugs, the old compounding pharmacy Leroy used. I parked two spaces away and pulled the camera out. Sure enough, when Bud stepped out of the truck, he had on his neck brace. I snapped more photos as he lumbered up to the entrance, moaning for effect. I waited a few moments, and just as I was about to follow him inside the pharmacy, Bud stumbled right back out the door. A younger man in a white smock, who I assumed was the pharmacist, guided him by the elbow.

"Goddamn it!" Bud's face looked even redder now, and he yanked his arm away. The pharmacist let him go and took a wide stance at the door.

"You need to leave, sir."

"My doctor is on vacation," Bud pleaded. "He'll vouch for it when he gets back. You can see I'm struggling here, brother. My neck—look, just look at my truck!"

The pharmacist pointed toward the highway. "Sir, like I told you last time, unless you have a doctor order you a refill, I can't help you."

A few people had gathered in the parking lot to watch as Bud kicked the tire and cussed. I didn't need to follow him to know he was probably headed to the Walmart pharmacy next, maybe the H-E-B in Colburn if that didn't pan out. I felt a flicker of rage thinking about Jacinda selling her husband's pills around town. Addiction to this crap was not Jacinda's fault, her contributions more like a drop in a deep dark well, but damn. Look at the waves, all for some cash. A knot formed in my throat like I might cry—I didn't know Bud Nelson from Adam, so why was I so upset? So disappointed? I swallowed hard, dutifully snapped more pictures as Bud ripped the brace off and banged his fist on the hood of the truck. The insurance company had all the proof they needed.

Chapter 17

I keep a cardigan and pointy-toed flats in the bullet, in case I wander into a situation where I need to look slightly more presentable. Maybe adding a necklace, a fresh swipe of lipstick. Being my mother's daughter, I usually have a little color on my lips. But even with my backseat provisions I worried I'd be underdressed for the women's group luncheon, and I didn't have time to go home and change. Couldn't find the hairbrush I kept in the center console, either, so I parked at the end of the Richters' driveway and ran my fingers through my hair, trying to get the bump out from wearing a ponytail all morning.

I wasn't the only one scrambling. Bethany ran out of the side door to her house wearing a bathrobe and carrying a full trash bag in her hand. She swung the bag into the can and caught me sitting in the bullet.

"I'm not that early, am I?" I stepped out and looked at my phone. Ten till noon.

"Annie, thank goodness. Can you help? Just, like, bring the pizzas out? I started setting up on his parents' back patio. I think we're good to go otherwise."

"Sure," I said, following her inside. The house was in the same shape as last night, except worse, because she hadn't done the dishes from breakfast. Grease-spotted boxes from Pizza Hut sat stacked on the stove. "No more disturbances last night? You sleep okay?"

"No—and yes. But, jeez, too much wine," she said, swallowing an ibuprofen. "Haven't had more than a sip or two in I don't know how long. Lord help me, they're going to be here in less than ten minutes—"

"Just go get dressed," I said, though I had wanted to question her about Jacinda—and what she thought about her selling drugs—before the others arrived. Had Jacinda been selling to church members? Worse, staking out and poaching from the recovery meeting? Even if Bethany didn't know, something told me that if nothing else she'd have a strong opinion on the matter given her outpouring the night before. "Hurry up, I need to talk to you about something," I added.

"Okay, okay!" Bethany said, rushing upstairs.

I carried the pizzas outside and down the flagstone path toward the main house and the gently sloping backyard. Honeysuckle gathered on the low picket fence like white bunting, a yellow rose climbed a wrought-iron archway over the gate, and a cinnamon-barked crepe myrtle shed delicate white blossoms on the freshly mown grass. There was a large patio with a stainless-steel grill, a fire pit, and several long wooden picnic tables. Against the side of the house was a fold-out table covered with a disposable plastic tablecloth. Bethany had set out paper plates, plastic utensils, and a pile of napkins with a rock on top so they wouldn't blow away. A scuffed plastic ice chest was on the ground beside it filled with water bottles and sodas.

When Bethany had said "luncheon," I hadn't realized it would be this casual. Maybe I wasn't underdressed, then. I laid

out the pizza boxes, made a sad little pile of the red pepper
flakes and Parmesan packets, and as I did, Bethany came up
beside me and tapped my shoulder. She wore a coral-pink shift
dress, that again, while conservative, was tight and slightly ill-
fitting. My mom used to do the same thing—refuse to size up,
claim it was motivation.

Bethany frowned. "Girl, what happened to your jeans?"

"Damn it, I forgot," I said, my face warm. I'd sat on the ground
while staking out Bud Nelson's place. I felt along my back pocket
and found it crusted with mud. "Don't guess you have anything
I could borrow?"

Before she could respond we heard the sound of gravel crunching under tires, car doors opening and closing. We walked
around to the front porch to see about thirty women arriving at
once in a caravan of Tahoes and Explorers, all on time to the
minute. Amid the flurry of cheek kisses and one-armed hugs,
I slunk to the corner of the yard and took a wet napkin to my
pants. Naturally, it made the stain worse. Now I really did look
like I'd crapped myself. I tied my cardigan around my waist,
feigned ignorance, and rejoined Bethany so she could introduce
me around. About half the women were my mother's age, but
even the younger women were older than Bethany and me, except for the recent graduates, of course, and one woman I recognized from high school.

"Grace, how are you?" I asked when she hugged me. Grace
Dawes wore a shift dress like Bethany's, and her bottle-blond
hair in a shoulder-length bob she'd curled and hair sprayed
into loose waves. Around her neck was one of those nameplate
pieces that said "Mama," and in her ears, the dangly Kendra
Scott earrings that were everywhere now. The promise ring
she'd worn through high school had been replaced by a dia-
mond that looked like a bauble from a gumball machine it was

so large. I looked around at the other young women—all pretty, skinny, armored with tasteful sameness. The Grace I remembered from high school was religious, but not popular by any means. Had attended the Church of Christ, not Hillview. She'd worn skirts cut below her knees that I'm pretty sure her mother had sewn, wasn't allowed makeup or piercings. We were lab partners in biology, and, united by a shared love of old movies, became friends.

"Doing great," she said, looking at me a little funny. Cautiously, maybe. "Steve's mom was late picking up the baby this morning and I almost didn't make it. I'm glad I did."

"Congratulations on the new addition," I said, remembering from Facebook that the baby was her and her husband's second. I smiled, racking my brain for how to explain my presence. "Well, I've been spending some time with Bethany," I said.

"Oh, I've been praying so, *so* hard for her," Grace said. She clasped her hands together and squeezed her eyes shut, and for a moment I thought she was about to make me pray with her right then. She opened her eyes and stared into mine. "We all just love Bethany—I don't know what we would've done if we'd lost her, too. What John David would have done. It was clear to me the moment he brought her to worship there was something"—Grace paused, her eyebrows knit together—"special about her. Look at her, she's just gorgeous."

I nodded, glancing at Bethany out of the corner of my eye. She stood at the edge of a group that had formed by the drink cooler, wiping her hands on the front of her dress as she fished out a water bottle from the melting ice. Her smooth, chestnut hair swung over one shoulder, shiny in the sun.

Grace's eyes drew down. "Kendall was supposed to host today. She was head of the missionary committee. That girl really dove in with both feet when she and Michael joined the church leadership. She had a servant's heart."

"That's what I've heard," I said, wondering if she'd also meant it as a slight dig at Bethany.

"Gives me chills all over again. It's been such a hard time for all of us, really."

"It's terrible, I know," I said, fooling with the arms of my sweater around my waist. "Also, jeez—Jacinda?"

"Jacinda Moore." Grace let out a long sigh and shook her head. "That poor woman. Just awful she got herself killed."

Got herself killed—again, an interesting way to say murdered. I wasn't sure if it was that the word "murder" was indelicate, or if it was a subtle indication that Jacinda had deserved what was coming to her. I lowered my voice. "You knew her, right? Who do you think would've done it?"

Grace clasped her hands together. "Oh, goodness, that's right! I heard you're a cop now? Dang, Annie, look at you!"

"No, I'm a private investigator," I said, blushing for some reason. "I am looking into Jacinda, though."

Grace nodded furiously. "Anything I can do to help. Though I have to tell you, she and I weren't close. You remember I started coming to Hillview when me and Steve started dating? When I went with his youth group on a mission trip?"

"Sure." The blow to our friendship had been her relentless campaign to have me join youth group. All the pressure had made me uncomfortable. That and the idea that she needed to save me. That I was doomed if I didn't play board games and listen to Switchfoot with them on Wednesdays.

"Well, it was Jacinda who took us down to Mexico. She was a hoot, as my mother would say." She looked around and crinkled her nose up. "Honestly, though? I have no clue. She left the church. I think she was close with the music director, Pastor

Brad. You could talk to him. Or maybe you should ask Bethany. The two of them were kind of close there for a while."

"Is that so?" It was one thing to call a dead woman a bitch when she'd been taunting her, another if the two of them had been friends. "Grace, do you know anything about Jacinda selling drugs?"

"My goodness. Are you serious?"

"Yeah, turns out she was selling pills," I said, noticing that while a little shocked, Grace readily believed me, which I thought spoke volumes. I took out my phone and pulled up Charlie's picture. "You're sure you don't know anything about it? Know a man named Charlie who she might've been seen around with?"

"Uh, no. And no, nothing about her dealing drugs." Grace shook her head after studying the picture. "But you heard about the last trip to Mexico? She went on a bender in the town where they buy supplies and didn't show up the next morning when she was supposed to supervise the construction project. She didn't show up for a couple days. Scared everyone. They thought she'd been kidnapped."

I shook my head. "It sounds like she was going through a hard time?"

"You could say that, yes," she said, her lips pursed. "I know it must have been hard after her husband passed away."

"Hey, y'all," called, startlingly, a man's voice. Heads turned and the chattering went down a notch. John David was home. He wore Ray-Bans that he slid onto the top of his head, pushing dark curls away from his face as he strode into the garden. His polo shirt was navy blue, untucked. It seemed to me there should be a rule about clergy wearing shorts like that, but I supposed if you had his muscled, tanned legs it would be more of a sin not to. Bethany extracted herself from her conversation with another woman and approached her husband.

"Good catching up, Grace," I said, and cut across the lawn toward Bethany. She had her back to me, and when I strode up beside her, I could feel her body tense.

"Hey, Annie," John David said, taking my hand for a moment.

"How was your conference?" I asked, then looked at Bethany, wondering if she'd told him anything about her panic attack last night over the phone. Her eyes narrowed and her cheeks tinted, and I thought the answer was likely no. I almost imperceptibly nodded, letting her know I would keep her confidence. I got it. Like she'd said, there was a lot going on. He'd just lost his best friends. And I knew what it was like not wanting to show the soft parts of yourself to others, to a man. With Wyatt, I wasn't sure if never seeming too vulnerable was my pride or something more cynical—a fear of what he might do with that kind of power over me.

"Good! Got home early. Figured I'd help out—Mom was tired after the drive. She and Kendall used to tag team these things," John David said, his voice wavering for a moment. "I do feel like a bit of an interloper, though. This is supposed to be for you ladies," he added, smiling sheepishly. He looked over my shoulder as the woman Bethany had been speaking with hurried over and handed him a Coke. Bethany and I stepped to the side when a group of women brushed past, giggling and squeezing his shoulders.

Just then, John David's eyes landed on the single folding table stacked with pizza boxes. The pizzas had been sitting out for a while now; a string of cheese had hardened on the top box, a big fly hovering over it. "Oh. Pizza Hut?" he said, and looked at Bethany. "Aren't these things usually, ah, a bit more catered? You know you can always use the card, honey."

"I didn't place the order in time," she said, looking away.

Bethany had messed up and I could feel myself sweating for her. Knew from our conversation last night that this luncheon—really all of her interactions as preacher's wife, the job title—was, in her mind, about her not fitting in with these people. What really upset me, I realized, was that John David didn't seem to notice Bethany teetering on the edge with these short, shallow breaths. If he was disappointed, he recovered quickly. Smiled and took a step back, his presence somehow both aloof and intense at the same time.

"Let's eat while it's hot, y'all," he said to the group, waving toward the table. I tried to pull Bethany aside, make a joke about the whole thing, but she turned her back to me and busied herself with handing out plates and napkins.

As a line formed in front of the pizza boxes, I heard more than one woman say to Bethany, "Pizza Hut! I haven't eaten there in decades!"

Or, "But have you been to the new Italian place in Colburn? They have the gluten-free crust . . ."

Or, "Is there any salad?"

I found myself in line for food right in front of the two new grads who'd returned from the mission trip in rural Mexico. A bigger group of teens had gone down over spring break, but the two young women had apparently stayed on an additional month. They had tan lines around their wrists from where they'd worn lanyard bracelets and waterproof watches, their noses dusted with freckles. One still had wet hair from the shower and the other had gotten her blond hair tied into tiny braids with beads on the ends like she'd come off a Carnival cruise. They buzzed with that energy specific to long trips when you're unsure if you're really this tired from sitting all day, not totally sad, not totally happy to be back, and kept giving each other slow, meaningful stares.

I turned back and smiled at them. "How's it being home?"

They looked at each other, and when the one with the braids turned back, I could see tears in her eyes. "I'm sorry, it's just that we only found out about Kendall and Michael a couple of days ago."

"And Ms. Moore," the other girl added.

"Oh my," I said. "That's terrible."

"We didn't have reliable internet down there. We'd go check our email in town like once a week—they didn't want to upset us by telling us until we were about to come home."

"I'm so sorry."

"Thank you," the one with the wet hair said, squeezing her friend's shoulder. "Excuse us."

I nodded, turned back to fix a plate, then stepped out from the pergola into the direct sun. I lingered at the edge of the patio, hoping to insert myself again, to gently pry for more details. But the two girls finished loading up on pizza, sidestepped me, and joined a group on the far side of the yard. Grace sat at the table nearest me. She smiled and waved me over, but I wanted to sit near the two girls. As I was about to trail after them, John David stood from his seat and clapped, his eyes roving the yard like a hawk's. I gathered I was supposed to sit down now and be quiet, so I took the seat next to Grace, and across from Bethany, who looked as hot and uncomfortable as I felt. John David said a prayer and then asked the two girls to give their presentation while everyone was eating.

The one with the braids stood with her hands in fists while her friend looped her arm through hers. "We were privileged to be God's servants to many poor families in Mexico. We're humbled that we were chosen to extend God's love through Jesus Christ to the Mexican people, and that He chose us to go into the world to make disciples."

There was a murmuring of approval, a couple of *amens*.

"After we finished with the construction projects and maintenance needed for our new sister congregation in Jimenez, Mexico, Carly and me focused our ministry on leading a Bible school program for orphans. I brought my laptop to show y'all the pictures and our slideshow, but—"

Bethany made a choking noise. "I'm so stupid, y'all," she said, spinning her head around to the group. "I didn't even think to pick up the projector and screen from the AV room. I'm so sorry!"

John David palmed his forehead in an exaggerated "oops!" motion, and the group burst into giggles. Bethany turned scarlet. I couldn't tell if he was this oblivious to his wife's discomfort, just trying to lighten the mood, or if he was punishing her a bit. Either way, I could have walked up and smacked his head a little harder.

"It's okay, Bethany! I'll put them up online," the girl with the braids said, then turned to her friend. "Carly, want to go ahead and tell them about the garden?"

The girl opened and closed her mouth a few times, but no sound came out.

"Carly?"

"I just—" The girl slowly shook her head. "I can't with this presentation. I'm sorry, but I can't. I know y'all have had time to reflect and to pray, but we can't stand up here and act like nothing happened. That Kendall and Michael and Jacinda weren't killed," she said, a sob jerking her chest. "That the whole trip didn't go to shit!"

For a moment, it was dead quiet. The only sound the girls' crying and the muted bark of the Richters' golden retriever begging to be let out of the house. Grace shuddered beside me, sweat beading on her hairline and upper lip.

John David stood and started to speak, but the girl put her hand out to stop him. "In small group we're supposed to share what's weighing heavy on our hearts. I'll try that now," she said, her breaths shaky. "Honestly? The trip was really hard. The building supplies went missing. And the church we were originally supposed to be ministering with was deserted. We spent the past month figuring out what to do about it, mad at Ms. Moore, mad that Kendall left us. And now they're gone? I feel sick—like, I don't even know what to think or how to feel! I'm so upset!"

The girl in braids was now full-on crying, snot and tears running down her face. A few of the women at the table were crying now, too, and the rest looked somberly at their greasy paper plates.

This time John David walked up to the two girls and practically forced them back to their seats. He moved to the head of the table, tilted his chin, and, his features softening, his voice lowered to nearly a whisper. "I don't know why any of this happened. I can't believe they're all gone—" He leaned forward and gripped the edge of the table for a moment. He shook his head, and bit his lip like he might cry, too. "We don't know the Lord's plan, y'all. We just don't. All we can do is accept the lessons He intended for us, and continue on with grace and humility. We must keep walking by faith, knowing that those we've lost are alive in our hearts as they mend. That we'll see them again for eternity. Put your faith in God. It's what we must do and how we will be rewarded in heaven."

The noon sun was over us, the air still. I could feel my scalp burning, the can of Dr Pepper in my hand already warm. I took no pleasure in the luncheon imploding like this, but I had to admit it was a little gratifying hearing the girls vent like that.

To hear John David admit he didn't have all the answers, even if his speech was a bit patronizing. I also felt deeply the need to search for meaning in times like these—it's what motivated me to do what I do. But there was a difference, I thought, between controlling the narrative and restoring order. To me, restoring order meant stripping away all the lies. It meant staring down the objective truth—I couldn't say for certain if what Hillview preached about divine plans was true or false, but neither could they.

John David looked at the girls and put his hand over his heart. "You two are so brave. And I can see you are so tired. Go home, girls, get some rest. Honey?" He used his hand as a visor and looked at Bethany. "Let's bring out the cake, and I'll lead us in a moment of prayer—"

"I didn't do a cake," Bethany said, her voice strained. She looked up at John David and cleared her throat. "I didn't think to get dessert, honey. I'm sorry."

"Oh, well. That's okay," John David said, though his smile visibly slackened. "Well, why don't y'all go on and get seconds then, and we'll—"

"Wait!" Bethany bolted up from the picnic bench and turned toward the main house. She whipped her head around to face John David. "I just remembered there's cookie dough in your mom's freezer, I'll pop them right in!"

"No, no!" the other women muttered. "Don't be ridiculous!"

John David, too, looked at her like she was a windup toy that had gotten stuck in the corner of a room, its wheels spinning uselessly. He stepped toward her, laughing a little. "Honey, it's really okay," he said, and pulled her in for an embrace. Bethany was shaking and seemed on the verge of tears. But when she looked at his face, she smiled and started laughing, too.

"Gosh, they're just the sweetest," Grace said.

Before I could think better of it, I raised my eyebrows at her. "Are they?" I said, my voice tight.

"Can't say I blame her for trying so hard." Grace leaned toward me, sighing. "You know, I think we're all a little in love with the preacher's son."

Chapter 18

I left not long after Bethany admitted to a pounding headache and excused herself to lie down. John David had led her inside, gently stroking her hair. After the trash was cleared away, the group relocated into the main house for a prayer session and Bible study. I chose not to stay, given it wouldn't be an opportune time to ask more questions. I had itched to get out of there, had longed to go straight home. But now, my apartment was making me sneeze. I couldn't see it, but knew there was mold. Had to be it, given the rain. Festering in the walls, black spores releasing into the dusty air returns like a slow poison. I dropped my keys in the wooden bowl I kept on the counter as Tate darted between my legs. He'd gotten less skittish in the past day or so, had taken to chasing and eating the crickets. "Good boy," I said, moving out of the way so he could pounce on one.

After I had showered and changed clothes, it was all I could do not to take a long nap. I poured myself a glass of ice water and drank it while I stared out the sliding door to the balcony at the parking lot. I felt irritatingly close to something. Jacinda clearly had a lot of dirt I could sift through. I was especially curious about the Mexico disaster, but I also needed to angle back to Charlie. Jacinda selling her husband's pills made me wonder if there was more to her firing him than poor performance. Pastor Brad said it was because Charlie was caught using again. But what if Charlie was dealing? Her competition? My phone vibrated, and glancing at Wyatt's name, my heart lifted. Just as quickly it panged—I felt bad I hadn't called him first. But maybe it was good I'd had a few days; our argument the other night, in retrospect, was seeming like less of a big deal.

"Wyatt? You okay?"

"Yeah, just taking a breather. Thought I'd say *hey*."

I smiled. "How's Nana?"

"Fine. You wouldn't know it from talking to her. She moans every time she sits or stands, but tell her the dog's got out and she jumps right out of that recliner and books it down the hall. She's asked after you, too."

"Tell her I've been thinking about her," I said. Over Christmas I'd driven out to Alpine with him and his family to visit. His grandfather had taught history at Sul Ross for many years and they'd retired to a small ranch on the outskirts of town. I'd known Wyatt's parents for years, his mother had been my high school English teacher, but even with the aunts and uncles and cousins I'd felt right at home. I remembered his excitement driving me around the ranch and showing me the rocky outcrops where he and his brother had played as kids, the pride on his face when I tasted his grandmother's prickly pear jelly or admired his grandfather's floor-to-ceiling bookshelves. There was also something about being in the high desert—the yellow hills harsh against the sky, a blue so blue it ached, a violet dusk gathering on the valley floor below. We were so far away from everything. Many times, I'd wanted to go back there, to sneak out onto the roof of his grandparents' house again, to map the stars on a black, windswept night with only his arm around my waist to anchor me.

"How're things going with work? Did you find the guy?"

"Well, not physically, no," I said, pausing. How much to divulge? Now that I had a big case of my own, I needed to decide on a few things. There was no such thing as investigator-client privilege, and nothing had been classified by the police as far as I knew, but I decided to keep the details on a need-to-know basis. "I've got a few leads. Been a long few days, though."

"Good. Well, good you've got a lead, I meant," he said. When I didn't add anything, he cleared his throat. "What do you think about dinner tomorrow night?"

"Yes," I said, feeling heat creep up my neck, also worrying he was going to ask if I'd thought more about his bigger proposition. "But, um, I'm actually working now. Kind of need to—"

"Got it," he said, his voice unusually clipped. "We're about to make supper here, anyway."

"Oh, what're y'all—"

"I'm gonna go now, too," he said, then sighed. "Annie, are *you* okay?"

I bit my lip—I hadn't told him anything. He didn't even know about me finding Jacinda. I paused for a second, then said, "Yeah, I'm fine. Look forward to seeing you tomorrow." I wasn't as afraid of unloading my dark thoughts on Wyatt as, say, my mother, and I didn't assume that he wouldn't understand. Back then, I would've said the distance I put between us was to protect him, but really, it was always about me.

He disconnected, and I leaned back against the sliding door. Opened Instagram without thinking and scrolled distractedly, the way one picks at a scab. My skin felt tingly, my clothes too tight—flitting through other people's stories wouldn't lessen that restlessness. Right as I was going to close the app, my thumb hovered over a post: graduation pics taken in a sunny, open field, portrait mode fuzzing out the busted arena and the mud. The rodeo fairgrounds. Realizing then who might know a thing or two about local dealers, I grabbed my keys. I needed to head toward town.

Tyler Thompson's family owned a feed store at the end of Second Avenue, the point where Garnett's streets thinned to gravel then dirt, and the houses grew farther apart a few blocks from the high school football field. It used to be a thing—when football practice let out, the guys went down to Tyler's family's store to pilfer chips and candy from the register and hang out in the empty lot where customers backed up their trucks to load them with hay bales. More kids would show up, Tyler's older sister and her boyfriend would buy beer, and then the roughhousing would start. People slowly peeled off as the night wore on, and always, a handful of girls stayed too late, hoping for a shot with Tyler. But he was already half gone by then. Too smart to get attached to someone in Garnett.

I walked inside the store and was affronted by the strong smell of alfalfa and birdseed. Tyler's sister was behind the register. She wore her hair in a messy bun at the very top of her head, like she had as a teenager, but was now about fifty pounds heavier and had a baby on her hip. A second kid rolled Tonka trucks across the polished concrete floor. Her eyes brushed over me. "Help you?"

"Is Tyler around?"

She turned and looked at the clock on the pegboard wall behind her while the baby stared at me, a long string of drool hanging off his lip. "Uncle Ty! Uncle Ty!"

His sister smiled. "He's probably around back. If you see him, tell him his break ended five minutes ago," she said, and used her sleeve to wipe the baby's face.

"Thanks," I said, and went out the back door. There was a half-empty bottle of Gatorade on the step, but no Tyler. On a hunch, I started walking toward the rodeo fairgrounds where I'd recognized him a few nights before. Headed west down an unpaved alley and into a vacant lot behind the high school, the late-afternoon sun slanted into my eyes until I was under the shadow of the stadium scoreboard. I remembered Tyler's speech at his graduation—he and Nikki and Wyatt were in the same class—which he'd given as valedictorian. A train had interrupted. The railroad tracks were just south of the field, and usually when a train passed the speaker would be caught off guard and continue reading even though no one could hear them. Tyler, though, had had stage presence. Gave the audience a knowing, exasperated smile. Deadpanned, "I'll wait."

I reached the big gravel parking lot for the rodeo fairgrounds, and could see in the daylight that the metal chutes and bleachers, once painted white, were chipped and rusted. Past the arena, near the pavilion Nikki and I had sat under, Tyler paced back and forth across the grass, hands on his hips and breathing hard like he'd come in from a run. Despite the heat, he wore Under Armour beneath his gym shorts and his Red Raiders T-shirt, and dark tube socks that went up over his thick calves. His reddish-blond hair was pulled into a ponytail and curled at his temples where he'd been sweating.

"Tyler, hey," I said as I approached. "Remember me?"

It took him a minute. His skin was broken out, and his once sharp jawline had disappeared. "Annie? Man, it's been a long time since Mr. Meyer's class. How's it going, girl?"

"Fine. I didn't know you were back in Garnett," I said, and smiled. "Did you come home right after graduation?"

"Didn't graduate," he said, looking down and laughing a little. "Had too much fun and decided to take a break. I'm sure you heard like everyone else that I was off the team. That was rough. Been a few years, though, so maybe not?"

"I heard," I said. He'd missed something like three of six field goal attempts in the first two games and got cut. It had never occurred to me that being off the team was that big of a blow. He'd been a walk-on. Hadn't even gone to Tech for football, but was on an academic scholarship. Looking at him, at the red patches on his cheekbones, I realized being cut was a big deal to him, though. And of course it was—all that glory dimmed out in such a public way.

"Choked," he said as he rolled his shoulders back and shook out his arms. "Yeah, I'm still nursing an injury from back then, but soon as that's healed up, I'm going to get back in shape. Go to tryouts at State. Finish up my degree down here then get the hell out."

"That's all great," I said. I worked to keep my face neutral, to not betray my thought that he was lying to himself or that I was—even though I had no right to be—disappointed in him.

"But enough about me," he said, his eyes narrowing. "Heard you work for the sheriff's department or something, right? What're you doing wandering around out here? Perp go thataway?"

"I'm not a cop and I actually wasn't wandering. I was looking for you. Saw you here the other night."

His shoulders drooped back down, and he shifted on his feet. "I don't know what you're talking about."

"What was in the bag?" I stepped closer so our eyes met. "Don't bullshit me, Tyler, come on."

"I need to get back to the store before my sister gets mad," he said, stepping around me.

I swallowed hard, hoping he'd buy my bluff. "Fine. Don't tell me," I said to his back. "But I bet the coach might have some questions once I post the pictures that I took of you and that dealer standing right in the headlights."

He spun around and stared at me. "Even if I believed you, you wouldn't mess with me like that."

He was right, of course, but I stood my ground. "Try me."

"Pain relief," he said after a moment, shrugging. "I need them until I work through this injury. Why? Do you want some?"

"No, I just wanted to know if you ever bought pills from a woman named Jacinda."

"Oh, her," he said, eyebrows raised. "She picked me up outside a meeting once. Didn't see her again after that, only her errand boy would come when I texted her."

I held out my phone with Charlie's picture, careful not to let him grab it and try to delete the incriminating photos that didn't exist. "This wasn't him, was it? Charlie?"

He squinted at the screen and nodded. "Didn't give me a name, but that's him. It was only a few times I bought from her. They fell off the map and I went back to Eli and his bullshit."

The name Eli scratched at the back of my mind—where had I heard it recently?

Tyler frowned. "You don't really have a choice around here, least not right now. It's too bad. Lady had real oxy, not the pressed crap that he pushes. Liable to kill someone—you heard about Ms. Harkness?"

I nodded.

"The pills she OD'd on were cut with fentanyl. It's hard to come by legit pharms these days. Jacinda told me she had a prescription she took around, even drove all the way to Florida a few times where they're real lax, coming back with whole suitcases of it."

"Jesus." My heart beat faster. I had that same sensation I'd

177

felt after seeing Jacinda's body in the river: like I'd hooked a nail on a loose thread, unraveling the seam faster than I could stop pulling it. I had to find a way to tie it off. "And Eli—is that the guy you were with the other night?"

"Why do you need to know all this? Shit, you are a cop."

"I'm a private investigator. Working for my granddad."

"Guess that makes sense," he said, looking at me for a moment. "You were always quiet, but not shy. Know what I mean? Listening to everything. Too high-minded to be called sneaky, but—"

"I'm not sure I should be flattered by this analysis," I said, though, in a weird way I was. Being around people I grew up with was something I both hated and loved about living here: it felt good to be known. Like you had actually mattered to someone. But it also made you feel like you couldn't ever change.

"Yeah, maybe not." He smirked. "You need to stay away from that guy, though. He finds out about those pictures, you and me both are screwed."

"I don't want to scare you, but . . ." I paused, taking a deep breath to steady my own nerves. "Jacinda was murdered. Her errand boy, as you called him, is also missing."

Tyler bent at the waist like he was going to be sick. When he stood upright his face was bright red. "You don't mean to scare me?"

"If you won't help, I'll still find him, so—"

"I don't know where that mean motherfucker lives! I don't hang out with him. We're not friends. Here's his number, so you just leave me out of this from now on," he said, handing me his phone. "Promise?"

"Okay." I punched in the number and handed it back. "You know his last name?"

"Yeah. He's a Wallace."

My stomach flipped. Wallace. Bethany's mom's last name. That was it—Eli was the name of the stepbrother she'd told me about. "He grew up around here?"

"Yeah, he was in my sister's class." Tyler grimaced, looking east toward the scoreboard for a moment. "It's funny, isn't it?"

"What?"

"Round and round." He laughed half-heartedly, drawing a circle with his index finger. "Everyone leaves—you, me, hell, Eli went to prison, so that counts—and now we're back. I'm surprised you stuck around."

"Me, too, some days."

Tyler looked at me, his eyes searching. "Hey, what're you doing tomorrow night?"

"Seeing an old friend of yours, actually. Wyatt Reed," I said, tucking my phone in my pocket. "Y'all ever talk anymore?"

"Like I said, round and round," he said, then rolled his eyes. "Ah, nope. But tell him I said hey. Tell him I said good for you, man."

I couldn't tell if he was hitting on me or making fun of me. Maybe both. That was how he'd acted in high school, too—cutting you down to build you up, keep you guessing. Not being sixteen anymore, I didn't find it attractive. I stuck my shoulders back and handed him one of my cards. "If you think of anything else, you call me."

"So official." He snickered, and I felt stupid for giving it to him. "Maybe I will call you."

The sun warmed the side of my face, and illuminated the red in Tyler's hair, in the uneven stubble on his chin. "See you," I said, walking backward until I was at a safe distance. Back and back until I could turn and run.

Chapter 19

"Feeling better?" I pulled down the visor and reached in my purse for my sunglasses.

"I'm fine now," Bethany said. On the other line, I heard her shuffling things around, closing a door. "John David and I were about to sit down and go over his calendar. Busy week ahead— wedding season. Can I call you later?"

"No," I said. "I need to talk to you about your stepbrother and Jacinda. I didn't want John David to see a text, so—"

"Hey, babe! Yeah, I'll be right there!"

"Bethany, go outside for a minute."

"I'll meet you at the café later, okay? I'll call you when I'm leaving the house."

She hung up and I dropped the phone in the seat. Drove the short distance between the feed store and the courthouse square, parking in front of our office building. Mary-Pat was getting into her black Silverado as I was getting out of the bullet. The low-hanging sun filtered through the live oak branches, and I had a feeling of being on an endless loop, the round and round Tyler had described. This was the very spot I'd started my day just after it rose. Maybe I was exhausted, or maybe seeing him had gotten me in a high school state of mind, but I thought of our home cross-country course, the one that ended at the starting line. Feeling the tailwind of adrenaline, that wobbly sensation in my legs after I'd stopped running but like I could keep going, going.

Mary-Pat tossed her bag on the bench seat and turned to face me. "What's happened? You look a little spooked."

"I feel a little spooked. Wondering if my client hasn't told me everything she knows."

Mary-Pat looked up at the trees bathed in orange, and shook her head. "They tend to do that. Doctor up the truth."

"That and now I really don't think it's a coincidence that Charlie was seen near Jacinda's property the night she died. Apparently, he worked two jobs for her. One was selling pills."

Mary-Pat turned her head sharply. "That could be big. Have you told Garcia?"

"I'm about to."

"Good. What else have you got?"

"I went ahead and finished up the work for the insurance guys," I said. "Will type up the report, then I'm thinking I might drive up to Idell to see about Charlie's family and friends. It's where he grew up."

"Idell, huh. Small world," Mary-Pat said. A property she owned was up that way, I remembered. "Well, if he's alive, might be he's hiding up there."

"That's what I was thinking," I said, rubbing the sore spot on the back of my neck. I'd been tensing my shoulders all day. "Hey, do you know a local dealer named Eli Wallace?"

"I know a Doug Wallace. Owns one of the liquor stores out by the county line, also been known to sell pot. Think he had a son, might be the same."

"Yeah, I think that's the one," I said, pulse quickening, remembering that Bethany's stepdad had been named Doug. "I'm wondering if Wallace might be involved somehow. Sounds like Jacinda and Charlie moved in on his territory."

"This is getting seedier and seedier." Mary-Pat shook her head. "None of this is what I had in mind when I asked if you wanted to take this case solo, Annie. If you want out, now's the time to say so—"

"No way," I said without hesitation, though she was right. This was so much bigger than what I had signed up for back in the office with Bethany, and yet I couldn't let loose of it. Tyler's description of me in high school rattled around in my head. Maybe I was destined to do this work, and not just because of my last name. That kind of long-eyed view filled me with a strange pride. But Tyler had also made me deeply sad. I couldn't forget the boy I knew in high school—the distance between his two selves seemed wider to a person like me, and it made my heart hurt. He'd done his best to make me feel like a failure for being back in Garnett, like him. But I wasn't—I knew I wasn't, if for no other reason than I had work to do now. I really believed I could fix it. I'd find out what happened with Jacinda and Charlie and the pills, and if I did, a better version of him, of this entire goddamn town, would come right back again.

"I'm headed to pick up your grandfather," Mary-Pat said, opening the door to her truck. "Think I'll make us supper. Do I need to set another place?"

"Can't," I said. "I'm meeting Bethany."

"Call me tonight, then. Don't let me worry."

"Yes, ma'am."

* * *

Whenever we ate together, my aunt Jewel liked to shake her head at my plate and tell me that one day my metabolism would slow down. Good thing that day was not today, I thought, polishing off a chicken-fried steak platter. Bethany had told me to go ahead and order, that she'd be there soon. It was nearly nine, the café quiet and near empty except for a trucker at the counter nodding off into his eggs, me, and a woman and her young daughter seated across the room splitting a piece of cobbler. I'd had time in the office to do some cursory searches on Eli Wallace, and I'd found a local news story from five years ago. Like Charlie Kingman, he'd been to prison, but not for drugs.

According to the report, he'd beaten another man to a pulp in a bar fight, and when the guy went down, he hit his head on table corner and died. The charge was downgraded to involuntary manslaughter and Eli had been sentenced to two years at the state prison out near Parr City. The fact remained that he'd killed someone—and if he'd killed before, who's to say he wouldn't commit such violence again? Maybe he shot Jacinda in a rage. Pushed her truck into the river to cover it up. Stomach in knots, I'd called the phone number Tyler gave me before my nerves completely won out—I'd have a better chance at talking to him, I reasoned, than the law. What if I were this close? The number was not in service, so either Tyler had given me a fake one or Eli had ditched the phone. The bell over the door chimed and I felt a rush of warm air against my back. I turned around and saw Bethany.

She sank into the chair opposite mine. "Man, this place never changes."

"Did you know Tyler Thompson is back in Garnett?"

"Uh, no—well, yeah, maybe. Think I heard that. Why?"

"I saw him earlier. It's beside the point, though," I said, back-tracking. I didn't want to shit-talk Tyler. I handed her a menu across the table. "Eli Wallace is your stepbrother, right?"

She wore her long brown hair pulled into a low ponytail, and though she'd done up her face, I could see she was a little pale. She'd changed from her dress into the expensive yoga pants meant for showing off your butt, not exercise, and an oversized pink T-shirt. She threw the menu on the table and frowned. "Yeah, that's him."

The woman at the other table had been watching us. She cautiously approached, tapping Bethany on the shoulder. "I'm a big fan of your husband's," she said, twisting a paper napkin in her hand. "He has this way with explaining the scripture—well, I don't have to tell *you* that—but Pastor John David, he brought me back to church, made me want to change my life. Saved my life, really. I just love him."

Bethany raised her eyebrows, then smiled, quickly gaining composure. "I'm rather fond of him myself," she said in a warm, funny way that somehow didn't come off as sarcastic. She'd clearly had a lot of practice.

The woman had food stuck in her teeth, which somehow made her standing there pouring her heart out even more un-bearable. "Gosh, you're even prettier up close, Mrs. Richter! The two of you set an example for us all with your marriage," she said, and then looked at me. I didn't know what to say, and couldn't bring myself to embarrass her by pointing to her teeth, so just kind of stared at her. "I didn't mean to interrupt y'all's sup-per," she said.

Bethany stood and pulled her in for a hug. "Thank you, sister. I'll look forward to seeing you on Sunday."

"I forget you're basically a celebrity now," I said as soon as the woman was out of earshot. "Maybe we should've met at my office, but I know from experience that she can't hear us from over there under the box fan."

Bethany rubbed her eyes with the heel of her hand. Realizing she'd smudged her mascara she licked her thumb and ran it over her lower lids to fix it. "I don't know why I came here at all if you don't have anything on Charlie Kingman's whereabouts or his family. I'm exhausted, Annie."

"Let's get back to Eli," I said. "You knew about his conviction?"

"Yeah, I heard. It makes me sick. But I don't have anything to do with him. We never spoke after Momma kicked Doug out," she said, pressing her lips together. "And I haven't seen him since that day at church. Why?"

"Did you know he's a drug dealer?"

She looked around the room. "Yeah, well, he's always sold weed. Some of his dad's moonshine, too. So, sure, I guess so."

"He's into heavier stuff now." I made eye contact with her. "So was Jacinda Moore. You calling her a bitch the other night hit differently after Grace Dawes told me you and Jacinda were friends."

"I did call her that, didn't I?" Bethany's eye twitched. "But back up, Jacinda was into drugs?"

"Yeah—"

"Mrs. Richter!" Dot hurried through the swinging doors that led to the kitchen, tripping over her clunky white Sketchers to come take Bethany's order. "My word, your husband's sermon last week was one for the ages!"

"I thought you were here Sundays," I said. When we'd worked together, she loved to bitch about the big groups that would come in after church and altogether tip two bucks.

Dot looked down at me like the devil himself had jumped up and bit her. "Hillview streams their services now. Anyway, hon, what'll you have?"

"I'll tell him you said so." Bethany smiled at her. "Just water is fine, thanks."

Dot poured her a glass from the pitcher, left mine half-empty, then hauled ass to the stool behind the register so she could play Candy Crush or whatever it was she did on her phone.

"Anyway." Bethany shook her head, then looked at me with deadpan eyes. "Grace Dawes is a fucking dork."

The sip of water I took shot up my nose.

"You know she is." Bethany smiled mischievously, fiddling with her straw wrapper. "Really, though, I didn't know Jacinda was into drugs. Knew she partied. John David and Kendall both told me she let loose on that last mission trip."

"What exactly happened?"

"Well, I wasn't there," Bethany said, her eyebrows knit together. "But the construction supplies were stolen, and according to Jacinda, there were some financing issues. So, she went into town and had a few too many or something. Spent the night away. Long story short, John David drove to meet them in Del Rio to patch things up and bring them new tools, and the whole thing was a bit of a headache. Not that he minded. The missionary work is so important. I think the whole thing with Jacinda was not actually that big of a deal, though people got all bent out of shape about her behavior. Um, what's the phrase I'm thinking of . . ."

"Pearl clutching?"

"Yeah, that's it. Jacinda has been going down there for twenty years, has friends in the area. She and her husband had a house there, one of those places they keep quote, unquote 'working on' to avoid paying any taxes. She wasn't in any danger."

"Right," I said, watching her.

"I shouldn't have called Jacinda a bitch. She was actually pretty down-to-earth. People got all defensive around her, thought she was pushy and loud, but she was just straight with you. When John David and I got together, she was the only person with the balls to be honest with me. Told me his mother and her inner circle wouldn't like me as much as his ex, who he'd been with since like middle school, and that they'd see me as a rebound, but to ignore them. Said they'd come to love and accept me given time," she said, and her downcast eyes welled. "I took Jacinda seeing me so clearly as a sign that she cared, but now I think it was to judge me."

"Speaking of adages, what's the one about glass houses?" I moved the last bite of mashed potatoes around on my plate for a moment. "I think Jacinda and your stepbrother—and Charlie Kingman—were either working together or were each other's competition."

"Jacinda was dealing?"

I looked at Bethany. She seemed genuinely surprised, but then again, she'd obscured the truth before. "Yes," I said. "And I wonder if that day you saw Eli at church, he was there for her, not you."

"Oh." She blushed. "Maybe."

"Even if Jacinda was going to tell people about your relationship to him, people know you can't choose your family. Everyone would understand," I said. What I didn't say was that they liked having someone to save. That it made them feel better about themselves. That church people—hell, most people— loved a redemption story.

"Uh, hello? You see how they put John David up on a pedestal, and me by extension?"

She was right, of course. I glanced at Dot scrolling through her phone and singing "Amazing Grace" to herself.

"It's not just Eli being trashy, or even that he did time," Bethany said. She bit her lower lip and winced. "He and Doug come from a long line of organized criminals. Like, Doug's dad was on *America's Most Wanted* once. He's doing life in Huntsville. Back in the day they ran moonshine and gambling rings, robbed, killed people. Smuggled black beauties up from Mexico."

"'Black beauties'?"

"Speed. I shouldn't be surprised Eli's taken up the family tradition. Like, I bet some of the older church board members if you said the name Wallace would— Oh, Lord. You can't tell anyone we're connected, Annie."

"I won't," I said, and sat up straighter. "But, Bethany, if you really think Eli could be coming around your place, this is more serious than I thought."

"I know," she said, lip trembling.

I drummed my fingers on the table, a nervous habit. "So, you think Jacinda had planned to blackmail you, then? Why?"

Bethany had started crying, her tears darkened with mascara. "The construction contract, maybe? Money? I know she was pissed about the new rec center. Furious at John David's dad. I don't know," she said, her breaths shaky. "But this is the only secret I have. Thing is, we—me and Momma—we knew Eli and Doug were doing all kinds of illegal shit; we just didn't care. I was such trash—"

"Oh my God, Bethany, stop," I said. "You were a kid." I reached across the table for her hand, but she stood and picked her purse up to leave, watching Dot from the corner of her eye to make sure she didn't see her crying.

"Bethany, just wait—I don't think you should be driving like this."

"I'll be fine," she said.

"You don't seem fine."

She leaned down to hug me, her tearstained cheek sticking to my hair. "You know, you have one of those faces, Annie. Or maybe I've just known you so long—anyway, I think I needed to get that off my chest. I actually feel a lot better now. Maybe you should be the one in ministry."

"No way in H-E-double hockey sticks."

Bethany wiped her eyes, smiling weakly. She looked out the picture window. Three of the streetlamps had been knocked out during the storm, and the square was dark, only the yellow bulb over the café door lighting a strip of the sidewalk. "I've been thinking a lot about family lately. Especially after seeing Eli again. Think it's partly why I wanted to spend my birthday weekend at the cabin. That time was on my mind—I wanted to remember it wasn't all bad, that we had fun, too. Look what happened. It's all my fault."

"No one predicted the river ever coming up that high. No one. Come on, I really think you should sit a minute—"

"It wasn't just Doug hitting Momma. Eli, he was awful to me. Verbally abusive, you know? Threatened to do worse if I told on him. I remember being weirdly angry Momma didn't realize what was going on. Like she was supposed to be psychic? But, I mean, it happened right under her nose."

"Bethany," I said, standing. "Let me get you a coffee, or if you have to go, let me drive your car."

"No, no, I'm fine. I'll talk to you soon, Annie. Let me know when you find Charlie or his folks," she said, and shielding her face with her hand, walked out into the pitch-black night alone.

Chapter 20

I woke late, still unsettled by Bethany's admission and my lucid dream. One I'd had a lot the past few weeks. In it I'm eight, and it's the year of the El Niño flood. We're at the old house that backed up to the creek. My mother runs out into the driving rain, yells at me to get in the truck, but I run the other way, toward the tin-roofed shed. The water comes up to my waist and I stop, trapped—both by the water and my indecision—and unable to make it either to the shed or back to the truck, I drown. Last night, though, I'd realized I was dreaming and kept going, waded toward the shed, but when I reached for the door handle, it turned into a snake and I woke feverish and sticky-skinned, a little dazed, the feeling not so unlike a bad hangover.

After enough coffee to set my teeth on edge, I had it in my mind to locate Eli Wallace. Thought I'd start by trying his dad's store off the state highway. Price, the county to the west of ours, was dry, so there were a handful of dive bars and liquor stores right on that stretch of highway. The beer-way, people called it. Doug Wallace's store, Eagle Beverages, as one might guess, had a big bald eagle painted on the side of it. It was a cinder block building the color of dust with bars on the windows. The gravel parking area in front of the store was empty, and the Reddy Ice cooler by the door looked busted. The sign was flipped to open, but the lights were off inside.

When I pushed through the door, a bell chime announced my presence, and I called out with a hello. Nothing. No music was playing, and I couldn't see anyone behind the counter, either. "Mr. Wallace?" I said, my voice nearly echoing it was so quiet. I told myself I was at Doug's store to inquire after his son, and by extension Charlie Kingman, but another part of me wanted to confront the assholes for what they'd done to Bethany and her mother. And now, secondhand fear and guilt gripped me—she was right, no one from church should know. It was none of John David's business, either, in my opinion. Given the threat of the truth coming out, it also had occurred to me that Bethany had a motive to kill Jacinda. But if that were the case, why tell me about Jacinda's threat in the first place? Why, then, would she tell me about Eli and his family at all?

"Hey, there's a customer!" I tried again.

The place was familiar to me, though I didn't think I'd been here before. I'd had my first drink of alcohol—that I remembered, anyway—outside a store like it. I was six or seven. Leroy had taken me across the river to go fishing and I was thirsty after being out in the sun, so he'd given me his last beer to sip on while he went inside for a fresh case and a Coke for me. He was in the store long enough that by the time he came back I'd finished the can and was dizzy, smelling like beer and a crushed bag of Fritos I'd found in the glove box. My dad was particularly furious, and my parents didn't let me go fishing for quite a while after that.

The sun coming through the barred windows illuminated the wine bottles on the top shelf, orange price tags stuck over the labels, the dust so thick it gave new meaning to the word "vintage." Once-white floor tiles were warped and I caught my toe on one, brushing against a flimsy rack of airplane-size bottles of flavored vodka in radioactive shades of pink and bright blue. Who actually bought these? Guess if you needed a quick fix. My face burned for some reason, thinking about Leroy again, and I remembered Tyler had said Jacinda picked him up at an AA—or was it an NA?—meeting. Pastor Brad had also talked about her using New Beginnings as a place to locate laborers for her construction sites. Maybe Brad was in deeper than he let on. He was, after all, the person who introduced Charlie and Jacinda. I halfway dismissed it—the man was way too sincere, I thought—still, I made a mental note to take a closer look at him.

The register had a piece of computer paper taped over it with CASH ONLY written in Sharpie. A free wildlife calendar from the First Bank of Garnett was tacked onto the wall, along with a framed photograph. I recognized Eli at once, though he looked younger than in the mug shot I'd seen online. He stood next to an older bald man, who I assumed was Doug. Hunting rifles in their arms, a dead buck between them. Both men had prominent cleft chins and the same long nose and tight-lipped smile. I looked around the register for a bell to ring, a nervous feeling building in the pit of my stomach, and clocked a second exit behind the counter. I had thought it would be okay given the daylight hour, given this was in fact a legitimate business—but maybe I shouldn't have come here alone. I looked at the shelf below the window, and as I did, I saw something move outside—a flash of red, a shirt or a ball cap maybe—and went to the exit. I pushed, and it opened out to a grassy area. Beyond it was a small trailer partly obscured by a stand of mesquite. There was a buzzing, pounding sound coming from it—heavy metal music.

A hand closed around my arm and yanked me backward. My heart thumped in my neck so hard I could barely hear. I turned to see who the fingers digging into my skin belonged to, and was confronted by a large man in green army pants, black shirt, and red bandana tied around his head. His face was the one from the photograph—Doug Wallace, I was certain. I yanked my arm back, but he tightened his grip. "Let me go," I said, still too shocked to even feel scared.

"You ought to explain yourself, sneaking around my god-damn place," he said, filmy teeth bared.

"Let me go or I'll scream," I said.

"Who would hear you?"

Sweat pricked my skin. I looked at the trailer. Doug laughed, spit gathering at the corners of his mouth. "That's my place and I live alone."

"The sign said open. This how you treat customers?"

"You're not a customer if you're fuckin' stealing from me."

"I'm not here to steal from you. I came to talk to you."

"Whatever." He let go of my arm and shoved me. "Get outta here, girl."

Shaken, arm stinging where he'd twisted the skin, I turned to go. No, I told myself, and stopped. "Hey," I said. "You're Doug, right?"

He narrowed his eyes and crossed his arms over his bulky chest.

"I'm looking for your son, Eli. Can you tell me where to find him?"

"Why?"

I pulled out my phone and found Charlie's picture. "This man is missing. I think Eli might know where to find him. He look familiar? Name's Charlie Kingman."

Doug's eyes grazed the screen. "Nope."

"What about a woman named Jacinda Moore, she—"

He looked over my shoulder, watching the store. "Nope."

"You didn't let me finish. Let me show you—"

"I said no! Damn. I don't know the company he keeps and I don't care."

"Hey. Like I said, Charlie's missing and Jacinda's been killed, okay?" I angled my body so he could see my face. In his black, dilated eyes I recognized fear. I took a step back, unclenched my jaw, and tried softening my voice. "Please, help me? For all I know, Eli's in danger, too."

Doug sucked in his lower lip, stared off for a moment, then shook his head. "Naw. Even if I knew where Eli was, I wouldn't be telling that to you. You think you know me, but I don't know you. Other than you're a wannabe thief."

I took a deep breath, unsure if what I was about to say would work for or against me. "I'm a friend of Bethany Keller's. She and Eli have been back in touch. That's how I heard he might know about Charlie and Jacinda. She's worried about him."

"Bethany?" For a split second, Doug's face softened. "How is she?"

"She's doing great," I said. "She's married now and is really happy."

"Good for her." He shifted his weight from one foot to the other, then shook his head. "But I don't know where Eli is."

"You have a number for him?"

"I thought you said they were in touch."

"Yeah." My face felt hot. "But he's not answering her, so—"

He huffed through his nostrils. "Listen. You better get. I don't buy half the shit you're saying."

"Well, maybe the next time it'll be the sheriff asking after him. If he's mixed up in this trouble, it's better he comes forward on his own."

Almost imperceptibly, I noticed his arms went rigid. The hair on the back of my neck stood up. I looked over his shoulder to the trailer and saw no movement, no shifting of the curtains or shadows moving across them. Doug fiddled with something in his pocket before pulling it out and shoving it back down again—a knife. The handle was smooth bone, and right above his thumb on the handle was a silver star. Doug grimaced and shook his head. "Go on, now."

This time, I listened. Massaging the spot on my arm where he'd grabbed me, I hurried around the side of the building instead of going back inside, tall weeds scratching against my jeans. When I rounded the corner, I could see the bullet was still the only car in the gravel lot.

I reached for my keys, and right as I clicked the fob to unlock it, I heard gravel crunching, felt a rush of wind as someone ran up on me from behind.

His sweaty, calloused hand covered my eyes. His arm, thick as a tree branch, circled my waist. My feet dragged in the gravel and I could taste the dust kicking up, smell the Listerine and cigarettes on his breath. I planted my heels as hard as I could and felt his arm release from my waist, but before I could pull away, I felt a jolt of cold. Something hard pressed into the soft underside of my jaw. A stinging sensation as a sharp edge drew lightly down my neck.

He held the knife at my throat.

"Please," I whimpered. "Please let me go."

He moved his hand from my eyes to my shoulder, and I blinked hard against the green spots forming in my vision.

"No one threatens me," Doug hissed in my ear. "Don't you ever threaten me or my boy with the law again."

"I won't," I said, and as I did, he pressed the flat side of the blade down against my pulse point. A truck rolled past on the highway, thank God. Afraid to make any sudden moves, I prayed for the first time in a long time, willing the driver to stop.

Brake lights.

The truck swung wide and turned back toward us. I still had the key fob in my hands—I clicked the panic button, and as the horn blared and the lights flashed, the truck getting closer, Doug let me go. I rushed to the door, my hands shaking as I reached to open it. I locked the doors and put the key in the ignition as fast as I could.

Reversing, I looked in the mirror and saw the dust swirling around him. The hunting knife clutched in his meaty fist glinted in the sun, and I could hear him yelling after me, "Don't you ever threaten me again!"

Once I'd driven far enough out, checking my mirrors until I was certain Doug Wallace hadn't followed me, I felt like I could breathe again. Heart cranked up to a hundred, I hit the gas pedal and drove the back way with no destination in mind. An hour later, I ended up circling Leroy's neighborhood like a homing pigeon.

I pulled into the driveway and caught sight of him on a ladder. A stepladder on the porch, but still. I parked and ran toward the house. "What's gotten into you?" I said, my voice high and shaky.

Leroy turned to look at me, and a pair of smudged reading glasses he rarely wore slid down his red, bulbous nose. "Hand me that drill bit," he said. His tool kit was open on the ground and his walker parked next to it.

"You shouldn't be up there."

"Bought me a security camera," he said, pointing to the ripped-open box on the ground and nearly losing his balance.

I reached out and put my hand on his back. "Why don't you wait and let Daddy come help you?"

"No," he said, swatting away my hand, and again wobbled dangerously. Something about how I had my neck craned to look up at him, or the panic still fluttering in my chest, I felt hot and dizzy all of a sudden, like I might throw up.

"You look like you seen a ghost," Leroy said.

"I'm— I'll be right back," I said, and went into the house, making a beeline to the kitchen for some water. I took a long drink, my breath fogging the glass, and touched the place on my neck. A nick, hardly a scratch, but I could still feel the pressure of the blade and the way my heartbeat had thrummed against the metal. He was just trying to scare me—maybe if I told myself that enough times, I'd believe it. I closed my eyes, listened to the click of the ceiling fan and the hum of the fridge. Breathed in the woodsy, sweetish smell of pine-paneled walls, air-dried laundry, and the cedar disks Mamaw used to leave in the closets. I was safe now.

I heard Leroy come in, the bathroom door open and close, and the faucet turn on. He hobbled into the kitchen with a wet rag. "Thanks," I said, flinching when he placed the rag on the back of my neck. I took a deep breath and told him everything. He nodded as he listened, went to the fridge for a beer, and handed me one, too. "Doug's a dumb lout likes to pick on women. Damn it, you shouldn't have gone out there by yourself."

How was I supposed to do this job if I couldn't work alone? Or if I was afraid of people like the Wallaces? I knew I could've handled the situation better, but I wasn't about to apologize or stop what I was doing. Not now. I have a contrarian streak that I'm not so sure I should be proud of, but that's one way to motivate me—tell me no. I cracked open the ice-cold can of Budweiser, which tasted good going down, but went straight to my head. "What're you so afraid of?" I asked.

"Little darlin', you get cornered and—"

"No, I meant with the security camera. Did you hear someone again?"

"Not since the time I told you. It's that little things seem off, misplaced. Makes me feel like I'm losing my damn mind."

"Inside the house or out?"

"Both," Leroy said, motioning me to join him in the small living room. I sat on the couch and he sank into his favorite recliner and popped the footrest. He reached over to the side table and straightened the lamp and Kleenex box, his TV remote and candy jar full of black licorice. "Just a feeling like my things are out of place. It's more than likely nothing. No need to worry."

I wasn't sure if he meant worry about his memory or the prospect of a break-in. "It's probably good to have a security system, anyway," I said.

He pointed his thumb toward the storm door, his two slobbery dogs pawing madly at it, hoping we'd toss them a rawhide. Andy was a big German shepherd mix and Barney was a terrier mutt, both strays he'd found wandering on the place out across the river. "Used to be the only security system I needed," he said, chuckling. "Fools bark like hell at a squirrel but sleep like the dead when a stranger walks past the house."

I got up to let them in, their tails thumping on the floor when I turned toward the pantry.

"If there was a thief, they'd probably knock open the gate for him," Leroy said, the pair settling down on either side of his recliner with their treats.

Thief. It had taken me aback, seeing myself through Doug's eyes for a flash—me, a threat?—like a cloudy reflection on water's surface. My skin was still tender where he had twisted my arm.

"It's my understanding the Wallaces have a history around here. You knew them?"

"I remember when Doug's father, Jimmy, went into hiding. I like to have thought we'd never get him," Leroy said, then drank some of his beer. "He was tough. A terrible person, but smart. Might be it skipped a generation. Doug is no outlaw. Just a mean old dumbass. Doesn't surprise me he'd cover, though. They've probably still got a bit of a family business going. None so loyal as blood."

I leaned my head back against the sofa, the patchwork quilt that covered it soft and cool against my cheek. I was in Mamaw's spot by the window, the cushion still formed to her though she'd been dead years now. We hadn't gotten used to it. The house had turned into a neglected museum exhibit, all her knickknacks—mostly porcelain hummingbirds, a few souvenir shot glasses, and a pair of tiny bronzed cowboy boots I found hard to believe were once my dad's—sat on the shelf, strung together with cobwebs. But I noticed that the pile of mail and unpaid bills that had lately devoured the coffee table was gone, a neat stack of stamped envelopes in its place.

I scooted onto the middle cushion. "I feel a little stuck. Any ideas?"

As was his nature, Leroy pondered the question for a few moments before speaking, long enough this time to make me wonder if I should ask again. "Focus your energy on talking to other known associates of Charlie," he said, clamping his hands on the arms of the recliner. "Forget about Jacinda Moore for a bit."

"Finding Charlie and learning who killed Jacinda I don't think are mutually exclusive."

"Might be you're right," he said, burping into his fist. "Given what you've told me, you're probably right. But you know what I mean. Change up your tactic when you feel stuck."

"I hear you." I looked around the living room, at the Remington prints and family pictures on the wall, their glass frames blurred by dust. Leroy pitched himself out of the recliner and went to the wooden cabinet where he kept his vinyl. He picked out my favorite, Patsy Cline, and swayed as he stood over the turntable, looking out the window.

"Saw you got the kitchen cleaned up, a few bills paid," I said.

"Your old man," Leroy said, his face drawing down. "Been coming by a lot lately. Wish he would let me be."

I suppose I understood a thing or two about pride. But it irked me Leroy was making it difficult for my dad to be the bigger person. There was a picture of the two of them the day my dad joined the Garnett police force, wedged on the shelf between my grade school portraits so it was halfway hidden. Taken maybe a year before the wreck that resulted in my dad's back injury and allegations of misconduct against Leroy, along with decades of pent-up frustration between the two. "Have you and my dad ever tried just talking about what's really bothering you?"

Leroy turned the volume higher on the turntable.

"I'll promise to be more careful if you promise to let your family help you out," I said, really meaning that he ought to go easy on my dad for a change. "None so loyal as blood, right? I'd like to think *we* can look out for each other, can't we?"

"You offering to finish installing the cameras?"

"Fine," I said, though I made no move to get up, only listened to the old songs play, my eyelids growing heavy. I couldn't quite sleep—I couldn't quite get over my feeling that safety, here, anywhere, was nothing more than an illusion.

Chapter 21

Wyatt dropped the tailgate and pulled a cooler from the bed of the pickup. "Guess we could try the new Italian place in Colburn if you'd like, but I think this'll be better. You like steak, don't you?"

My eyes darted to the rust-flecked campsite grill. It looked like an animal had at one point nested in it, but I figured the heat would kill off any really bad germs. The spot we parked at out across the river for our date was more of a rest area than a campsite, but there were picnic tables, and a view of the water and the escarpment to the northwest that at sunset would turn purple then blue. I nodded, happy with the selection.

Wyatt uncorked a bottle of red wine that he poured into two metal camping cups. "First things first."

"Fancy," I said. "Here's to your summer break."

We toasted, taking each other in. The light hit his hazel eyes, bringing out the green, and he smiled with his whole face. "Remember that one time we came out here—I think it was right after school let out—and we caught the new volleyball coach on a date with Mr. Brown?"

"File that under things that can't be unseen," I said and laughed. "Shoot, I was actually thinking about Mr. Brown the other day. You remember Heather Ellis? She's taken his place as the new librarian."

"I think I knew of her more than I knew her."

"Didn't you go to undergrad together?"

"She was a senior when I was a freshman. And I don't think she was as excited as I was to see someone else from back home. She was kind of popular, actually, or well known. Always leading sit-ins, organizing protests. Pretty cool."

"I mostly remember the purple hair," I said.

"Heather was the one who tied herself to that tree they were cutting down outside the high school, wasn't she?"

"I totally forgot about that. Yeah, that was her," I said, thinking about our last encounter, her hurrying along with her head down in her loose slacks and black loafers. Heather Ellis had gotten a lot less radical and outspoken, it seemed, but her community garden, her digital literacy programming, it was a kind of activism, I thought. Activism minus the loudspeaker. She and Wyatt reminded me of each other, I realized. He'd always gotten into causes, or rather, one cause: the river. He'd spent much of his first semester at State waist deep, monitoring the river's wild rice. Wyatt also knew that doing the right thing was doing it over and over, often quietly, hoping it amounted to something. I took a sip of wine, warmth spreading from my chest out to my limbs. "So, should we walk before you throw those steaks on?"

"Sure," he said, taking my hand. He kept close to me, and when his arm brushed mine, I felt a flutter in my stomach. The closer we got to the river, the softer the ground became, and the sound of the current filled my ears. The Geronimo was still swollen. Running fast and muddy, whitecaps peaked like milk foam on coffee. We needed to hurry if we wanted to catch the sunset from the ridge—it wasn't so late yet, but the shadows were deepening. Sunlight ebbed away from us and a purple hush fell over the grass.

"It's crazy seeing the river this high. We were out here, what, a month ago and it had stopped flowing? Was totally dry up north of here," I said.

Wyatt shook his head. "Wasn't dry. Looked like it, but actually the water drains into the fissures and gaps in the limestone. The Geronimo keeps flowing underground."

A subterranean river. I looked down, imagining, surely, the pulse beating back against my boots, an echo of the unseen current humming in the tall grass. "I didn't know that."

"It's true." Tree branches groaned in the wind like old men, the birdsong dimmed, and a twilight sky stretched on forever. Wyatt stopped midstride and picked up a worn-smooth rock, rubbing it between his index finger and thumb. "Have you seen that new development, just over east of here?"

"Yeah, the town homes. They look really nice," I said, wondering if he was about to suggest we look at one. The topic of moving in was still ticking between us. I pictured clean white walls and stainless-steel appliances, empty rooms to hold all kinds of promises and what-ifs. "Heard they'll be expensive," I added, my hands starting to sweat.

"Even if I could afford it, no thanks. I was talking with the foundation director and apparently all the dirt they moved and all the vegetation they took out is mostly to blame for how bad those apartments downriver flooded," he said. He'd been working for a trust set up by the university that advocated for the health of the river and local ecosystem. His studies were on communities and water, so it was the perfect fit, and partly why he'd chosen State. He shook his head, staring out over the water. "Makes me sick."

"Like six people died—hell, a whole family drowned," I said. "He's sure?"

"There'd have been damage regardless. But not so swiftly and so high up. The grading changed the floodplain. I think people forget that what we've done affects the way water flows. People forget that rivers, even spring-fed ones like the Angel, are composed of runoff to an extent."

I felt flushed with anger, remembering the muddy, gutted units. The broken chairs, the child's toys, the spray paint on the wall . . . "How did the plans get approved by a surveyor in the first place? The county?"

"I don't know, but someone ought to be held accountable," he said. "All this development here, by the university, too, it's only going to get worse. More landowners should do like the O'Briens west of town and do a conservation easement. I meant to tell you, me and some of the others from the foundation are going to the ranch end of next week, maybe stay the weekend. We're gonna paddle out to this island to camp. Take a look at native plants, stuff like that."

"Ever since the flood, I've been a little afraid of the river, especially at night," I said. We walked into a stand of trees, and I felt the temperature drop, if only slightly. My stomach twisted with this sense of foreboding, this feeling like we were perpetually between disasters. And we were, if you thought about it. The planet was warming and the storm fronts growing stronger, our town was dying, and we were all sellouts. Or something like that.

"That night." Wyatt stopped and turned toward me. "You never did tell me what happened. Or what happened to your car. I saw the hood's dented."

"You didn't ask," I said, snappier than I meant to sound.

"Sorry."

"No need to apologize," I said. "I was scared is all."

"Yeah, me, too." He dropped my hand and we climbed up a stone bluff dense with cedar and cacti, neither of us speaking. I'd always felt like the true marker of a good relationship was if you could be quiet with each other. We had always had that. But I wasn't sure if this was a good silence yet—it felt companionable, but I was beginning to doubt it, and something told me I should brace myself for the summit. For what he'd say next. After all this time, I couldn't always read him. That ineffable quality, though, is what always drew me back. We made it to the top, stopped, and looked out over the rock walls, gouged and scarred from the river that night. Wyatt whistled, took the rock out of his pocket, and arced it over the fast-moving water.

"You and me. We're in this weird spot, right?" he said, facing me. "I'm sorry for the dumb shit I've done, or not done."

"I know," I said, my entire body feeling like a clenched fist. "Me, too."

"Before you get mad, let me say something. I think part of our problem is that you don't trust me—"

"That's not it," I said, angry he'd told me not to get angry. "I just don't want to be so serious all the time, you know? Like I see Nikki and Sonny and instead of wanting to play catch-up I can't help but wonder if I even want to get married."

"I don't remember proposing."

"You know what I mean. Living together."

His face stiffened. "So, I take it your answer is no?"

"Not right now," I said, tears stinging the corners of my eyes. "It doesn't mean I don't want to be with you, though."

He looked at the ground for a moment. "Okay, I can take that. But it's not even all about living together right this instant. It's about you not, like, wanting to grow this thing between us," he said, and reached for my hand. "You're my person, Annie.

I've always known that. But there's this cloud hanging over us whenever the future comes up. I'm sorry, I had other ideas about tonight, and what to say to you to fix it. But I just don't think I can keep doing this. I'm sorry."

I stared at him for a minute. A minute, maybe more, as he rambled on until I fully grasped that he'd broken up with me. I couldn't think—I didn't argue. It was a physical sensation more than anything else, a wooziness and a yo-yoing in my stomach, like hitting the drop on a roller coaster.

"Fine," I said, and drew back my hand.

He called after me but I kept going, skidding downhill, stomping through the tall grass until I reached the truck, kicking myself for not driving.

The lights were on in the living room, the curtains still open, and I could see Nikki and Sonny laid out on the couch. She hadn't texted me back yet, but I didn't care. I couldn't stay in that empty apartment, not now.

Nikki was halfway out the door before I was even up to the top step. I looked at her, biting down to keep my eyes from welling.

"Damn it, get in here," she said, pulling me in for a hug.

"Sorry," I said, then took a deep breath. "Y'all are busy."

"We're not doing anything but watching TV and eating bad takeout."

"So, a Wednesday?"

"Yeah, yeah." She laughed a little. "Well, was it you or him that did the breaking up?"

"Him," I said, following her inside the little pink house, the two-bedroom bungalow that had been her grandmother's before she passed. Sonny hadn't had a ton of stuff when he'd moved in, and much of the furniture was Nikki's, not mine, so the place was mostly the same as when I lived here, only different jackets and shoes by the door, and it smelled a little guy-ish now, like Irish Spring and socks.

"How do you feel?"

"Like shit," I said.

Sonny sat up and leaned his head over the back of the couch. "How 'bout them apples?"

"Ignore him." Nikki rolled her eyes. "He's drunk as a skunk. Went out with that guy from next door. He's also a vet."

"He's single," Sonny said, lying back down and laughing.

Nikki threw a pillow at him. "Shut up, dumbass. It's not funny."

"It's okay," I said. "Maybe I should get going."

"Don't you dare," Nikki said, grabbing my wrist and pulling me toward the kitchen. "There's a bottle of wine open and we're gonna make cookies."

I noticed an envelope on the kitchen table, addressed to me. Remembered I'd never gotten around to forwarding my mail or updating my license. I slid my finger under the flap. Junk mail, of course. "Chocolate-chip, I hope. 'We'? Lord knows he's not going to be much help."

"Bethany's here," Nikki said, and poured me a glass of wine. "She's in the bathroom. Come on, let's sit."

"Oh. I didn't see her car," I said, feeling even more now like I'd intruded, and queasy remembering my last conversation with her. I wasn't sure how much Nikki knew about her stepbrother Eli, if anything.

"She got her nails done at the salon and we rode back together," Nikki said. The TV was tuned to the baseball game, but Sonny's head was under a cushion. His shirt was off, revealing the shiny, puckered-looking scar tissue that ran from the base of his neck down his back. I knew he'd been badly injured during his last tour, but I'd never seen the scar. I'd also never seen him like this. Drunk, sure, but he was acting not himself now. All inhibitions seemed gone. Maybe that meant he was *more* himself—but I'd always thought on the occasion that Leroy veered over the line, when he was mean, he turned into someone he was not. I preferred thinking that, anyway. Nikki poked his arm and he rolled over. "He's not listening to us. Sit and tell me everything."

"Well, the mood was off to begin with," I said, pausing. I guessed if Sonny was going to be my cousin-in-law, I should be more comfortable around him, but I still felt weird spilling my guts. "Wyatt started talking about those new town homes on the river. Apparently, it's coming out that the grading caused the flooding to be much worse downriver. Downriver where those apartment complexes were decimated. You know, where people died? I think he and I were both worked up and sad and it just went downhill from there—"

"Ignorance is bliss," Sonny interrupted, sitting up and scooting closer to us on the couch. He massaged the back of his head. "That's what freedom is."

"You're a font of wisdom."

"Don't make fun of me, Annie." He stared at me for a moment, his eyes bloodshot. "It's true. That's what freedom is. Me and him were saying just that. Like, when I was in Afghanistan? I realized no one back home knew what the shit was happening. 'Cause if they knew, they'd have to have an opinion. They'd feel terrible."

Nikki rubbed his shoulder. "Babe, I think you should never drink gin again. Sorry, Annie."

Sonny shook her off. "Seriously, though! The fact that we could be fighting a war for this long and it doesn't affect you? That's freedom, baby!" He started to stand, but kind of rolled off the couch and stumbled toward the bathroom just as Bethany came out of it. She sidestepped and he pushed forward, barely making it to the toilet before he vomited.

"Hey, girl," Bethany said, crinkling her nose at Sonny's bent-over figure. "You got here just when the fun started."

"Hey, Bethany," I said, then turned to Nikki. My appetite—for cookies, or anything really—was gone. "I'll go."

"Yeah, I better get him into bed." Nikki looked around the room, her cheeks turning pink. "Let me know when you get in, okay?"

I nodded, feeling the roller-coaster sensation again. I think I expected Nikki to put up a fight, maybe even come with me, and I was shocked to find my hand on the door and it opening. I stepped out onto the concrete porch and took a deep breath. Night-blooming jasmine curled around the neighbor's chain-link fence, perfuming the warm air. I missed living on this street. The pecan trees and mature sycamores, the purple-and-gold pinwheels and hand-painted *Go Steers!* signs stuck in the grass. I fished in my purse for my keys, but as I did, Bethany came outside.

She handed me my wineglass, brushed the top step as best she could, folding her sundress under her legs. Her manicured nails were gently rounded and the palest pink, like loose petals. "I wasn't really ready to call it a night yet, either."

"I'm sorry I don't have any updates on Charlie to give you."

"It's okay," she said. "You'll find him. After we talked the other night I kind of like prayed to him. Not literally, but I thought, *please keep us safe,* and it was his face I saw. Despite it all, I keep thinking of this Charlie like he's my guardian angel keeping watch," she said, shivering.

Keeping watch. My scalp tingled. "You're positive you've never seen him before the flood?"

"Yeah, we went over this."

"Sorry. I'm a little scattered," I said. "It's just—"

"Nikki said you and Wyatt broke up," she said. "I'm sorry."

"Yeah." I sat next to her and took a sip of wine, but it tasted sour, like the bottle had been open too long. "Tonight he says I don't trust him anymore. Maybe he's right that I don't want to be this open book. Like I can't be fully myself around him, if that makes sense."

"I think I get it."

"I'm just not ready for a big commitment."

"Annie," Bethany said, bumping her knee against mine. "Are you afraid of commitment, or are you afraid of asking for what you want?"

"What do you mean?"

"I mean you're afraid of the good, mushy love stuff. Like, you're afraid you won't get what you want and then you'll feel worse for having let yourself want it bad. I feel the same way. Like, all the time I do."

"Maybe," I said, my chin quivering. I squeezed my eyes shut, but the floodgates had opened and I couldn't stop myself from crying. "Damn it, I'm sorry to bombard you like this when you've got enough going on."

"Oh, Annie," she said, leaning over and hugging me. "It's okay."

"I do feel kind of relieved, though," I said, and drew in a sharp breath, unable to fend off another crying jag. I've always been more likely to have an emotional—often inappropriately timed—breakdown in front of strangers. The stakes are lower. If they judge you, if you lose them for being real, then whatever. Not that Bethany was a stranger, but she and I hadn't been close, not until now. Or maybe she was simply there. I could hear Nikki and Sonny play-fighting and laughing through the door, and felt a surge of gratitude toward her.

"If you're relieved, then it's a sign this is the right thing. Live and let live, girl!" She smoothed my hair back, tucking a strand behind my ear. "You're free as bird!"

The sun was gone now and moths floated around the bare lightbulb above us. *Free.* I was free—but Sonny wasn't wrong, I thought. Without Wyatt I might feel like someone new. The problem was the light in his hazel eyes, the goofy grin on his face when he made a layup, the way he reached into the river to feel the cold current running through his fingers, to grab hold of it— all these parts of him felt like parts of me, too, and I never could unlearn them.

Chapter 22

There comes a point in an investigation—sometimes, not always—where the subject grows overfamiliar in my mind. If Bethany saw him as her guardian angel, to me Charlie Kingman was a ghost. I couldn't quite see him, but I felt him humming in the air around my head. When she'd said he was watching over her, it occurred to me that it might also be literal: who's to say Charlie hadn't gone to work for Eli Wallace after Jacinda fired him? What if he were by the cabin that night to find Bethany, relay a message for him or corner her for money? There was a tangled knot of unknowns in my mind, and I hoped that seeing his hometown, stealing a glimpse into his past, might at least grant me some clarity.

That is, if I didn't straight up find him here.

Speeding down an empty highway, alone, I felt like I was in a movie—that's what people did in movies after a breakup, wasn't it? They got the hell out. The farther north I drove, the more the grass dried and the trees shrank. It made me dizzy, the heaven-to-earth ratio so unbalanced in favor of wind and sky. Houses spread farther and farther apart until I counted miles between two somewhere between Abilene and Lubbock. By the time I was coming up on Charlie's hometown, there were just a handful of cars on the blacktop. FRIENDLIEST LITTLE TOWN IN THE BIG COUNTRY, a sign at the Idell city limits proclaimed. There was an open Dairy Queen and an Allsup's nearer the interstate, but the main drag had been shuttered and looked beat to death by wind and dust.

Mary-Pat owned property up this way. I'd visited, oddly, during the last big flood. The El Niño flood. Like in the dream I'd been having, my parents and I evacuated only to return to a huge amount of damage. They needed me gone while they worked to repair it, and out of desperation—I don't know why I wasn't sent to Leroy's, though remembered I couldn't stay with Nikki because their house had also been damaged—they asked Mary-Pat to babysit. She had evacuated up here already and drove halfway back to meet my mom and take me with her. I cried hard—it was the middle of the night and I was scared—but when we were nearly there, the sun rose, and it was like something broke open in me. I remember feeling exuberant. Shaky from the adrenaline still coursing through me after having escaped the rising creek, and in the light of day, powerful, like we could do anything.

I went to Allsup's first. The man behind the counter didn't know any Kingmans and the store was empty. I hung around the parking lot for a bit, but the only folks coming and going appeared to be truckers. Dairy Queen was next. I figured I'd earned an ice cream even if no one had any useful information for me. Inside, there were a couple of old men seated, their cowboy hats and their denim jackets placed over the booth back, their lunch trash piled neatly in the little plastic baskets. On the other side of the restaurant sat a woman talking on a cell phone, the towheaded baby in her lap gumming on a french fry.

The cashier looked to be about sixteen. She fooled with the rubber WWJD bracelet on her wrist before catching herself and putting her hands back at the ready to enter my order. "Welcome to DQ! What'll you have?"

"Oreo Blizzard, please," I said, handing over my debit card. "I'm in town looking for someone. Do you happen to know any Kingmans living in Idell?"

The girl rolled her tongue over her braces and punched in the order. "Yeah, but Mr. and Mrs. K both passed."

"I'm looking for Charlie Kingman, or anyone who knew him."

"Hold up. You know Charlie?"

I spun around and saw the woman who'd been on her cell phone was standing right behind me, refilling her drink cup at the fountain. She looked to be in her late twenties, maybe a little older, and had on leggings and a black spaghetti strap top I was pretty sure was intended to be worn as underwear. She held her baby in one arm and a slouchy, hippie-style purse slung over the other shoulder.

"No, but I've been hired to find him," I said.

"He was my best friend," the woman said, shaking blue-streaked bangs out of her eyes. "Charlie Kingman, I think about him all the time. He all right?"

"Annie," I said, my heart beating faster. "I'm a private investigator. I don't exactly know if he's okay or not. Mind if I ask you a few questions?"

"Kasie. Wow, um, guess I got a few minutes before we have to pick her brother up at school, so sure," she said, and nodding at the cashier, "Later, girlie."

The teenager stuck her tongue out at the woman, then held my Blizzard upside down before handing it to me. I said thanks and followed Kasie outside. She sat heavily on a picnic bench seat and handed the baby a teething ring from her bag. "God, I haven't seen Charlie in forever. I've texted him, tried messaging him online. Either he ignores me now or got a new number. I think about him a lot, I'm being honest."

"Really?" A little nervous, I swallowed a big bite of ice cream too fast and felt a brain freeze. "You grew up together?"

"Known him since kindergarten. We were supposed to leave Idell together. Start a band like we'd dreamed about. Then I had my son, and well," she said, shrugging. "Charlie didn't just want to leave, he needed to leave. I wasn't mad, given the circumstances."

"The Mr. and Mrs. K that girl mentioned—those his parents?"

"Yep. Both teachers at the high school. Mr. K was also the football coach. Died in a car wreck a few years ago. Guess Charlie either couldn't or wouldn't make it to either of their funerals. They were awful to him, though. Kicked him out, didn't even give him time to pack."

The sun beat down on my neck and my Blizzard had already started to melt, a sticky trail running down the side of the cup onto my finger. "Because of the drugs?"

She sighed. "There was some of that, sure. But they found out he was queer and that's what set 'em off. Don't know how they didn't know already. Guess they were in denial. Assholes."

"That's really sad," I said. "No wonder he stayed gone."

"Yeah. Everyone was a shit to him since middle school. Nicknamed him 'sister,' stuff like that. Charlie, though, he was tougher than he looked. He was so special." She paused, reddening a little. "He was so good-looking, real sweet, too. Mostly he kept his head down. He had his own life that he kept quiet, even from me and our group. One night not long after we'd graduated Charlie got picked up by an undercover cop at the truck stop off the highway. He didn't get charged or nothing but his dad beat the tar out of him. We only talked a few times after that. Told me he got a job at a club in Austin. Said I should join him, too, but I couldn't just then, and we fell out of touch."

"What about any other family? Anyone he would've kept in touch with?"

"Uncle Ross, maybe. He'd probably know more or might even still talk with him. He lives at the old drive-in," she said, and bent over to pick up the teething ring the baby had tossed. As she did, I noticed a tattoo on her lower back—a blue rose.

"The rose tattoo? You get those at the same time?"

She started humming, and at my puzzled look, smiled. "Blue roses! Like the Joni Mitchell song! You catch up with Charlie, get him to play for you. He's real talented. Too shy to do anything with it, but he has a great voice. We were into all the folksy stuff growing up. He had the look, too." The baby patted her chest and she looked down at her phone. "Dang it, it's nearly three fifteen. I better get. If you find Charlie, tell him it's okay to come home, all right? Tell him it's okay now."

Idell ended. You could blink and miss the half I hadn't seen. There weren't outskirts here. Only red dirt roads off the state highway petering out into open fields of cotton. A big white square like a ship's sail loomed on the horizon, and it seemed like I'd be driving forever to catch up to it. Closer, rips in the screen—hail damage, bullet holes—seemed to contract and expand, exposing the blue of the sky beyond. A wooden sign at the theater's entrance read THE STARLITE IS NOW CLOSED. THANK YOU FOR 50 YEARS OF GREATNESS. There was a single-wide trailer parked behind the old box office. I parked next to a green sedan that the wild grasses had grown up around.

A man in his late sixties wearing brown repairman coveralls unzipped to reveal a stained undershirt opened the door before I had a chance to knock. Unshaven, small in stature with long gray hair braided into pigtails, he looked like what would happen if Willie Nelson had a down-and-out twin brother. He eyed me suspiciously. "If you're the lady who called from the bank you can turn right around."

I looked down at my jeans and high-tops. "You think I look like a banker?"

"No."

I smiled. "Ross, right? I'm here about Charlie Kingman. Mind if I ask a few questions about your nephew?"

"Charlie!" He threw his hands up dramatically. "Man alive, come on in."

I probably should've been more nervous going into a trailer out in the middle of nowhere—there was a rifle propped by the door and the air smelled like skunky weed and unwashed dishes—but he offered me a chair opposite his at the dinette table cluttered with papers and rolled-up film posters, and I accepted.

He rubbed his hands together and smiled. "Want a pickle?"

"Uh—"

He pointed to several jars of jumbo-sized pickles on the stove that sat next to industrial-sized cans of nacho cheese dip and plastic buckets of Red Vines. "Go on, help yourself. Closed six months ago and I'm still working my way through all the loot from the snack bar. Closed! Can't believe it most days."

"Awful sorry to hear that."

"Charlie, he worked the drive-in every summer. Work all night then sleep all day was our way of life. We'd get up in the afternoon and play the guitar, talk about the movies, then it was time to do it all over again. My favorite thing was to have him go bang on the car trunks to make sure kids wasn't sneaking in without a ticket. Embarrassed him to no end, but gave me a good laugh."

"Have you seen Charlie recently?"

The old man shook his head. "I keep thinking now that my brother is gone, he might come back, but I haven't seen him in over a decade. Been on the wind, you might say. Sure like to have broke my heart, but Charlie never did want to be tied down. He and I are a lot alike. We come alive in the nighttime," he said, and riffled through the stack of papers. He held out an eight-by-ten framed school picture. "Had this hanging in the box office, embarrassed him to no end. I sure miss that boy."

The boy in the picture was eight or nine and had short, nearly white-blond hair, fair skin that made his deep blue eyes pop out at you, and a narrow, serious-for-a-kid's face. Ross breathed heavily, his hands quivering as he took back the picture, gazed at it again, and I felt a pang in the center of my chest. "I'd hoped you might know where he's at these days," I said.

"Charlie had a rough time of it for a few years. Addicted to meth and got popped, did time. A nice couple owned a construction company down in Garnett hired him and kind of took him in after he got out. He spoke really highly of them—Jake and Jackie, think he said their names were. Seemed he was doing pretty well for himself once he got clean. Or so I thought. Shoot, I hope he's okay now. Last we talked I— Now, who did you say you were? His sponsor?"

"Annie McIntyre. I'm a private investigator. A concerned friend sent me looking for him," I said, wincing at the half truth. "People are worried about him. Seems he's gone missing."

"Wow, okay." Ross's face went pale and he was silent a moment before scooting out his chair and going to the sink. He coughed. "Something to drink?"

I shook my head.

He shivered and downed a glass from the tap. "Charlie called me for the first time in, I don't know, a year or more, just the other day. Tuesday. Called me from a pay phone, wouldn't say where. Told me that it might be the last time I heard from him. Said someone tried to kill him."

"Oh, my," I said, pulse quickening. This meant Charlie was likely still alive. "Did he say who?"

"No, no. And shoot, you showing up like this makes me think I should've taken it more serious—I thought he was on that crap again, out of his mind. Upset me, but I wasn't so surprised. Oh, Lord. Is that true about someone trying to kill him?" He set the glass on the table and paced the narrow room.

"I don't mean to frighten you, sir, but it very well might be. What else did you talk about?"

"Shoot, not much," he said, and smacked his hand on the wall. "I was really ticked off, thinking he was high again. Lord, forgive me if that boy's hurt and in trouble. Lord forgive me."

"I'm going to leave you my card," I said, standing. "You call me if you hear from him again, all right?"

The old man rubbed his hands over his tired eyes and nodded. "Thank you, darlin'. I will."

"Bye now." I closed the door to the trailer softly behind me and breathed in the fresh air. My chest expanding, I felt charged up and sad at the same time—at the possibility of finding Charlie alive, at his apparent pain. I'd come up here expecting to hear, if anything, how much an addict and a drug dealer like Charlie had ruined lives and relationships, or that he was always trouble, that he was likely dead. Instead I'd found the folks who loved him.

Leaving the Starlite, I drove west. I could go anywhere. I could be a different person alone on the road, but I drove out toward Mary-Pat's place and idled in front of the house. It was empty, but well-kept. Think she had renters part-time. She'd bought the property when she worked for the sheriff's department up here and never sold it. Her first job, and the one she left when she decided to return home. The windows and doors were curtained, and a row of shrubs planted for privacy nearly obscured the metal windmill and short gravel driveway. Beyond it, I knew, was a door to the storm cellar, painted red and flush with the ground. A place I only returned to in nightmares.

The week or so I spent with Mary-Pat that fall felt radical to eight-year-old me: I'd never traveled much before and it was like we had now climbed closer to heaven, getting out of the floodwaters and up onto the high plains, the Llano Estacado before us limitless. The first day, Mary-Pat went to Dollar General and came back with an off-brand Barbie and a plastic bucket and shovel I wasn't sure what to do with, then left me to my own devices. Gone most of the day, but at night she fried us chicken, took me visiting with old friends of hers I'd never met and haven't seen since then. I hadn't wanted to leave. Had finally started to feel safe again. But toward the end of our stay, it came a bad storm. Probably the same front. It hailed, and just as quickly ended. The air felt stoppered—it wasn't right—and then, the sky turned green. A tornado. Instead of climbing higher, we had to go low. When Mary-Pat swung the cellar door open, the light showed crazy lines and figure-eights drawn in the sand by rattlesnakes, spiderwebs the length of my arm, mousetraps full of bones. She had to physically pull me down those steps. My heart had hammered as the door swung shut and we were plummeted into total darkness.

I put the bullet in park and took out my phone.

"Garcia."

"Sheriff, it's Annie McIntyre. I've got solid reason to think

Charlie Kingman is alive. He called his family just last week. Said someone had tried to kill him."

He let out a low whistle. "Wow, look at Nancy Drew. Looks like you did a good job."

Annoyed, I nearly said "No shit, Sherlock," but remembering my talk with Mary-Pat, decided against it. "Guess the search and rescue on the river was a waste, now that we know he didn't drown."

"Not a waste," he said, and I could hear him printing something from his desk, the clank of a spoon stirring in a coffee mug. "Where is Charlie now?"

"Somewhere in hiding. Don't have more details yet," I said. "You think it wasn't a waste, why?"

"Because it looks like we found the gun that killed Jacinda Moore."

Chapter 23

I kept checking my phone, hoping for a text from either Garcia or Mary-Pat. There was a rattling inside me knowing that Charlie was alive out there, somewhere, and that I might be the one to find him. It was too soon to have heard back about the gun—whether it was in fact the murder weapon, or who it belonged to—but I couldn't help myself. Plus, folding napkins was boring as hell.

"I keep thinking how lucky it was that we didn't have cell phones when I was a girl. I would've missed out on so much, staring at my lap," Aunt Jewel said. She put out a fresh bowl of water for her toy poodle crouched under the table gnawing his tail. Jewel had her back turned while she worked, but kept sticking her neck out to glare over her shoulder at me. Her white hair was freshly rolled and teased up so the top of her head looked like a pile of cotton balls.

"I'm putting it away," I said, and went to give her a hug. Mean as she was, there was something that softened me to her that day. Maybe her pressed pink suit and the smell of her tuberose perfume undercut with baby powder, or the fact that she'd had that little dog groomed and its nails painted pink for the occasion. How hard I knew she'd tried. I put an extra leaf in her dining table so she could pile it with trays of deviled eggs, dips, chips, refrigerator pickles, and little sandwiches with the crusts cut off. For sweets, she'd made tea cakes, lemon bars, and pecan fudge.

"Think I heard a car outside," I said. "Dang, it's nearly two o'clock."

Jewel drummed her nails on the butter-yellow tablecloth. "That better be your cousin. Sonny's people show up first, I'll have a fit."

Nikki, arms full of flowers, kicked the front door closed behind her. "Y'all ready?" She wore a pretty white sundress and had one of the pink carnations tucked behind her ear. She beamed until her eyes landed on the CONGRATS NIKKI & SONNY banner that I'd hung over the table. "Damn it, Annie, that's totally crooked. What's wrong with you?"

"You're right. Sorry," I said, and moved a chair over to fix it, but it was too late. Sonny and his mother came inside at the same time as my aunt and uncle, followed by Leroy, my parents, my other cousins, her other bridesmaids, and a handful of Sonny's people. I shrugged and moved the chair back, checked my phone one last time, and went to pour Nikki a drink. I placed the cup of sangria in her hand, trying not to interrupt her conversation with an older relative of Sonny's. I could tell she was nervous—she kept wiping her hands on her dress and giggling—and I didn't want her to lash out at me again. By the entryway, my dad stood talking with Leroy. I went to the kitchen and came back bearing more refreshments.

"Thank you, little darlin'," said Leroy, and cracked the beer can, his eyes darting over my shoulder.

"Where'd Daddy go?" I said, and set his Dr Pepper on a side table.

"The buffet. Seems he's in a mood." Leroy patted his round belly and whistled. "I'm surprised Jewel consented to these folks tramping on her white carpets in their shoes."

"Hope your socks match. She might make an example out of you," I said, leading him inside. We talked a bit with Sonny, who didn't seem to remember the other night, saving us both the embarrassment, and then Nikki's dad, my uncle Curtis, before I could successfully isolate him to discuss the case. I'd called both Leroy and Mary-Pat when I was driving home. When I'd told them Charlie was alive, they'd both reacted the same way: they were only more certain it was no coincidence that Charlie had gone missing the night that Jacinda was murdered.

Leroy sat on the couch, sliding a bit on the plastic cover. "You know, Ears, I keep thinking there's different reasons to hide. A difference between running scared and running to cover your sorry behind."

I nodded and sat next to him.

"What I'm saying is you shouldn't jump to assume Charlie was the triggerman. Remember what I told you about seeing all angles," he said, watching me. "Remember that intuition and bias are not the same. You need to be clear-eyed now more than ever."

"I don't assume Charlie is guilty, of course I don't. He said someone tried to kill him: maybe whoever killed Jacinda was coming for him, too. But I do think there's a decent chance he killed Jacinda, given the circumstances that we know of," I said. "A more than decent chance—"

"Lord. What on earth's the matter with him," Leroy said, looking over my shoulder. I turned and saw my dad had fallen asleep sitting up in a recliner, a plate of food precariously balanced on his lap.

"Jeez—Daddy?" I said, walking over to him, and when he

didn't respond, I touched his shoulder. His eyelids fluttered open and he leaned forward, pressing deviled egg onto his shirt front. "You feeling okay?"

"Fine," he mumbled, setting his plate on the coffee table. He got up and turned toward the bathroom. "Excuse me."

Momma, who'd been spot-cleaning a spill on the tablecloth with club soda and a rag, swooped in. "He's exhausted. Up all night," she said, and put her hand over her mouth like she was telling us a secret. "His sciatica. Damn near freezes his whole leg up."

I shook my head. "Maybe he should've stayed home. Has he taken his muscle relaxers?"

"Yes. He's fine, sweet pea," Momma said. I used to think her insistence on his being fine was to protect his ego. Maybe it was. But I also think now her insisting Dad was fine was about *her* pride. I think it embarrassed her how much she propped him up—she didn't want to burden me with it, too.

"You're all getting old and falling apart like me," Leroy said. "Say, Tina, pass me a plate of those cookies."

"Getting old. It's the damn truth." Uncle Curtis sat down and scooted his chair closer. "I tell y'all about how I took the diverticulitis . . ." he said, drawing out each syllable, a preamble to a very detailed story he always managed to share right when folks were eating.

The front door opened, and in walked Bethany and John David, shouting "Congratulations!" at the same time. Nikki skipped over to greet them, kissing Bethany on the cheek. Sonny and John David shook hands and clasped each other on the back. The four of them looked so happy. And why wouldn't they be? It's just that I had this weird sensation I was watching them play dress-up. Something about how John David stiffly placed his hand near the small of Bethany's back, or the practiced way Nikki took Sonny's arm with one hand hooked under his bicep and the other placed on his forearm—like posing for a prom portrait—was both sweet and a little awkward. It reminded me that I've never been good at playing the part. I thought marriage must be like a game of house, that you both had to keep committing to the bit. I knew myself to be steadfast—that wasn't what scared me. It was that something out of my control might come along and shatter all suspension of disbelief.

"I need a refill," I said, leaving Leroy to go to the kitchen. I was pretty sure Wyatt wasn't coming, but he hadn't been *un*-invited. I checked the clock on the stove, realizing even if by some small chance he did drop by, it would be unlike him to show up much later than this. He was the type of person who came to a dentist appointment thirty minutes early, happy to read a paperback in the truck, both because he hated being late and because he kind of liked waiting. It was good to be bored sometimes, he'd say, grinning. Or that he liked being in his own head. I was about ready to be out of mine, I thought, taking a gulp of sangria and ladling more into the ridiculously tiny punch cup that was part of a set Jewel had me get down from the attic.

I turned to see Bethany had followed behind me. "Annie," she said, tapping me on the shoulder. Something was different—she'd gotten bangs. A possible distress signal, but she'd parted them to the side, I assumed to obscure the jagged red line above her eyebrow. She wore a high-necked gingham dress, pearl earrings, and wedge heels that made her half a head taller than me. "Maybe it's not the time or the place, but any updates?"

"You look cute," I said, sensing that with Bethany, compliments were the best way to disarm. She was going to be put off by the fact that I hadn't told her immediately Charlie was alive, but I had my reasons. He no longer was a ghost. I didn't know yet if he was a killer—or hell, if he was tied in with her ex-stepbrother. The less she involved herself, I figured, the safer she'd be. "Yes, there is an update," I said carefully. "Yesterday, I found his next of kin and—"

"Annie! That's huge!"

"Yeah, I know. There's reason to believe Charlie's alive."

"Oh, my," she said. "He's alive, you're sure?"

"He survived the flood, anyhow. Made contact with an uncle a few days ago."

"Do you know where he is?"

"No, and that's something I need to talk to you about: he's wanted as a murder suspect, Bethany. I'm going to keep looking, but there won't be any warm and fuzzy reunion with you two after I find him. It'll involve the sheriff. If that bothers you, maybe you can simply rest easy knowing he made it."

"No, I understand. But I want you to keep me in the loop. I'll keep paying you."

"Well, you haven't paid me anything yet."

Her face turned pink. "Oh, Jesus. You sent me that invoice days ago and I totally forgot. I'll come by your office with a check."

"No, I'll come to you," I said. "Your father-in-law is in his office at the church during the day, right? I have something I want to talk to him about."

"Uh, sure. Come by around noon," she said, and fanned herself. "Wow. He's alive—I don't know quite how to feel, knowing he might be this bad guy."

"I understand," I said, noticing her face looked sweaty and her neck had that splotchy pattern again. Even if he didn't kill Jacinda, her honey-haired Jesus was not that—he never was. She could move on, yes, work out her survivor's guilt, but there would have to be a shift in her heart.

"What's going on in here?" Nikki said, bounding into the

kitchen. She put a hand on each of our shoulders. "Annie, pour this girl a drink."

I was about tired of Nikki acting like maid of honor was code for servant, but I reached for the punch ladle.

Bethany grabbed my wrist. "Is that spiked?"

"Better believe it."

"None for me then," she said.

Nikki narrowed her eyes. "Since when are you not drinking?"

"Well." Bethany let out a deep breath. "Since I found out I was pregnant."

"Holy shit, girl!"

"I know! We're really excited!"

"Congratulations," I said, making a conscious effort to pick my jaw up off the ground and smile. "Dang, Bethany. You must've just found out?"

"Was at the doctor's yesterday," Bethany said. "Still, let's keep that bottle of wine just between the two of us? Thinking back, that might've been why I was so worked up. Hormones, right?"

Nikki squealed and hugged Bethany tightly. "Let's tell everyone the good news!"

"No, no, I don't want to steal your thunder today," Bethany said. "And it's still really early. We've only told John David's parents."

"Can we tell Sonny? Come on, let's at least go tell my mom," Nikki said, taking Bethany's arm and reaching back for my hand. "Annie?"

"Right behind you after I fix myself a plate," I said, my heart beating funny. It was strange, I knew, but I was a bit overcome— not unhappy for Bethany, but taken aback. Maybe because I'd known her since we were kids, it felt strange to me knowing she'd be someone's mother. I swallowed hard, leaned against the kitchen counter as she and Nikki shuffled through the swinging door together. I moved my elbow and glass clanked behind me—dishes were starting to pile up in the sink. I'd also noticed the food could use refreshing from the surplus platters stacked and Saran Wrapped in the fridge. I told myself I'd hung back in the kitchen to work, keep the party in full swing, but really, I didn't think I could walk out there and be the kind of friend I knew was required of me.

I'd been working for a while when Jewel came up behind me and turned the faucet off.

"Now you want to play hostess? Get your little behind back out there," she said. "Besides, I call dibs on the dishes. I'll do them tonight before bed."

"Oh, but—" I felt antsy, sweaty just thinking about rejoining the party. The sound of Sonny's booming laugh through the door made my head hurt. "You don't want me to give you a running start?"

She put her arm around my shoulder. "Thing is, I actually like doing them late. Busies the hands. Makes me forget how sad I am everyone's gone and left."

"Sad? That's the best part."

She pinched my waist. "You're a wicked girl."

I smiled, though I'd known what she had meant. How the shadows could turn blue and lengthen, how alone, the nighttime could last forever. How a chill might set in on a night like this when all the people and all the noise would suddenly be gone. And I knew what it felt like to be left behind. There were already fractures in the wall I kept around me—I felt them snap and widen, threatening to take the whole thing down if Jewel asked, even jokingly, when was I going to get engaged or what I'd done to scare off all the boys. Wriggling out of her grip, I reached under the sink. "I'm at least going to take out the trash," I said, and left out the screen door with the bag in hand.

A neighbor was doing yard work, and the smell of gasoline and fresh-cut grass carried on the light breeze. The cans were around the side of her carport. Here I dropped the bag in and stooped to pet the old tomcat that Jewel claimed wasn't hers—claimed he wasn't hers, yet put kibble and water out for him every morning, and had started calling him Whiskers. Then I heard footsteps on the gravel driveway. A car door closing. Bethany and John David stood in front of her SUV, his arms wound tightly around her shoulders, her hands clutching his lower back. Were they already leaving? Maybe they needed a break from the crowd, like I had. They stood like that for a few moments, swaying slightly, and he kissed the top of her head, then her cheek. I replaced the trash can lid as quietly as possible. I felt then that the two of them would be okay. Out of such trauma and sadness had come new life—what could bring more of a renewed sense of purpose? I let go of a breath I hadn't realized I'd been holding for Bethany. But when she lifted her face from John David's shoulder, I saw that she'd been crying.

Chapter 24

"The gun was Jacinda's. Registered to her late husband," Sheriff Garcia repeated, the road noise on his end making it hard for me to hear.

"What do you make of that?" I asked, pressing my other ear closed with my finger.

"Doesn't change much about my theory that we're looking at the man from the security camera footage at the casino, or at this Charlie who worked for her, but it does make it more difficult to prove it, either way. I better get going, Annie. You'll fill in Mary-Pat for me?"

"Yes, sir. Will do," I said and hung up. I worked my jaw back and forth a moment. I'd be willing to bet Charlie had access to Jacinda's things—her gun—at some point, given their relationship. Hell, could he be the blurry figure on the casino tape? Of course, there was still Eli Wallace to consider. I kept thinking about how Jacinda had alienated herself from any friends, how she'd threatened Bethany. I needed to know more about the construction work, and—I thought while peering at the white steeple through the windshield—her breakup with Hillview.

The phone felt hot in my hand. It was 12:09 p.m., past time to meet Bethany, so I got out of the bullet and walked the long blacktop parking lot toward the green grass and topiary bushes of the church campus. Campus—the fact that they referred to it as such indicative of its size—was laid out in a circle, smooth concrete sidewalks from fellowship hall, the office building, and the Sunday school rooms spokes radiating out from the massive sanctuary at its center. The new construction was to the right of the Sunday school building, connected via a covered walkway sectioned off by sawhorses and orange cones.

I walked into the Sunday school building. Hillview ran a day-care center, and Bethany had started teaching a few days a week until they found a replacement for Kendall. I came to a door with a poster taped over it that said *This Little Light of Mine*, covered with tiny handprints and construction paper candles. I peered through the glass panel and saw the classroom was empty. The whole building was eerily quiet. I pushed open the door and waited for ten minutes or so, looking at the watercolor art on the wall, the God's eye–style yarn lanyards hanging from the ceiling, and the plastic buckets of crayon nubs and glue sticks lined up on the tables. I accidentally stepped onto a trail of Cheerios some little hand had dropped, smooshing them into the rainbow-patterned rug. As I bent down and did my best to clean it up, I decided I ought to wait outside. I dialed Bethany, but her phone went to voicemail. Texted, then wandered the hallways for a bit, toward the youth group rooms.

The door at the end of the hall still had Michael's name plated on the front. My chest felt tight every time I thought about how those last moments in the cabin would've been, the surrealism of the river rushing in, knowing you were trapped. There was a plastic inbox hanging on the door, and crumpled at the bottom was a sticky note, *outgoing, thanks*, penciled on it. My heart

jumped in my throat—his handwriting, probably. A sliver of
life, ephemera that touched me for some reason, and I pocketed
it, turning to the bulletin board hanging on the wall. Tacked on
it were posters for sleepaway camp and a trip to Six Flags at the
end of the summer. A picture of Michael, his wife Kendall, and
a group of kids in tie-dye VBS shirts squealing with laughter.
Another of the pretty, waiflike Kendall and a pack of teenage
girls hovering over a group of Mexican toddlers. I understood
that the mission trip was also to perform charitable works, but
still, it felt icky to me in a white-savior kind of way. The arro-
gance had always bothered me, and my shoulders tensed up—I
shook it off and kept walking toward the next building, stopping in front of John David's office.

The door was closed and the lights were off inside. Before I
went to find her father-in-law, I checked my phone again for
anything from Bethany. It was now half an hour past when she
said we would meet. Beginning to worry, I typed out another
text when the door opened from the inside. "Shit," I said, dropping my phone.

The Reverend Richter stood in front of me, looking down.
Silhouetted by the window at his back, his face was dark so I
couldn't read his expression. "Can I help you, young lady?"

My heart raced like I'd been caught doing something wrong.
"Sorry," I said, bending to pick up my phone. "I didn't hear
anyone."

"Come in," he grumbled, motioning me inside John David's
office.

"We met at the flood relief drive, I'm—"

"Yes, I remember," he said. "You're Leroy McIntyre's granddaughter." He flipped the overhead light on. There was something less imposing about him now. Maybe it was being without
the robe and stole—his gray T-shirt was damp with sweat and

tucked into track pants, and he had a towel slung over his shoulder. He looked less burly and stout, frailer even, and overweight.

"I had an appointment to see Bethany," I said, my voice trailing up as though it was a question. "Guess she forgot."

"Bless her, she's got a lot on her mind these days."

"Yes, I know she's pretty traumatized," I said, and seeing his eyebrows furrow, remembered. "But lifted up by the good news. Congratulations—your first grandchild?"

"Yes, thank you, dear. It's true that grief doesn't stop for joy, and joy doesn't stop for grief," he said, and I nodded, remembering how I'd seen her yesterday by the car. It had to be overwhelming, all those conflicting emotions. The Reverend coughed and patted his face with the towel, then pulled a Hillview T-shirt from an open cardboard box wedged behind the bookshelf. "Excuse me. I needed a clean shirt and knew my son had some swag, as they call it. Was trying out the new fitness center we put in— Bethany's pet project, actually. She's been teaching aerobics and ah, Zumba, here a couple of afternoons a week."

A nervous laugh tickled at the back of my throat picturing the man doing a cha-cha step. He reached into the fridge under a shelf behind the desk, and pulled out another of those water bottles with the Hillview logo on it. "Something to drink?"

"Thanks," I said, twisting off the top. "Sir, I had an appointment with Bethany, but I also wanted to speak with you about something."

His brow furrowed before he smiled. "Of course."

"The Parsons Memorial Rec Center—it's a pretty big project. Hope this isn't a sore subject, but through the course of my investigation I've become a bit involved with the Moore case. I was wondering if you could tell me why she lost the bid. Just seems like her company would be a natural fit to do the work," I said, trying not to lead too much. I needed to know if her losing the bid was about the money, or something else. Bethany had said Jacinda was furious at John David's dad, so much that she considered Jacinda might blackmail her over it. That to me seemed more personal than what John David had allowed when I asked about it the first time.

The Reverend frowned and threw his hands up. "The others came in at a much more reasonable price. Like I had to remind Jacinda, we're a church, not hotel financiers," he said, sweat glistening under his eyes. "She had been acting erratically the past few months, long before, so I wonder if she got mixed up with the wrong people."

"You're probably right," I said.

"Yes, well," he said, nodding seriously. "Between you and me, it wasn't just the high bid that ended our work with her. Jacinda let the business go into turmoil after her husband grew ill and passed away. It pained me to distance myself from her, but she seemed intent on taking her frustration out on everyone around her, myself included—you see, I couldn't trust her with a project of this scale and importance to our church community."

"She did a good job on those new town homes over by the river, though, wouldn't you say?"

He looked up at me, his mouth open for a moment. "Oh, sure. The whole council agreed the development would really add a lot to Garnett and might invite retirees, or even younger folks with disposable income who could commute or work remotely. It really is scenic. Will improve the property values all up and down that stretch of river."

"You're on the city council," I said, thinking out loud.

"I am," he said, his chest puffing up. He chuckled. "Sounds like I'd better work on my reelection campaign."

"Crazy thing, I've heard that the development might've worsened the flooding? Did the city council know about that risk?"

I asked, and could tell by his narrowed eyes it came out like an accusation. I needed to work on my "light" touch. There were lots of challenging parts to this job, but for me anyway, the hardest often felt like asking questions. How to draw someone out varied from person to person, moment to moment, and the tones and silences that Leroy used didn't always work for a young woman—people got angrier when I pressed, thought I was rude when I stared.

"Lord, no. Of course not. I've never heard anything about that," he said, and before I could open my mouth, he huffed and wagged his finger at me. "Someone is clearly spreading falsehoods. It's that radical liberal university group, isn't it?"

Radical liberal? Really? A laugh escaped—if anything, the Riverkeeper Foundation was apolitical, if not a bit conservative, helmed by an ancient professor and a couple of wealthy ranchers. But the Reverend's jaw tightened, and the laugh died in my throat. "Uh, no," I said, lying. "It's just talk going around."

"Wouldn't surprise me if it was that university group with their agenda. One thing that stays the same is that people are afraid of progress. Anyway, Ms. McIntyre, I've got a bit of writing to do before I go home. I need to clean up and get back to my own office."

"Of course," I said, and put my hand on the doorframe. I was testing this man's temper—his body had gone rigid, his fingers pressed hard into the arm of the leather desk chair. A voice inside my head said *go, go go*. But I was already here, and who knew when I'd be granted an audience with his highness again. I tilted my head and smiled. "You've been so generous with your time. One last thing, sir, then I'll go. You said that Jacinda had taken out her frustrations on others at the church—what did you mean by that?"

"Right." He raised his index finger and finished his water

bottle in one gulp. Cleared his throat, looking out the window. "I suppose it was the last mission. She went on a bender and disappeared for two days. Caused a logistical nightmare, not to mention rattled the kids. When she came home and I expressed my concern, and frankly my outrage, she went off the rails. Denied it all and said that others had been acting much more inappropriately. Which of course was not true."

"Inappropriately how?"

"She wouldn't—or more accurately, couldn't—give me any details."

I stared back at him with raised eyebrows.

"She made it up," he said, his face splotched with red now. "Slinging mud to assuage her guilt. The more I think about it, the sadder it makes me. God rest her soul."

"It sounds like the trip to Mexico was pretty rough."

He straightened his back and took the gym towel off his shoulder, snapping it. His nostrils flared and he stared back, his eyes boring a hole in me. "It is missionary work, not vacation. Comes with the territory. Now, I believe that's enough talk about Jacinda for one day. I'm up to my neck in work, Ms. McIntyre."

"Of course. I'll try Bethany again," I said, sweating now myself. "Thanks for your time, Reverend." I stepped out into the hallway, and right as I was about to call her one more time, my phone buzzed with a text: Wasn't feeling well and went home. Can we meet up later?

Fine, I replied, and fast-walked out of the building, a nervous feeling in the pit of my stomach. Since I was near her place, I decided to drive over to Mary-Pat's. She didn't answer her phone, either, but I made a left out of the church parking lot and headed over anyway. Swore I looked both ways, but right after I turned, I looked up and saw a red pickup truck in my rearview, right on my bumper. The driver must have pulled out after me from either the parking lot or Farm-to-Market 22, which was right past the church. I needed to pay better attention while driving. I tossed my phone in the passenger seat, and when I checked the mirror again, saw that the truck had dropped back.

When I pulled up to Mary-Pat's, she still hadn't checked her phone, and acted a little ambushed when I got out of the bullet. It was her day off, and I'd caught her out in the yard gardening. Maybe ambushed is not the right word—she was stuck in her own head for a moment or two, but perked up when I told her about the call from Garcia and my meeting with the Reverend.

"He seemed awful defensive about Jacinda—and about the town homes," I said, and plucked a sprig of rosemary from the plant curling over the edge of her stone-lined garden bed.

Mary-Pat took her gloves off and put her hands on her hips. "City council might not have known about the risk, but then again, John very well might've since he owns that land."

"Wait, what? The Richters own the town homes?"

"The land. Used to, before he sold it to the developer. He also owns that little complex next to River Oaks, what's it called? Rancho Vista, I think."

"River Oaks and Rancho Vista both were decimated. Maybe he didn't know about the flood risk, then," I said. "Wow, the Richters must be pretty wealthy. Wealthier than I thought."

"They've been in the area forever. Yep," she said, and stretched her arms out to the sides, fanning herself. She mopped her forehead with the hem of her oversized cotton button-down and motioned for me to sit on the porch. She walked to the front door of the century-old limestone farmhouse. "Getting to be too damn hot to be working in the middle of the afternoon."

I hadn't known Mary-Pat was a gardener. There were lots of things I supposed I didn't know about her—by her design, not mine. She liked her privacy, and as an investigator, was pretty adept at maintaining it. I crushed the rosemary between my thumb and forefinger and inhaled. Under the shade of the oak tree next to the house, the day felt springlike, less like the beginning of summer's endless heat wave. Mary-Pat returned with a pitcher of lemonade and two etched glasses filled with ice. She'd tucked a lavender stem in each. "My mother's set. Can still see her carrying it out for me and Daddy, leaning over the rail to cut the lavender. Little things make the difference, she'd say."

"Thanks," I said, taking a sip. "That's really good."

"Fresh squeezed, like she used to make it."

"On my day off I usually stay in my pajamas and rewatch *The Office* for the fiftieth time," I said. "You're like Martha Stewart."

"There's a reason why I haven't invited you in," she said. "I can barely walk through there's so much shit piled up on the floor. Never cared for housekeeping. Being outside, though, those are the chores I like. You know I never did go fishing the other day—we can get your old granddad on board, we might could fish the tank on his neighbor's property. That's the secret to my good soil. Fish fertilizer."

It's also what Mamaw had done with the guts—she'd marry them to the dirt with her bare hands. Leroy and I would come back sun-weary and starving after a morning at the tank, clean the fish in the bed of his truck over newspaper, let her take care of the rest. She'd fry up catfish with a cornmeal batter, serve it with slaw and summer tomatoes, cantaloupe, and a piece of white bread in case you got a bone stuck in your throat.

"I think my granddad wants to go out to the place. I just don't know about that leg," I said. Bumble bees swarmed and dumbly knocked into foxgloves and irises. There was a birdbath in between the two beds, chickadees playing, their feathers fluffing up when they shook. A blue jay swooped in and heckled the tinier birds, pushing them out of the water. "You haven't said what your thoughts are on the gun being Jacinda's," I said.

"I don't know. Might make it likely Charlie's our man. Maybe he would've had opportunity to steal it from her when he was in her employ."

"I thought that, too," I said. "Though, it just occurred to me Garcia didn't say she'd reported it stolen." There was a squawk and I looked back at the ruckus in the garden. Now there were two jays in the birdbath. Charlie's round eyes in that school picture had been the same startling shade of blue.

"You'll find him yet," Mary-Pat said, shaking the ice in her glass.

Watching her pour, I felt the knot in between my shoulder blades loosen. "You consider yourself religious?"

"You sound like the man on the late-night television."

"I've been spending all this time with the Hillview people," I said, and took a big sip of lemonade.

"I still consider myself a Christian, I suppose," Mary-Pat said. She smiled, but her eyes drew down. "Grew up Baptist. Before my folks came around to politely accepting—meaning mostly ignoring—my 'lifestyle,' as they called it, they insisted I get private counseling with our pastor. It was humiliating, pray away the gay type stuff—and, oh, I've never felt like stepping foot into any church since, much less the one I grew up in."

"I wonder if Charlie's parents ever regretted how horribly they treated him, or wished they could've gotten him home."

"Who knows?" She pinched her eyes closed and leaned back into the rocker. "A few folks, that I knew of anyway, were living a lie inside the church. Marrying someone they shouldn't have.

It's a hard choice sometimes, deciding to be free." She sighed, and waved her hand. "To be free of all that."

"You did," I said. "Did you ever want to settle down with someone?"

"Yes and no. I've wanted both, at different times. With Lynn, I suppose I might have. My first serious relationship. But she had a kid and an ex-husband, and it got to be too complicated. I don't know why I'm telling you all of this, nosy parker."

"Maybe I'm getting better at my job."

"About time."

I smiled, watching her for a minute. "Hey, I was meaning to tell you. I drove past your old place when I was up in Idell. Remember that time I stayed with you?"

"Yeah, you could throw back some food even then," she said, and laughed. "I liked to have never got you to calm down after going in that cellar."

"It scared me. It was dark and creepy down there, obviously, but also, I was a little confounded. We'd just barely escaped the flood—I felt more than scared. I felt doomed."

"I don't know about being doomed," she said, looking up at the trees. "But no, you can't ever outrun the storm."

Chapter 25

I had to find someone who'd known Jacinda and Charlie in the same context. Someone who'd seen them interact, who could tell me of their dynamic—was it like a powder keg, ready to ignite? Who was in charge, really? After I left Mary-Pat's, I went back to work. Searched county records for permits, anything I could find on the town homes project, and recognized a name on a list of subcontractors immediately: Juan Ramos was an old friend of Leroy's. When I drove to his house, Leroy agreed to call the guy and arrange a meeting if I let him pick the place.

The band had finished setting up, and the longtime owner of the VFW bar, Jimmy Ryland, sat on the edge of the stage. On nights when there was live music, the tables got pushed to the walls to make room for dancing, and the joint turned into a honky-tonk called Yesterday Once More. Leroy looked, if not happy, relaxed. Better than I'd seen him look since the paranoia about a break-in had begun. Juan seemed to be enjoying himself now, too. He was a tall, wiry man who wore his salt-and-pepper hair in a low ponytail. He had brows so thick they partially obscured his eyes, and a beard that he rubbed between fingers flecked with bits of white paint. He was the finish work guy Jacinda had hired. He sipped his beer and leaned back, aware Leroy and I were hanging on every word. "See, I called them her puppy dogs. Jacinda Moore collected men like that," he said.

There was a screech of feedback—Jimmy stood and took the microphone, tipping his cowboy hat. "Now introducing, the Four Horsemen!"

Juan turned around to see, and I squinted in the bright neon, recognizing the young guys dressed in bandanas and black western wear from Mixer's. They were short a player. An older woman, who I thought might be one of their mothers, was seated in his place, a steel guitar in her lap. "Actually, we're called Petrified Triangle now," the lead singer said, pushing his thick glasses up the bridge of his nose.

"No one cares. Damn, son, just play something already," Jimmy said, waving his bony arm over his head. He hopped off-stage, and the band launched into their first set without another word.

Leroy nodded along to the music approvingly. "Sound a bit like the Everly Brothers." He stopped peeling the damp label of his beer bottle and looked across the table at Juan. "Go on, tell us more about Jacinda's crew."

"Charlie and that other dope, Trevor Sutton, they worked on her crew, right, but they also would go get her lunch every day, hold her phone and check her appointments. Anywhere she went, one of 'em was close by. Like two toothless personal assistants. Wasn't nothing new for her and Jack to hire from the county jobs program, or that church rehab, but after Jack was gone the relationships seemed less than professional if you ask me."

"Who's Trevor Sutton?" I asked.

"I don't know him, not really. He either got fired or moved

on," Juan said and shrugged. "But he was this big, ugly-looking dude. Heard she got in an argument with this contractor hadn't paid her yet and she sent Trevor over to threaten him at home."

"Damn, that's pretty bold," I said, heart beating faster knowing I needed to find this guy now, too. "Well, I was under the impression Jacinda had a lot of people angry with her . . ."

"Yeah, yeah," Juan said, growing more animated. "Like I said, really unprofessional. She herself owed money around town. Even tried pulling that with me—putting off my check for that big paint job—but I wasn't having it. We get to talking and she tells me she's in the hole like six figures."

Leroy let out a low whistle.

"Wow," I said, remembering Garcia had said the same thing about massive amounts of debt. "She was a gambling addict, wasn't she?"

"Yep. Sad, you ask me. She liked to hit up this casino outside Ruidoso a couple weekends a month. Tried to get me and the wife to go with them once, but it's not our scene. Makes me a little sad for some reason."

I leaned forward, watching him. "And did you know she was dealing drugs?"

"No." Juan looked between me and Leroy, his eyebrows moving up and down like two caterpillars. "Seriously?"

Leroy nodded.

Juan slapped the table. "Damn, I had no idea. Guess people really do get desperate when it comes to money."

"Ain't it the truth." Leroy finished his beer and started on a second round he'd already had me fetch for them.

"Honestly, I thought she was *on* drugs," Juan added. "Would miss meetings, or come to the site all spaced out, these big shades on. Crazy mood swings. That last big job barely got done."

A couple of older men came in and took the table next to

ours. They had a bottle of Jack that they passed around—the VFW was beer and setups only—and stared at Leroy. "Hey, Sheriff," one of them said. "What're you, a wallflower now?"

"Shoot!" Leroy smiled. "I reckon so."

A pair of women wearing boots and tight jeans with their hair teased skyward joined the men. After a bit of sweet-talking from the women, the two couples hit the dance floor. Leroy watched quietly for a moment, his smile tensing into a grimace. Under the table, he palmed his bad knee and shook his head. "Anyhow. Those new town homes look mighty fine," he said, turning back to Juan. "Miracle they didn't get washed out."

"No kidding, man, Jacinda had those guys build a moat around the property. We all thought she was crazy, but it was actually a good idea. It probably saved them. They moved a lot of dirt to get the foundation way up above the river."

"Yeah, well, it also changed the floodplain, so no, it wasn't a good idea," I said, my voice rising. "Did Jacinda talk at all about that? What all that grading would do?"

"I didn't hear nothing about it," he said, looking taken aback by my tone.

"It worsened the flooding. It—" I stopped short and took a breath. Juan hadn't done anything wrong, and he was of no use to me if he got defensive. Jacinda probably hadn't known, either. But it made my stomach turn thinking about the wreckage at the apartments downriver, knowing the ultimate price that had been paid.

"All I know is that the paint looks primo," Juan said, and grinned. "Hey, Annie, your dad ever tell you about the time he worked for me?"

"No, he hasn't," I said truthfully. Dad had had a lot of odd jobs since quitting law enforcement, so the fact that he'd painted houses didn't surprise me.

"That was probably before you were born," Leroy chimed in. "Might've been the summer before he hired on with the department. Even back then he couldn't hold down a damn job. If I recall correctly, he refused to paint some woman's kitchen a color he didn't like. Went so far as to lecture her about it," Leroy said, his eyes closed as if picturing the scene, a laugh bubbling up to the surface.

"Damn, that's right," Juan said, letting out a hoot of laughter. "Shoo boy, it was ugly, have to admit. Think it was bright green and orange. Looked like the Nickelodeon colors. But I had to let him go after that. Crazy kid."

That he'd been let go also did not surprise me. It didn't matter anymore, and my dad probably didn't even remember the incident, but it annoyed me the way Juan and Leroy laughed at him. And the part about him not being able to hold down a job was mean-spirited.

"Unlike that hothead father of yours, old Juan here's an artist." Leroy pointed to the other man with the neck of his beer bottle. "You know he did the bank mural?"

"So, as an artist, you must get frustrated when people make decisions in poor taste?" I knew I was being oversensitive. But I didn't think it was appropriate for Leroy to constantly berate my dad in front of other people, especially when Dad wasn't here to defend himself.

"Course I do." Juan smiled and looked at me for a moment. "Speaking of poor decisions, I stay out too late and the wife will chew me out." He reached for his wallet, but Leroy stopped him. After they said their goodbyes and Juan left, I looked at Leroy. He sat slumped in his chair with his cane propped on his lap.

"I better find this Trevor Sutton," I said, skin prickly with nerves. "Might have a beat on Charlie's location."

"And might know of any fights he and Jacinda had," Leroy said. He tapped his boot on the table leg to the rhythm of the song. "Surely wish I could have a night out like the old times."

"Me, too," I said, shrugging out the tightness in my shoulders. There was something about the honky-tonk that yanked my heart around. The steel guitar and the fiddle, the neon. I had to admit it was hard not to cloak my love in three layers of irony, but I loved this place purely, and I loved it faithfully, the way you love the albums you played as a kid in your room on repeat, when no one else could hear you belt the words out.

"One more round and then we'll leave," he said.

"Fine. But by the way, you need to let up on my dad," I said, finishing my first beer, which had turned lukewarm in my hand. Earlier when I'd picked Leroy up, I saw that the carport was fixed and the truck had been towed. Dad had followed through, just like he said he would.

"Come on now. We was just having a laugh," Leroy said.

"Not just that. You know, him trying to help you around the house?"

"He doesn't need to use me to make himself feel better," Leroy said, his voice uncharacteristically sharp.

"Jesus," I said, louder than I meant to. "He's trying at least. Why can't you reciprocate?"

"You're right. He's a good man, your father. Better man than me." Leroy took a long pull from his beer and set the bottle down too hard. "But it's high time you knew the truth. That he's always resented me for doing what I could to look out for *him*."

"What do you mean?"

"He was driving that goddamn night, not me," Leroy said, his voice raspy and tight, as though the words had hurt coming out.

"What night?" I said, my unease building.

Leroy looked at me with one eyebrow raised, knowing that deep down, I already knew what night he meant. "He'd been drinking on duty. It was a bad wreck, a miracle we weren't killed. When the officer came, I had us both out of the vehicle, told him it was me who'd been driving."

"You protected him."

"Only time I've lied like that," Leroy said, unclenching his fists. "Think I'd do it again, too, if only I didn't sometimes think I should've let him take responsibility. Living with it all knotted up inside him's a burden. I reckon he's drifted too much since then."

My whole life I'd understood that the car accident that had injured my dad's back—with Leroy at fault, specifically—to be the bedrock of their discontent. My dad not finding a new career, Leroy losing his. I wasn't sure yet how to process this change to the narrative. "Why didn't you tell me until now?"

"It wasn't my place to. But you're an adult, and honestly, I'm tired of being seen as the bad guy," Leroy said, looking back at me. His eyes were shiny and black, like two polished marbles.

"I guess I thought his sobriety was like a protest against—"

"Me?" His shoulders slumped. "In a way, it is. But he's an alcoholic like me. Only he has an iron will."

I couldn't think of anything to say. Knowing that my dad fought against addiction—not to mention the weight of what he'd done—made my heart sink. No wonder he found it hard to see Leroy. Hell, the whole family. The fortitude it must take to be around that many people drinking. To be in this tiny town, the kind of place where the only thing to do was drink. Had he kept it a secret that well? Or was I completely oblivious? I knew, like all grown kids do, that my knowledge of my parents, of who they were before me, was heavily filtered, bits of truth like grit caught in a sieve. But this was different. I wasn't feeling betrayed so much as sorry, stupid even, for not understanding.

If Leroy noticed my eyes brimming, he didn't say so.

"I did it so he wouldn't have charges brought against him. So that he might work again," he said, sighing. "We were working a homicide. A young man who'd been missing. The case got sidelined by our bullshit. Took the department a year to close the investigation . . ."

Leroy rambled on about the case, but I wasn't listening. He'd said he was tired of being the bad guy—but how did his telling me my dad's secrets against his will make him better? I'd known without knowing, I think. Was afraid of the truth. But really, there was nothing to fear. What had happened between Dad and Leroy was knowledge, context, but it was the past. Sitting in that old honky-tonk as the guitars whined, as the dancers moved across the creaking wooden floorboards with soft, artificial light cast across their faces, the past was as real a place as any. But it was only a mood, only a feeling. It couldn't hurt you. Of course, chasing it could occupy you to the point of madness.

"Come on. How 'bout another cold one?" Leroy said, and when I didn't reply, he laid his hand open on the table, halfway offering it to me, his fingers lightly shaking. "That's enough of that talk. I'm sorry, darlin'. I was a fool to bring it up."

"Let's get out of here," I said. My chair nearly tipped over as I pushed it out too quickly and walked toward the bar. I paid our tab and waved at Leroy to come outside with me. I didn't want to drink here anymore. Or anywhere, really. He followed a few paces behind because of his cane, and I should have slowed down to walk with him, but I didn't.

Outside it was only dusk, though it felt like it should be three in the morning. It felt like when you're in the middle of the dance floor at last call, disoriented when the fluorescent lights come on and you can see all the trash on the floor, the rips in the booth backs, how the walls are nicotine-stained and grimy. I unlocked the bullet and opened the door, but Leroy hung back. His skin was faintly blue in the shadows, his Stetson silhouetted against the beer signs in the window, and I realized that for once, Leroy looked cowed. Telling me the truth wasn't only about him and Dad. It was about me and what I thought of him. He'd never really let me—or anyone—in this much.

"Come on," I said, extending my hand. "Let's go."

Chapter 26

As difficult as finding Charlie Kingman was proving to be, finding Trevor Sutton was easy. I'd first gone about it the traditional way, pulling records and seeing if any addresses listed for him were current. They were not. He was no longer required to check in with his parole officer and she also did not know where to locate him. But when I found his Facebook page, he replied back to my message within an hour. I wouldn't have the element of surprise on my side, but at least he'd agreed to meet. Unfortunately, he worked graveyard at the cement plant now and wasn't off again until the next morning.

The day stretched out ahead of me. It's something I both loved and hated about being an investigator: the bendy sense of time when you didn't have a set schedule or anyone watching you while you worked. I kept track of my hours, took notes to provide the client with, but it usually didn't matter whether those hours were nine to five or middle of the night. You'd think the arrangement would make you inclined to work less and be more efficient, but mostly there were no boundaries between work and home. I closed the laptop and rubbed my eyes. Neon confessions replayed in my mind with the strange texture of a dream, Leroy's voice warbling in my ear like a broken jukebox. Sooner or later I'd want to hear my dad's side of things, but right now I felt too blue and too wrung out, but also charged up. I was mad at Jacinda, mad at Charlie, the Wallaces, and strangely, Tyler Thompson. Even the thought of Pastor Brad at New Beginnings made my skin flush. Maybe anger wasn't quite it—I think I resented that they weren't so unlike my dad and Leroy. Ever since my talk with Tyler, I'd had the half-formed notion that solving this case would help fix the drug problem in Garnett. Make an example of the dangers Jacinda had fallen prey to, maybe. I wasn't so naïve to think it was that simple, but the association was there, churning in the back of my mind. It was better than feeling as useless as I did now.

Tate jumped onto the cushion next to me. I scratched behind his ears, but instead of settling down he batted his paw at me and meowed, staring pitifully into my eyes. I moved the laptop and he vaulted off the couch and ran to his dish. Foolishly, I thought he'd warmed up to me enough to sit on my lap. More foolishly, I realized as I was opening it that I was down to his last can of food.

I didn't feel like driving to Colburn to go to H-E-B, so once again found myself at Walmart. The whole way over, a red pickup truck had followed behind me. It could've been a coincidence—I certainly wasn't the only person going to Walmart—but as soon as I spotted the truck in my rearview, I'd felt goose bumps break out on my arms. A beater, at least a decade old, with tinted windows—it looked like the one that rode my bumper when I was leaving the church. I didn't know who would be following me, but I'd definitely pissed off Doug Wallace, maybe others. After I turned quickly into the Walmart lot, they sped on down the highway. Whoever it was knew to hang back. If they were following me, that is.

I'd nearly finished shopping when I saw Heather Ellis from across the store. She was combing through the sale rack in the men's clothing department, and I held back a laugh as she examined the 24 BEERS IN A CASE T-shirt I'd seen the other day. I pulled my buggy up alongside hers. "Hey, stranger. Find something you like?"

Heather jumped and touched her chest. "Annie," she said, her oversized glasses turning her eyes into saucers. "I didn't see you there. What's up?"

"Needed a few things." I noticed she wore jeans, a slouchy V-neck tee, and sandals. "You have the day off?"

"Have to work tomorrow, so yeah, taking today off. The librarians and assistants rotate once a month, but I'm like a hamster on a wheel. Any change to the routine always kind of throws me off my game."

"I know what you mean."

She held up the beer shirt and another that had a bald eagle clutching guns and an American flag in its talons. The combination reminded me of Eagle Beverages and I shuddered—for real, though Heather thought I was joking—and she laughed. "Think I should get one of these for my dad?"

"Hell, get both," I said. She had a pair of jeans, a black hoodie, boxers, and a flannel shirt in her buggy. I found it a little odd, her dad being the bank president. I couldn't see the man I knew owning a hoodie. An off-brand Walmart hoodie, at that. He probably needed some kicking-around-the-pasture stuff; the Ellis place was out in the country, a couple hundred acres that they ran a few head of cattle on and a big, redbrick house set behind a windbreak.

"Dad wouldn't ever buy new clothes if me or my mom didn't occasionally grab a few things for him." Heather laughed again. "So, how's the search going?"

"Getting closer," I said. "Only a matter of time at this point before someone catches up with him. Hopefully, for his sake, it's me or the law."

"Jeez. Hope so. Guess drugs will do that—get you mixed up with the wrong people."

"Drugs?"

"Oh, I just assumed," she said, her eyes going wide again. "I mean, based on what you've told me about him. Is that bad?"

"Well, you're right," I said, watching her. "Charlie was mixed up with that."

She nodded, meeting my stare. "I'm glad to know you're close. I figured you must be good at working for your granddad if you decided it was worth sticking around in Garnett. Or at least like it?"

"Uh, yeah, I think so. And thanks," I said. "I'm going to keep trying anyway."

"That's all we can do," she said, and tossed a pack of Hanes T-shirts into her buggy.

I said bye and pushed mine forward. Heather wasn't telling me something, I worried—I was willing to bet she'd recognized Charlie from the library after I sent her his picture. Why, though, wouldn't she admit to that? It would be understandable enough, a mistake. Sometimes, it's better to ask the question when you have more to lean on. I wasn't sure yet what I would be accusing her of, not really. I continued down the aisle, stopping when I saw an endcap display of multicolored prayer candles. The tall jars with the Virgin of Guadalupe on the front, or Jesus, or that painting of a guardian angel hovering over the bridge while the two children cross it. I really did believe I was, if not close, going in the right direction. Why then, were my hands shaking? I picked a candle out as a kind of talisman, the one with Jesus opening his robes to reveal the rays of light shooting out of a bloodred heart. I picked out the one that looked like Charlie.

By the time I left the store, the sky had turned. There was a dip in air pressure, a few stray drops on the asphalt, and the sun slid behind a cloud, edging it in silver. It smelled like rain, and my mind went to Wyatt a few days before the flood. Wind at his back, his light brown hair fanned onto his neck, his T-shirt pulled tight around his shoulder blades. The sun had been out all day but I'd known it was coming a bad storm: electricity in the air, and a raw, frayed-edge feeling under my skin. "Petrichor," he'd told me, tipping his head up. "Not rain you're smelling, but bacteria and plant chemicals that are undetectable until rainwater releases them into the air." And in true Wyatt fashion he'd gotten that longing look in his eyes, said, "There's this whole other universe we haven't been paying any mind to."

He must be camping at the O'Brien ranch by now. I considered texting him, but quickly changed my mind. I refused to put myself out there like that, not after he'd been the one to break up with me. I pulled up to the railroad crossing right as the arm went down and lights started flashing. While a rusted, graffitied train lurched down the track, I checked the forecast instead. Rain all weekend. I shivered and rolled the window up. As I drove over the bridge toward home, I felt a headache coming on, the pressure behind my eyes building like the storm clouds now snuffing out the sky. What would happen to this town, if not even a month later, the river rose again?

There had been no sign of the red truck from earlier. Still,

I took the long way home, onto the back road past River Oaks. It was still empty, the units gutted. I slowed down when I saw that Rancho Vista, on the other hand, had a construction crew out front. I parked the bullet on the shoulder, hoped the ice cream in the backseat wouldn't melt, and walked onto the property. An older man wearing dusty jeans and a hard hat leaned against a new F-350, talking on his phone and smoking a cigarette. The nice truck combined with the way he seemed to be watching the others made me think he was in charge.

He saw me coming up on his right and ended the call. "Help you, miss?" he said, eyebrows raised.

"Are you the foreman?"

He nodded at me, giving the "wait a minute" finger to another man in a hard hat coming up toward my left.

"I'm curious about these apartments, you're rebuilding them?" I asked, and stepped forward, not letting the other man edge me out.

"That's right," the foreman said, and stubbed his cigarette in the dirt. He looked up at the clouds. "Hopefully it doesn't just get wrecked again. Happens a lot, but what are you going to do? Money's only for rebuilding, not relocating."

"You must be contracted with FEMA, then. You're doing the other complex, too?"

"Nope, we got the bid through the owner's private insurance company. Don't know about the other place, but I bet they didn't have flood insurance. It's not required. No one else out here is working with private insurance adjustors to my knowledge. Now, I don't mean to be rude, hon, but we're losing daylight here," he said, and motioned the other man forward.

"Thanks," I said, and walked back to the bullet grinding my jaw. Damn. If the owners of River Oaks knew they were in the floodplain, maybe they'd have gotten the upgraded insurance, too. Given the fact that Reverend Richter owned both the land sold to the developer for the town homes and Rancho Vista, it seemed he must have known what was coming. Known and still didn't care that people's homes—people's lives—could be lost.

I called Mary-Pat and she picked up on the first ring.

"He knew," I said, turning the ignition. "The Reverend. The selfish jerk knew about the flooding risk that would come from building the new town homes. He took out a private flood insurance policy on the Rancho Vista complex—why else would he have done that?"

"Well, that's not—" She paused, and I pictured her chewing her lip like she did, gears turning. "It's not illegal, I don't think. Seems like he might get sued for damages, but no, I don't think that we're talking about insurance fraud. A flood, or tornado—or any act of God as they call it—is still out of his control. It's not like he committed arson, then collected the insurance."

"I know, but that's the type of character accusation that could lose him his city council seat," I said.

"Not to mention ruin the reputation of the church. You need to be sure before you do anything with the information," Mary-Pat said.

"As the builder, Jacinda would have been privy to that knowledge. She even had them dig these ditches—basically a moat—around the town homes. What if she threatened to expose the Reverend? She needed cash. Maybe she attempted some kind of blackmail," I said, my heart racing. Excitement mimics anxiety, though—I felt a little dizzy, and all the budding trees leaned over the road looked overly bright, everything in view too sharp, too close. It was Bethany. Her bruised, carefully touched-up face. Her tears when she'd told me about Eli, and her small, hopeful smile when she'd told me she and John David were expecting. The Richters were more than her in-laws. The Richters, that church, they were this whole idea that she aspired to, and it pained me thinking that it might go away. Just slip through her fingers, and after all she'd been through.

"It's all certainly worth looking into," Mary-Pat said carefully. "Where does that leave Charlie?"

"I'm not sure yet," I said, and checked my mirrors when a speck of red appeared in my periphery. A red pickup turned onto the road not a minute after I flashed past.

"Be careful, Annie. John Sr.'s one of the more powerful men in this county. I don't know who all has allegiance to him, but it might include the law. Keep this between us, for now."

"Okay," I said, and she hung up. She was right. I'd let it lie while I worked a different angle. I dropped the phone in my lap, peeking in the mirror again. It was the same red pickup; I was sure now. My palms started sweating. I didn't want whoever this was to follow me home, so I sped up, but the truck did, too, shortening the distance between us. I kept going down River Road for a few miles, toward the highway. I went over the bridge and around the curve as fast as I dared. I remembered there was a private dirt road up ahead that cut through to the highway, the turnoff right before the intersection at RR 30. I hit the gas and turned quickly, hoping the dust I kicked up would be somewhat obscured by the cottonwoods bordering the road.

It worked. I reached the highway and still hadn't seen the pickup in my rearview. After a few miles I turned off and pulled into the Texaco to get my bearings. Being followed was such a violating feeling. It made me want to both hide and turn around to chase them back.

Turn around. That was it.

I needed to seek, not hide. Earlier I'd considered my next move going to the feed store, leaning on Tyler again for more on Eli Wallace's whereabouts. I couldn't follow Tyler now, though—he knew me and my car. But I could think of someone else who might be paying their dealer a visit here soon.

Chapter 27

Bud Nelson's front door was open. From my hiding spot in the trees I could see inside the house. The floor was cluttered with plastic storage containers and trash bags. He had the TV on. I squinted to see what he was watching—Dr. Oz, it looked like—when he finally came tumbling out. He had on saggy carpenter jeans, loafer-style house shoes, and a white undershirt loose around the collar like it had been worn for a few days. No sign of the brace. He hitched up his pants, stuck his wallet in the back pocket, and slammed the door behind him, not bothering to lock it. I waited until he turned right onto the road before running toward the bullet, which was parked behind a tree a quarter of a mile back. I had no idea if my hunch that he'd be buying pills at some point would prove accurate, but I decided I would keep after him until I had a better idea.

His first stop was the drive-up teller at First Bank of Garnett. I idled in a parking space, hoping my mother wouldn't walk out and recognize me; it was nearly five, so she'd be getting off soon. I waited and watched Bud take the plastic tube from the slot and remove a small stack of bills. Then we were back onto Main Street, headed west. Main Street turned into RR 30 and the tiny lots with low-slung, single-story houses turned into fields of maize. The lower parts of the stalks were yellowed from being underwater for too long, and the hay fields were overgrown, the farmers unable to cut and bale while the grass was still damp. Bud took us up over the fault line where the land was hillier and the road twisted like a ribbon in the wind. Nearly to Parr City, he braked hard and put the truck in reverse. I eased into the other lane, passed him on the left, kept my speed down, and watched him in the rearview. He reversed until he turned right onto an unmarked dirt lane. Nervous he'd caught on to me, I took my time before making a U-turn and following.

I'd lost him. The trick I'd employed yesterday was used against me. That is, if he even knew he was being followed. I kept driving down the narrowing dirt road, but my stomach flip-flopped—I worried I'd force a confrontation with this man I didn't know with no plausible explanation as to why I'd also be out here, in the middle of nowhere.

The road had taken a lot of damage from the storms, and was completely washed out in places, with deep ruts the width of a car. I couldn't go as fast as Bud could in a truck. Distracted, sweeping my eye side to side, I accidentally drove right into a pit in the center of the road, bouncing in the seat and wincing as my tailpipe scratched against the ground. The road pitched steeply upward, and on the down side, curved around a thicket of mesquite, rocks, and cacti. I still hadn't seen Bud. Around the bend I saw a metal mailbox to my right and a gravel drive-way with no gate. The faintest cloud of white caliche dust hung in the air. Seemed worth a shot. The driveway went straight uphill, so I accidentally came right up on Bud's truck pulled off to the side. In a clearing before me were a bunch of vehicles in varying states of rust and disrepair, including an old blue school bus, and parked beside it, a newish slate-gray truck. Off to the side of the clearing was a dirty, once-white bungalow that had been partially burned down.

I reversed until I was out of sight, parking behind a big juniper bush and hoping no one had heard me. I figured if I cut through the trees and came around the opposite side of the clearing, I could get close enough to see what was going on. I took my keys and my phone and walked the hills that were electric green with spring growth, bent low among the scrubby cedar and cacti. I stopped at one of the cars on cinder blocks at the edge of the clearing and crouched behind the rusted bumper, peering around the side. A double-take—Bud's shiny bald head was bobbing up and down inside the school bus. I couldn't see anyone else without coming out from around the car. I needed to make a dash for the burned-out house. The side where the most damage was looked like a gaping mouth—white boards dangled like broken teeth over the black void.

I got down on my knees and crawled between the cars until I was close, then made a run for it, sucking wind, my heart pounding though I'd only gone a short distance. It was hard to tell how recent the fire was—there were half-burned boxes of photos and clothes in the living room, but the rain and wind had swept away any ashes or smoke smells. The house was likely built around the turn of the twentieth century. An old-fashioned woodstove, crown molding, and floral wallpaper were at odds with the violence of the damage—a hole had exploded in the ceiling, the carpet singed, drapes ripped. There was evidence of recent activity: cigarette butts on the floor, a crumpled fast-food bag, and an Amazon box. Crouching below the front window, I could see the school bus clearly. Outside was an awning and a small unattached deck made out of unfinished plywood with no railing. I could see through the window that some of the seats had been replaced with a hammock and a table. Bud stood in the middle of what once was the center aisle. To his right, back turned, was a broad-shouldered man with a head of dark hair underneath a red ball cap. I couldn't be certain, but based on the night at the rodeo fairgrounds, and the pictures I'd seen, I thought it could be Eli Wallace.

Bud walked out of the bus, and the ray of orange sunset that had broken through the clouds beamed him in the face. He stopped and blinked, dazed-looking. Maybe high already. Eli—I could see his profile clearly now and was certain it was him—hopped off the last step and shoved Bud to the ground.

"You sack of shit. Think I can't count? Open your wallet," he said, and stomp-kicked the back of Bud's knees with the heel of his boot. Bud wailed, and instead of getting out his wallet, staggered back onto his feet and tried to run for it.

A second man—not Charlie, to my dismay—came out of the bus and watched the scene go down with his arms crossed. Scrawny and pale, he wore basketball shorts and no shirt, his boxer shorts bunched up over the waistband. Eli was tall and lean, defined arms and shoulders visible through his thin T-shirt, and he quickly overtook Bud. Used one arm to hold Bud back, and with the other, pulled a gun.

No, no, I silently screamed, throat choked, unable to move, think—

Eli pistol-whipped Bud to the back of the head, and gun hitting skull made a wet, cracking sound. Bud gurgled once, then dropped into the dirt. I grabbed my cell phone from my pocket. No service—and I was maybe twenty feet away. Call and they'd hear it. I crouched down lower and tried to calm my breathing, to think. Typed out a text to Garcia and to Mary-Pat, but it failed to send.

"You're the one had to make it difficult," Eli said, hoisting Bud up so he could reach into his pocket. He fished out his wallet and shoved him. "Now, get your fat ass out of here."

"Come on, man," Bud said, his voice slurred. He held a hand to the back of his head. Blood seeped through his fingers and dripped onto his clothes, the dirt. "Shit, man. Help me!"

"He said get," the scrawny man said, and ran forward, kicking Bud in the shin at full force.

"All this trouble . . ." Eli clicked his tongue. He still had his gun drawn. He spit in the dirt and wiped his chin with his sleeve, a smile forming. "Next time's gonna be double the price."

Bud swayed and nearly toppled over, one hand still cupping the wound. He threw up and stumbled down the driveway while the two men laughed. I didn't know what to do. Every fiber of my being wanted to take my chances and run to the bullet, call 911 as I peeled out, but I couldn't risk them catching me. Not after what I'd seen.

Waiting for the sun to go down felt like the longest hour of my life.

Eli and the other guy sat outside on the makeshift deck while they drank beer and smoked. They had heavy metal playing, loud enough that I couldn't hear a damn thing they said. I hoped they would get in the truck and leave, but also kind of didn't, because I worried then they'd spot the bullet half-hidden in the juniper bush. Still squatting below the window, my legs started shaking, then went completely numb. All the panes had been blown out by the fire, and broken glass littered the once-green carpet, now mottled brown with mud and speckled with black mildew. So, I couldn't sit, but I thought if I scooted sideways with my head tucked beneath the sill, I could make it to the wall, stand, and stretch my legs.

The music cut off. Startled, I lost my balance and fell forward onto my knees. The glass poked through my jeans, but I didn't think I'd been cut. Stupidly, I pressed my palms against the blackened sill to get my balance and the force of it rattled the window frame, slamming it closed.

"What was that?"

Eli's voice.

Oh, God, I thought, curling into myself and taking the last sideways step out from under the window. I spun around and pressed my back against the wall. I couldn't tell if the old-timey floral wallpaper was damp from the rain or it was my sweat soaking the back of my T-shirt.

"I didn't hear it. What?"

"The house. Sounded like something fell over."

My heart boomed and my breath caught in my chest. *Please don't come over here, please, please—*

The front door whined on its hinges. Boots stepped over the threshold, glass crunching under heel. A half-closed pocket door was the only thing separating me in the living room from Eli Wallace in the hall. I couldn't see him, but I could smell him—musky aftershave, cigarettes. He cracked his knuckles, shuffling farther inside the house. I could see the staircase from where I stood, and Eli's hand, leathery and wide, clamped down over the singed-black baluster.

He pushed the door open.

I held my breath and slid to the corner so the door opened onto me. The knob grazed my arm, but he didn't push it open wider. He stood in the center of the room with his back turned to me. Walked to the old woodstove, bent in front of the grate, and opened it. Over his shoulder I saw a plastic grocery bag half full with smaller plastic bags of what looked to be pills, three or four stacks of cash, and another handgun. Eli opened the Amazon box to the right of the stove. When he moved the flaps down, I could see what looked like a small metal telescope with a hand crank. Tyler had said Eli had been known to sell counterfeit pills cut with fentanyl. Maybe that was the press.

 I was sweating so badly now I worried he could smell me, feel the heat radiating from me. I breathed slowly through my nose, willing my heart to stop beating so loudly, racking my brain for what to say when he eventually did turn around. Should I make a run for it now, while he was bent down? As I was about to make a break, Eli closed the grate. He stood, but instead of coming back toward the front of the house, he turned to his left. He went out the way I'd come in, through the burned-out, wall-less kitchen, never once turning back.

Dusk's purple shadows turned to black, and though Eli and his buddy were still drinking and shooting the shit outside, I decided to creep back through the trees. I paused, briefly, for one last look behind me. Something had nagged at me, and then I realized it was the newish truck parked in front of the bus. In the dim light thrown from the deck, I could see the plate was bright yellow—not a Texas plate, but a New Mexico plate. I zoomed in as best I could with my phone and took a picture.

The bullet was exactly as I'd left it, and I breathed deeply the scent of crushed juniper that carried on the cool night air. Drove out as fast as I dared, and dialed the sheriff.

"Garcia."

"It's Annie McIntyre," I said, then hit the damn pit in the middle of the road again. The bullet bounced so hard my teeth chattered. Up ahead I saw headlights—my heart slammed against my rib cage and I eased off the road, narrowly avoiding a low barbwire fence—and cut mine.

"Annie?"

"Yeah, sorry," I said, flattening myself against the seat back. "So, there's this guy, Eli Wallace, he's a dealer—"

"Wallace. I know that name."

A dark-colored sedan passed by at a decent clip. They obviously didn't know about the pit up ahead, either, and I didn't think they'd seen me. Just in case, I drove away slowly with my headlights off until I couldn't see their taillights in my rearview anymore. I explained to Garcia about seeing Eli at the rodeo fairgrounds, what Tyler Thompson had said about him, and Bethany noticing him at church when she was with Jacinda. I left out the part about Eli being her ex-stepbrother. "Eli and his buddy, they're selling pills, maybe more, out here. Their stash is in the house, in the woodstove. He seriously injured this guy," I said, a fresh surge of anger making my skin tight and hot. "Also, you said you were looking at a man seen with Jacinda in the security footage of a casino near Ruidoso—did you catch his vehicle? I ask because there's a truck here with a New Mexico tag."

"We only got a partial," he said sharply. "Dark four-door?"

"Yeah. I'll text you the picture."

"You did the right thing backing off and calling me," Garcia said, and I could hear him snapping his fingers at someone. "This is good work you've done, but you're lucky no one saw you. Even if those plates don't match, I'm heading out thataway now."

"Okay, good," I said. But instead of feeling relieved, I felt a rush of panic. "I still haven't found Charlie Kingman."

"You have any new leads?"

My neck pricked with heat. "I'm still working on it."

"That's okay. We'll know more after we get Wallace in and start pressing. Thank you, Annie. Be careful now."

Garcia disconnected. The clouds had rolled back in, obscuring the moon and stars. I couldn't see much beyond my high beams, and I inched along. Damn, had I really driven this far out? My legs trembled, and I felt a wave of pure physical exhaustion wash over me. But my mind kept buzzing. *Go, go, go.* As guilty as Eli Wallace was looking, Charlie had to be involved, and he had to be found. If he wasn't an accomplice, he was likely a witness and his life in danger—why else would he be hiding? Finally, I rolled out onto the highway and picked up speed. Flying down the blacktop, no cars passed and no one was behind me, yet I couldn't shake the feeling I wasn't alone.

Chapter 28

Trevor Sutton sat on his couch drinking a beer at nine-thirty in the morning. "There's coffee left on the stove if you want it. My girlfriend makes it before she goes to work. Me, I'm trying to wind down," he said, rolling the can between his palms.

"I'm fine, thanks." I was tempted, but knew another cup would make me twitchier than I already was. When I'd driven up to the trailer park—heavily damaged from the flood and near empty—I realized I could have asked that we meet somewhere public, the element of surprise blown already. All I knew about Trevor Sutton was that he'd been muscle for Jacinda and that he was a felon. But when I'd messaged him I had it in my mind that I could learn more if I saw his place, if not find Charlie. I sat on the edge of the armchair he offered me, keeping my body angled toward the door. "So, Trevor, how long have you been at the plant?"

The microwave beeped and he walked to the kitchenette. "Two months. I like it, though it'd be nice to be on days, for me and Steph to have the same schedule. Maybe next month. Sure you don't want nothing?"

"Really, I'm good," I said, looking out through the mini blinds at the gray sky, thinking it was too warm in here. "The night of the flood, you were working the same shift?"

Trevor sat back down holding a soggy-looking burrito on a paper plate. "Yeah, got trapped out there. Couldn't make it home for over twelve hours. Had to sleep on the pack house floor. Sucked."

"Before the plant, you were working for Moore Construction, right?"

"For Jacinda, yep. She and I didn't get along—and I don't mean that in any suspicious way or nothing, her being killed and all. We just needed to part ways. I felt like I was being taken advantage of."

"Really." I tried to keep my voice light, gossipy. "She ask you to do something illegal?"

"Yeah, well"—a laugh scratched at the back of his throat— "I'm not at liberty to say, Miss PI."

"Come on," I said, leaning forward. "I know she was selling pills."

He stared at me with his lips pursed. He was a big guy with a moon face and blue eyes so light they almost looked clear. He took a bite of his burrito and shrugged his shoulders. "Was she?"

A bead of sweat rolled down my back. "The main reason why I'm here is to ask if you've seen your old coworker, Charlie Kingman, at any point in the past month."

"Shit, no," he said, dropping the burrito onto the plate and wiping his hands on a wad of paper towel he grabbed off the coffee table. "Honestly, I've been worried about him. We lived together for a bit."

I sat up straighter. "When was this?"

"Months ago. Before me and Steph got together, he lived here with me. This is my aunt's old place. Charlie and me met at a halfway house after we'd both got out."

I looked around, imagining Charlie sitting at the chipped Formica table, watching TV on that very couch, but it was hard—he was beginning to feel less real and more like a ghost again. "While you lived together, did he have any friends, or was he dating anyone?"

"No. I didn't even know for the longest time he was, uh—"

"Gay? Were the two of you ever—"

"No, no way—I mean, I don't care about that, I'm no bigot. I'm just into women," he said, his voice rising to a loud pitch.

"Was Jacinda? A bigot, I mean."

"I don't know. She was churchy, but I don't think she cared. Two of them, they were real close. I knew it'd be awkward with me and Charlie when I quit, but we pretty much stopped talking when he moved out. I think he thought I was rejecting him, but it wasn't nothing personal. He was an okay dude. It was Jacinda that I, well, I don't need to talk ugly about the dead."

"Go on, I'm not judging."

He took a drink of beer. "Well, she was manipulative. Thing is, when you get out of prison, sometimes you need those old boundaries. You get used to structure. Being out, it can feel like you have too many choices and it's real stressful always acting right. Know what I mean?"

I nodded. It was exhausting writing your own script sometimes. I'd felt something like that after graduation, not knowing what to do next, frustrated that real life wasn't a meritocracy like school. My twenties so far had often felt like a long sigh.

"So, that's how Jacinda got you under her thumb." Trevor grew more animated, setting down his beer and talking with his hands. "She'd bad-mouth the guys who had, like, lives? I think her caring and all was real, but she wasn't my mother or my girlfriend, you know? You'd be around her at work all day, then feel like you had to accept the dinner invitation from her, which she'd pay for but constantly remind you that she was paying, then she'd text you the rest of the night when you finally got home. She was funny and nice and all, and probably lonely after her husband died, but damn."

"What did she text you about?"

"Reminding you to do shit, mostly. Criticizing the work you'd done that day, then saying how you were in her nightly prayers and that she loved you. Weird shit like that. Charlie, though, he ate it up."

I paused for a moment. "Do you think Charlie killed her? Maybe she pushed him too far?"

"Charlie? No," he said quickly. Raised his eyebrows at me like I should already know better. "I've known people who've snapped. Met guys in prison who seemed normal but come to find out they butchered their girlfriend. So, I don't know one hundred percent. But I really doubt it. The two of them was thick as thieves. Like, if I didn't know better, I'd think they were dating."

His initial reaction told me a lot—beyond the two of them being close, he didn't think Charlie had it in him. "What was he like?"

Trevor smiled and looked down like he was remembering something funny. "He was shy around a lot of people. Kept his room neat. Could also be a dick sometimes, but who isn't?"

"He had a temper, then?"

"No, not really. Not like you're thinking," he said, rolling his eyes. "Like leaving an inch of milk left in the jug instead of throwing it away."

"He wasn't mad when Jacinda fired him?"

Trevor shook his head. "She didn't fire Charlie. She just took him off the books, paid him under the table. He was set to get a raise, if you know what I mean. Like I said, she wanted us to do her, uh, bidding, not worry with construction work. Me, I wasn't into it."

"Got it," I said. There went at least the most obvious motive, money. "There's one other thing I've been trying to figure out—where was Charlie staying after he moved out of your place?"

"This old Airstream camper parked out at Jacinda's. Was painted this retro pink color. A hipster's dream—the two of them planned on making it some kind of tiny house Airbnb. Rich people love vintage, you know. Charlie stayed in it rent free while he was working on it," he said, then finished his beer. "Feel hot in here to you?"

I nodded, sweating bullets now.

Trevor got up and opened the front door so the breeze could come through the screen. He looked back at me and yawned. "Get cold when I'm tired. I don't mean to be rude, but—"

I stood and grabbed my purse. "Right. You must be exhausted."

"Yeah," Trevor said, and looked relieved. "I'll walk you out."

The half of the trailer park closest to the river looked tossed. Like a giant hand had scooped everything up, shook, then threw it down like dice. Camper shells, roof shingles, nails, shreds of insulation, pipe fittings, even a toilet tank, were scattered over the grounds. A twisted metal clothesline outside Trevor's window bent toward the sky like some kind of demented modern art installation. "You're lucky your place was okay," I said.

"Should've seen it earlier. I've cleaned up a lot, but yeah, I know." He took off his sweatshirt and my eye landed on a tattoo the length of his forearm. A red-orange phoenix outlined with blue, like the inverse of a flame. He caught me staring and pointed to it. "Charlie drew this for me."

"Rising from the ashes, right?"

He shrugged, laughing a little. "Eh, thought so at the time. Charlie was emo like that, too. I'd just gotten out, felt like I needed to do something to commemorate it. But I don't know. Now I don't think you learn so much from the bad as you do from the good. Know what I mean?"

"Sure," I said, wondering if he was right, that maybe pain was not the great teacher it was cracked up to be.

"Actually, I think I'd rather forget all the shit that's nearly killed me." He laughed again. "Still like the drawing though. Looks badass, if I may say so."

"You may," I said, and unlocked the bullet.

I drove to Jacinda's. I was almost certain I hadn't seen an Airstream, or any type of trailer or camper for that matter, but I needed to be sure. I also was certain that if there was one still parked out there, the law would have searched it. But had they known what they were looking for at the time?

It seemed like overnight the pale buds and the bright, new green of spring on the trees had unfurled, deepened to the mature shades of summer. The sky, too, was fast-changing, darkened now with gunmetal clouds. I stepped out of the bullet and walked into the tall grass behind the house. There were no signs of life from either of the buildings. It occurred to me that the bedsheets tacked over the windows of the barn were likely meant to hide any packing or storing she had done with the pills.

She was manipulative

Wanted you under her thumb

Trevor's disdain for Jacinda echoed in my head. Despite all I'd learned, despite my anger at her for spreading that poison around, I'd felt prickly, defensive when Trevor had spoken like that. And here I was again. The menacing throb of the river through the trees, the shadow of the barn—it had me twisted up. There had been something intimate about having sat here with her body. I'd known the moment I saw her she'd been dead for some time, but all the same, a light had been extinguished when I spotted her through the window of the truck. A moment of perfect stillness disturbed. There was a godlike vanity to it, I knew, feeling like my discovery had made her death real. But still, I was yoked to her. I couldn't shake that.

I made a mental note to mention Trevor Sutton to Garcia, to have him request the cement plant's time cards from the night of the flood. A faint popping noise—I thought I heard tires on the gravel and stopped midstride. The house and top of the driveway where I'd parked weren't visible from the road, so I hadn't worried too much about someone seeing me. I walked back and looked around the front of the house and saw nothing.

"Damn it, Charlie," I said aloud to the trees. "If I don't find you first, someone else will."

The first drops of rain brushed my cheek, gentle as a kiss. But I knew better. Looking at the swollen river between the trees, my heart beat faster. *Medicine after death,* Leroy had said. It was all too much. I swept my eyes over the grass as I walked. There was a patch of dirt nearer the downward slope toward the water. The patch looked to be about the size of a small trailer, though it was hard to know for sure. An Airstream could have been moved by the floodwaters, I supposed, but wouldn't someone have spotted it by now? The river was still high, but after the second search and rescue, I doubted it would still be in the water undetected. There were no visible tire treads, but someone might have hitched it to a truck and moved it weeks ago, the tracks faded by now. Maybe even Charlie himself. He could be anywhere by now. Blindly driving around looking for an Airstream trailer, even if it was distinctive-looking, seemed like a fool's errand.

What other choice did I have?

Chapter 29

After a few hours of fruitless searching, I stopped at the Texaco for gas. The sun peeked in and out, the wind had stopped, and the smell of diesel fumes and dust hung in the air. I dug around for a water bottle that had rolled under the front seat, but it was hot and tasted like melted plastic, so I decided to go in and get a Coke. There were two other cars at the station. One was a black Ford truck with a horse trailer hitched to it, the other was a Pontiac, a bright blue Grand Am with peeling, tinted windows. I was about to open the convenience store door when a woman charged through from the other side. She wore dark sunglasses, and her high ponytail was dishwater blond, nearly the same shade as the ribbed tank top she wore tucked into camo-print hunting pants. "Excuse me," I said when she stopped in the doorway, blocking my way.

"Oh my god! It's you," she said, then turned behind her to a second, dark-haired woman, who I couldn't see as clearly. "It's that goddamn *snitch*." The blonde took off her sunglasses and I recognized her as Tyler Thompson's older sister.

Before I could put any distance between us, she walloped me in the face with her purse.

There was something solid inside and the metal chain hanging from the zipper whipped me in the eye. The blow was hard enough—and shocking enough—to send me stumbling backward, and I fell off the curb, landing hard on my arm. I'd felt brain jostle against my skull. I'd never been punched in the face before and was surprised to see stars, like in the cartoons. My nose smarted and I felt a dribble of blood on my upper lip. Covering my face with the arm I'd landed on—and which was also bleeding and sore—I used the other to prop myself up. "I don't know who you think I am," I said, standing unsteadily. "Or what the hell you have in that bag."

"You're the one who got my brother arrested. You set him up. He saw you driving out there last night."

I'd thought the dark sedan that passed me on the dirt road seemed familiar. "They arrested Tyler—Tyler and Eli Wallace?"

"He got caught up in some raid last night. We had to bail him out at like four in the morning."

I had also given Garcia Tyler's name when I'd told him what I knew about Eli. So, it was my fault, in a way. My stomach twisted with guilt, but I stuck my shoulders back. "I'm sorry. I didn't know he'd be there."

"Tyler's in sad trouble now," the other woman piped up. She looked me up and down, biting her lip. "Then again, someone like Tyler? He'll probably get court-ordered rehab, not time. Maybe his license suspended."

Tyler's sister whipped around. "Like that's not a big fucking deal?"

The bell on the convenience store door chimed, and out stepped the driver of the horse trailer. The two women turned around and

I took the opportunity to run for the bullet. The driver, a scrawny teenage boy, looked between the three of us and turned right back around. I kept one hand on the door as I looked over my shoulder at Tyler's sister and her friend, my shock and fear calcifying into anger. "If you come at me again, you're gonna have another problem. It's not my fault your brother's gotten mixed up with the wrong people."

"You have no idea, do you?" She stepped forward, and her friend grabbed her arm to hold her back. "He was really trying. He was going to go back and finish his degree."

"Come on. Your friend's probably right," I said, tasting blood, my face tingling and hot. "He'll get clean. He'll get the help he needs now."

"Huh, yeah, like we never thought of rehab. Where do you think he relapsed the first time? All I know is, I better not see you at my family's store ever again."

She gave me the finger and the two of them got into the Pontiac and sped off. I felt bad about Tyler—I didn't anticipate him getting caught for possession. But Tyler was an adult and he made his choices. He screwed up. If his sister was so concerned about him getting arrested, she should have intervened sooner. I told myself these things, too defensive to see any other response—namely, to extend any empathy to either of them. My face throbbed. The raspberry on my forearm burned. I found a stash of fast-food napkins stuffed in the center console, tipped my head back, and held one to my nose. After the bleeding stopped, I pulled up the local news site on my phone. Sure enough, the headline story said the Garnett County sheriff's department had recovered weapons, pills, and heroin from a private residence near Parr City. It also said that a suspected dealer was a person of interest in another "high profile case"—so, the plates must have been a match—and that the man was still at large. My breath caught in my chest.

Eli Wallace had gotten away.

"I'm okay," I said, avoiding the swollen face in the mirror. "I'm nearly home."

Mary-Pat breathed heavily on the line. "They'll catch Eli here soon enough. Until they do, Annie, you need to watch your back. If Tyler and his sister knew you were responsible for the tip-off, I'm sure Eli has heard your name, too."

"I can't really lie low right now," I said, and told her about the Airstream trailer. As I pulled into my complex's parking lot, my phone pinged with a text from Bethany. Maybe she was finally ready to write me my damn check.

"That pistol your granddad gave you," Mary-Pat said. "From now on, keep it with you in the car."

"You know I don't like that," I said. "I've only shot a gun like twice in my life." I knew I should let Mary-Pat take me for target practice sometime, but at least for now, I felt that being armed would only be me borrowing trouble.

"Annie."

"I'll think about it," I said, hanging up and stepping out into the late-afternoon heat. The humid air cloaked me like a second skin. There was a ripple of thunder in the distance, and a low, scraping noise. A boy rode a scooter in wide loops around the parking lot, but otherwise it was empty of people. I entered the stairwell and stopped. I could see through the railing at eye-level a pair of ratty women's running shoes standing in front of my door. My pulse quickened. I was about to run back to the bullet when a female voice said, "There she is!"

I laced my car keys between my fingers and walked up the remaining stairs.

The woman was short and thin, barely taller than a kid, but she had a forceful presence—something about the way she leaned forward, snapping gum. The guy with the greasy bun who'd startled me a few days before stood a few feet behind her, leaning on the beige vinyl siding. I looked at my front door, but nothing seemed amiss. At first, I thought I saw smoke coming from the side of the building, but it was only laundry steam, the air perfumed by dryer sheets.

The woman stepped forward. "Me and my boyfriend live in the unit right below yours. We saw some guy looking in your window. Like a prowler."

"Oh, God," I said, gripping my purse strap.

"Yeah," she said, her mouth hanging open so I could see the blue wad of chewing gum. She pointed to her right, where there was a support column joining the railing of the landing with the railing around my balcony. "I was coming out to water my plants and hear something above me. I see this guy standing on the railing, kind of hugging the pole, one foot on your railing, the other on this side. Scared the crap out of me. When I called up to the guy, he swung his leg over and ran down the stairs. Cops haven't come yet."

"Whoa—" It was like someone flipped the on-switch with Man Bun. His dull eyes lit up as they raked over me. "What happened to your face?"

My palms started sweating and my keys slipped against my skin. I touched my finger to my nose and felt a fresh drop of blood. "I'm fine," I said. "Well, sort of. I guess I'll talk to the cops when they get here—"

"If they get here," the woman said, rolling her eyes.

"Right," I said, looking out over the parking lot. Garnett's police force didn't have a stellar reputation to begin with, and recent funding cuts and only a handful of newly recruited, underpaid officers only had made matters worse. "Did you happen to notice anything about him? You said it was a guy, right?"

"Yeah. I mean, I think so. Kinda tall. Wearing a hoodie and a ski mask. That's what scared me, how I knew something was wrong. White guy—I saw his hands. Drove off in a red pickup. That's all I saw."

The red pickup—shit. This wasn't some random creep. My legs felt weak, and I fumbled toward my door with my keys pointed at the lock. "Thanks for looking out. Sorry, I don't think I've ever come down and introduced myself before."

"Don't even worry about it," the woman said. "Know you'd do the same. You sure you're okay, though? Want him to walk in with you?"

I looked over my shoulder and Man Bun nodded in agreement. "I tend bar at the Longhorn's off the freeway. Don't have to be in till five, can stick around if you need me to."

That explained the noises at four in the morning. I felt bad that I'd rushed to judgment, that I'd been afraid of him that night he'd been blocking the stairwell. Then again, I was taking their word for everything right now—all I knew was that they were posted up by my door when I came up the stairs. "I'm fine," I said, and pushed the door in with trembling hands. "I'll let you know what happens with the cops."

Inside, the air was different than the sealed, air-conditioned smell I was used to. It had the mineral smell of wet earth, and was warm. The guy had broken in. The sliding door to the balcony was open, a swipe of mud-caked grass on the carpet, but not enough to make out a footprint. The lock on the door had never worked right, and the dowel rod I'd placed on the track to keep it latched hadn't, either, apparently. I slid the door closed. Grabbed the Maglite I kept in a miscellaneous drawer in case I needed to defend myself, swallowed hard, and checked the bedroom, the bathroom, even the closets. Poor Tate hissed at me from under the couch, but no one else was inside the apartment.

The TV was still there, and the locket and opal ring that had been Mamaw's—the only real jewelry I had—were still on my dresser. My laptop was open on the dining table, but I remembered that I'd left it open, right next to it my spiral-bound notebook.

My notebook—it was upside down.

I flipped through ruled pages dented with the hard press of my blue pen. The last page I'd written on had a small tear along the perforated edge, the tiniest water mark and smudge to the ink that hadn't been there before, as though someone's wet thumb had rested on the page. The same page where I'd written down contact information for Charlie's uncle Ross, scribbled a drawing of a rose, and logged my hours for the past few days. I ran my fingers over the laptop's touchpad and the screen brightened. I'd left open a browser with a bunch of tabs. One was my email, another the Facebook message thread with Trevor Sutton, which I knew the intruder had read—along with who knows what else—because under my profile it said "active" less than an hour ago. Whoever had broken in wasn't looking to rob me or attack me. They were on a fact-finding mission.

They, too, must be looking for Charlie Kingman.

It was no secret around town that I was looking for Charlie— and what better way to find him than to follow in the tracks of the person paid to do so? All they'd need to do was gather up my clues and connect the dots before I did.

I downed a glass of water and an ibuprofen, tasting blood when I swallowed. I needed to get cleaned up before I did anything else. Wetting a rag in the bathroom sink, I surveyed the damage. My nose looked a little swollen, but it wasn't so bad. Worse was the raspberry on my palm and forearm from falling backward onto the asphalt. I scrubbed the dirt and gravel out of the wound, my anger rising as the raw skin prickled and stung. I needed to get out of here. I didn't have time to wait on a police officer to tell me what I already knew. There was too much riding on Charlie to let him lurk in the shadows much longer.

Besides, I was pretty sure if I didn't get to Charlie first, his body was going to turn up like Jacinda's.

Thunder boomed and wind whistled through the gap between the buildings. I heard the sliding door open fast along the track, thudding into the wall. Heart in my throat, I ran out of the bathroom. But it was no one—the latch was simply busted. Instead of figuring out a way to secure the door, I walked out onto the balcony and leaned over the side, wind whipping my hair across my face. Who had been here, looking at what I saw? Tall and white didn't exactly narrow it down, and while my first thought was someone young and agile—Eli Wallace, I feared most—it wasn't exactly a feat of athleticism to climb from the stairwell to here. You'd crack your head open like a watermelon if you fell, but the top bar of the railing was nearly a foot wide, and you wouldn't even have to let go of the column before planting your feet onto the balcony.

Tate rubbed against my calves. I picked him up and scratched behind his ears, and for once he didn't resist. I felt the warmth of his body against my chest and listened to his soft steady breathing. Rain, the smell of it, was like a heady perfume. Gathering clouds blotted out the sun, and miles off, a sheet of heavy rain ripped a seam in the sky. That strange mix of shock and inevitability came over me. There was something about violent weather—awesome in the Old Testament sense of the word, being at the mercy of a fast-changing sky—that still excited me more than it scared me. It felt wrong thinking that now. But as the storm gathered strength, I wanted to be in it. To witness the acts of God. In my bones I knew I needed to return to the floodwaters. That I was still missing a piece of the hours leading up to and immediately after the river crested. That if I wanted to find Charlie, I needed to go back to that night.

BETHANY, ONE MONTH EARLIER

The clouds broke and scattered in the wind so suddenly that the warmth of the sun on her shoulders stopped Bethany in her tracks. She and Kendall carried four camping chairs and a cooler and walked down the embankment toward the river. The Geronimo ran fast and high, and the surface of the water, a dull blue-gray just moments before, now shimmered.

"Let's hope it stays nice like this," Bethany said, popping out the legs on the chairs and planting them in the damp grass. "Forecast says there's a thirty percent chance of rain tomorrow. Not bad odds."

Kendall wrapped her arms around herself and rubbed her shoulders. "Brought a swimsuit, anyway. I'm so ready for it to warm up."

It had rained all week, and all week Bethany had waffled over whether or not to cancel their reservation. But they were here now, and she breathed a sigh of relief seeing that shock of blue sky.

Kendall picked a stick up off the ground, twirled it over her head, and whooped before flinging it into the river.

Bethany laughed. "That's the spirit."

Kendall skipped over and hugged her—to Bethany's surprise—and when she pulled back, Bethany could see Kendall's eyes brimmed with tears.

"Is everything okay?"

"I'm late," Kendall said, wiping her eyes, grinning wide. "I'm going to take a pregnancy test when we get home. It's only been a few days, so I don't know, but I think this time it's real. It's different. I can feel it."

"Oh my gosh, Kendall," Bethany said, and tears now pricked her eyes. "That's so exciting."

"I haven't said anything to Michael yet. I don't want to get his hopes up," Kendall said, whispering though neither of their husbands were within earshot. Kendall and Michael had been trying for two years now, and it had taken a toll on her, Bethany knew. They all knew—she was always talking about it in nauseating detail during small group. It had taken Bethany aback, Kendall and her church girlfriends' openness about such things. It wasn't prudishness—the conversations were decidedly unsexy—but a nagging fear of the eye being turned on her. She had in her head this idea of a great, roving eye looking down on her that made her sear with heat. She thought then about her mother, who'd always said that their family's clannish, private nature was on account of the Scots-Irish blood on her grandmother's side. After living with her, though, Bethany thought her grandmother was just a bitch.

"Pray that we're so blessed," Kendall said, and squeezed her hand. She sat in the chair opposite Bethany and kicked off her sandals, smiling expectantly. Bethany's upper lip started sweating. She knew what Kendall was thinking—were she and John David trying for a baby? John David's relatives—the whole congregation, for that matter—had been dropping hints since she and John David got back from their honeymoon, but now they were straight-up asking. They weren't *not* trying, but she wasn't using an app to track her fertile days and taking vitamins and all that like Kendall. She was secretly relieved it hadn't happened yet, and guilty she felt relieved. It wasn't that she was unsure about John David. The opposite, really. Sometimes she wondered if she had room in her heart for more than him. It scared her how much she loved him.

"Hey, river rats," John David called from up near the house. "How's the water?"

Kendall leaned back, the tendons in her neck straining as

she turned her head upside down to see him. The delicate white skin on her throat was so pale Bethany could see the bluish hue of her jugular. Kendall giggled and stuck her tongue out, and John David squeezed her shoulder as he approached. He sat down in the chair between the two of them and smiled. PDA often made Bethany anxious, but without thinking she grabbed the collar of John David's T-shirt and pulled him in for a kiss. His lips brushed hers, and she resisted the urge to dip her chin and nestle into his neck, sun-warmed and familiar, and close her eyes.

He smiled and leaned back in his chair. "So, are y'all hungry? Mike's firing up the grill."

"Starving," Kendall said. "We picked up some kielbasa on our way in—and oh, I made that German potato salad you like, Bethany!"

Bethany nodded and smiled, but her mind was elsewhere. Something about the mention of the grill gave her an odd feeling—she tried to remember, had they cooked out that weekend she'd come with her folks? She remembered smelling charcoal and cooked meat, sitting on a picnic bench while air-drying in her swimsuit, and the good/bad sensation from scratching raw the constellation of ant bites on her bare feet. She also thought about Eli for the first time in weeks without any queasiness. Just his face at seventeen—unlined and clean-shaven, those twin dimples in his cheeks when he laughed hard.

The wind picked up and John David looked out over the choppy water. "We probably shouldn't go tubing, but if you girls are up for it, we could take out the kayaks. I found some life vests in the closet upstairs."

"Sure," Bethany said. "Anything to get out of the cabin. I'm sorry, y'all. I remembered it differently."

"Oh, come on. It's not that bad," Kendall said.

John David raised his sunglasses, pushing his dark curls up off his forehead. "I'm going to pretend I didn't see a few mouse droppings in the cabinet."

"Ew! No! Let's hope they're old," Kendall said, giggling. "Well, you can't beat the décor. There's one of those singing largemouth bass things hanging in our room. Remember those?"

John David laughed and shook his head. "Actual cigarette burns on our blanket."

"Just some questionable stains on ours."

"I didn't notice. How gross," Bethany said, suddenly sticky and cramped in her plastic chair. She sucked on an ice cube and looked toward the trees.

John David reached into the cooler for a Lone Star Light—he'd never been much of a drinker—and shrugged. "Whatever. After Easter, I just want to relax."

"Amen," Kendall said, then closed her eyes and stretched like a cat, raising her arms and arching her back, her toes curling around the leg of John David's chair. Her hair looked like spun gold in the sun, and when she caught Bethany staring at her, her cheeks tinted pink.

"Bethany!" Michael jogged down the embankment, his legs looking more gangly than normal in his pastel shorts. Michael was cute—all the girls in youth group had little crushes on him, tittering whenever he left the room—but he was also kind of goofy-looking. His features worked in concert, but at certain angles—Bethany watched him come toward her, his glasses sliding down his nose, and couldn't help but hope for their sake that the baby favored Kendall. "Your phone's ringing," he said, handing it to her.

"Hey, Dad," she answered brightly, though her stomach had flip-flopped when she saw his name on the screen. It still felt weird calling him Dad. She often slipped and said "Reverend" and he rarely corrected her. The Reverend's voice was staticky—she had like one bar out here, the others none—but she heard him ask if he could speak to John David. He'd been trying to get in touch with him directly, but his phone was going to voicemail. Bethany handed him her phone and he walked off with it, trying to get better service up near the road. Michael sat in John David's chair and leaned over to take Kendall's hand in his. Bethany stood and stretched. "I'm going in for more ice, y'all want anything?"

"No, I'll be up in a minute," Michael said. "Actually, Bethany, while you're up there can you turn the sausages?"

"Sure thing."

From the kitchen window, Bethany could see the river and also John David pacing up and down the gravel road. He stroked his chin and bit his lower lip. She knew the motion—it was what he did when he didn't want to do something, but was trying to put on a good show. John David would do anything his dad asked of him, without hesitation, so she knew before he'd said anything that he would leave to attend to pastoral duties. It had been happening a lot since the church hired Michael as youth pastor and promoted John David to executive pastor. It was to be expected, but it was hard with him gone all the time. And at home he was tired. He'd tried to explain it to her once, about how after a day of giving himself to others he was emotionally spent, and that he needed no one to need him for the rest of the night. She'd lately started having daydreams about him dying. Not fantasies, but, like, practice runs. She'd get so worked up over him being in a car accident that hadn't actually happened, she'd start crying real tears.

Bethany walked out onto the patio and opened the lid on the grill. The way the sausage casings grew taut, the fat sizzling—it jangled her nerves. She pinched her nose and looked up. As quickly as it had turned blue, the sky darkened. At her back, the sun eked out a few rays, and the cypress trees along the riverbank turned orange, a startling contrast against the slate sky. The wind came to an abrupt stop, like God had turned the off-switch on a fan. Her ears popped. The stillness pressed down, and the bottled-up air felt charged. Kendall and Michael would see two pink lines on a pregnancy test when they got home, and in a few minutes, John David would walk back to the cabin and break her heart. It was all happening, but for a moment, Bethany was reminded of why she loved coming to the river so much—it was that moment when she was swimming downstream, the current carrying her, and she ducked her head under the surface of the cold, clear water, holding her breath, looking up at the wavering light and feeling outside of time and space for as long as her lungs could stand it.

Part III

ANNIE, ONE MONTH LATER

Chapter 30

By the time I'd gotten to the county hospital, the wind had blown heavy-looking clouds in, masking the sun's slow descent. Intermittent rain pinpricked the sidewalk as the parking lot lights flickered on.

I thought again about the night of Jacinda's murder. About the river rising over the hood of her truck, water weeping through the seams of the windows and doors until the cab submerged with a final, heavy suck. And Bethany, not even a mile away, clinging to a tree for life. How Charlie had been pulled into the same cold depths—how he had managed to make it out of that raging river alive, I didn't know. He'd at the very least be injured, I was certain. No one had reported seeing Charlie that night, much less aiding him, but what if he'd managed to walk to the main road? Would he have hitched a ride to seek medical attention?

I entered the lobby, shivering at the polar blast of air-conditioned air, and asked to speak to the head admitting nurse. I was led by a receptionist around the counter to a cubicle where I waited for nearly forty-five minutes, and just as I was about to hop over to the vending machine for a coffee, a woman came around the corner, her tight-lipped smile betraying no warmth. "She said you were looking for someone? I'm sorry, but I haven't had any ambulances with unaccompanied patients today," she said, and sat heavily in the chair across from me. Started to put her feet up but stopped herself. Over her shoulder I could see the double doors leading to the exam rooms and the ICU at the end of a short hallway. Garnett County Hospital was small, and the general consensus was that if you could make it to Austin or San Antonio, you should. Garnett had one regular floor, an ICU, and a long-term care unit, but there were no more elective surgeries and the maternity ward had closed. It made me a little sad thinking that no one would be born in Garnett anymore. The nurse eyed me warily. The laminated ID pinned to her scrubs said her name was Tami.

"Hi, Tami. I'm actually wondering if you can tell me if a Charlie, or Charles, Kingman was admitted any time in the last month," I said, smiling hopefully.

She put a pair of those oversized blue-light glasses on, turned to her computer screen, and typed. "Nope, sorry."

"What about an unidentified male patient? Here's his photo," I said, and handed her my phone. "I think he might've come in during the aftermath of the flood, a few days later tops."

"Lemme see," she said, and stifled a yawn. She looked at the screen for a few moments before handing it back. "Well, we had a couple of John Does that night, but they were older and Hispanic. No, this one really doesn't look familiar. I would remember his face. It's distinctive. Sorry, sweetie."

"Thanks anyway," I said, unable to hide my disappointment, and tried to remember I wasn't the only one who might be tired and fed up today. Persistence is as much a part of the job as luck or timing, I knew, and I knew that I needed to keep going, think of a different angle than this one, but time was running out. The nurse coming back with nothing made me want to bang my head on her desk.

She took off her glasses and massaged her temples. "I was here all that day and the next few. Lord, that was a long night," she said.

"Yeah?"

"We lost power long enough that we worried about the emergency generators going out," she said, perking up. "Of course, it was busy, too. Had a congestive heart failure patient come in that night with fluid on her lungs, she was asking for her last rites as the lights started blinking and it went dark for a minute."

"That's scary. I hope that she went peacefully, despite that," I said. Something scratched at the back of my mind when she mentioned last rites. It was why John David hadn't been at the cabin when it flooded—I remembered he'd gone to be with an elderly congregant who was dying. "The patient, was her name Parsons?"

"I actually shouldn't be sharing that kind of personal information," the nurse said, and looked curiously at me. "But by the grace of God, there is a Mrs. Parsons still here with us. You know her, too?"

"Sort of," I said. Lenora Parsons—the same as the church trustee whose name graced the new rec center at Hillview Christian. I was almost certain she had been the one that John David had gone to see the night of the flood. "Since she's still here, can I visit her?"

"I bet she'd like that. Poor lady hasn't gotten many visitors," she said, pointing toward the double doors to the hospital floor. "Room 104."

I walked down the corridor toward the long-term care unit, resticking the visitor pass onto my shirt. I wasn't sure what to expect, but the thing about luck and timing is that you had to make the odds good for yourself. Anyone, however loosely associated, was good for questioning. You don't know until you know, Leroy liked to say. I stopped in front of room 104. The door was open a crack and the lights dimmed. I rapped my knuckles on the doorframe, and a wisp of a pale, white-haired woman scooted up on her pillow. "Come in," she said.

Her eyes were red and I could see then that she had been crying. "Is everything all right?" I asked. "Should I go and get the nurse?"

"Don't do that," she said, dabbing her eyes and nose with a tissue. "I'm just sick of being alive!"

"Well," I said, coming to stand next to her. "Not sure I can help you with that one."

She smiled faintly. "Lenora Parsons."

"Annie McIntyre," I said, and took her slight hand in mine. Her skin was papery, bruised purple where an IV had been stuck, and cold to the touch.

"Been waiting on my son-in-law to bring by my granddaughter. Lord, how I wish it were Don bringing the girl."

"Don's your . . . ?"

"Husband. He died last year. I've been sick for so long, I— I always thought, always hoped I'd be the one to go first. I'm ninety-four years old now. Ready to get to heaven and see him. More than anything. The doctors all thought this was it, but *it* was a month ago now and I'm still here."

"You go to Hillview Christian, don't you?" I said.

She touched a gold cross resting at the hollow part of her clavicle. "You do, too? Is that who sent you?"

"No, ma'am," I said. "Not regularly, anyway. But it's how I recognized your name. I was speaking with the nurse and she said you came in the night of the big flood?"

"The doctors said it was time"—she let out a long breath that turned into a cough—"I specially asked for Pastor John David to come, for him to be by my side. Such a lovely young man. Maybe that's why my wretched old self is still here. Punishment for putting that poor, sweet man in danger. His father finally made it out here, the stern old Reverend, and I could tell how distraught he was. He felt badly he'd told John David to come here in the first place. Told the nurse his son had gone off the road trying to get back into town, that he was stranded. I could tell he thought me so selfish."

"Oh, ma'am, I'm sure that's not true," I said. The hair on the back of my neck stood up. John David hadn't made it to the hospital. Didn't he say that's where he'd been? Maybe he'd said he was on his way to the hospital. That made sense. He wouldn't have been able to get back to the cabin by the river, either way.

Mrs. Parsons wiped away another tear and I looked around for a tissue to offer her. "I'm just so, so tired," she said. A cough rattled her entire body and she squeezed her eyes shut after the effort. "Remind me of your name again?"

"Annie," I said, looking at the plastic pitcher on her bedside table. "Would you like some more water?"

Mrs. Parsons shivered and pulled the blanket up to her neck, shaking her head.

"Thank you for talking to me," I said, my throat feeling tight. "I'm sorry you don't feel well. Are you sure I shouldn't get the nurse for you?"

"Lord, please take me," she whispered, and turned to face the wall.

Outside, the night was a seamless, socked-in black, the parking lot lights tiny specks blurred by the downpour. I looked both ways and saw that I was alone. I hitched my purse high up under my arm. The bullet was parked at the far side of the lot and I'd have to make a run for it. The puddles splashing my ankles were warm from the asphalt, but the water beating against my face felt cool, almost cleansing on my skin. By the time I slipped into the driver's seat I was soaked. I wrung out the ends of my hair and wiped my eyes, sitting for a moment listening to the rain pelt the windshield. Mrs. Parsons had looked so helpless—and I couldn't help but think of Leroy and that aimlessness of the heart I knew he also felt.

I turned the radio on and put the bullet in reverse. Headlights shone into the rearview and I braked hard. The rain was blinding, and I hadn't been able to see this person was right on my bumper. When they reversed and turned, I could see more clearly. A pickup truck. I yanked my head around—in the split second before they put the truck in gear and sped off, I recognized the red beater. I couldn't make out the driver, but I did see briefly the lower side of the tinted windshield.

Right above the registration, a Hillview sticker.

Chapter 31

Bethany stood on tiptoe and moved her fingers along the top of the doorframe to John David's office. "I don't know why he bothers," she said, and pulled the key down. She unlocked and pushed open the door, flipped the overhead light on, and motioned me inside after her. It was half past nine, a gray, rainy morning, and John David was down the hall in a committee meeting before the service.

Bethany wore a simple white dress with bell sleeves and an empire waist. She placed a hand on her stomach and frowned.

"Feeling better?" I asked.

"Mostly. Felt a little queasy after breakfast."

"And the other day?"

"Oh, right. Sorry. And sorry for ditching you. I, um, ran into Kendall's mother in the parking lot," she said as she slumped down into John David's desk chair. She squeezed her eyes shut. "Annie, she looked awful. Terrible. Seeing her really set me off. I felt so, I don't know, angry? Like, horrified I was alive and not Kendall. Had to get out of here. Couldn't even tell her about the baby. She's going to be hurt I didn't tell her myself."

"I'm sure despite all she's lost she'll be happy for you. But I understand why it'd be uncomfortable," I said, bouncing my knee distractedly. I hadn't been able to come down after leaving the hospital. Despite securing the sliding door and stashing Leroy's pistol in my nightstand, I couldn't sleep in my apartment. At dawn I'd gotten out and driven around again, searching for the painted Airstream. Nothing. When I pulled into the Hillview lot to meet Bethany and get my check, I drove around for a few minutes searching for the red pickup, but again came up with nothing. My skin had that achy, raw-nerved feel. My mind stuck in the numbed-out place where exhaustion meets wit's end.

"No, you don't get it. It would deeply hurt her," Bethany said, then leaned forward on her elbows. "My mentor, she leads the women's group here at church, she said— I'm sorry, is this too much—"

"No, go on," I said, crossing my legs to stop the nervous bouncing.

"I told her I've felt like I couldn't carry on, and Annie, she put her hand on my forehead and said all I needed to do was get through today. 'That's your one job,' she said. So, I try to remember that. Seems like I take steps forward and steps backward, but it works. I just remind myself to put my trust in God, my marriage, and John David. Over and over again—"

"Walking by faith?" I said, and nodded up at her father-in-law's book.

"Exactly," she said, not detecting my note of sarcasm.

"If this is none of my business, ignore me, but was this pregnancy a surprise—or?" I said, reddening as soon as the words escaped my mouth, knowing that I'd been rude. Like starting a sentence with "no offense, but," as though it actually blunted what came after. "It's just, Nikki told me that you used to say you weren't sure about kids."

I expected Bethany's eyes to change. To darken and dart around like the old Bethany's would have, but she met my gaze and smiled. "I did tell Nikki that one night. Probably after too much wine. Lately I've been thinking it has something to do with Momma going so young. It's a terrible thing, losing a parent. I don't know if her heart condition was genetic or not," she said, turning her face toward the window. "Mostly I worry I won't be a good enough mother. But I have to trust in God's plan for us. I've been needing to exercise my faith for a long time."

"Your mom's illness, I mean, that's an understandable reason to worry," I said, not sure why I wanted to play devil's advocate with her. "Not that I think you won't be a good mom, Bethany, but you're allowed to feel conflicted about the whole thing. Do you feel conflicted?"

She turned back to me. "Sure. But it all changed when I found out about the baby. Kind of clicked into place. And especially since I've survived this, like, freak disaster, I think it's important for me to move forward with my life. To stop questioning everything and not be so afraid."

"Guess I've always been more of a what-if type of person. Maybe that means I'm cynical."

Bethany tilted her head, studying me for a moment. "You can still be a what-if person. Maybe you start wondering instead though, what if something good happens? That's what you have to do when you love someone. Go all in. You know what I mean?"

I started to say something, but no words came out.

"Annie?"

Prickly heat broke out on my chest and neck. I did know what she meant, knew it in my heart, but still, something in me held back. I made a helpless motion with my hands and shrugged.

"Hey," she said, reaching across the desk. "How're you feeling about the breakup?"

"About the same," I said. The sun must have broken through the clouds; a shaft of light shone in through the window, warming my shoulders, and it occurred to me, with some embarrassment, that I'd been waiting for Bethany to ask about Wyatt. That I'd been plying her, all the while feeling surly because I needed to vent, too. That what she'd said about love felt like pressing down on a bruise. The hurt was already there, and I had an impulsive need to keep dwelling on it.

"Chin up, girl. It'll get better," Bethany said. She squeezed my hand, then looked at the clock. "Oops, I better get over to the sanctuary. Here I am rambling and you still need to get paid!" She opened the top drawer of John David's desk and rolled her eyes. "You wouldn't guess it, but John David's a total slob. Hold on, I know the checkbook's in here somewhere."

She dug around and pulled out a set of car keys—the key fob had the Toyota logo on it—with a bunch of other tiny metal keys, a red rabbit's foot, and an oversized bottle opener in the shape of a bucking horse that said THE WILD MUSTANG. "Someone must have lost these," she said, putting them back in the drawer after staring at them for a moment. She found the checks and made one out to the firm.

"Thanks," I said, standing. "So, those aren't John David's keys?"

She shook her head and shrugged. "Staying for worship?"

"Not today," I said, pausing with one hand on the doorknob. "Hey, Bethany, what car *does* John David drive?"

"We rode in together this morning, but usually he takes his dad's old farm truck around. Little red beater. Why?"

"Nothing," I said. "I'll get out of your way."

Bethany stepped out after me, locked the office, and gave me a little wave as I turned the corner and looked back. My heart beat so hard I could feel it in my teeth. While there were probably hundreds of red pickup trucks driving around the county at any given time, and a fair share of them churchgoers, this was too much of a coincidence. I merged into the stream of people headed down the sidewalk toward the sanctuary, sat on a bench, and took out my phone. I googled "wild mustang" and "New Mexico," and sure enough, there was a Wild Mustang Casino and Resort located outside Ruidoso. In addition to the gun being missing from Jacinda's Toyota truck, I remembered Garcia had said the keys were never found.

There was only one way to find out if those were Jacinda's keys inside John David's desk. It would be risky to come back to the office during the service. There were simply too many people here. Plus, Bethany would be returning to the building with the children for Sunday school after the first hymn. My phone in my hand started vibrating, and it took me a moment to register the incoming call.

"Mary-Pat, you'll never believe—"

"Annie, are you with your grandfather?"

"No, what's going on?"

"I don't want to worry you, but—" Her voice cracked. "Listening to the police scanners, I heard them send squad cars over to his address."

Chapter 32

By the time I pulled up to the house, a Garnett city cop was standing on the porch with my father, who was bent at the waist with his hands on his knees.

I ran from the bullet up the gravel driveway. Dad's face was scarlet. I thought he was crying, but when his lips peeled back from his teeth and he brayed, "What're you doing here?" at me, I realized he was, in fact, laughing—loudly and inappropriately—which oddly made me even more upset.

"Crazy old man called the cops on his own son," he said, wheezing now.

The officer was about my age and about as confused and uncomfortable seeming. I crossed my arms and stared at him. "What's the problem, Officer?"

"Owner reported a break-in. I'm about to let it go, since he's decided to not press charges. Seems there was a misunderstanding," he said, wiping the sweat off his forehead with the sleeve of his uniform.

"Annie," Leroy called from behind the screen door, pushing it open. "What're you doing here?"

"Jesus," I said. "You've got to work on your paranoia."

Leroy stepped onto the porch and frowned, cutting his eyes away. "He came in uninvited and was going through my things. Took something wasn't his."

"You knew it was my dad? What the hell," I said, my blood pressure rising. In my family there was a code: don't air your dirty laundry in public. It was a betrayal on Leroy's part that an officer had been involved, even if he did think for some wild reason Dad was stealing from him.

"Everything *is* okay, isn't it?" the officer asked. "Do I need to—"

"No, it's fine. Sorry for your trouble," I said, standing slightly in front of Leroy.

Leroy stepped forward, nodded, and waved the young man on. "It's all right, son."

Dad let out a hiss of air and put his head in his hands. As the officer was getting into his patrol car, Mary-Pat pulled up in her Silverado. I'd let her deal with Leroy. "Daddy, I'll drive you home," I said. "I can come get your car later."

Dad walked to the bullet without another glance at Leroy. Sat in the passenger seat and turned toward the window. He reclined the seat as far as it would go, groaning as he stretched out his back. "He's losing his damn mind. Old fool. I went over to drop off some meals your momma made. Let myself in and called out for him, but no answer, so I figure he must be with you or Mary-Pat. Said he was in the shed out back and didn't hear me. Probably gave him a scare is all."

"This doesn't make sense, even for him," I said.

"Like I said, he's an old fool. We, ah, had some words."

"Right," I said, my face growing warm. I turned off the highway onto the bumpy, single-lane road that led to my parents' house out in the country. "He's been complaining about you prying—his words, not mine." My stomach tightened. I hadn't told Dad what I knew about the accident, and it occurred to me then that I might not ever.

"I know," Dad said, then sighed heavily. "I think he was trying to prove a point about his personal space."

A possum scuttled out into the road. When I braked the seat belt locked, digging into my neck. I sped around it and looked at the dash clock. Church would be letting out now, John David headed back to his office most likely. I didn't have time for this bullshit. We rode the rest of the way in silence, and when I pulled up to my parents' house, Dad unbuckled his seat belt and got out before I even had a chance to turn the car off. I considered leaving right then, letting this mess sit for later, but I also wanted to warn Momma off him. The house was tidied up, as it always was on Sundays, and I could hear the rumble of the clothes dryer going in the other room. "Think she went to the store with your aunt," Dad mumbled, then went to his recliner to sulk.

It was quiet and stuffy inside, dim and yellowy from a lamp left on, and the smell of the baskets of potpourri on the end tables combined with lemon Pine-Sol was sweet and overpowering. The change in air pressure when it rains always gave me a dull headache, but I could feel it growing stronger now. Dad picked up the remote and clicked the TV on. Intent on letting the events of the morning blow over, it seemed. But something nagged at me. "I know you don't want to talk, but what does Granddad even think you'd be after?" I asked. "He said you took something?"

Dad rubbed his eyes. "I don't know, sweetheart. Just forget about it."

I reached over behind his head and turned the lamp off.

"It's dark in here," he said. "Turn that back on."

"Fine," I said, clicking it back. Lamplight during the day

always made me a little sad. Reminded me of Leroy's house during Mamaw's hospice care, when she couldn't see well anymore and rarely left the bed, day hours melting into night hours and back again. I stood next to the recliner, waiting for Dad to speak, and when he didn't, I sighed. "I need to get to work anyhow. I'm on a case. Solo this time."

Washed in the blue glow of the television, Dad nodded silently, his eyes blinking back sleep. The fact that he never asked about my work bothered me, though I didn't want to admit it. He'd never wanted me to work for the firm, and so I did my best to not worry him. Still, it hurt that he didn't seem, if not a little proud, at least somewhat interested.

My head was throbbing now. I went to my parents' bathroom and opened the medicine cabinet for some Tylenol. I didn't see any, and as I was rooting through the drawers in the vanity, I saw that Dad's shaving kit was unzipped. Out poked an orange bottle with a white top. Curiosity got the best of me; as far as I knew, neither of my parents were on any medications. The bottle was from the local compounding pharmacy, Bluebonnet Drugs. I looked closer at the label. It was one of Leroy's.

The oxycodone he'd been prescribed for his leg injury.

I flew into the living room. In what felt like slow-motion, Dad's eyes clocked the bottle in my hand then moved up to my face, his skin losing all its color. He stood, fumbled forward, and reached for the pills, but I stepped back, holding the bottle behind me. "You lied," I said. "You did steal."

Dad spun around as the screen door creaked and slapped on the frame.

"I see my baby's here," Momma called out in a singsong voice. Plastic shopping bags rustled as she unloaded the coming week's groceries into the pantry. "Sweet pea?"

Dad lunged toward me, but I stepped behind the couch,

clutching the bottle so tightly the lid nearly popped off. Momma stopped her unloading and walked into the living room. Her short, tawny hair was slicked back from the rain and she smiled. "Sweet pea, why don't you stay for supper? Though you might have to stay the night. It's spitting hail."

I didn't speak, only looked at my dad, waiting for him to break.

Momma stood beside Dad, and the laugh suspended in her throat. "Dang, who died?"

"Go on, Daddy, tell her," I said, my voice croaky with tears.

Momma grabbed his arm. "William, what's going on—"

"I can explain," Dad said, his eyes searching mine, pleading. "Just let me explain."

After I called them, Sherrilyn and Curtis came over to help subdue both my parents. Dad had been cussing himself out, Momma joining in, both of them crying off and on, and I simply hadn't known what to do. Nikki had come along, too, hanging back in the kitchen with me while they talked it out. I could still hear low voices in the other room as Nikki pulled two plates down from the cabinet—she'd found leftover chicken in the fridge, and had decided to fry us up some okra when I admitted to her that I hadn't eaten all day. "Can't believe Uncle William thought he'd get away with it," she said. "Your granddad is crazy but he's not senile."

The afternoon light in my parents' kitchen was wrong, a kind of greenish-yellow storm light—or maybe it was Nikki at the stove with her hair tied back and not my mother. That zoom-out feeling when you bring someone home for the first time and it's like you're seeing it new, through their eyes. The chipped laminate counters, a fridge covered with gag-gifted magnets, old pictures, and a list of "important numbers" written in Momma's neat script. My great-grandmother's jadeite on the high shelf collecting dust. Walls the color of egg yolks. The red-checkered curtains and wicker chairs gave the house a country-kitsch look, I supposed, but the stuff was so familiar to me it had no aesthetic. It was simply ours.

"His back," I said, tracing my finger over the rings in the dining table. "You know, the doctor my dad saw said if he wasn't interested in surgery, she could refer him to a physical therapist, an acupuncturist, a masseuse, but he straight-up refused. Part of me thinks he likes being in pain. Likes being shackled to it. Pills are another way of his being shackled."

Nikki frowned, blotting the oil off the okra with a paper towel. "I don't get it."

"I mean there always has to be something wrong with him. What would he do if he suddenly felt better? He'd have no excuse not to move on."

"Damn, that's cold."

"I know," I said, and felt my face flush. "And I don't totally believe that. It's just that I've been thinking about this for a long time." I hadn't told Nikki what Leroy revealed that night at the VFW bar. It burned me up and I wanted to. But it wasn't my secret to tell. What felt harder to admit was that I was ashamed of my dad. That I was ashamed of me. I'd been superior—smug, even—when confronted with Tyler Thompson's sister. Worse, too distracted by my own bullshit to realize what was happening with my own family.

"Cut your dad some slack. Those pills are addicting," Nikki said with a little shrug, and proceeded to fix us both a plate.

As if it were that simple. As if he hadn't lied, stolen.

"It hasn't been going on very long, for what it's worth. He says he wasn't taking one unless he really needed it. Leroy had stopped getting the refills. Said it made him too loopy," I said, and burned my tongue on a piece of okra. The woman I'd sat next to at New Beginnings flashed across my mind. Her dry, worry-lined face. Pale lips trembling as she stood to speak, turning all that anger back on herself. I thought about my algebra teacher, Ms. Harkness. I thought about Tyler Thompson and Bud Nelson, my hatred for Eli Wallace, and even Jacinda, all of it metastasizing in my chest until my skin felt tight and my breaths were shallow.

"Is he going to get help?" Nikki asked.

"He's going up to Mary-Pat's place. It's where he went to be alone and dry out the last time he fell off the wagon, years ago. I didn't even know. I thought he was gone for a job that fall."

"You were just a kid. They probably didn't want to scare you," she said, reaching for my hand. "I'm sorry."

"I feel like I'm losing everyone."

Nikki squeezed my hand, and we sat like that for a few moments before I realized she was crying now, too. "What's the matter?"

She pulled her hand back and wiped her eyes. "You didn't say anything to Sonny, did you? About us talking to those guys at Mixer's?"

"No," I said, stung she'd think so. "But Mixer's isn't exactly the type of place you can be anonymous."

"Sonny asked me if I was sure! Who asks that during your own engagement party? I asked him why he was questioning me and he just shrugged. Said to forget about it, but of course I can't."

"Fair question," I said, regretting it as soon as the words left my mouth.

"Oh, for god's sake." She flicked a piece of okra at me.

"Sorry," I said, picking it up off the floor. "I'm not even thinking about both of your, um, indiscretions. I don't care about that if you don't. It's that you're really young, Nik."

"Doesn't mean I don't know what I want."

"Why rush, though?"

"Maybe I want to change! You enjoy acting like you're this free spirit, this unconventional outsider or whatever, but in fact you're the most rigid, controlling, goody-two-shoes person I know. Did it ever occur to you that *you're* being the immature one now? You accused your dad of not moving forward, but what about you? You know, Annie, life's not a dress rehearsal—"

"Wow," I said, my fork clanking on the plate. "Did you cross-stitch that on a pillow? I know we've been spoiling for a fight, but I don't have the energy. Not now."

"You started it," she said.

"Okay, fine," I said, rubbing my temples. "You're right about me. And honestly, I'm still upset about Wyatt, on top of all this."

"You need to tell him that." She crossed her arms, giving me the same look she and Bethany had as kids when they told me they were in charge because they were older. "You said you feel like you're losing people. But what if you *really* believed that? If something ever happened to Wyatt, if he wasn't around, you'd be out of your mind. Wouldn't you?"

My eyes teared up again as I pushed my food around the plate. I needed to get the hell out of here. It was nearly five in the evening now and raining hard. After a few uncomfortable minutes of silence, I rinsed my plate in the sink, and turned back toward Nikki. She sat with her chair scooted back, hugging her knees to her chest. "I have work to do," I said.

"Fine," she said, sliding her plate toward me. "I'd better get home. Sonny texted and said the river's just under the bridge at Salt Fork Road." She picked up her phone and keys from the table, put the hood up on her rain jacket, and walked to the back door. Wind gusted against the window, rattling the old single panes. It was true. I was losing everyone. Everyone that mattered to me had slipped like water through my grasping fingers.

Chapter 33

I took a sharp turn and my heart lurched with the car. I willed Wyatt to answer the phone, but of course he didn't. When Nikki said the river was nearly over the bridge at Salt Fork Road, I realized that was only of couple miles from the O'Brien ranch. The road smoothed out, and though it was pouring, I sped faster. As I was about to disconnect, his voicemail picked up.

"Hey," I said. "It's me. Just wanted to make sure you're okay. It's too dangerous to be out on the river right now. I don't know what I'd do if anything happened—so, just, cut the camping trip short if you haven't already? Please come home. I need you to come home, Wyatt, and we need to talk—"

I braked hard and skidded to a stop. A white GMC truck up ahead of me had started to reverse and turn around. The driver flashed their high beams and pulled up alongside my window, motioning for me to roll mine down.

"Get to high ground!" an older man yelled through the pummeling rain.

I tightened my grip on the wheel. "Road closed?"

"Not yet, but the creek's washed over the crossing," he said, his voice straining. "Where're you headed, hon?"

"Hillview Church," I hollered back.

"Go on take the county road toward Cedar Springs. You can loop back there and come the other way."

"Thank you, sir," I said, and rolled up the window. Shook the water off my arm, put the bullet in reverse, and followed him away from the rising creek. I remembered the phone in my lap and picked it up to end my message to Wyatt, but I'd already been cut off. Realizing I was tailgating—especially dangerous on these slick roads—I took a breath and eased my foot off the gas. I needed to be calm and clearheaded for what I was about to do.

By the time I got to the Hillview parking lot, it was nearly time for band rehearsal and youth music lessons. I'd spotted a flyer by the door when I was leaving that morning and knew this might be my only chance to get into the building while it was unlocked. The only chance I'd have to break into John David's office. I paused, bracing myself for the rain, praying I was right, that I was getting closer, and that Wyatt was not out on the river while the waters rose.

Inside the building, only one overhead light was on in the hallway. The band was setting up in the music room—I could see them carrying instrument cases and folding chairs through the pane in the door—and I scurried down the hall as quickly as I could to avoid anyone seeing me. As I was about to reach John David's office, I heard my name being called.

"Pastor Brad," I said, stiffening. "Good to see you."

"What're you doing here so late?" He stood in front of the band room door, holding it open for the group of teenagers that came streaming in from outside. They high-fived Brad, sloughing off rain jackets and tossing their wet umbrellas onto the ground, darkening the light blue carpet and giving the hallway a damp, sweaty smell. Brad watched me. He smiled, but his eyebrows knit together—suspiciously, I worried—and came closer.

"Met with Bethany earlier and forgot my bag," I said, and held out the canvas tote I'd planned on stashing any evidence in. "She told me the building would be unlocked if I came during y'all's practice."

"Well, glad to see you got it," he said, clamping a hand on my shoulder. "Actually, I was meaning to catch up with you. Ask if you were able to find Charlie."

"Nope." I shook my head and inched away, a little unnerved by his grasp on me. "He seems to have truly disappeared."

Brad gave my shoulder a good squeeze before letting go. "I hope he's well. This has been a hard year to say the least, hasn't it? And we're not even halfway through it. I saw the news about the police having a person of interest for Jacinda's murder. All this coming out about her makes me realize we weren't as close as I'd thought—I didn't know she was involved with drugs, I really didn't, else I wouldn't have had her hire Charlie. I should have seen it coming though, after that trip to Mexico. Not the drugs, but you know, her being so unhinged. But I'm sure you heard about that."

"No, not really," I said, fishing.

He looked over his shoulder, reached back, and shut the door to the music room. We were alone in the hallway and he came even closer this time, leaning against the wall next to me, close enough that I could smell his overly sweet cologne, acrid sweat underneath. "Well. It was a nasty rumor Jacinda started that luckily didn't get very far. She accused the pastor's wife of cheating on him while they were in Mexico. Said she caught her with a man at some hotel in the town where they'd go to make calls and get supplies."

My stomach dropped. "Bethany?"

"No, Pastor Michael's wife, Kendall. Like I said, a nasty rumor. That sweet woman would not—I feel wrong even bringing it back up, her being gone now," Brad said. "It's just with you looking into Jacinda and Charlie, I don't know—it occurred to me when I saw you that you might not have heard the whole story."

"How big of a rumor are we talking?"

"I hear everything around here, and far as I can tell it fizzled out before it took off. Jacinda came to us right before Easter service and they drowned the next weekend, so we all just dropped it I guess," he said, running a hand through his gelled-up hair, dusting his blazer with little white flakes. "Jacinda called a closed-door meeting with John Sr. and the pastoral leadership, excepting Michael. Very awkward. Not the type of thing you take lightly. It could have cost them their position in the church."

"Did Jacinda say who Kendall was having this supposed affair with?"

"No," he said, his eyes darting back and forth. "She said she 'didn't get a good look at him' and acted all weird and cagey, as if *she* wasn't the one who'd called the dang meeting."

The band's drummer poked his head out of the music room. "Hey there," he said, nodding at me. "Brad, we're gonna get started. We ought to let the kids go early. Their folks won't want them driving out late in this storm."

"Sure thing," Brad said, and caught the door with his toe. "You be careful out there, too, Annie."

"I will, thanks." I started walking down the hallway, but froze when Brad called after me again.

"Exit's the other way!"

"Oh, actually, I was going to use the restroom before I left," I said, sweat pricking the back of my neck.

He nodded, but before he closed the door, he paused. "And Annie, please don't repeat what I told you."

"Course not," I mouthed. Waved goodbye, and hurried toward the restroom at the end of the hall.

After twenty minutes or so of hiding in a toilet stall waiting for band practice to end, knees to my chin so no one would see my legs, the power went out in the building. The shock of utter darkness made me audibly gasp. I instinctively put my hand over my mouth, but even still, if someone came in, they'd surely hear my heart galloping. The music stopped, and Pastor Brad telling the kids to remain calm carried across the hall. When it was clear the power wasn't coming back anytime soon, they must have called it; the scrape of instrument cases dragging across the floor and squeaking rubber soles as they passed by followed soon after. When I was sure they'd all left, I stepped out of the restroom and walked in the dark toward John David's office. Rain pelted the roof and the rumble of thunder was so loud it sounded like a bucket of rocks had tipped over. Kendall cheating on Michael was scandalous, if true. *Her being so unhinged* echoed in my mind. Was Jacinda unhinged? Hard for me to say. But you couldn't pull talk like that without proof. Like Pastor Brad said, the accusation alone would have shattered reputations. Kendall would be judged by her community, be cast out, but it wasn't the gossip that would break her—no, it was bigger than that to a believer, which I thought Kendall truly was. Infidelity was a sin in God's eyes.

I stood in front of the office, ran my hand over the top of

the doorframe, and found the key in the same place Bethany had reached for it that morning. The air conditioner clicked on and I startled at the rush of air—the power was restored to the building. I didn't dare flip the overhead lights though, on the off chance someone returned. I opened the window blinds and the artificial light from the parking lot lamps spilled in, giving the room a cold, white-blue tint. My eyes adjusted to the shadows, and I went to the desk. The keys were at the back of a top drawer filled with loose scraps of paper, notes, stray pens, and binder clips. I held them out in front of me, the red rabbit's foot tickling my wrist.

But why keep the keys and abandon the gun?

The answer was probably in Jacinda's house, I thought, fingering the smaller brass keys on the ring. Maybe even a safe-deposit box. I sat for a moment at John David's desk, trying to imagine how that night might have gone down. What Jacinda would have said to him. How he could have easily wrangled the gun from her. And Charlie—had Charlie been a witness?

My eyes trained on a framed picture next to John David and Bethany's wedding portrait. The one I'd seen him holding when we met for the first time. Kendall stood between him and Michael, and based on John David's green-and-gold baseball uniform, I took it to be from their college years. I walked to the window so I could see the photo better, catching a purple flash of lightning in the dark sky. Kendall had her arms around each man's shoulder, but John David had his arm around her much, much lower. It was innocent enough, the pose as spontaneous-looking as the wide, laughing smiles across their faces, but something in the way John David's hand cupped her waist, how their hips tilted toward each other—

John David introduced them.

He loved her as much or more.

Were John David and Kendall having an affair up until her death, that might be exactly the type of information Jacinda Moore might have wielded—to an unintended effect.

A door opened and closed in the hall. I dropped to the ground and crawled under John David's desk. It was probably a janitor, or maybe one of the band members had forgotten something. I held my breath. Then, the door to the office opened. I tucked my legs tight to my chest, panicking, wishing I'd left the blinds closed—

"Get up, Annie."

I inched forward. "Bethany?"

Raindrops had collected on her waterproof jacket and slid off onto the rug when she moved. Her mascara ran, black lines drawing down from the corners of her eyes to her mouth. Her face was both pale and flushed at her nose and cheekbones. She looked like a marionette doll, working her jaw back and forth before she spoke. "I saw your shitty fucking car out there when I was picking up the flowers from the sanctuary. I didn't think you'd stoop so low as to sneak in here and, and—"

"And what?" I stood, meeting her eye.

"Those." She pointed at Jacinda's keys still clutched in my hand. "Give them to me."

She knew.

"No." I shook my head, pretending like I didn't feel as though I'd been punched in the stomach. "So, how long?"

Her lips puckered so they were almost white.

"Come on, Bethany. How long have you known? Was it when you saw the keys? That's when I figured it out. Well, I had my suspicions when I talked to Lenora Parsons," I said, pausing to catch my breath, to blink back the tears clouding my vision. "Tell me the truth. Did you know he killed Jacinda?"

"That bitch threatened to kill my husband. Pointed a loaded gun at him. It was self-defense what he did."

"Or was it way back when you hired me?" I shot back, unable to control the shake in my voice or the sharp recoil to my heart. Stupidly—like, of all the things to be upset about right now—it occurred to me I was verging on tears not because I was scared. It was because I believed Bethany and I had become friends. That I'd opened up to her. Maybe that's why I hadn't seen it. I clutched the keys tighter, the metal digging into my palms. "I know that's why John David's been following me in the red truck. Thinking I'd lead him straight to Charlie."

Bethany's eyes were also glassy with tears, but in hers I saw a steeliness I hadn't seen before. Her whole body stiffened and she leaned forward. Strands of wet hair clung to her outstretched neck like tentacles.

"Tell me the truth," I said. "Did you know this whole time? Is it why you hired me?"

A moment passed between us, a long stare. Bethany jerked her head, no, but it was too late. We both had realized it would be benevolent of her to lie, say no—that I couldn't stand it otherwise, and that she would give me that. Or hell, maybe it was true. I'll never know for sure.

"No. I hadn't figured it out. Not until I recognized her keys this morning. John David broke down and talked to me when I confronted him. He told me that he saw Jacinda's text message to me that night," she said. "He went to defend me from her, Annie! Then she pulled a gun on him, demanding money—he walked into a fucking holdup, okay? It was all my fault—all of it. Self-defense was what happened. He would never, never—we are good people, Annie, okay? John David, he's this special person. He—"

"Damn it, Bethany, he's lying to you! Think about the fact

that he rolled her truck into the water and didn't call the law. And what do you think he was going to do if he got to Charlie before me? Listen, I believe you when you said you just found out. I trust you, so you trust me, okay? Let's go to the sheriff," I said, my heart beating so fast I felt dizzy. "You need to do the right thing. You don't want to be an accomplice after the fact. Come on, if nothing else, think about your baby."

"That's exactly what I'm doing," she said, and it was like a light clicked off in her eyes. Her shoulders tensed back up. Stiffly, almost mechanically, she reached for the baseball bat on the shelf and turned back to face me.

The door was still open behind her. My canvas bag with my phone and car keys inside of it was across the desk. I'd have to push her aside to break free, run, and call for help.

"Bethany, please," I said, reaching for the bag, stepping closer toward her and the door. "Please trust me."

Before my hands could close around the straps, she raised the bat and swung wide. I ducked and stepped backward, grabbing the bookshelf and looking for something, anything to defend myself with. My hand closed around a hardcover copy of *Walking by Faith*, but before I could shield myself, she swung again. The bat landed across my jaw, sending me to the ground. My forehead hit the corner of the desk and I felt that boomerang sensation again—that jostling in my skull. A trickle of blood ran down my face into my mouth. Pain radiated from my head, my vision doubling until I closed my eyes and submitted to the darkness.

Chapter 34

I dreamed of water, of riding waves. I dreamed I was slipping below the surface, breathing through my nose, kicking my legs and pumping my arms, a steady current roaring in my ears, pulling me down, down—

And then I broke the seal.

My eyelids were crusted with blood. My head pounded and my jaw was so tight I didn't think I could move it, even if my mouth wasn't duct-taped shut. The fabric against my cheek vibrated—I was on my side in the backseat of a moving car. The seat buckle dug into my arm and my hands were bound behind my back with what felt like a rubber extension cord. I focused on the dash lights. The dark, silhouetted heads in the front seat.

"Hurry, please hurry," Bethany said, her voice hoarse from crying. She leaned her elbow on the console, reaching for John David's hand at the base of the steering wheel.

"Stop it," John David said, and swatted her away. "You want us to go off the road?"

"People drown all the time, but not all beaten up like this," Bethany said, moaning.

A chill spread from my chest out, like I'd sucked down a glass of ice water. They were planning on tossing me in the river. I breathed deep through my nose, trying to control the frantic pace of my heart, but my body shuddered with adrenaline. No way was I going out like this.

I moved my hands, and—oh, God, I moved my hands! The knot was not tight enough, the rubber cord too thick and slippery.

"Honey, honey," John David said, sanding down the frayed edges of his tone. He was using his preacher voice now. "Calm down. Pray if you need to. Just know that you're making this worse than it already is, carrying on like you are. It's plausible she got into it with a criminal, right? That's what you said."

"Us, John David. We're the criminals," Bethany said, bursting into tears again. "Oh, God, no—"

"Stop it," John David said, tossing his head to get a loose curl out of his eyes. Rainwater beaded in his hair and shone in the blue dash light, haloing his smooth face. He wet his lips and smiled. "I'm going to get us out of this. This is your mess, too, but *I'm* going to be the one to fix it, like always. Until then, for the love of Christ, Bethany, stop talking."

I turned onto my stomach, lifting my hands so that the loose part of the knot looped around the seat buckle. I pulled, getting just enough slack to slip my hand out. Peeling the tape off my face, I squeezed my eyes tight to stop from crying out.

"I know she knows more than she told me about this Charlie. That's her in a nutshell—always thinks she's a step ahead of everyone. That's been her since we were kids," Bethany said, sniffing. "Lord, please forgive me. I don't know how I'll even look at Nikki."

I scooted up on my elbows. Not enough for them to see my face in the rearview, only enough that I could see out the window.

The rain had stopped, and I could see a black-and-white road sign reflected in the headlights. We were on the farm-to-market road I'd been told to turn around and get off of. The low water crossing and the creek up ahead. The creek that fed into the river. If I was going to jump out of the truck, it had to be now.

Bethany spun around in her seat and grabbed my ankle. "Shit! She's awake—she's out of the bindings!"

I yanked my leg back, kicking at her and missing.

John David groaned. "Then hold her down!"

Bethany unbuckled her seat belt, but as she reached again, I sat up and slapped her across the face. "Wake up, Bethany! He's never been honest with you—he was sleeping with Kendall, for God's sake!"

"What?" Bethany drew back, holding a hand to her cheek. "What are you talking about?"

"Shut up!" John David said, then reached an arm around the seat. The truck swerved and he turned back, gripping the wheel again. "You're a liar and a swindler—I knew better than to hire you. You don't know anything."

"Oh, but I do," I said. "You know, I wondered why Jacinda came to you with the blackmail about the floodplain and the new town homes and not your dad. But she had double the ammo with you, didn't she? Caught you and Kendall sneaking around on the last Mexico trip. Came home, followed you, maybe took some pictures. Right?"

"You and Kendall," Bethany said. Dead-eyed, she faced her husband. "Is it true?"

John David was silent. Bethany started crying again, and as she wiped her nose, I scooted toward the door and gripped the handle.

"Is it true?" Bethany's sharp intake of breath sounded like it hurt her. "I said is it true, John David!"

"Damn it," he said, and laid his hand on the horn. "Both of you shut up!"

"She was pregnant," Bethany said, her voice barely scratching above a whisper. "My fucking God, she was pregnant and it was yours."

"Hold on, she what—pregnant?" John David spun his head to the side. "Oh, oh my God," he said, a sob jerking his body forward.

Bethany snarled and grabbed a fistful of those shiny black curls.

John David hit the gas and the truck careened sideways for what felt like an eternity before righting itself. We ran over the flood gauge, flattening it, and plunged down the embankment into the creek. I knocked face-first into the seat back, and nearly vomited, the pain in my head was so intense. The airbags had deployed, the powder filling the cab with smoke, but I could see over them that the water was already over the hood and rising. I tried the side door. Too much resistance. I rolled down the window and water rushed inside the cab. I hesitated, looking back. John David fumbled with his seat belt and Bethany moaned. Panicked, I thought if I could get out, maybe I could open their doors from the outside.

With no time to think, I squeezed through the window, using my legs to kick up and out. The creek swelled around me, my head barely above water. I blinked hard, eyes adjusting to the dark as the cold, muddy water weighed down my clothes and stung the cut on my face. I paddled hard to keep treading, my legs and arms burning from the effort. The truck was completely submerged. A warm stream below the surface suctioned against my legs, pulling me down—I had to swim diagonally across the current, and fast. My head pulsed with pain as I used all my strength to cut toward the trees, and I cried out when

I placed my feet down into the soft, grassy muck and waded, heels sinking, water sloshing into my panting mouth.

I struggled up the embankment, water lapping at my heels. The incline was so steep that when I collapsed onto my hands and knees, I was nearly upright. I looked over my shoulder, but couldn't see anything. The cloud cover and the humidity made the night feel airless, and it was a sealed-in dark, a storm-cellar dark. Weighing whether or not to dive back in, to try to open the truck's doors—that is if I could even locate the truck—I heard Bethany scream, John David yelling at her to swim.

Legs shaking, I steadied my arms and braced myself to continue on hands and knees uphill, hoping the land would level out, hoping I was headed toward the road where I could flag down a car, or a house where I could use the phone. My limbs felt like jelly. Knowing the two of them were at my back, knowing that eventually John David would overtake me, made my efforts feel futile and I had to shut off my brain to keep going. A low barbwire fence cut across the hillside. I took a deep breath and stood, swaying as I swung each leg over. When I stumbled forward, flashes of blue and red punctured the darkness. The farm-to-market road was before me. I was on the opposite side of the creek, right behind the church. The lights drew nearer and my body felt beyond the pain, numb. It was as though I floated down the crumbling asphalt to meet those flashing lights.

Chapter 35

Memorial Day weekend is the worst time to move. Everyone else has the same genius idea about that extra day. Loads of beer-and-pizza-bribed friends and unlucky relatives, the stairwell all arms and elbows, wilting cardboard boxes stacked on top of each other, heavy-duty trash bags slung over sweaty shoulders. I watched the U-Haul truck Wyatt rented reverse into a spot and nearly clip two cars in the process. Turning back from the window, I surveyed the drab carpet and avocado-green couch, the low wooden shelf full of books from college I never sold, my favorite blue mug, and my worn, spiral-bound notebook open next to my laptop on the pinewood table. The crescent moon of Tate curled up on a cushion. Wyatt was walking up the stairs, and for a moment, another smaller, scared version of me wished he weren't—I wished I could press pause, keep this small imperfect square all to myself, the anxiety of opening up the door to him almost crushing.

Before he could knock, I stepped into the bathroom. Splashed water on my face and took a deep breath. Several stitches later, the wound had closed. The swelling was gone, the bruising along my jaw a faded yellow. Wyatt had called 911 and sent dispatch toward the church that night. After hearing my voicemail and calling me multiple times with no answer, he knew something was wrong—he worried a car wreck—and in a way, he was right. The truck was not recovered from the creek for several days, but Bethany and John David had made it out alive. Selfless man of God that he was, John David had left his wife on the shore unconscious and barely breathing. I can only assume his plan was to run away; he was stopped by law enforcement at the on-ramp to the freeway about an hour later.

There it was—the knock.

"Morning," Wyatt said, a smile crinkling his hazel eyes. "Sonny said he and Nikki should be here in thirty. We could start unloading without them, but I thought we might want to have breakfast first."

I stood with my hands at my sides and my back against the door as he walked past me into the narrow kitchen.

"Annie?"

"Yeah, sounds good."

He held a box of kolaches from the Czech bakery in Colburn and a carton of orange juice that he set on the counter. He put his hands in his pockets and looked down at his feet before reaching into the cabinet. Pointing at the stack of mismatched plates, his finger shook. "These dishes okay to use?"

The way he bit his lip, how sincere he was just then—it broke me out of my shell. I wanted independence, but I wanted this, too. I had asked him to move in with me when his lease ended, until we could find—and afford—a better place. I had been as sure of it then as I was now, which is to say I knew it was the right thing to do and I had no idea if it would work.

But I knew I loved him.

I'd thought a lot about what Bethany had said about her and

John David that day I saw the key ring. About her faith. I think she was right about choosing love in times of uncertainty. My only wish was that she had chosen someone who had room enough in his heart for her. I put my arms around Wyatt. "I'm glad you're here," I said.

He rested his chin on top of my head, and I could feel his jaw tense. "Really? I worried you might've changed your mind on me."

"Nope," I said, and felt for the first time in a long time like I was at the beginning of something, not at the end or the weird middle. "Come on. We've got a big day ahead of us."

The Ellis place was far out, nearly to the county line. I parked behind a line of cars in a small field off the side of the long gravel drive. The party would be in the garden by the pool, as it was every year. I spotted my mother's dented blue sedan a few rows over.

Wyatt got out of the bullet and stretched his arms over his head. "You nervous?"

"A little. There's been a lot of buildup."

We walked into the backyard, the air hazy with barbeque smoke, full with about forty or so people milling about. Mostly bank employees and their families. Momma must have barely beaten us, still had her purse on her shoulder. She hefted a hollowed-out watermelon with scalloped edges, filled with fruit salad, onto a buffet table. I placed my hand on her arm. "Hi, Momma."

"Sweet pea!" She hugged me, then Wyatt.

Her boss, Mr. Ellis, came from inside the house, a thick canvas apron tied over his polo shirt and shorts. He placed his metal tongs on the table next to Momma's fruit salad. "Welcome,

McIntyres! Good to see you, Annie, it's been a few years." He looked between me and Wyatt. "And you are . . . ?"

"Wyatt Reed," he said, and stuck out his hand.

"My boyfriend," I added.

"Wait a minute," Mr. Ellis said, squinting his eyes at Wyatt. "You coached boys' basketball at the summer rec league last year, didn't you? My boy had the best time. Chase Ellis?"

I could see Wyatt's mouth twitch—he'd told me earlier Heather's little brother was a pill who made it clear he'd rather be home playing video games. "I remember, yeah. Chase had a lot of hustle," he said.

"Well, I hate that I missed the tournament." Mr. Ellis's eyes cut over to Momma. "Tina, where's William?"

Momma's face turned pink and she wiped her hands on the front of her daisy-printed sundress. "He's sorry. He just got back from visiting family. Got in very late last night."

"No need to apologize!" Mr. Ellis smiled and shrugged. "He's missing out on some good grub though."

"Well, he really is sorry. It's always a pleasure, you having us," Momma stammered. "Wouldn't feel like the start of summer otherwise."

"It's summer all right," he said, and fanned his face with a paper plate. "Should get better out here once the sun sets. Margaret's already by the pool with her feet in the water, girls. Wyatt, let's get us a couple beers and I'll grab Chase. I told him he's going out for JV this year and could use some pointers."

Wyatt looked back at me, quickly crossing his eyes, and I stifled a laugh. Once he and Mr. Ellis were out of earshot, Momma let out a long sigh. "I used to love these things. Now the thought of chatting it up with Margaret and her clique makes me want to claw my eyes out."

I looped my arm through hers. "How's Daddy doing?"

"A little green around the gills, but fine. Better, really. He and I just need time to catch up before"—she waved her hand around—"we did all this socializing. I don't want you to worry about him, sweet pea."

"I'll come by tomorrow," I said after a moment. "But, do you think he's still mad at me?"

"I don't know. He better not be."

"Annie?"

It was Heather. "There's someone I'd like you to meet," she said, motioning for me to follow her off the patio and into the yard. "Hey, Mrs. McIntyre."

"Have fun, girls," Momma said, worrying with her purse strap. She looked so tired. One moment I'd feel tender, miss Dad something awful, then I'd think about Momma all alone in that house, cooking supper while exhausted after a long day at the bank, and red sparks would light up my brain. I wasn't even mad at him—I was simply mad. I'd been talking with Momma about it some, and she kept repeating that addiction was a disease, that it was bigger than him. A disease, yes, but lately I kept thinking of the storm. That all my dad or anyone else who was struggling could do was try and take shelter when the sky turned dark.

"I'll be back, Momma," I said, and turned and walked away with Heather, bracing myself to finally confront the man who'd brought me all this long way.

Heather smiled nervously. "Bet you'd never take me for harboring a fugitive. How'd you figure it out?"

"Kept thinking about the clothes you bought. I didn't believe they were for your dad," I said, and meant to laugh, but it came out kind of stifled. "That and I realized all this land out here would be a pretty convenient place to hide an Airstream. Heather, I have to ask—why did you do it? I mean, hiding him like that was really risky, not just for you but also your family."

"To be honest, if I'd have known he would be wanted by police it probably would've been a different story. But he said he needed help, and—" She stopped and shrugged, meeting my eye. "He and I hit it off. I worked with him on several things when he first started coming to the library, housing, his résumé, things like that. You get to know a person. I trusted him."

"Did he tell you what had happened?"

"At first? Not the details, no. He told me he needed to stay out of sight, that he'd gotten mixed up with a guy who was dealing. He was worried, him being a felon, and didn't want to go back to prison. Said he'd made one mistake and that he'd lost everything in the flood. It resonated with me, I think, his needing a moment of grace. We have all this room, and it felt good to do something useful for someone. My life's felt pretty stalled out lately—and honestly, selfishly, all this was exciting," she said. We walked away from the party around the side of the house where there was a raised stone fire pit circled by wooden deck chairs painted in bright, beachy turquoise. "Charlie," she called out to the man seated.

His intense blue eyes roved over me and I felt my face grow warm. He was wearing one of the plain T-shirts from the pack I remembered Heather buying, jeans, and a pair of generic white athletic shoes she must have also gotten at Walmart. He put his can of Sprite down and reached for my hand.

"Nice to finally meet you," I said.

Heather made like she was going to sit in one of the chairs and stopped midway. "Oops, I forgot my drink. Annie, you want something?"

"Whatever you're having is fine, thanks," I said. She rounded the corner of the house and it was quiet for a moment. Charlie had a small frame but was muscular, compact. He had a cagey, nervous energy, and I noticed a slight tremor in his hands as he fooled with his earring and shoved his hair back from his face. His whole body seemed to vibrate, like a rabbit ready to bolt. He sat back down and gripped the armrests while I took the seat next to his. "So, enjoying the party?"

He let out a jittery laugh. "Yeah, I think everyone is more comfortable with me over here in the corner. Her dad looked like he was gonna stroke out when the missus introduced me to their friends as Heather's fugitive." He bounced his legs and pointed behind him. "Aw, but I shouldn't bitch. Heather and her folks are letting me stay until the trial."

"What's next after that?"

"Who knows? Been thinking I might visit my uncle up home."

I squinted and made out the painted Airstream toward the far fence line. Parked in the center of a ring of trees near a windmill, it was visible from the house, but not from the road. "I met your uncle Ross. Up in Idell when I was looking for you."

He grinned wide, a gap on the top row proof of the hard living he'd done. "Then I'm sure you heard about his drive-in. Old man wants to get it back up and running. He's apparently started a GoFundMe. Hell, might be worth trying. People love 'vintage,'" he said, making air quotes.

"Hey, you never know." There was a quick, cool breeze as the sun dipped. Out of the corner of my eye I saw Mrs. Ellis get up to light the tiki torches that ringed the pool. "I know I'll hear it all in the trial, and I've surmised some, but what exactly happened to Jacinda?"

"I miss her so goddamned much," Charlie said, snorting out a laugh. His face lit up in a pained, awestruck way like he'd been bottling it up. "Jacinda and me—we made a bad decision. Didn't mean she ought to have ended up killed."

"I'm sorry. I heard you were close."

"Yeah." He bent the tab on the can back and forth for a moment before placing it on the ground. He rested his elbows on his knees, cradled his face in his hands, and took a deep breath. "It was always the money. Then she owed this dealer in town, should've never gotten into business with him—anyway, it snowballed. No one was taking her bids, either, not after she fell out with Richter. So, she gets it in her head to blackmail his son. She'd caught him stepping out with another pastor's wife. Had him good. Pictures of the two of them saved on a flash drive, like in the movies. All that day she's bugging him to meet, and finally, he agrees after she starts to make good on the threat. See, Jacinda texted his wife."

I nodded, remembering that Bethany had assumed Jacinda's text was referencing her relationship to Eli Wallace. For as cold as I felt toward Bethany now, it pained me that she never even considered it might be John David who had done something shameful, not her. That she had blamed herself for what had happened, no questions asked. "And John David, he came over to y'all's place?"

"Yep." He held my gaze and shuddered. "Well, the state park down the road. Jacinda decides to bring her pistol, which was a big mistake. Two of them start arguing and she waves that thing around like a damn fool. They're on the ground pulling at each other, hitting each other, and bam! I wasn't even sure who pulled the trigger until he stood up. There was nothing to do. Killed instantly."

"That's awful."

"He chases me down the road, shoots once, but I'm faster. I was hidden in the brush when I see him drive Jacinda's truck to the edge and push it into the river with her in it. Goddamn cold-blooded bastard. It started storming and was dark, but he stayed out looking. I'm running, hiding, staying like one step ahead. Eventually the storm got bad enough that he high-tailed it, but I'm still too afraid to move. When the water came up to the trees, I ran out and took an ATV from the property still had the keys in it. But it was too late. Ended up climbing a tree."

"And that's where you saw the woman in the river," I said, a tight knot forming in my throat. "You saved her life."

Charlie's eyes were red and he looked down to wipe his face with the back of his hand. "I know."

"It was brave of you."

"I had no choice. I mean, of course I did, but in that moment, it was what I had to do. Didn't think twice. Shit, I thought for sure I was a dead man hitting that water. But I kept swimming, and then I saw the river had narrowed, dammed up from some big pile of wood and concrete. I was able to climb out."

"Why didn't you go to the police?"

He looked up, grimacing. "Because I know exactly how it would've gone down. I'm a felon. That pastor's word against mine? I was scared. And this man, his eyes that night—it was like there was nothing there. If the cops didn't believe me, man, I really think I would have conveniently disappeared not long after."

"You're probably right," I said. "Heard you're their star witness now, though."

He nodded. "That woman in the river—Bethany—that was his wife?"

"Yes," I said. "Bethany and I, we're not in communication, doubt we'll ever be again—but I've heard she's struck a deal with the DA, is set to testify against John David as well. Doesn't want to give birth in prison, I imagine."

"She really got herself in a mess."

"She sure did." Sitting across from her honey-haired Jesus,

it occurred to me that I didn't regret trusting Bethany. I didn't want to be jaded. Leroy didn't want that for me, either. If I was going to do this work, he said, I needed to be clear-eyed. Didn't mean I couldn't trust people, or that I wouldn't get burned again. It's hard work kicking the door to your heart open, but you have to, over and over. All the mention of her name had left me with was a hard feeling of aloneness. A feeling I couldn't shake the rest of the evening, or ever, really.

Chapter 36

The river was now low enough to cross, and the sky streaked with pink light as Leroy and I made our way up to the place early the next morning. We'd missed the bluebonnets, but the prickly pear had blossomed, and yellow coreopsis dotted the hillside like flecks of bright paint. The grasses were wet with dew and overgrown, nearly as high as my waist in some places. When the wind blew, the pasture on either side of us undulated like a great green ocean. The air was clean and sweet, and the dawn held all the promise that mornings tend to, but what was different that day was that Leroy had climbed the hill unaided.

He stepped over the stone foundation and scattered bricks—all that remained of the old house—stopped his humming, then turned to face me. "You know I want you to be the one."

"The one who does what?"

"Lives out here and uses the land. I've decided to update my will. Someone ought to clean the place up."

"Thought that was supposed to be you," I said.

He adjusted his Stetson and yawned, a laugh tumbling out of his mouth. "Not likely, little darlin'."

"I can't ever tell if you're serious," I said. "What about my dad?"
His smile faded. "What about him?"

"Have you talked to him since he's gotten home?" I searched
Leroy's face, but he gave nothing away, not even a flicker of
acknowledgment. "Well, don't call your lawyer just yet," I said
and shrugged him off, not wanting to argue. Maybe I'd accepted that Leroy and my dad's joint purpose on this earth was
to cycle in and out of these battles with each other. For so long
I'd thought of them as opposites, but now I could see they were
painfully the same—and that they cringed at seeing their re-
flections in each other. Did Leroy really want to bequeath me
this? Or was he trying to punish my dad? I think now that the
place was an idea, a feeling as much as it was a parcel to be split
up and willed down the line, but that day I looked out west
toward the escarpment, still purple in the early light, and felt
a secret thrill in my heart. Near the creek, we walked through
a stand of pecans, birdsong rising and swelling as we moved
under the canopy. I took Leroy's arm in mine to lead him down
the hill, even if he didn't need me to.

We drove over to the dirt road where Leroy's land ended and
the Shaver place started. There was another low water crossing
as the Salt Fork wound its way between the properties. We got
out to take a look around. A sandbar had moved to the opposite bank, and a naked ball of roots dammed the water. Twin
sycamores I'd loved lay on their sides, slanting the horizon. As
much as I wanted to believe I knew this place like the back of
my hand, the river never was the same, it was always changing,
and while I was sure there was something to be gleaned from
that, I only felt dizzy and a little blue as we walked. It took
me a long time to understand the difference between owning
a place and being of a place. The mud was studded with river
rocks. Red, putty brown, yellow with veins of gray, pale green.

I remembered being a kid and finding an arrowhead out here once—I didn't really care if I found one again, but I liked looking, liked to turn the worn-smooth rocks over in my hand. Leroy filled his pockets with stones and we kept moving, knowing Mary-Pat would be mad if we were much later.

The tank was high, full from the rain. I parked next to Mary-Pat's Silverado and we made our way to the water. The long tail of her silver braid swung out from her sun hat as she paced around the floating dock getting our chairs set up and the tackle boxes out. "Hey there," I called.

"Quiet, now," she said, and set her line.

"Didn't mean to scare them," I said more softly. A breeze—mineral-rich and cool, with no premonition of the blazing heat to come—rippled across the water.

We took our seats on either side of her. She had an ice chest stocked with beers, cans of pineapple juice, some bologna sandwiches, and chips. Leroy reached for a beer and Mary-Pat opened a bag of Fritos and peeled back the lid on some bean dip. "Want some?"

"It's seven-thirty in the morning," I said.

"Suit yourself."

"Hey, Pat," Leroy said, and leaned forward. "What did Garcia allow?"

"It's true about Eli Wallace," she said.

"You're kidding me," I said. Red heat broke out on my neck and chest, and I tugged the collar of my shirt. "They really just let him go?"

"His lawyer got them to drop the charges, yep. There wasn't much of a way to prove possession or intent to sell seeing how he wasn't caught on the premises, and no drugs were in his car or on his person. That land and the house on it had been abandoned for some time."

"What about the pill press? Couldn't they lift prints off it?"

"They never found one," she said. "Maybe he grabbed it when he ran, or maybe you were mistaken—"

"No, I know what I saw," I said, tamping down the desire to yell out a string of cusswords that would really scare the fish. Eli Wallace would go back to dealing, it was only a matter of time, and the poison leaching into Garnett would continue unfettered. I wasn't so naïve to think that if it wasn't Eli, it would be someone else. That locking him up was a Band-Aid. But I couldn't get out of my head the wet cracking sound when metal met skull. The smirk on Eli's face as Bud Nelson skidded in the dirt on his hands and knees—

"There's something else," Mary-Pat said, her head cocked. "I guess I'd better tell you, though I don't think you should pay it any mind."

"What?"

"Word's going around that you're a snitch, Annie. Eli's cellmate's a talker. Said Eli kept going on about getting his revenge or some bullshit. Garcia wanted me to let you know to keep an eye out."

"Let him try," I said, though my pulse ratcheted up a few notches. It was easy to be mad instead of scared in the clear light of day.

May-Pat waved her hand. "He's all bluster, if it's even true. He's not about to do something stupid so soon after getting off."

"Be careful nonetheless," Leroy said. "But I know you already are."

I shook it off and nodded, hooked a minnow, and threw out my line. It was quiet for a few moments except for the clicking of the reel.

Mary-Pat took a swig of her pineapple juice and sat up straighter. "Tell you what I heard about my neighbors: the old Reverend's resigned from city council. Those apartments and homes that got destroyed on River Road? He's halting construction on the church, moving some money around to start a fund for folks to repair or relocate."

Leroy let out a low whistle.

"That's great," I said. "Only took attempted blackmail, murder, and public humiliation. You can't take back what's happened."

"Better than nothing," she said. "I suppose."

Leroy sighed. "I reckon so."

My red-and-white bobber skittered once across the surface of the water, dipping down and up fast enough that I wasn't sure if I'd imagined it. The sun climbed higher, warming my back through the worn-thin cotton shirt unbuttoned over my tank top and shorts. I rolled my shoulders and took a deep breath, on the exhale banishing the odd, spiky feeling from my chest. Being out there, being with Leroy and with Mary-Pat—it gave me a self-sureness I didn't always have while I was alone. "Think they're biting?" I asked.

"Who knows," Leroy said, gazing over the silt-colored surface of the water. "Might be a big old catfish is circling."

Mary-Pat grinned. "You'll be lucky to catch a perch the size of my little finger."

My bobber moved again. Then, I felt it—a tug.

Acknowledgments

I'm fortunate to have worked with some incredible people on this book, and for that I'm especially grateful. I'd like to thank my brilliant and steadfast agent, Sharon Pelletier; my editor, Hannah O'Grady, for her guidance, and for lending such intelligence, vision, and generosity to these pages; Joe Brosnan, for his early enthusiasm for this book and for a series; Kayla Janas, Martin Quinn, and all of the talented, hardworking people at Minotaur/St. Martin's Press who do such a great job of getting books into the hands of readers.

I'm grateful for the friends and family who've supported and encouraged me. Over the course of writing this book, I became a parent. Mine had told me that my heart would expand in myriad ways, so much so it would be hard to describe. To my parents, Joe and Donna Tanner, all I can say now is thank you—for everything. For my mom, to whom this book is dedicated, I owe special thanks: without her caregiving and her words of inspiration I wouldn't have been able to finish it. Thank you to my best friend, my sister Olivia, for reading an entire draft in a weekend at the ninth hour, and for playing lunch lady. Thank you to my husband, Dane, for being a true partner and a wonderful father. And to Rosalie, thank you for being my light.